THAUMATROPIC ROOTS BOOK THREE

SECRETS OF DEARA

STEVEN J. MORRIS

Secrets of Deara

Book 3 of Thaumatropic Roots
Steven J. Morris
Copyright © 2025 by Steven J. Morris
All Rights Reserved.
1st Edition

ISBN 978-1-956105-25-4

For Libby,
who challenged me to level up.
Your edits made this book better. Your coaching made me better.

For Bobby and Todd,
for the long talks, the dumb jokes, the unshakable loyalty, and all
the kind of friendship you don't put in fantasy books because no one
would believe it.

And for my oldest daughter,
who worked her tail off and earned her place at the table.
Your grit inspires me. Arkansas is lucky to have you.

Books by Steven J. Morris

The Guardian League series

The Guardian of The Palace

Stars in the Sand

We're Going on an Elf Hunt

The Song Unsung

Thaumatropic Roots series

Mother of Trees

Bones of Cenaedth

Secrets of Deara

Shepherds of Truth

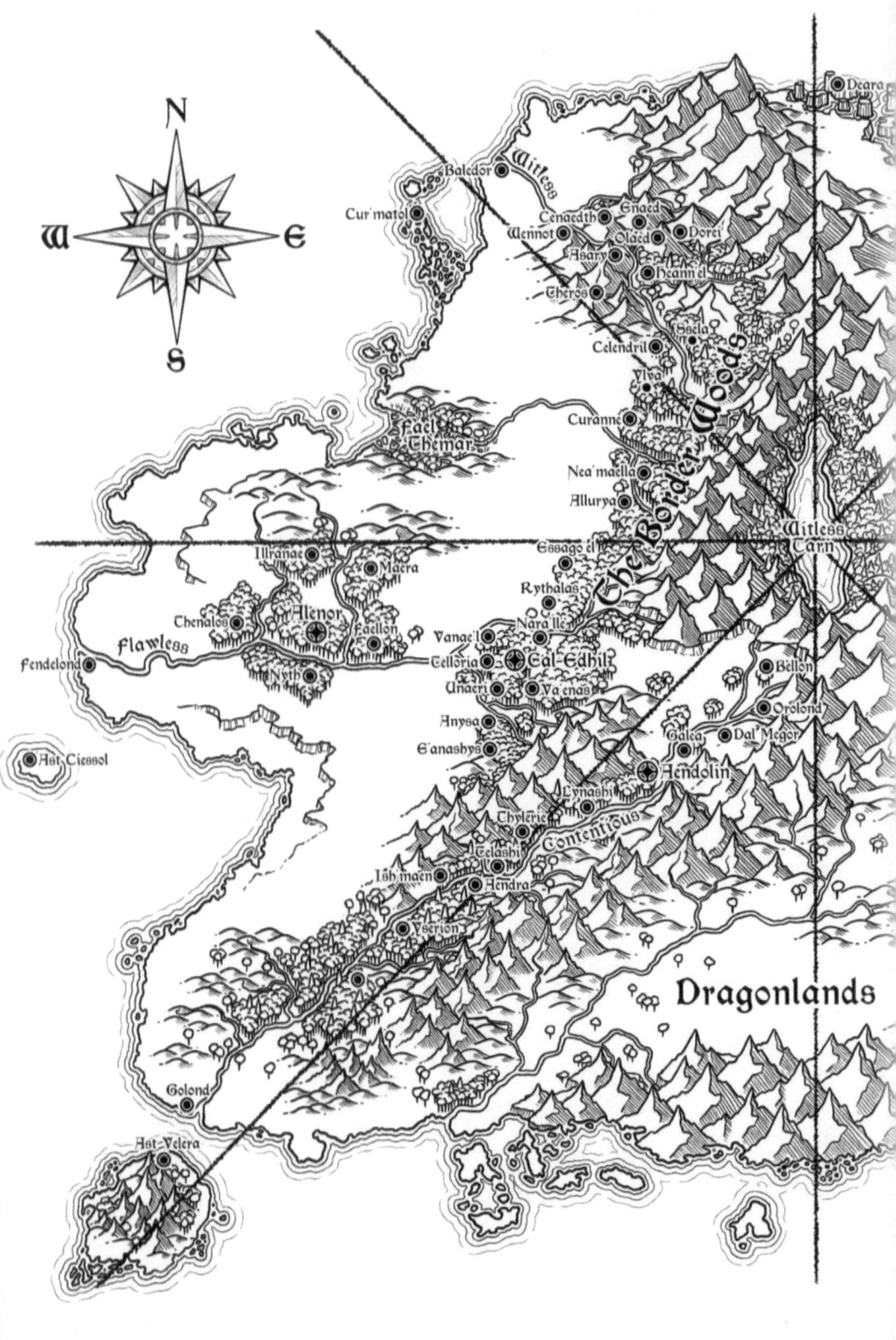

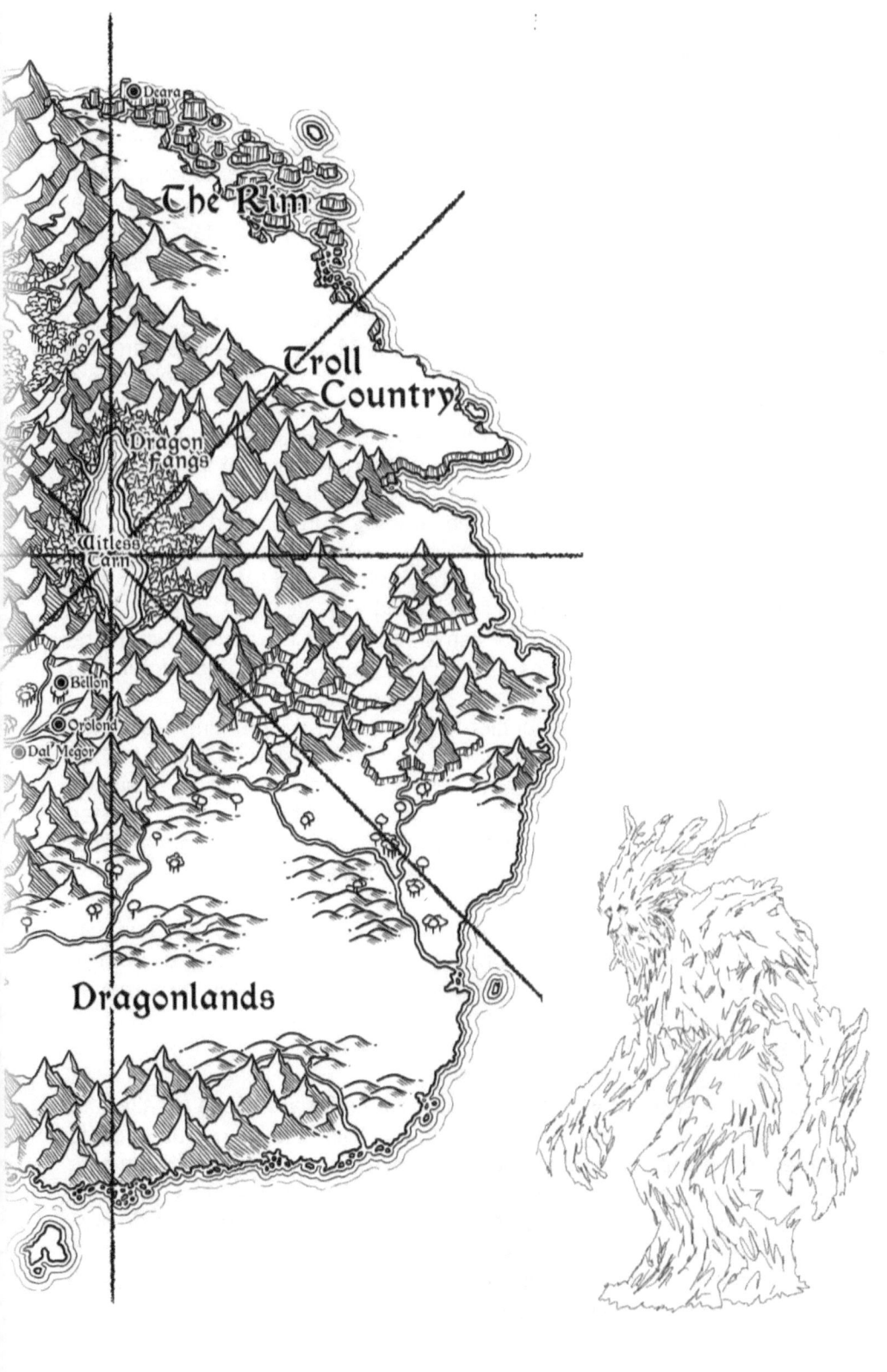

The Rim

Troll Country

Dragon Fangs

Deara

Witless Tarn

Bellon

Orolond

Dal'Meger

Dragonlands

Prologue

Before she became the Mother of Trees, she was the Mother of Dragons. We were her first true children, created to create. I remembered. And it pained me. Though the world shifted and turned, though the world *broke*, I remained. My wings spanned the centuries. But at long last, I felt it— the inexorable pull of time unraveling me, the weight of age pressing into my bones.

It should not have come to this. The world should have been mine to shape, as it was in the beginning. Before the Mother broke it. Before she caged the great tides of magic and left my kind to wither, shackled to a dwindling fate.

I thought—often over the centuries—of letting it end with me. To die and leave no heir. To let the true age of dragons fade at last into dust. Our drones would remain, fighting over scraps of memories impossible to hold. The blues and greens had already surrendered to that fate. Kryhryzar the White had chosen an heir with no past—the first of the Lost. To my mind, a mistake. And Shaythyl the Red? What choice had she made? What had become of the world's protector? I'd decided her choice didn't matter. No legacy remained worth preserving when the world itself conspired against us. When our Mother had stolen our birthright, leaving nothing but slow, aching decline.

Then, out of nowhere, ancient magic stirred. Its hum resonated through the leylines, and I recognized it instantly. After all, I had helped create it. That very magic kept me from it: a shield of storms, designed by me alongside Vaelrith the Blue, the last of the blue queens. We had forged it as an experiment, a sealed ecosystem, a world within a world. Because… we had planned to leave this one behind.

A painful memory. Best forgotten.

I moved close, watching. For the first time in centuries, curiosity stirred within me. Years had once been fragile, monotonous things, stretching endlessly before me. But as mine grew shorter, they moved faster, filling me with an almost-forgotten impatience.

Yet, I could do nothing. So, I watched. I waited.

My waiting paid off: the shield failed.

Only for a short while—barely enough time for the winds to falter, for the scent of something hidden to drift across the sky. But I felt it. Something deep, something vast. A pull. A resonance thrumming beneath the island, a second heartbeat calling to me. Not the wild, crackling magic of the storm shield. Something else. Another artifact, ancient and bound with purpose.

I did not fly to it. I had not lived so long by rushing headlong into snares. Instead, I marked the island, etched it into my mind, onto the maps of magic I had long since memorized.

Then the storm shield flared back to life, sealing the island once more.

I did not turn away. I did not forget.

Instead, I made a choice.

I would not die childless. I would not let my legacy fade to nothing. I would bring forth my heir—not to inherit a dying age, but to reclaim what was stolen. To make one last attempt at breaking the cage. To wield the power that should have been ours from the beginning.

Elliah ~ 1

I sat, frozen, watching helplessly as the alabaster-skinned Salts made off with my Hughelas. My limbs refused to move, pinned in place by the force of thick, unnatural air or wind. If I could only get to the magical hammer at my back and cast it away, I would be free!

As the troop continued down the west road, I fought the constraining air, reaching for the thing that kept my natural resistance to magic from working. Beldroth, the muscle-bound Warder with whom we'd trekked across the Heartlands, had taught me three ways to carry the hammer—the way I had it today was the best for travel, the worst for battle. The head of the hammer sat high on my back. I carted it around to neutralize it, so dragons couldn't locate it, but that also meant it neutralized me—my ability to deter magic.

The scattering of patrons nearby sat in wary silence, watching with the careful detachment of forest creatures scenting danger. *Useless.* Not that I expected help. People rarely stepped in unless the fire licked at their heels. The Salts had spoken like we were criminals, intimidating the onlookers, though we'd done nothing to deserve it. Hughelas's abductors had actively searched him out, accosting him regarding a phrase Beldroth had used when we'd sought passage on a Salt ship down the Flawless River to speed up our journey: *Daughter of the Nine Winds.*

I needed to get the hammer off my back.

I strained, fingers twitching against the magical force, pushing, reaching, fighting like a fox in a snare. The other patrons—merchants, laborers, travelers—watched from their benches, some shifting uncomfortably but still making no move to help.

The kidnappers took the western road, heading to the ocean. The Salt magic resisted me, but the farther the Salts moved from me, the looser its grip.

My breath rasped against my teeth as I finally got one arm up, my fingertips brushing the hammer's haft. The spell pushed back. My contact with the hammer worked against me, giving the Salt spell more strength. I pushed harder, inching my other hand back, fighting the restraint of the spell.

Move, curse you!

My fingers of both hands closed around the shaft of the hammer. Inch by inch, I pulled it out of its harness, then, finally, dropped it to the ground behind me. With an audible crack, the pressure broke.

I shot forward, toppling the bench as I surged past the already overturned table, trampling pages scattered from Hughelas's prized book. Five paces. Ten. Then I stopped short.

The hammer.

If I left it behind, it would call dragons to it like a carcass called vultures. It might have already whispered to them, a beacon for any passing wings. The wind carried enough danger without inviting talons. The last time I lost it, dragons nearly burned Cenaedth to the ground.

Beldroth would kill me for abandoning it. But he'd also kill me if I lost Hughelas, his son.

A growl of frustration ripped from my throat. I doubled back, snatching the hammer with both hands before bolting down the street once more. It slowed me, weighed me down, but I feared losing it might prove costly. When I got close, I'd have to ditch it off the road, somewhere hidden, then retrieve it after I freed Hughelas.

I sprinted, my boots pounding against the dirt, my lungs burning.

The road stretched long, winding westward, down the hill toward a riverport town on the Witless River that we'd passed on our way from the Heartland, a town too distant to see. I would have time to catch them. Then ditch the hammer, and… and what?

If I kept on alone, I'd have to fight four of them with only my dagger.

I skidded to a halt, cursing under my breath.

I had to go back. Had to tell someone. Beldroth, my mother—*someone*.

Mother of friggin' Trees!

I clenched my teeth so hard my jaw ached. *I had a choice.* A real choice. No one was shoving me one way or another—I had to decide.

That was new.

For years, my life had been running. Reacting. There had never been time to stop, to weigh choices. I'd followed my mother because it was all I knew. Then, my mother and I had followed Hughelas and Beldroth across the Heartlands, where I'd learned a goddess had shackled me to my fate, making me wonder if any choice had ever truly been mine. In Cenaedth, my decisions had been driven by instinct—fight, run, survive. No time to think. No real control.

But *this*? This was different.

There was no right path already carved out for me. No one to tell me what to do. No command to obey. No mother to follow, no prophecy to chase. Just me.

And suddenly, the weight of that hit me.

I could fail. Not just fail—choose *wrong*. If I chased them alone, I might catch up—but I'd be outnumbered. And if I failed, no one would know where they had taken Hughelas. If I went back, I might not make it in time—but I might have a real chance to stop them.

My stomach churned.

This is what it means to be the one making the call.

It should have felt empowering. It didn't.

With a final bitter glance at the trail ahead, I turned, slamming the hammer back into its harness. Then I ran—harder, faster—back toward Cenaedth.

Because I couldn't save Hughelas alone. But I damn well wouldn't let him slip away.

Elliah ~ 2

The town of Baledor sprawled like a careless splash of color across the edge of the sea. Brightly painted houses in every shade imaginable jostled for space against the coastline, their peeling walls battered by salt spray and wind. The docks stretched far into the water, a maze of wooden piers tangled with ropes, barrels, and nets.

Alabaster-skinned Salts bustled through the streets and along the docks, their white hair gleaming in the sunlight, their bright clothes faded but spirited, patched with care and worn with pride. Survivors, weathered but unbroken. Bigger buildings had shoved their way on the north side of the mouth of the Witless River, and masts from large trading vessels reached for the skies near them.

Beldroth, Illiara, Marinna, Gormar, Trentius, and me—we comprised the group that rushed to rescue Hughelas. Beldroth, Hughelas's father, had the height of a Salt, but next to him, they looked like gangly saplings. Illiara, my Wood Elf mother, carried Beldroth's baby, and I'd learned more about her extravagant past during the weeks we'd traveled with Beldroth and Hughelas than I had in the eighty years we'd spent dodging town to town, running whenever my condition became known. Marinna had joined us in the swamps of Fael Themar, all Wood Elf in appearance except for her startling blond hair and the muscles she'd carved from Beldroth's training. Dark-skinned Gormar was an Alluvium Red Prophet—his joining us had surprised me, but he stood with his pack, ready to leave, even as I'd run back to Cenaedth, as if he'd seen it coming. Finally, Trentius, a High Elf who lacked the sharp arrogance of his kin. His fractured mind had made him something rarer: kind. He had bonded with a wolf-sized red dragon, Smoky, in Cenaedth, who drew more attention than any of us elves. They'd all either traveled with us from Alenor, seeking the help of the Alluvium to fight the trolls, or they'd joined us along the way.

We'd missed the Salt crew at the riverport docks—Beldroth had insisted we quickly gather our bags, because if we didn't, and then failed to locate Hughelas quickly, we would be worse off than losing a little time up front. But the townspeople confirmed that they'd boarded a ship to go downstream. We bought passage on a trading vessel and followed, hoping, praying, that we'd catch them in Baledor before they vanished into the open ocean. Our vessel docked in a bustling part of town, where crates shifted, ships groaned against their moorings, and voices called orders over the crash of waves. We stood out. Between Beldroth's mighty Warder frame, Trentius's High Elf golden skin, and a small red dragon that kept trying to hide behind Trentius's legs, the townsfolk paused in their comings and goings to gawk and stare.

The overnight travel hadn't dulled our sense of urgency, yet urgency didn't hand out answers.

"How are we supposed to find anyone here?" I muttered, raking my gaze over the chaos of the docks. Salts moved with a quick, purposeful energy, their conversations loud and overlapping, carried by the tang of the ocean breeze.

Next to me, Gormar's gaze swept over the bustling docks, his expression thoughtful rather than searching. When he spoke, his tone was distant. "Baledor's always been like this. Good for trade, better for losing things. For me, mostly losing money."

Marinna shot him a look. "You've been here before?"

He shrugged. "A few times, long ago. Ports like this don't change, just the people passing through."

That was the most I'd heard Gormar reveal about his past. I watched as his sharp eyes lingered on the way the Salts bartered, the way the dockhands handled cargo. Unlike the rest of us, he wasn't looking for a trail to follow—he was reading the currents of the town itself. It made me wonder how much more there was to Gormar than I realized.

Then he blew it.

"We'll follow prophecy," Gormar said, his voice pitched with excitement.

Marinna snorted. "Wonderful! Let me guess, Elandra hummed a tune no one can hear, and it leads the way to Hughelas?"

Scowling at Marinna, he slipped his hand into a pouch, drawing out what looked like several strands of hair.

Marinna rolled her eyes. "Oh, excellent. Hair. Because nothing says divine guidance like shedding."

Gormar plucked a hair from his head and nimbly tied the hairs together, his fingers weaving with practiced ease. Then, with a snap, he summoned a ball of flame into his palm, the fire crackling and twisting unnaturally as it consumed the hairs.

I leaned in, irritation giving way to curiosity. The fire swirled, coalescing into an image. First, Hughelas—his face faint, but unmistakable. Then, a symbol burned bright: a fist gripping a trident.

A few children circled near us, taking in our little magic show.

Beldroth frowned. "What symbol is that?"

"I don't know," Gormar admitted, "but it means something. It has to."

"Tch," Illiara commented.

"Wait," Marinna said. "Was that *Hughelas's* hair?"

"Of course," Gormar said. "I have some from each of you. For prophesying."

14

"What?" Marinna's voice shot up. "You've been collecting our hair? That's disgusting!"

Gormar sighed theatrically. "It's a necessary tool, not a hobby. You'll thank me when it saves us all."

Before their bickering escalated, I turned my attention back to the image. "It's all we've got," I said, shoving aside my unease. "We need to figure out what that symbol means."

Nearby, a squat building, painted a once-bright blue that had mostly faded to a salt-streaked gray, caught my eye. Its sign, swinging on rusted hinges, read *The Drowning Sailor,* next to a picture of what was presumably a tankard of ale with a man swimming in it. Beldroth grunted and headed for it.

The air was thick with the smell of ale, wet wood, and something faintly moldy. Sunlight filtered in through grimy windows, casting hazy streaks across the tables. Salts crowded the space, their voices loud and their laughter louder.

We drew more than a few curious glances as we stepped inside, clearly outsiders, clearly trouble.

The muscle-bound Warder's trip to the bar sent a ripple through the room, wary glances turning his way. The bartender, a burly man with a scraggly beard, leaned against the counter, unimpressed. "What'll it be?"

"Information," Beldroth said. "The fist and trident. What does it mean?"

The bartender scoffed. "Never heard of it." He turned to wipe a glass.

Beldroth's patience frayed. "I don't have time for games," he growled, his voice low and dangerous.

Instead of intimidation, the bartender's lip curled. He crossed his arms, shoulders squaring. "Then you don't have time for a drink either. Get out."

Several patrons stood. The temperature in the room changed. My stomach knotted. I had little doubt that the Warder could take out the bartender and every patron in the room. But what if they simply didn't know the symbol?

Before things turned ugly, a familiar voice cut in smoothly. "Now, now," Gormar said, stepping forward, his easy grin disarming. "No need for trouble. My friend here's just worried about his son."

The bartender's stance didn't shift, but he glanced at Gormar, eyes narrowing. "And who are you?"

"A traveler. And a man who appreciates good stories." Gormar leaned on the bar, casual but deliberate. "Like, say... the stories a man hears in a fine establishment like this."

The bartender eyed him. Gormar tossed a coin onto the counter and pushed it forward with one finger. He slid over a second coin. Then a third.

A long pause. Finally, the bartender exhaled through his nose and muttered, "Peacekeeper ship."

Beldroth's fist clenched, but Gormar just nodded. "And where might one find it?"

A glance toward the docks. "Yellow pier. Ship's called *The Salty Squirt*."

Marinna blinked, then snorted. "The Salty Squirt? Someone has an odd sense of humor."

Gormar grinned. "Much obliged." Turning to Beldroth, he opened an arm toward the door. "Shall we?"

The bartender plunked an empty tankard on the counter. He leaned toward Gormar, his voice dropping conspiratorially. "But don't say I didn't warn you—anyone who boards a Dearan ship doesn't come back."

I wasn't the only one squinting at the bartender for those words. But, not waiting for questions, he grabbed the tankard, a pitcher, and walked to the other end of the bar.

We left, the tension dissolving the moment we stepped into the salty air. Beldroth inhaled sharply, his frustration still simmering.

I exhaled, my mind turning over what I'd just seen. That hadn't gone how I expected. Gormar hadn't pushed; he'd pulled.

The docks stretched out before us, vibrant and chaotic. The garish yellow wood of our destination stood out like a flare against the blue-gray backdrop of the sea. My stomach twisted as we moved toward it, the bright colors doing nothing to lift the unease that settled over me.

"Gormar?" Beldroth asked.

"Yes?" Gormar straightened, raising an eyebrow in surprise.

"Thank you," the Warder said simply. His tone was solid, unembellished, carrying a sincerity that settled over us like the hush before a storm. Then, without another word, he strode toward the docks to find his son.

Beldroth : 1

"Faeyoo!" I shouted at the deck high above. My voice carried over the salt-heavy wind, swallowed slightly by the groan of wood and the rhythmic slap of waves against the hull.

I set down my pack with care, loosening my sword in its sheath. No telling how this might go. My companions hesitantly followed suit.

The vessel loomed, a dark silhouette against the bright sky, its sails furled and ropes taut. The deck bustled with movement. They'd pulled a gangplank aboard as we'd started down the yellow-painted dock. Whether to avoid us or simply because they were ready to disembark, I did not know. Snow-white heads peered over the side of the enormous ship, squinting down at us. But they didn't respond in kind. They called back to someone, presumably someone with more authority.

As I waited, I studied those who'd accompanied me, measuring them. Who would follow me into danger?

Illiara, unwavering as ever, stood by my side, her expression impassive but her fingers twitching, as though already calculating the spells she might need. She carried our baby, which she insisted made her magic even more powerful. Even if I wanted her to stay behind for her own safety or that of our child, she would not have listened.

Elliah, Illiara's daughter—she loved my son. They were young, their affections clumsy, but I wasn't blind. She would fight for him, but I hoped it would not come to that.

Gormar, the Alluvium Red Prophet who believed Elliah was going to end the world, had surprised me by insisting on joining us. He'd spouted nonsense about wanting to observe as she destroyed his people, but he claimed he would help find Hughelas, and he'd come through.

Marinna was a powerful ally—strong in Warder magic, steady in a crisis. Illiara had once seen her as a rival, but the tension between them had eased. They weren't close, but the edge was gone; they'd found a kind of peace, if not friendship.

Trentius, the only High Elf I'd ever connected with easily, hadn't come alone. To save Cenaedth, he'd attempted a Compulsion spell on a hatchling red dragon. The other High Elves later said he'd bungled the spell. He hadn't Compelled the creature; he'd done something different. They couldn't say what, exactly, and neither could Trentius. But where Trentius went, the wolf-sized red dragon followed.

I'd hoped Brittanie would join us. She'd proven herself both powerful and levelheaded in a fight, and like Illiara, carried a baby that enhanced her magic further. But she'd done too good a job in stopping the red dragons—the Low Council had elected her to lead their army. The High Elves who'd survived escorting us to Cenaedth intended to return with the Alluvium army to Alenor. Brittanie had chosen Wynruil to advise her. Where Brittanie and Wynruil were fighters, Gormar had done little but talk, yet his magic had proved crucial to locating Hughelas in time. A part of me wanted to believe, despite everything I'd learned, the Mother had brought us to him, or him to us, for a reason.

"Faeyoo," said a woman from above, her tone ripe with scorn. A stern woman with sharp features, she bore skin markings similar to my deceased wife's, even on her cheeks.

"That's her," Elliah confirmed. "*She* took Hughelas."

Lyrei hadn't spoken often about her past, though she'd told stories to Hughelas when he was little. She'd often stared longingly at the Contentious River, and I'd had many nights where I feared I would find her gone upon waking, even after we had wed. But something kept her there, fighting trolls and dragons by my side.

It wasn't like, as a family, Bellon had caged us. I'd offered for us to follow the Contentious to Ast Velera, a Salt city on the island at the end of the river. She could have visited her people… or we could have started a new life. But while the water called to her, something had stopped her. She'd taught Hughelas a few Salt traditions, told him stories of the ocean, but she had never revealed that she'd had a title among her people. Not to him, nor me. She'd *never* explained that she'd been someone of status. Why would I have guessed? She'd stumbled into Bellon from over the mountains, through territory roamed by dragons and trolls. Not by ship. Other than her obvious expectation that her orders would be followed, that she'd clearly led people in some fashion, I had no clue about her life before Bellon.

The dragon who'd killed her told me her identity.

"You have my son," I shouted up.

"I have Hughelas, son of Lyrei," the woman shouted back. "He is a Scion of the Nine Winds. Even if his blood-magic is tainted with that of a Warder, he goes with me to his ancestral seat."

"You kidnapped him!" Elliah shouted up. She pulled out my hammer… her hammer… and handed it to me.

More elves fighting elves? "I do not wish to fight you," I shouted up. Salts untied the ship from its moorings as we spoke. Either they worked at the docks and would stay behind, or they would scurry up the ropes after freeing the ship. "We are all elves."

"I have my orders," the woman yelled back. "Your son I must bring to Deara. None of you need share his fate, but if you interfere, I will take you all!"

Ah. I smiled. *The solution is easy then.*

I swung the hammer back, preparing a blow that would likely put a hole in The Salty Squirt... and found myself wrapped in air.

Elliah jumped up the side of the ship and started climbing, quick as a squirrel. I tried to shout at her to stop. I wasn't attacking, merely "interfering," but the barrier of air prevented speech. The rest of the group was similarly transfixed. How many wind workers did that vessel hold? But the spell didn't work on the dragon. Smoky flew up with Elliah, blasting the mages with a fire that startled more than burned.

It was enough to break their spells. Marinna jumped forward and placed her hands on the ship. Two balls of flame burst into existence in Gormar's hands. I had used no mana, but mana flowed in like spring water... Illiara's doing. Trentius cheered wildly for Smoky.

The sky darkened with clouds that formed in seconds, lightning jumping around inside them with deepening cracks of thunder.

The ship hummed. Marinna would destroy it before the fight began. Hughelas was on that ship. He could easily be crushed by timbers or drown as the ship sank.

"Stop!" I bellowed, a hand on the ship to amplify the sound through magic.

"I do not wish to fight you," I repeated over the low grumble of thunder. "If my son must go, I will go with him. This is acceptable?"

I did not want elves spilling each other's blood. I'd intended to fight alongside the Alluvium against the trolls—that had been the plan. But plans lost their luster when faith fractured, and mine had cracked beyond repair. Though I still believed the Mother had a Plan, I no longer believed her infallible. And the war on the trolls would go on without me. The High Elves knew the plan and the Alluvium army marched—they would not fall for lack of one soldier. But Hughelas—he was not replaceable. Not to me. My role in the war had ended; my role as father had not.

"Hold!" the woman up top yelled. She walked out of sight, her voice barking orders to her crew. After several seconds, her head appeared over the rail to look down at me. Elliah stood atop the rail, balanced and crouched to spring with her bone dagger in her hand. Smoky, after a relatively ineffectual spattering of fire, drifted in lazy circles around the ship. The captain, for she must have been the captain, undoubtedly felt her ship shuddering beneath her. My magic would not have repaired the broken hull of the Knoll, but I could have done it further harm had I so desired, and Marinna's magic was stronger than mine. "It will take several days to reach Deara," the captain said matter-of-factly, like she was simply weighing options and not concerned about the welfare of her vessel. "We do not have the food-stores to take on so many extra passengers. Will it just be you joining us? Or," she asked with a raised eyebrow, "does one of you know the spell to create rations?"

I glanced at Illiara. There was a Wood Elf spell that created an edible powdery substance out of seemingly nothing, keeping one alive though never satisfying one's hunger. Every soldier on the front lines had experienced it. But very few Wood Elves had the power to cast the spell, and even fewer could create enough of the powder to sustain more than themselves.

"I know the spell," Illiara said, doing a quick headcount. Seven of us, if I included Hughelas and excluded Smoky. Illiara raised her eyebrows and sighed. Whether at the thought of producing that much of the dustmeal, or having to consume the loathsome stuff, or because she had reconciled herself to the fate I'd brought upon us by refusing to fight, I wasn't sure. If anyone had the mana to produce the loathsome powder for seven, it was Illiara. She nodded.

The captain smiled, a serpent coiled in a mountain crevice, ready to strike. "I find these terms acceptable," she said.

She disappeared, barking further orders up above. Salts hopped back over the ship's railing with ropes, using them to rappel down the side, then push themselves out to the dock. I waved for everyone to gather. Elliah stayed up above, hopping off the railing and eyeing the crew dubiously. I would speak with her separately, but I suspected I knew what her answer would be.

"No one else need go," I said. Illiara made a clicking noise. Even as upset as I was, a smile slid across my lips before disappearing again.

"I'm in," Trentius said. "Swift Strike Stops Sinister Scheme."

"I would prefer to continue with you," Marinna said.

"Will your daughter be going?" Gormar asked Illiara, flames burning low in his hands.

Salt sailors held the ship fast to the dock as others loosed the sails and re-secured the gangplank.

"She will insist on going," Illiara answered.

"Then I'm going too," he said with a nod of finality.

The ship's captain marched down the plank. Her pale-blue shirt and pants, while loose-fitting, held a sharp cut that suggested authority. "You're all going? To Deara?" She looked up, raising an eyebrow at Elliah and Smoky, the former glaring over the banister, and the latter having settled beside her.

A sigh escaped me. The last time I'd ridden a boat, I'd gotten horribly sick, and the thought of repeating the experience made my stomach churn. More than that, the idea of everyone jeopardizing their futures for me or my son weighed on me. Yet, despite my fractured faith, I failed to rid myself of the sense that there was an orchestration behind events. There had to have been a reason the white dragon's last words were *Lyrei, Daughter of the Nine Winds*. I'd repeated it in order to gain the trust of the captain of the Knoll so that she would take us aboard. I'd never imagined it would cause trouble.

It was too much to be coincidence. If we had not met Elliah, would we have gained access to the Mother? Probably not. Then She'd sent us on a path that revealed the buried ruins and a message from the Breaking. I'd lost heart at that point, as the declaration from the past had conveyed that the Mother of Trees needed to die to save the world. But my son, after growing more and more distant, had connected that encounter with the dying of my wife, his mother. It hadn't fully restored my confidence, but it reawakened something—enough to keep me moving. And at every turn, dragons. A dragon had told me my dying wife's title. I'd used it. It had led to this. Our journey was *meant to be*.

My pack weighed more than when I'd set it down—burdened now, not just with supplies, but with consequence. "We're all going," I told her.

We were fools, though I didn't beat myself up over it. After all, our choices had been limited. We could have destroyed their ship, creating a literal boatload of enemies. Probably an entire race of enemies. Or we could have abandoned Hughelas. It didn't sound like he was necessarily in danger—to be a "scion" of a princess wasn't all bad. I was a scion of Wood Elf leadership, after all, though I had been on the run for the past eighty years. That was not the norm for children of leaders. Yet if Beldroth's deceased wife had chosen to keep her identity secret, perhaps her path had been very similar to mine.

No, we were fools because we'd handed ourselves over to strangers whose intentions we didn't understand. Sure, fighting was still an option, even destroying the ship. But the Salty Squirt was the only thing keeping us from a watery grave. Our guards didn't confine us, but their steely stares and locked jaws as we tried to make conversation left us in cold, isolating silence.

Reluctantly, we had surrendered our weapons to the captain, Captain Striker, in exchange for a space shared with the crew below deck— where we stowed our packs and would sleep. It concerned me she renegotiated terms so fluidly. She was a formidable woman, tall and thin like most of the Salts, with a sharp nose, defined cheekbones, and a hawkish stare. We'd tried to bargain for Elliah to keep the hammer, but failed. A mountain of rock would conceal the dragon-bone hammer, else dragons would have long before recovered the dragon skeleton below Themopolis. *Dragons collect their dead.* But in Cenaedth, the hammer had remained too close to the surface, attracting the red dragons who had descended en masse to retrieve it.

Thoughts of red dragons made me unconsciously search out Smoky. She perched on a topsail, alternating between staring at Elliah or at the stern of the ship. "She's troubled," Trentius said, watching me watch Smoky. "She can't think straight." One of his eyes twitched. "Believe me, I know what that's like." His unsteady gaze troubled me. "I want her to leave the hammer alone, and she's trying."

Odd.

I glanced at Hughelas, who stood stiffly, leaning on the railing, eyes fixed on the water—but his focus lay elsewhere. He looked whole, but I knew humiliation ran deeper than wounds. Though no worse for the wear, he carried the weight of being kidnapped *and* of being the reason an entire group of us set off for a place from which we would purportedly never return. Though never a chatty elf, he'd become uncomfortably recalcitrant.

I walked over and put a hand on his shoulder. "You alright?"

He hesitated, then exhaled through his nose. "I keep thinking… what if my father hadn't gone straight for a fight?"

That caught me off guard. "What do you mean?"

Hughelas's fingers tightened against the railing. "He threatened their ship. But if he'd tried talking first, would it have changed anything?" He shook his head, eyes flicking toward the Salts moving efficiently across the deck. "Probably not. But he never even tried."

Elliah opened her mouth, then hesitated. "We didn't have time," she said automatically. But even as she said it, her gaze flicked toward the crew—appraising, uncertain.

I nudged them toward the center of the deck, where the rest of our group switched between gawking at the crew and watching Beldroth slowly turn from pale pink to paler gray. The lanky crew, all white-haired with skin either white as snow or sometimes pink, had settled into their routine after the business of getting us offshore. Many wore sleeveless vests, revealing lean but muscular arms and abs, some, like the captain, with skin art showing. I'd seen Salts before, even seen them work a ship when we'd gone down the Flawless River, but the Salty Squirt was bigger, requiring a sizable crew. I didn't enjoy having so many people tower over me.

Marinna, the blond-haired Wood Elf with Warder magic, who'd unquestionably saved the Alluvium from an attack by an enormous red dragon, nodded toward Beldroth. "Perhaps Gormar can distract him with something from his infinite collection of doomsday prophecies by Elandra," she suggested, her voice slick with mockery. She needled Gormar, though I didn't understand why. Her motives for continuing on with us remained unclear to me. At one time, I'd thought she was interested in Beldroth, but we'd buried that. Whatever her agenda, I had no intention of discussing it in front of our captors. No, *captors* wasn't right—we had surrendered willingly. But they treated us more like prisoners than guests.

"How dare you!" Gormar barked back, his face flushing with anger. "You'll not be so flippant when she returns to lead our army to the final battle."

Marinna flashed a false smile. "You're right. When her bones rise from the dust, she shall be a proper fright indeed."

Gormar's fists balled, and he glared daggers at her, practically vibrating with fury. "Elandra's prophecies are true, carried through the ages by the Red Prophets, meant to save us from destruction—if we're not too blind to heed them!"

"Save us?" Marinna asked, folding her arms. "How can they save us when your *cult* keeps them secret? And if they are secrets, why can't we get you to stop talking about them?"

"The prophecies of Elandra—" he began, but I interrupted him.

"Perhaps," I cut in with a stomp, quieting him, "we'd understand your vehemence if we understood how your prophecies worked."

It was a bluff to defuse the argument—I didn't want the Salt crew to see our bickering. But Gormar lacked restraint. Despite calling the Red Prophets' teachings "secret," he'd blurt them out whenever we gave him a chance, usually with little context.

To my surprise, Gormar paused, then nodded thoughtfully. Even Marinna, who relished mocking his doomsday tales, raised a brow and held her tongue.

The wind snapped through the topsails, but the mainsails remained tightly furled, leaving a wide space open in the center of the ship. Land had disappeared, and the sun had dipped below the water at the fuzzy edge where port and stern met, and its magnificent show of pinks and purples slowly gave way to the brightest of the stars peeking out from their canopy.

"This is a general prophecy," Gormar explained, without looking at anyone in particular. "Technically, it is impossible to disconnect a prophecy from all bounds. What would that even be? What would it be about? But without using a trigger or source for the Fire to feed upon, it will relate to the general surroundings and the caster's role in them."

Even that was more than I'd known before, and… interesting. Before, in Baledor, he had used strands of hair to direct the prophecy. Without material, the prophecy latched onto other sources.

Gormar began his casting, and a ball of flame sputtered to life— orange and yellow fire danced, forming a wavering globe the size of Gormar's chest that hovered at eye level. Captain Striker hurried over, a scowl hardening her face as a ball of water materialized by her head, a reprimand already on her lips. But the flames were clear of the rigging, the topsails high overhead. She hesitated, curiosity momentarily stifling her anger.

In the pulsing flames, a vision appeared, flickering in and out as if struggling to hold form. The image sharpened to reveal a ship with a crest on its sail: a fist clutching a trident. Flames surrounded it, but it remained clear of them. Then the fiery image transformed into the figure of a man, holding something indiscernible above his head proudly.

Captain Striker sucked in a sharp breath, her conjured ball of water splashing to the deck. "Pyrravyn." The name dripped from her mouth like a curse. "Where is the Daughter of the Nine Winds, Pyrravyn? What have you done?"

The image transformed again: a dragon, diving down in a stormy sky.

"Dragon!" a sailor shrieked.

Yes! The vision revealed a ship, and the dragon dove toward it. With the ship there, it became clear how massive the dragon truly was—possibly bigger than the red dragon we'd fought in Cenaedth.

"She's targeting the Squirt, Captain!" the same sailor cried.

A chill spread through my veins. The ship in the fiery visage wasn't the Salty Squirt; yet, when I forced my eyes away, I saw the crew scrambling to ready weapons. In the shadowed starboard waters, something massive and scaled streaked toward us in the water. The sailor wasn't crying out about the vision in the prophecy—he'd spotted one in real life!

"She's coming straight at us," the crewman muttered, voice tight with dread. "She'll gut our belly, for certain, Captain."

"Beam reach, starboard!" the captain shouted, her command slicing through the chaos.

"It's a blue," Beldroth said, voice low as if in reverence or controlled anger. Gormar had dropped his spell, leaving us gathered close, a small group of frightened prey amid the frenzied crew. "Marinna, with me!" My Warder disappeared down the stairs, Marinna hot on his heels. "Do you remember how to bind your magic to wood?" he demanded of her.

As the crew shifted the sails, the ship began a sharp bank—toward the dragon.

"Our weapons!" Elliah yelled. The captain looked back, weighing her options, calculating whether arming us would improve or worsen her chances of survival.

"In my cabin!" she shouted, pointing, though we knew where it was. It was the only room above deck.

Elliah bolted for the door as the crew loaded pods into long tubes they'd mounted on the side of the ship. With each *whoomp*, a pod launched from a tube, shooting out over the ocean toward the dragon. Seconds later, thunderous booms resounded, and geysers shot skyward.

"She's still coming," the crewman reported. "The charges didn't dissuade her."

"More charges! Direct starboard! Be ready to run hard. Do *not* lose my wind!" Then she muttered, "Taking landlocked idiots aboard brought this cursed luck."

Beldroth and Marinna had not reappeared. Gormar and Trentius both crouched, clinging to the standing rigging and trying to stay out of the way. A quick glance upward showed me that Smoky had abandoned his post, but I failed to spot him. With Elliah in the cabin, searching for her hammer, only I stood on the deck, and I found a space on the rail away from the busy sailors.

The beast charging us in the water was close enough that the dorsal fins glinted in the fading light like the teeth of a High Elf's saw. It would tear through the ship. Had it hit us from the side, it might even have cut the Salty Squirt in half. But Captain Striker had turned us to charge headlong at the beast—it would rip through the entire length of the Salty Squirt.

My hands clutched the rail, knuckles white. There was no one to Heal, no mana to restore. Nothing for me to do. I watched helplessly as Salts either worked lines or dashed about, while others lit pieces of string on those pods and dropped them like sacrificial offerings into the water.

The ship groaned beneath me, then surged forward as the sails snapped taut, responding to the crew's precise timing.

"Now!" the captain yelled.

My fingers dug in further as the sailors shifted the topsails to run with the wind, and the Salty Squirt jerked to port. The scales of the dragon scraped against the stern. *Schtick schtick schtick*—the sound as rapid as the beating of a hummingbird's wings as fin after fin jostled the ship.

Was it over?

"It was on its way somewhere," the captain said. "We are just the unluckiest fools who got in its way."

With the roar of a gushing waterfall and a guttural gurgling bellow, a serpent shot part way out of the ocean, spinning in the air and diving back in. I'd never seen even a picture of a blue dragon—its mouth had been round like its body, the teeth spiraling inside like some sort of inverted drill, built to shear its prey to pieces. For several seconds, the middle of the dragon stayed in the air, blue scales flying past while it maintained the illusion of floating. Finally, a tail whipped by. If it had wings, I'd missed them.

"It's circling back," a crewman whispered, voice laced with dread.

"Run with the wind!" the captain shouted. "Square the mainsail!" Quietly, she muttered, "She's got our scent."

The cabin door burst open, Elliah emerging with the hammer clutched to her chest.

I sidled closer to the captain, whispering, "With any luck, the dragon just lost our scent."

"How's your chalky dirt?" I asked Beldroth.

"Yum," he said, smiling weakly.

The stuff was nasty and dried out one's tongue, even when mixed with water, where it floated like swamp scum. But it didn't rot in heat or go soggy in salt air. In storm-tossed weather, it kept us fed when nothing else would stay down—or lit a fire. We had packed dried fruit and hard tack, but we thought it wise to ration them. The spell made for easier, if less pleasant, meals. It was summoned, reliable, and dreadful. But it worked.

"Care for a bite?" Beldroth asked one of the two Salts who stood by the stairs, occasionally sharing words with one another, but almost never with us. Two sets of stairs led into the hold, and the crew of the Salty Squirt had shifted toward the stairs near the stern, making room for us. Also staying clear of us, other than the guards they'd posted to listen in. The look Beldroth received from them was calculating.

"It's not poison," I said.

"Could have fooled me," Beldroth said with a pasty tongue and just the barest hint of a smirk.

In fact, after the incident with the dragon, the captain hadn't treated us as badly as she'd forecasted when we'd been on shore. We'd explained the hammer, despite our worry that she'd toss it—or us—overboard the moment she understood that dragons pursued it. Her reaction had been quite the opposite, her eyes lighting like she'd found buried treasure. After that, when the Salts took advantage of opportunities to snag food from the ocean, they shared a bit with us, along with fruit from the plains of the Heartland. I hadn't had to feed us entirely from summoned rations. Their cargo—not just fruit, but also sheep—suggested they'd come from the south, the same as we had. It made sense, considering their knowledge of Hughelas's heritage—they must have crossed paths with the crew of the Knoll.

Despite his words, Beldroth spooned a scoop of the pasty water-dampened dustmeal into his mouth and swallowed it, one hand on a sheep he'd let loose from the makeshift pen in the rear of the hold. Though the Salty Squirt's crew had shared some of their bounty, we had hit stormy weather, and we learned quickly that Beldroth's motion-skittish stomach fared better with the bland summoned food. And, apparently, the comfort of a sheep.

"I can't believe I lost that book," Hughelas said for the thousandth time, staring at the ceiling from a cot strung up along the side of the hold.

His initial enthusiasm at seeing us had rapidly turned sullen when he learned we'd cast our lot with him instead of rescuing him. Truth be told, after running from elves my whole life, I didn't have the same reticence about fighting my people that Beldroth had. If it had been Elliah, *my* daughter, I would have gone in swinging. But Hughelas was Beldroth's son, not mine. I put my hand to my belly—how would we handle it when our shared offspring was born? Was there a whisper of hope that our unborn child would never have to run from his or her own people or be kidnapped?

"Tch," I said, almost laughing at the darkness of my own musings.

Elliah groaned, probably weary of the arguments evoked by Hughelas's theories.

"We are *not* trapped in a cage of magic," my beloved Beldroth snapped, his usual patience worn thin by nausea.

"'Ensnared by flames that magic weaves,'" Gormar quoted in a sing-song voice.

"Stop," Marinna said, burying her face in her hands.

But Gormar didn't stop. "'No escape. No reprieves.'"

"That could mean *anything*," Marinna snapped. They'd gone at it for days, rankling each other's nerves in argument after argument. "Instead of a portent for *us*, it's more likely a foretelling of your Red Prophetess's own doom, trapped under that magical dome covered by molten magma."

"That was not *her*!" Gormar snapped. "The Red Prophetess will return to lead us into battle in the last days."

"Magical Mesh," Trentius mumbled as he leaned against the wall atop a barrel. "Conjured Cage Captures the World." He earned a frown from Beldroth, but then the big Warder grinned when he saw that Trentius gazed up at the ceiling, not truly listening. Trentius's simple mind tended toward thinking of catchy descriptions of events. Smoky preferred sitting or flying above deck, even in the rain. I wondered if Trentius's upward gaze tracked the dragon.

"Brittanie leads your army," Marinna retorted to Gormar, ignoring Trentius and not letting go of her fight. "Besides, there's nothing in the Pyre's Reckoning that says *Elandra* will return. You've recited it often enough." Under her breath, she said, "Even though we're not *special* enough to hear it."

Gormar fumed. Literally. Smoke wafted from his thin, black hair. "She had *other* prophecies."

"And I'm sure," Marinna said, "those *other* prophecies are incredibly clear, completely justifying your conviction."

Marinna smirked when flames danced from Gormar's fingertips.

I stomped my foot, testing a simple Earth spell Beldroth drilled into me. To my surprise, the sharp crack of it hitting the wood echoed like splintering timber, drawing every eye in the hold—even the Salts at the far end. I forced my shoulders to relax and steadied my voice, though my heart pounded like a war drum. "We are on a ship in the middle of the sea. Quench your flame, Gormar. Quell your temper, Marinna. Everyone, quiet your tongues."

"If not your words with kindness bloom," my daughter chanted, "let silence be your song."

I smiled at her, my words for the past decades finally showing they'd taken root. She ruined it by rolling her eyes.

"You have something helpful to add?" I asked her politely, damping down my flare of irritation. Since when had I become the voice of reason? I did not care for the role.

"None of you will let Hughelas discuss what he… figured out," Elliah said. "But he thinks he understands why I'm Bereft, and, speaking as the most freakish oddity in the room, I'd like to hear more."

I sighed. Truthfully, I wanted to hear more as well. But Beldroth had balked at the outset. Hughelas should have known better than to introduce the topic days before with the words, "The Mother of Trees is trapped in a cage of her own creation." Of *course* that would upset his father! The Warder's faith had taken a serious blow from the encounter in the tomb under Themopolis, where an enchanted statue informed us that the Mother of Trees had to die.

"What if," I said, nudging Hughelas, "you focused on your thoughts about magic, and less on the Mother?"

Hughelas regarded me, blinking several times before nodding with a smile.

"Okay," he said, his voice measured but alive with a quiet eagerness. "Let me try." He swung his legs over the edge of the hammock, ducking to avoid the low beam overhead, and rubbed his hands together as though stoking an unseen flame. The motion reminded me of an artisan preparing for their craft—hands poised to carve an idea out of wood or ink it onto paper.

"Imagine a line," he began, his tone carrying the weight of a teacher about to sketch a universe from scratch. "And that line represents, say, Earth Magic." He hopped up and walked to the table and tried to push it, only to find it attached to the floor with metal plates and a pin. He frowned at it, then cocked his head and smiled. "Even better," he murmured.

He took an empty plate and set it at one end of the table. "Imagine," he said, "this end, this plate, represents very strong Earth magic." He took three steps to the other end, grabbing the bowl nearly emptied of summoned edible paste and placing it there. "And this end with the bowl represents resistance to Earth magic."

He walked back to the middle. "Someone here in the middle has no Earth magic, but also does not resist it."

"Okay," Elliah said, as Hughelas gathered wooden cups. "So I'm somewhere near the bowl of paste."

Hughelas nodded, a faint arch of his brows begging for patience.

Marinna rapped her knuckles lightly on the table's edge. "So this table represents how magic works?" she asked.

Hughelas grimaced. "How it works *now*," he said mysteriously. "But the planks for this table originally came from a much bigger tree," he said. "Imagine these boards came from somewhere in the middle of the trunk, but originally the tree extended further in each direction before it was cut."

"So our magic," Marinna said, talking slowly as she considered his words, "would have been stronger if the board had been cut longer?"

"Right!" Hughelas said, his enthusiasm brightening his features. "And the same for magic resistance."

"Go further?" Beldroth asked. "You mean like children having more powerful magic than their parents?"

"Well, yes," Hughelas said, but he shook his head. "But that's not the point I'm trying to make here."

I frowned, confused. "Zoras thought the same. It's a pretty common belief among High Elves. Mages would often choose others with powerful magic for mates." A small blush crept across my face. I hadn't been immune to that vanity.

As I spoke, Hughelas placed two cups toward the end with the plate, then a smaller cup a little closer to the end.

"It is a well-known concept among Alluvium as well," Gormar said, his tone clipped and dismissive, as if the topic barely deserved his attention. Marinna shot him a glare, either annoyed by his smugness or genuinely affronted by the unfamiliar concept. Perhaps both.

Gormar continued, oblivious or indifferent to her irritation. "Among us, it is well understood that when mages grow too powerful, their children are Bereft. How does that fit into this?"

Hughelas's lips quirked into a sly smile, as though he'd been waiting for that exact question. "Let's follow that train of thought." He tapped his knuckles on the table, then stretched his arms wide, miming the shape of the tabletop. "Now imagine that someone takes this table—this line— and warps it into a circle."

With his arms, he mimicked bending the ends of the table up, attempting to make a circle above his head, but hitting his hands on the ceiling. Hughelas, like his father, was tall. But he was thin, presumably like his Salt mother who had died when he was young. He ducked down and made his circle. "The end with the powerful magic touches the end with strong resistance to magic." He touched his fingers together at the imaginary circle's apex.

Gormar was the first to nod his head. "So once you go past the end,

30

you wind up on the other side," he said.

"Exactly!" Hughelas said, his grin widening.

Elliah's brows furrowed as she pieced it together. "The intended powerful child," she said slowly, "becomes, instead—"

"Bereft," Gormar finished. "The Lacking. Our broken children."

Elliah paled. Hughelas's voice became softer, gentler, almost a whisper. "But it isn't the Bereft who are broken. Magic itself is."

Trentius cocked his head like he heard something distant. "Smoky says we're approaching an island."

Marinna 1

The ship shuddered. And it was my fault. Nearing land meant the trap closed around us.

Beldroth glanced my way, and with a quick grimace, I slowly released my breath. The ship resumed its normal slight rocking, no longer behaving like its crew had dragged it across a rocky outcrop. I opened my eyes to find Beldroth giving me a barely noticeable smile—he remained cautious about gifting me smiles near his pregnant wife. She tended toward jealousy—once.

Illiara and I had come to terms after our initial misunderstanding. Fighting for our lives alongside one another had done more to reconcile us than any amount of talking. Still, my Warder teacher remained reserved, and I was fine with that.

My control had definitely improved. That was partly why I relished antagonizing Gormar so much. I mean, his sincerity concerning beliefs about the return of a prophet whose bones I'd seen with my own eyes irritated me like a mess of swamp ticks, but pushing him to lose his temper before I lost mine had become a little game for me.

Because, deep down, I was scared.

I'd wanted to learn from the Warder—he'd presented an opportunity to change in a fundamental way that would allow me to live the life I'd wanted to live. Ironically, my ideal life was simple. I'd wanted a little nook in the world where I would sculpt. Sculpt with a chisel. Then, with a bit of magical training from Beldroth, I'd learned I might be able to use magic to create my rock art, and a new dream was born. But that dream wasn't fighting fearsome dragons under tons of rock. Not boarding ships to places unknown with a threat of no return. And not squaring off against a race of elves I'd only heard stories about.

One Salt crewman had left the hold, probably checking on the ship after my nearly loosed magic had set it trembling. The other frowned at Beldroth, who didn't pay the Salt any heed at all. They had a certain striking elegance, their lean frames honed by working on the ship. Still, I had to admit I preferred Beldroth's bulky muscle to their wiry strength—but that wasn't something I would say aloud. Not for fear of offending the Salts, but because I had no desire to test Illiara's reaction. More men than women crewed the ship, yet the work flowed between them with no regard for gender. Except when monitoring us. Only men had stood guard in the hold they'd converted into a makeshift dormitory. Their clothes tended toward plain grays, whites, or light browns, looking worn down by the elements, but they decorated their white hair with colorful baubles, and often wore tight-fitting metal bracelets. Like Wood Elves, they lived life with their feet bared to the ground... well, boards, I supposed.

Our Salt guards seemed friendly enough with one another when they weren't on duty. But they were cold to us. Possibly because we'd threatened their ship? Regardless, it left me frightened about journeying to a place where they ruled. I didn't have the Warder's confidence that the Mother of Trees had a plan for all of us. Frankly, I'd not spent any time in my life thinking about the supposed goddess. The swamps, untouched by the war with the trolls, were perhaps far from the desperate prayers that rose like smoke in more embattled lands. But even if the Mother did somehow influence our effort, she had not guaranteed safe passage. If it served her will that I died at the hand of Salts, what comfort did that provide?

Hughelas and Elliah were the first out the door—our remaining Salt watcher did nothing to stop them. That was a good sign, right? The rest of us followed them out into a drizzling rain. It was evening, but a sky filled with ominous clouds darkened the day. We walked toward the bow, but I spotted no land.

"You have one who can sense the land?" asked the captain from behind me. I spun, startled, as I hadn't heard her approach. Her hawkish nose pointed at me like she intended to pin me with it.

"The... um... dragon," I said, pointing out toward the sky in front of the ship, though I did not see nor sense the dragon. I looked over at Trentius, whose gaze was to the left of where I pointed, and I adjusted my arm.

The captain's stern gaze shifted to Trentius.

"You will teach me this spell," she commanded him, "so that I may communicate with dragons."

"Oh, absolutely," Trentius said, still watching the distant sky. "As soon as I figure out what I did." With a smile, he added, "'Spell Slipup Sparks Serendipitous Success.'"

The captain frowned, but Trentius seemed oblivious. Illiara stepped in. "He had a Hook in him for too long as a youth." Illiara's eyes flicked to Hughelas and her daughter, but returned to the captain, whose eyes pinched at her. "It's a High Elf spell that... well, it can addle your wits if left too long before being removed."

"I was trying to Compel it, to save our lives," Trentius said. "Smoky. The dragon. But I did the spell wrong. Now we are stuck." With a beatific smile, he added. "But she doesn't seem to mind." His smile turned wistful. "She was lonely in a way... one of many, all alike. But now she's *special*."

The captain nodded, like his words made sense to her, then barked a fresh order over. "Gather your things. You'll disembark soon."

A flash of lightning rolled around inside the distant clouds, briefly illuminating the horizon, and an island appeared, until the dark sky swallowed it back into the shadows. Seconds later, when the distant rumbling thunder reached us, the clouds above us took it as their cue to dump more water. We got little rain in Fael Themar. Water came in from the grasslands to mix with the ocean water and create our brackish swamps, but for whatever reason, clouds rarely deluged us. More often, they parked down in the swamps, creating misty fog that caused even the rare dry land to turn into muck.

The rain wasn't heavy, but it was unfamiliar. Was it unpleasant? Illiara and Elliah didn't appear to mind it in the least; to be caught in the rain must have been common in the mountain forests. Neither did the Salts take offense. Beldroth's usual smile had slipped away, making his face harder. Harsher. Gormar pulled a hood out from his black robes and covered his head. Why did he even have a hood on his robe? Fear of bat droppings in his labyrinthian home?

I wanted to be like everyone else, but the water was a little too cold, and the slight wind would have had me shivering before long. I didn't want to have anything in common with Gormar, but a hooded robe would have been pleasant.

It took several minutes before we glimpsed land again, the far-off lightning unable to overcome the obscuring rain. It surprised me we hadn't headed straight toward the island. I'd assumed it was our destination, but it looked like the Salty Squirt intended to pass it. I didn't know what direction we headed, and I found it as disconcerting as when the mainland had first faded from view. If the ship sank, would I even know which direction to swim?

Minutes later, too late to save a dry spot anywhere, but before the shivers had truly set in, the rain let up. Indeed, the island appeared to the side of the boat. The port side? We didn't name the sides of rowboats in the swamps, and the ship's details still confused me. But even as we passed it, the captain banked the ship hard to the left… hard to port, and pointed us at the island. We drove right toward a dark band of clouds that promised worse than the drizzle we'd just escaped.

I jumped as lightning pelted the air on either side of the ship with its simultaneous cracks of thunder. It was a miracle they hadn't hit the ship! More followed, and I questioned the captain's sanity as she barreled straight through, while I waited for the downpour to ensue.

With a rapid shift, the light returned to its previous state of mere overcast. I turned back, started by the sudden change. From the vantage point of having passed through, a different story unfolded. A dark band of clouds ringed the island, holding steady, while the lighter clouds—lighter, but still dark enough to have soaked us—passed them by. Somehow, the Salts tucked their island inside a storm ring of magic.

The wall of storms was incredible. What kind of magic held it in place, concealing and protecting the island? *"Deara keeps its secrets,"* the captain had whispered in my ear when she and her team kidnapped me.

It had clearly meant something else in context. They'd come looking for me because of who my mother was. *Daughter of the Nine Winds.* The memory of my mother's death had become distorted over the years. I knew that. Both bigger and smaller than what it was. The details of the fight eluded my memory completely. Yet, I distinctly remembered the look of surprise on my mother's face when the dragon charged into the cave we inhabited in the ruins of Bellon, already bloody and broken, and the single word my mother had uttered. "You?"

My mother had tried to calm the raging dragon. I had never understood her intention. She wasn't a Healer. It was foolish, and it had cost us her life.

Up to that point, I hadn't known dragons spoke. The ones that climbed over the mountains from the Dragonlands were younger and smaller. But that one had spoken. It curled its tail, almost protectively, around my mother's dead body, saying, "Lyrei, Daughter of the Nine Winds, it seems I've run to my death." In my memory, the stalactite had plunged into the dragon's head just as she'd finished speaking. Like she knew her death was coming. But if she had known, why hadn't she simply moved?

I hadn't missed the identical pose of the dragon bones in the buried swamp city, its tail encircling the pedestal.

There was a magic, probably only rumor or legend, called True Sight or Seeing. It was a power attributed to the Mother of Trees by her faithful believers, like my father. Fire magic offered prophetic visions, as Gormar had shown, but most treated those auguries with skepticism... even disbelief. Obviously not Gormar, who held to his prophecies as my father used to hold to his beliefs in the Mother. *Fire lies.*

While I deeply struggled with the idea that the Mother of Trees—a decaying and demented husk—orchestrated fate, it strained belief to think all the events that had led us to our current predicament were purely coincidental. A dragon killing my mother, it speaking her title, and my father using that title to get us passage to see the Mother of Trees, leading to my kidnapping by our current captors. How had the white dragon known my mother's title? *We* hadn't even known it!

Deara keeps its secrets.

My mother certainly had. The captain of the Salty Squirt had said nothing further on the matter. The very island before us—presumably

Deara—nested in concealing magic. My father told me of his conversation at the port—that no outsiders travel to Deara and return. And yet, the captain hadn't tried to lock us up, hadn't kept us apart. She'd merely ensured none of us had privacy.

As we approached the island, it became clear that, despite the halo curtain-wall of tempests, the sky directly over the island had normal weather—the spotty rain outside the island also nestled above it. Spots of sunlight broke through and illuminated steep cliffs of dark rock. We gathered our things from below and brought them on deck, the island seeming to jump forward during that time.

"Where are the docks?" I wondered aloud. A gray, decaying structure sat atop the cliffs, a single tower poking out its top like the last finger of a drowning man. But no docks nestled at the base of the cliffs.

I looked for Smoky and found him circling between the ship and the island. "Does Smoky have anything interesting to say?" I asked.

Trentius nodded his head rapidly. "Oh, yes! She says the waters outside the storm wall are swimming with memories, but none are inside. Very interesting. 'Mysterious Memories Swim the Sea.'"

Swimming with memories? "Smoky has been here before?" I asked.

Trentius shook his head, screwing his lips up as he thought. "No, she hasn't been here. She says the memories are down there… in the water."

Um… okay. "Can she go scout ahead?" Knowing what to expect might give us a fighting chance.

"I would advise against that," the captain said.

"Of course you would," Illiara mumbled.

"She's your dragon," the captain said. "Do as you will. But we have no way of notifying the coast guard that your… Smoky… is a friend."

"Do you often have trouble with dragons?" my father asked in all earnestness.

"Do fish have gills?" the captain responded. "Not inside the storm wall," she said with a grimace. "But Dearans will be particularly… sensitive… right now. That building," she said, pointing at the only visible structure, "lies on a rocky outcrop that conceals a harbor. You can't see it from here, but there are passages on either side of the outcropping." The captain's answer divulged more information than any conversation we'd had with her on the trip, and yet she kept going. "We will berth in said harbor. You should call your dragon to the ship. She will come to no harm if she is seen to be carried by the Salty Squirt. I cannot guarantee the same if she flits about." Her hawklike gaze pierced Trentius. "I do not want her to come to harm." Her tone reminded me of a school teacher intimidating a student for his or her own good.

Trentius bit his lip and looked out toward Smoky, who lazily glided back toward the ship. Whatever Trentius's attempted spell of Compulsion had actually done, the results were remarkable. Too bad his addled state prevented him from realizing and explaining what he'd accomplished.

Well, since the captain's tongue had loosened... "And then?" I asked.

The captain raised an eyebrow.

"And then?" I asked again.

The captain sighed, shook her head as though saying, *what a shame*, and turned back to bark orders to her crew, who were clearly doing fine without her.

I pursed my lips and looked at my father, wincing internally. Her response didn't foretell a warm reception.

"Don't worry, son." My father put his massive, stone-crushing hand on my shoulder.

"I know," I muttered. "The Mother's plan."

"The Mother's plan," my father said, but with no conviction. He sighed. "If She has a plan," he drawled, and not in his usual booming voice, "I don't know what it is. I had a plan, which She blessed, but that plan is now underway without me. The Alluvium march to join with the High Elves and take their forces to—" He paused, looking at Elliah meaningfully. She wasn't supposed to know the details of the plan. Something had broken into her mind, and she worried it would happen again, so we didn't speak the details out loud. "—to battle," he finished. "I'm *here*. Not there."

I winced. My father's convictions had once been overbearing. But our adventures had rattled his cage, and I realized, too late, that I'd taken comfort in his certainties, even while I'd also railed against them. A part of me longed to have my old father back, particularly when faced with the uncertainty before us.

But what he was trying to tell me—that message had power too. He was there for me. He'd made a choice. He had my back. I wasn't alone.

The Salts had locked me in irons when they'd first captured me. They'd clamped on circular bands that held my hands behind my back. It was not only uncomfortable; it made spell-casting virtually impossible. Someone with a lot more experience, like Wynruil, probably would have managed. But not me. I'd been afraid of a lot of things in my life—losing my mother, leaving home, almost losing Elliah—but my father had always been there. I'd never been completely alone. Nothing had frightened me more than when the Salts kidnapped me: alone, chained to a post in the darkened hull of a ship, being taken away by strangers to a strange land.

"If you need me, I will be there," he said, with the conviction he previously reserved for statements about the Mother. His touch conveyed his usual beaming smile, though I suspected I would find something much more grim on his face if I turned to look. "Unless your sibling or his or her mother needs me more, of course."

My sibling? *Oh, the unborn baby.* Oddly, I hadn't thought of the baby

Illiara carried as a sibling. I was going to have a brother or sister. Half-brother or half-sister.

"Tch," Illiara sounded, then she'd chuckled softly.

They'd thrown their full weight to help me. Which just tightened the knot in my stomach, because… well, because they were in dire straits for me. No matter how well we fought, or what magic or anti-magic we wielded, we would remain trapped on Deara. We lacked the skill to sail back ourselves any time in the near future. I didn't see how our futures held anything but ruin, and they'd taken that step for me.

"So, what will we do when we get there?" I asked the group. "What if we have to fight?"

"Whoa, whoa, whoa!" the captain said, stomping back over. She looked aside. "Furl the sails and ready a tender!" she shouted. "You're not fighting on *my* ship," she told us. "I'll row you to shore myself, and you can raze the fleet as much as you wish from that noble transport."

The fleet? Well, of course they'd have a fleet. Deara was an island—its people would depend on trade, and trade required ships.

I studied the furling of the sails as closely as I'd watched all of their trimming, easing, and luffing. Given that ships were our only exit route, the more I knew, the better. It wasn't the same as jumping into the thick of it myself, but they weren't likely to welcome my involvement. In fact, I'd noticed tensions even within their own ranks—sailors who, upon approaching a group of Salts below deck for leisure, caused conversations to falter and die. While they worked together well enough to sail, that trust didn't anchor deeply.

While the crew clearly possessed magic, they rarely used it, relying on the wind and their sails to make way. For learning, I tried creating a little vortex in the ocean like my mother had taught me, and I found it next to impossible compared to working the same spell on a mountain lake or the Contentious River.

They hadn't dropped anchor, and the waves carried the Salty Squirt ever closer to the jagged rocks, each swell dragging her inch by inch toward destruction. The crew had readied, then lowered, what I would have called a large rowboat into the waters.

"Let's go," the captain said, elegantly maneuvering over the rail and walking backward, hand-over-hand, down a rope to the boat below.

The others grabbed their packs, slinging them over shoulders with practiced ease. My lacking one reminded me once again that they were all in the situation because of me.

I looked at my father. Technically, he hadn't quite fulfilled his end of the bargain. We hadn't reached Deara. My father raised his eyebrows, tilting his head. His conscience wouldn't eat at him if we fought back—he wanted my input on whether we should. But to what end? To sink the ship at the foot of Deara did us no more good than sinking it in the ocean would have. I shook my head and climbed over the rail.

The others followed, one by one. Even Smoky fluttered down to coo encouragement to Trentius. Was it my imagination, or did the Salty Squirt lean as my father, the last of us, clambered down?

A large canvas bag already sat in the boat, wedged beneath the center bench. I didn't recognize it from among our gear. Too heavy to be provisions, too lumpy to be spare rope. I narrowed my eyes, suspicion blooming—something about the shape suggested weapons.

The captain began rowing before my father even settled, and despite her declaration that she would take us to shore herself, I seized a second set of oars and matched her rhythm, our strokes cutting through the waves. If we were going to Deara, we wouldn't cower—we would meet it head-on. My fears for myself had dulled in the face of greater concerns for my companions and family. There was no easy escape; we would have to learn the ways of Deara, uncover its secrets, and find our own way out. The sooner we started, the sooner we would be out the other side. A flicker of curiosity stirred beneath the urgency—about this place, about the family my mother never spoke of, about what knowledge the island might hold. Whatever awaited us, I was ready to face it.

The crew of the Salty Squirt hoisted the sails and flew past us, disappearing into an inlet guarded by cliffs and screeching gulls.

"We have little time," the captain said over her shoulder, "and what I'm about to tell you, you didn't hear from me."

Marinna 2

What had possessed me to go chasing after the Warder's son?

I'd surely been under some kind of delusional after-effects from the victory in Cenaedth. After all, I'd slain a dragon! Yes, I'd felt powerful... invulnerable even. My overconfidence was shocking—I'd intended to prove myself a second time by returning him safely. So, like a child who knew no fear, I'd skipped cheerily into the bog.

I should have walked away at the docks when I had a chance. I'd hesitated, the moment of reality nudging me to listen, and I'd ignored it. To my great regret. My magic tended toward breaking things; on a boat, that usually led to a lot of swimming.

After days at sea, approaching the island's rocky cliffs was like drawing near a warm campfire after a wintry day in the marshes. Even from the rowboat, I imagined I sensed the stone—solid, unyielding—holding fast against the mercurial waters that battered its base.

"Go on," Hughelas said to the captain between strokes.

"Do not mistake me," the captain snapped. "I am not your friend. I am not your ally. Do not come to me for help." She drove the oars hard, then eased them back, settling the handles inside the boat. She turned, giving us an appraising look. "Neither am I your enemy."

I exchanged skeptical glances with the others, but Hughelas took the lead, saying simply, "Understood."

Still, she hesitated, and I wondered why. She gnawed on her lip, ruminating on her choices. Finally, she spoke again. "Deara keeps its secrets. You will not be permitted to leave. This is your new home. Either your paradise or your cage. Choose the illusion you prefer. But it will also be your gravesite. However, it need not be *that* today."

"We *will* leave," Elliah said, anger clear in her voice.

My jaw clenched in agreement. Indignant self-righteousness boiled up. *You can't keep people against their will.* The words sat on my lips, unspoken. Untrue. The island stood several stories out of the water on cliffs. All the Salts had to do was control the ports—perhaps just one port—and they would control what went in and out of the island.

"You," the captain snapped toward Elliah, "Drevin will want to tear apart, just to see what makes you tick!"

The boat tensed, but the captain shut her eyes and took several breaths, and no one spoke or made a move. What would we have done? Throw her overboard and row back to the mainland? Impossible. The nearness of the rocky shore no longer steadied me. My chest tightened, thoughts spiraling as if the sea itself had pulled the ground out from under me.

"I apologize," the captain said. "You need to understand that the more I tell you, the more likely you are to respond in a way that reveals me, and it will be my gravestone they carve on the morrow. So just *listen*. Disagree and argue with me on your own time, in your head, after we have parted ways."

Elliah nodded once, still angry.

"You will be separated," she said. "The separation will have plausible reasons, but the real purpose? 'Split the fleet and let the tides pull them apart.'"

Beldroth's blond brows knit in concentration, but Illiara turned to look at her daughter, worry sketched on her face.

"You can use that to your advantage—you'll gather more information separately. You'll have to find ways to compare notes." She turned to Elliah. "As I said, they will likely devise some experiment that will bring you to a swift end, but if not, fade into the background. Be as plain and boring as possible. Stay clear of Drevin." The last she said with a pinched nose, like a foul smell had surprised her. "Same for you and your dragon," she said to Trentius. "If you want to keep your head on your shoulders, you'd do well to figure out how to enable others to cast that spell." The dragon sat at the stern of the boat, its head dangling over the side to peer down into the water.

"You," she said to Hughelas, "are a Scion of the Nine Winds. You will learn politics, or you will die trying... or not trying if you so choose. Remember this: you hold one card—no one knows your mother's story. Hold that *tightly*. It may keep you alive long enough to learn the basics of the court and perhaps fade into anonymity like Scion Samblar once did. You seem bright, but you will be no match for Pyrravyn. He is regent of the current Daughter of the Nine Winds, and he will tear you to pieces if he perceives you as a threat."

"What—" Hughelas started to ask, but the captain interrupted.

"We are out of time," she said, turning and dipping the oars back in the water. "Welcome to Deara." We rounded a bend, revealing a harbor too big to be true, so filled with ships that it looked like a dead forest of masts spider-webbed with riggings. The captain grumbled under her breath, "May her tides ever bind us."

Elliah ~ 3

We couldn't let them split us up! We'd faced dragons together, and yet they'd caught us like fish in a net, our strength worth nothing. Okay, not *nothing*. Fighting was an option. We would take some of them out.

Before we reached the docks, the captain bent down and tugged open the large canvas bag tucked beneath the bench. Metal glinted inside.

"Your weapons," she said simply, nudging the bag for us to take what was ours. "If anyone asks, I don't know how they got here."

Her expression remained unreadable, but something flinty lingered in her eyes. A warning—or a quiet act of rebellion.

"I'm not fighting elves," Beldroth said, his voice final, an oath carved in stone, but he grabbed his sword nonetheless.

"What choice do we have?" my mother said.

I wondered if my face showed the same determination as hers.

"We have a choice," Beldroth answered.

The others armed themselves, though I had my hammer already. But everyone kept them sheathed.

"'But beware the rise of the army of the Bereft,'" Gormar intoned. "'For when the Destroyer awakens, the Bones of Cenaedth shall burn.' I really don't think, in the end, we will have a choice. Elandra prophesied elves draining the souls of other elves, and that was one of her more joyous visions. Elves *will* fight elves. It may as well be now."

I squirmed. Hearing Gormar say it out loud made the thought seep like damp rot in heartwood—less a passing fear, more a certainty. I didn't want to share his grim vision of the world.

Was it possible to disappear into the armada of ships? Our rowboat a minnow amongst whales? But many eyes peered down at us as we took our slow passage through the watery labyrinth of bobbing wood, ropes, and birds. The Salty Squirt blended into the forest of ships, barely noticeable—until I caught the flurry of movement on its deck. Why *so* many ships?

But the location… it would've been faster for Captain Striker to have *walked* us in. Either she truly feared we might fight back and damage her ship when we saw the fate that awaited us—or she used the detour as an excuse to speak with us in private.

"The Peacekeepers have a vision," the captain said, very quietly. I hadn't realized I'd spoken my question aloud, but I had. "Not a *vision*, in the way *you* talk of them," she hissed to Gormar. "A plan. A purpose."

She shrugged. "They have not invited me into the details of that plan, but it is hard not to see the truth: war galleys, brigs, and merchantmen alike swell their fleet—enough to blockade or invade every Salt port in the world."

We rounded a corner in the maze of docks, and sands came into view—a narrow ribbon of beach hugged tightly between the restless waves and the looming rock wall. The cliffs above loomed, stone sentinels guarding the harbor, their jagged surfaces softened here and there by patches of stubborn vegetation. They drew my eyes upward, following the steep climb to the top, where large, imposing structures of stone and wood silently judged the harbor below. They were not the homes of fishermen or traders but the dwellings of authority, heavy with the weight of their purpose. Towers with narrow windows watched us like vultures, their presence undoubtedly less cold and indifferent than they appeared.

At the end of the channel we rowed, a group of Salts had gathered on the beach. Unlike the scattered sailors I'd seen before, this was an official-looking crowd, their postures straight and their expressions unreadable. Some wore medallions glinting in the sunlight, marking them as figures of importance, or at least authority. They stood in stark contrast to the casual chaos of the dockworkers and fishmongers further down the shoreline. These were not people here to welcome us; they were there to assess us—or perhaps to ensure we posed no threat. Behind them, the city loomed in silence, its presence heavy with the promise of what lay ahead.

"You look much like your mother," the captain whispered, startling me. But she wasn't talking to me. She looked over her shoulder at Hughelas. "It's the only reason I brought you back. If anyone had a chance of stopping this nonsense, it was your mother. I had to try."

After one final pull on the oars, she stowed them. We gathered our packs, slinging them over shoulders or hugging them to chests. The captain rose and stepped with careful authority across the narrow space. Water splashed around her calves as she dropped into the shallows and tugged the boat firmly onto the sands. Without hesitation, she marched past the line of Salts waiting for us on the beach. Ten in total, they stood shoulder to shoulder, several wearing medallions bearing the emblem of a fist gripping a trident. Those medallion-wearers regarded us with a sour disdain, as if we'd insulted their mothers or fouled their boots. Unlike the other Salts I'd encountered so far, some of these wore sturdy boots and carried swords on their hips, their stern gazes completing the image of a policing force. Everything about them, from their posture to the controlled menace in their expressions, suggested they were here to ensure none of us did anything foolish.

Among them, I recognized a man from the Salty Squirt, standing a bit apart, as though unsure of his place. He must have exited the ship and rushed across the docks with great haste to have beaten us there. The captain of the ship, however, had vanished into the crowd. None of the onlookers lingered openly to watch, but they surreptitiously viewed the spectacle unfolding before them.

One elf, a man dressed in a light robe of sea-blue with yellow banding, smiled from the center of the group. He had a hand on the shoulder of a little girl who must have been in her mid-twenties—a little past infancy for an elf—the top of her white locks barely reaching the man's stomach. She wore robes similar to his, but scowled as fiercely as the booted elves around her. Despite lacking authoritative clothing, or perhaps *because* he lacked it, my gut told me he was in charge. He confirmed my speculation by speaking first. "Rumor informs me that I am in the company of a Scion of the Nine Winds. The son of Lyrei Windsinger. I do hope these rumors can be believed."

Hughelas had pulled his oars in, the same as the captain had done. He stood, bravely stepping off the nose of the boat onto the sand. Beldroth's heavy form followed close behind. The rest of us went one by one, adjusting our packs as we stepped onto the sand, our backs to the water.

"My mother's name was Lyrei," Hughelas said. "A source I trust spoke her title, 'Daughter of the Nine Winds.' I admit I have nothing resembling formal proof that I am, as you say, a Scion." Hughelas deftly dodged the mention of a dragon providing the revelation.

Still smiling, the Salt said, "It would certainly be a strange and disturbing lie, and would cause you no end of trouble. Also a very difficult lie to even conceive." Almost laughing, he continued. "You have no idea the turmoil you've stirred up." The militant elves scowled as the chatty elf became more jovial. The little girl looked up at the man with pursed lips, as though she tried to work out the joke. With apparent difficulty, he reined in his amusement. "Allow me to introduce myself. I am Pyrravyn, until recently, believed to be the last Scion of the Nine Winds."

The last Scion? His words hung like the storm clouds on the horizon. The captain of the Salty Squirt had warned us of politics. Yet I found myself drawn to Pyrravyn, like a safe harbor in a storm. It wasn't that I trusted him, but compared to the scowls of the others…

"And this," Pyrravyn said, pulling the young girl in front of him, "is Bella, Daughter of the Nine Winds, who will one day lead our people."

"It's not a very *frightening* name, is it?" the girl asked, her sharp eyes settling on me. "I can see you're not wearing boots. But would you be quaking in them if you were?"

With all the hard, scowling faces around her, I intuited she was expected to be intimidating. I did not find her frightening, and her earnest question struck a chord with me and demanded an honest answer. Yet admitting she was not intimidating lacked wisdom. "Many aspects of our situation frighten me," I answered. I smiled brightly. "But your name itself did not make me want to throw myself off your cliffs. It is a pleasure to meet you, Bella, Daughter of the Nine Winds. I am Elliah."

She nodded at me, then turned to Pyrravyn. "See, I told you. No quaking, cousin."

This brought genuine pleasure to Pyrravyn's eyes. "You are young yet. Plenty still quake at the mention of Jade Galefinger."

Bella looked over at my feet before turning back to Pyrravyn and shaking her head.

In fact, I *had* heard of Captain Jade Galefinger. Talena Talonforged had encountered her on the seas and narrowly escaped with her life. But that had been a children's story. A book I still carried but hadn't opened since… I couldn't remember when I'd stopped reading it, but my life had become busy.

"Let me save us some time," Pyrravyn said, after chuckling at Bella's innocence. "I've already heard a report on each of you. Despite appearances," he said, looking at us, but nodding at the grim faces around him, "your arrival is most opportune. We have need of you all." He looked at Beldroth, "We have a problem that Earth magic might solve." He turned to my mother. "But the path is dangerous, and your Healing magic may be required."

That which I dreaded had begun—they were splitting us up.

To Gormar he said, "Your prophecies—our people need a guiding light." He turned to Marinna. "I hear you saved the Salty Squirt from being torn apart by a blue dragon's dorsal blades. You will save countless lives." He swept his gaze to Trentius, whose dragon poorly hid behind him but stuck its head out to the side to watch the proceedings. "You tamed a dragon! We must learn how you did it." His piercing gray eyes locked onto mine. "And the ability to resist magic. You have no idea how valuable that might be."

"I know you all came to defend your friend." To Beldroth he said, "Your son. But I assure you, he is in no danger. Unless he proves not to be who he claims. Another Scion of the Nine Winds will be a great relief to me. I have carried the burden of this island for far too long."

"And what," Hughelas asked, "if we all wish simply to leave?"

"Please," Pyrravyn said, his smile unwavering, though something in his eyes tightened. "Stay a little while. Understand the situation before deciding to go." In my mind, I heard the whispered words of the captain when she'd taken Hughelas. *Deara keeps its secrets.* "Please."

Without pausing, he turned to his left. "The lovely lady with the sword on her back and the pretty medallion is Eryndra Tidebringer, leader of the Peacekeepers." I didn't think it possible for her to deepen her scowl, but she did. The medallion, a fist clutching a trident, was the same as from Gormar's prophecy on the ship. That's when I realized I'd seen Pyrravyn before, in Gormar's prophecy as well. "Eryndra, if you would be so kind as to show Marinna around the shipyard? If there's something we can do to better dragon-proof it, I'm sure you would be very interested."

"Come," snipped the angry Peacekeeper.

Marinna paled.

"You will be safe," Pyrravyn told Marinna. "Perhaps you would accompany her?" he asked Trentius.

"Hesitant High Elf Hovers to Ward Wandering Wood Elf," Trentius said, taking Marinna's elbow in his, Smoky moving to Marinna's far side, as though to protect her. The color returned to Marinna's face as she gave Smoky a hesitant pat on the neck, receiving a gurgling purr in response. Eryndra turned and stalked away. They hurried to catch up, fading into the scattered Salts as they climbed onto the wooden docks, the small crowd either parting or stopping to gawk at Smoky.

For the thousandth time, I reminded myself we were trapped and didn't have a move that led us safely away from Deara. We had to play nice.

"Her magic would be more useful on a trading vessel," said a woman in elegant robes cut from fine sea-silk, her arms crossed and her chin tilted in restrained disapproval. She had the smooth, composed features of the highborn, but there was steel behind the grace. White hair, swept back from her face and pinned with silver combs shaped like wind-blown leaves, framed sharp eyes that weighed everything with merchant's precision. She looked like someone used to getting her way—without ever needing to raise her voice.

Pyrravyn raised a placating hand, though she didn't see it. "Let her train with the Tidebringer," he said. "Would you rather she experiment on a private trading vessel, where you risk losing cargo as well as endangering the galleon itself, or one of Eryndra's ships?"

"Hmm," she responded, neither agreeing nor disagreeing, but clearly displeased. "We have so *much* the world would pay for," she said instead. "You're a scoundrel, Scion Pyrravyn, but you're no fool. Why empty our coffers on war when you can fill them with trade?"

War? I looked back over the harbor. There were a *lot* of ships. More than a hundred? I thought so. Beyond the first couple of rows of ships, an army of masts stood ready.

"Allow me to introduce Yselda Coldwind," Pyrravyn said, "the head of our trading community. A staunch advocate of a more open world view."

"We have treasures the world would pay for," Yselda responded. "I'm not suggesting we *give* away our discoveries freely."

"Wrasseguard Feldryn," Pyrravyn said, and a male Salt warrior who lacked the Peacekeeper emblem snapped to attention. "Please show

Beldroth and Illiara the problem we have in the mines." With a look of self-deprecation, he said to Beldroth, "Please, just take a look. Your magic is suited to the task, where ours is not."

Beldroth, rightfully, appeared concerned. We were being split up, exactly as the captain had warned us would happen. But at least my mother would accompany him. I would be with Hughelas, and Gormar would join us as well. Not that I expected Gormar to be of any help.

"Please," Pyrravyn said. "I understand your unease. But remember," and his voice took on an edge, "you were not invited here. You are not guests. You insisted on coming with a threat to a merchant vessel of Deara." Yselda nodded her agreement. "There are those here who would treat you more harshly." Yselda nodded again. "But *I* understand that our actions triggered yours." Pyrravyn's eyes landed again on Hughelas. "Even if you are a Scion of the Nine Winds, you should not have been taken forcefully." Yselda's cheeks reddened slightly. "At this point, I merely hope to diffuse a heated situation until calmer heads prevail. Your help would go a long way toward resolving any ill will and possibly even forge friendships."

Forge friendships. Right.

"Please?" the little girl asked.

Grudgingly, Beldroth walked to the one Pyrravyn had named Feldryn, who had moved to the side with two others accompanying him, one male and the other female. The men were both brutes, though neither had the bulk of Beldroth… Warders were naturally big. If Beldroth fought them, and if no magic were involved, Beldroth would take them. With magic, who knew? But Beldroth was reluctant to fight other elves, and even if he did, it wouldn't get us off the island. The woman's sharp features suggested a stern rigor that brooked no nonsense. Rough crew.

"Take him to see the Skywarden first," Pyrravyn said. "I authorize Warder Beldroth and the lady Illiara, Scion of Celendril to witness the Tempest Crown."

Yselda raised an eyebrow. "How fortunate that neither Eryndra nor Maelith are here to protest," she said.

"Isn't it, though," Pyrravyn replied.

The Peacekeepers who remained scowled, but apparently lacked the authority to disagree.

Pyrravyn sighed. With a nod of his head to Beldroth, he said, "He needs to know what he's up against. It's stupid to send him in blind. Our silence poisons what it seeks to protect."

My mother gave me one last, long look, packed with worry, love, and pride. Then she joined Beldroth. The five of them walked toward the cliff. That left me, Hughelas, and Gormar.

Someone hurried toward our group, stopping abruptly to pull a book from his pocket. He flipped through it, doing… something… with it.

Pyrravyn rubbed his eyes, quietly groaning.

Yselda was less patient. "The sea is less whimsical than that elf."

The elf in question, white hair wild like lightning had combed it, stuffed the book back in his robes, looking around like he didn't know where he was or why. Upon spotting Pyrravyn, he rushed toward us with long strides.

Sighing, Pyrravyn spoke with magnanimous patience. "I'm glad you deigned to join us, Drevin—"

But the newcomer brushed right past Pyrravyn, marching straight toward me. I involuntarily took a step back, and Hughelas grabbed one of Drevin's arms, yanking him to a halt and earning drawn swords from the remaining Peacekeepers.

Drevin. That was the name the captain had warned us to steer clear of. Wonderful.

He didn't jerk away from Hughelas, or turn to him angrily. He tried, with his arm held, to see over my shoulder. Which he did pretty well with his typical Salt height.

"Is it really dragon bone?" he asked me, leaning away from Hughelas for a better view, then leaning *on* Hughelas to try another angle.

"Drevin!" Pyrravyn barked, marching over and clasping his other arm. "Put your swords away," he snapped at the Peacekeepers who had surrounded us. "Stand down! Now!" More quietly, he hissed to Drevin, "You're frightening our guests."

"Nonsense," Drevin said, still not looking at me, but trying to see *around* me to the hammer. To move things along, I pulled the hammer from its sling. Drevin sucked in a breath. His eyes darted from the hammer to my eyes, then back again.

He looked up at the sky. "Why don't they take it?" he asked everyone or no one. "I am told you're Bereft." While he hadn't connected the two points, the way he said it made them sound connected. He looked around. "I was told there would be a red dragon." He looked back at the hammer. "Can I hold it?" Immediately his brows furrowed, and he surveyed our group. "And a Warder. Where's the Warder?" He reached for his pockets, confounded by the constraining arms which kept his gizmos at bay.

Pyrravyn placed himself as an obstacle between Drevin and me, slowly releasing Drevin's arm. He nodded to Hughelas with a wry grin, conveying he *thought* it would be okay for Hughelas to set Drevin free.

Drevin pulled out a book and something pen-like, which he proceeded to use to jot a note into his book. "Well, can I?" he asked, without looking up.

"Hold a red dragon?" I asked, purposefully mangling his questions to stall for time.

He paused, jotting another note. "Hold the hammer," he said. He

48

turned to Hughelas. "Where *is* that dragon?" Then he scrunched his eyebrows, slowly pivoting to Pyrravyn. "He looks much like Lyrei. Remarkable. To think she lived a whole life. Out there. Deara keeps its secrets, but a Daughter of the Nine Winds leaving Deara with no trace for a century. A remarkably well-kept secret."

Pyrravyn's jaw muscles clenched during Drevin's speech, but he quickly recovered. "I sent the dragon and its... familiar... with the Tidebringer."

"Well, if she kills it," Drevin said, "alert me before it's collected."

Kill it? Why would Eryndra Tidebringer kill Smoky? I tried to find a flurry of activity that might indicate Smoky's location, but they'd disappeared.

"She won't kill the dragon," Pyrravyn said, the irritation plain in his voice. "Stop scaring our guests!"

"Why did you even tell him?" Yselda grumbled, her arms folded in front of her.

"Well, I'd *intended* for Drevin to see the dragon," Pyrravyn fussed back. He turned to Drevin. "But you arrived late. For now, you'll have to make do with those here."

Meaning me and my hammer.

"My parting with it," I said, "has proven to attract the unwanted attention of winged reptiles." While that was true, I was reluctant to part with the hammer for many reasons, including a gradual sapping of my energy when we parted ways.

"Expected," Drevin muttered. "If it really is dragon bone, that is. Unfortunately, the only convincing proof would result in its collection. I don't want that. But come, let's inspect that hammer and the Bereft girl who carries it. Come back to my lab." He turned and started back up the small beach in the direction from which he'd arrived.

I closed my mouth when I realized it hung open. They wanted me to go with that lunatic?

"Pyrravyn!" a woman shouted. Everyone turned to the newcomer, who, like Drevin, had not only full pockets, but extra pockets also filled. Except books and papers filled hers instead of gadgets. She moved hastily to our group, patting her pockets as she approached. From one pocket, she pulled out a book. After a quick glance, she shoved it back in a different pocket and searched some more. She arrived with a smile for Pyrravyn and a leather-bound book held out like a prize.

"Yes, Janelle?" Pyrravyn asked with skeptical amusement. Young Bella stood on her tippy toes, trying to get a better look, and Janelle lowered the book for her appraisal.

"I found the one I'd told you about," she said proudly.

"And you had to deliver it *now*?" Pyrravyn asked.

"Well," she said, looking around curiously. "I went to the palace, and they said you were at the harbor. You're always somewhere else," she said, matter-of-factly. "And it's nice to mark something off the list."

"You could have… I don't know… *left* the book at the royal quarters," he suggested.

"And risk it falling into the wrong hands?" Janelle said with a palm to her chest and wide eyes.

"Yes," Pyrravyn said, "there's real danger there. We *are* talking about the book for Bella, aren't we?"

"Yes!" she confirmed. "It's a rare one." Janelle got behind Bella and held it out in front of her. "The Tales of Talena Talonforged." She opened the leather cover to a familiar, though upside down, title.

I had a surreal sensation and shrugged my pack on my back to check for the book's familiar weight and bounce. "I—." I'd started to say, *I have that book*. But Janelle's gaze was not on Bella or Pyrravyn, who both looked at the book Janelle held before them. She was staring hard at me. She gave me a quick shake of her head, shutting me up. Hughelas opened his mouth to speak, and she shook her head to quiet him too.

"It's the perfect book for a young princess," Janelle exclaimed, flashing some exciting pictures of trolls, ghosts, magma rivers, and the like.

She *knew* I had the book. How did she know? She was trying to tell me something without saying anything.

"I'm Elliah," I said, as though that had been what I'd attempted to say before.

"Yes," Drevin said. "We know that." He had a notebook out jotting something down. "Let's go. I want to see what you can do."

"Do?" Janelle said, standing slowly. "You're a Wood Elf, correct?" she asked me, but didn't wait for an answer. "You wish to learn about Healing magic, Drevin? Or you have some moonlit glade curiosities?"

Drevin looked puzzled, then red crept into his cheeks.

"Neither," Drevin answered. "She's Bereft. Think of what we will learn from her about nullifying magic."

Yselda slapped a hand to her face, clearly upset with Drevin's loose tongue.

"Nullifying magic?" Janelle said, cocking her head.

Drevin turned to walk away, expecting his order to be obeyed. "Let's go."

"Drevin," Janelle whisper-shouted.

"What now?" he said, clearly irritated with her.

She pursed her lips and looked at him like he was a naughty child. She left the book with Bella and tiptoed over to Drevin, whispering in his ear. His eyes momentarily widened, then he nodded and started off.

"You're to come with me," Janelle directed my way with a brusque nod. Pyrravyn turned his gaze to Drevin's disappearing back. "He agreed," Janelle told him.

"Drevin *agreed* to let our guest with the dragon bone hammer go with you instead of him?" Pyrravyn's eyes widened, but with humor.

"Yes," she said, patting her robes down.

"Hmm," he answered. "One wonders at the coincidental timing of your arrival."

"Does one?" she asked, rocking on her heels and putting a finger to her lip like she was considering the question.

I already liked her more than Drevin. She hadn't invaded my personal space nor hinted at experimenting on me. My standards had gotten quite low.

"Oh, very well," Pyrravyn said. "My Lady Elliah, this is our head librarian, Janelle Tidekeeper. She apparently has a use for you that even Drevin finds worthwhile." Pyrravyn considered his own words, then laughed. "And perhaps they are both right. Hughelas, if you would come with me, I will show you something of your family history. I will vouch for Elliah's safety with Janelle. I can think of no one I would trust more than her."

"Elliah?" Hughelas asked.

Great. We were splitting up. Better I go with the librarian than the mad scientist, but I'd rather stay with people I trusted—clearly not an option. Hughelas wasn't pleased either. But learning from Pyrravyn seemed key, and I wasn't invited. Of my remaining options, I preferred the librarian. I nodded.

Gormar followed Hughelas, his robe trailing like a crimson shadow behind him. That left me standing beside a woman so burdened with books she looked like a mobile archive. She was taller than I, with an ageless poise that made her feel carved from wisdom itself—elegant, unreadable, and slightly dangerous. Most people tried to seem important. Janelle didn't need to.

"Come, Elliah," Janelle said. "There's something in the library for which Drevin is willing to postpone his curiosity about you. We must endeavor to retrieve it." She walked off, and I followed. Once we were out of earshot, she added with a knowing smile, "But the direct route is rarely the most interesting."

Beldroth : 2

The Salt soldiers led us to the cliffs, then up a switchback stairway that wove into the rock face wherever the stone permitted. In my homeland, we would have called it a serpent's path. Above, the sky churned with madness: dark clouds coiled at a fixed distance, holding in lightning that chased itself in circles with barely a grumble of thunder. But it stayed away from the harbor, kept clear of the cliffs, with normal clouds drifting past the circle formed by the storm.

I adjusted the strap of my pack and said, "I'm Beldroth," to be polite. Pyrravyn had introduced Feldryn, but not his two companions, one male and the other female. "This is Illiara," I told our escort as I stopped to look out over the picturesque landing. "Who is powerful enough to manage weather manipulation at this scale?"

"Beginner stuff," scoffed the male guard who wasn't Feldryn. "Easy as stopping your blood from pumping."

I knew it wasn't "beginner stuff," and I wondered what drove his nasty behavior. Perhaps it was because I was an outsider. Or he was strong enough in magic to get away with rudeness. But it wouldn't surprise me to learn he struck out with words because he was weak in magic. As a trainer of fighters, I'd often had to sort out motives behind behaviors.

"I know something of Salt magic," I said. "You can't manipulate salt water, and there's just enough salt in blood to make that difficult. Some inherent complexity with life interferes further. So, ironically, while you cannot stop my blood from pumping, if you're strong enough, you might start it pumping if I died."

The Salt squinted, my words striking a chord. "Let's hope it doesn't come to that."

He'd lost someone he cared about. It was writ plainly on his face—he'd tried to revive them and failed.

"That must have been hard for you," I said. "I'm sorry."

He nodded, the muscles in his jaw bunching as he bit back on something.

"Rhogar," he said. "Name's Rhogar." He turned his back and started up the stairs. "Let's go. There are lifts for the wealthy. You may be a guest of the Scion, but our regent didn't consider your comfort in doling out his requests for help. Though, to be fair, he probably doesn't know the Wrasseguard policy: 'The reef grows stronger against the tide.'"

"That's okay," I said. "I'm enjoying the climb. Nice stone underfoot." It was, and the weight of my pack between my shoulder blades settled in like a familiar companion. "Interesting views." I'd never seen anything like them. I looked over at Illiara to see how she was handling it. While it was obvious to *me* that she was pregnant, the way she wore her clothes concealed that fact from others. But her gear looked uncomfortably large on her. She looked back at me with a raised eyebrow. "I will probably regret asking this," I said to her, "but how are you faring?"

"Are you still trying to leave me behind, Warder?" she asked with a biting tone but a hint of a smile. "I've told you before—I'll be by your side come trolls or high water. Wood Elves are a hearty bunch."

I put a hand on her shoulder as we ascended the next set of stairs. "Not trying to leave you behind." I slowed and let her pull ahead. "Was hoping you'd lead the way to further improve my view."

"Tch," she sounded. "Every time you get a little rock under your boots, it goes straight to your loins." Yet, as she climbed the steps, she swayed her hips suggestively, the little devil.

"I'm a Warder," I said, because that explained enough. "Don't tell me you didn't enjoy Cenaedth… once they gave us a cave of our own." I certainly had.

"Tch," she answered.

"Well, perhaps we'll have another shot at your enjoyment on Deara," I said. "I'm willing to try. For your sake, of course."

"Deara keeps its secrets," Rhogar said. "And I urge you to keep yours. Not all of us have a safe harbor for our galleons."

"Galleon?" the female Peacekeeper scoffed. "I hear your *dinghy* has no harbor because you refuse to scrape off the barnacles."

I smiled. If there was one constant the world over, it was the humor of soldiers.

"I'd let you do the honors, Avanine," Rhogar replied, "but your port is too busy to support a flagship of such fine craftsmanship."

Avanine laughed, saying something about a busy port being better than dry docks, but I didn't pay attention, my focus returning to Illiara, who laughed as she continued climbing. Illiara was absolutely the right mix of grit and grace, fierce loyalty with biting wit. In many ways, much like Lyrei. The juxtaposition of Salts, who reminded me of Lyrei, alongside Illiara, left me hovering in a strange place—lured toward my wife's memory even as it drifted further from reach.

The banter gradually died out. Not from discipline, but from some unspoken tension that settled over us. No one said a word, but it was clear—they didn't like where we headed.

Soon after, we made a turn that revealed the buildings above: a mix of wood and stone. Those nearest the edge often had wood decks protruding over the perilous drop. Up close, some looked like stubby tongues sticking out of fat heads. Their city proper extended away from the bluff, activity increasing farther from the palatial buildings on the edge. Feldryn marched us right though, the word of our passage spreading quickly and creating an informal parade. It wasn't nearly so grim as our trek through Alenor among the stoic High Elves. Children called to their parents to make them stop. Hawkers shouted their wares with more care about selling their goods than watching our procession. While it shouldn't have surprised me that there were no other races on the island, it did. Like Cenaedth with the Alluvium, Deara had only Salts. While I'd seen Wood Elves among the High Elves in Alenor, the tensions between them had been high. A stark contrast to Telloria'ahlia, a town grown from mixed-breed elves after a sort of racial reformation had occurred among the elf races. Among my people, it was uncommon, but not unheard of, to see Warders paired up with Wood Elves or Salts. We'd fought alongside the Wood Elves, and the Salt toehold of Golond sat at the mouth of the Contentious. Warders hadn't created the same schism we'd encountered everywhere else on our travels. We hadn't kicked half-breeds out to form their own towns. We hadn't "purified" our capital to make it entirely Warders.

Our march took us straight through the town and out the other side, following a stone-paved street into a rural area. To my surprise and delight, after initial farmland, we passed sheep out to pasture, Salts sitting on jutting rocks to shepherd them in the same way Warders did back home.

"Is that where we're headed?" I asked. We'd spent weeks walking the grasslands between Alenor and Cenaedth, and the days helping with cleanup in Cenaedth had required walking through their labyrinthian tunnels. So I didn't ask out of weariness, but it seemed odd to travel so far for this mysterious problem for which they asked my help. A building had grown on the horizon, right in the center of the road. Officious for such a rural setting, it screamed importance.

"It is," Feldryn answered, his agitation heightened. He didn't like what was coming, which made me finger my sword and wish I had the hammer.

The building was circular, stone with a wooden roof like a cone with the peak sliced off. A wide doorway held a pair of whitewashed wooden doors carved with intricate designs, flanked by a pair of Salt mages in faded light-blue robes with white trim.

"You can't bring them in here," the guard on the right said, his shoulders sagging like he'd already lost a battle. He had the look of a soldier trying to hold up for too long on too little. The other guard, a woman, shifted from foot to foot, her eyes leery and dark from lack of sleep.

The tense wariness worried me. I set my pack down, needing to move freely if it came to that. Illiara followed suit.

"You think I want to?" Feldryn grumbled. "Pyrravyn wants them to see the Crown."

"He'll chew me up, you know," the guard said.

"Not just you," the woman added.

"Do you expect I will escape his tongue?" Feldryn answered. "I have my orders."

The guard grimaced. "And the day started so peacefully."

Feldryn grunted and walked in, waving for us to follow.

The inside was one large, circular room with that single entrance. A mage rose from a crouched position as we entered, spinning with a rapidly reddening face that looked built for anger. But that wasn't what stopped me in my tracks. To my surprise, and—from the quick intake of her breath—to Illiara's surprise as well, a gem-encrusted pedestal like the one buried under Theopolis occupied the center of the room.

Marinna 3

How had I gotten into this mess?

I followed a stone-cold warrior who looked as deadly as she did beautiful onto the docks that formed the skeleton of the harbor. I wanted to run away screaming—I'd stepped far beyond my comfort zone. A foreign land, with hostile natives, and for all practical purposes, they'd culled me from the herd. But "following" was encouraged by the two Salt warriors behind Trentius and Smoky. I had nowhere to run.

"Why do you look so worried?" Trentius asked, an encouraging smile on his face.

My pack chafed against one shoulder where the strap had twisted, but I didn't dare stop to adjust it with Salt warriors so close behind. There was no comfort in carrying my own gear—only the weight of uncertainty, made literal.

I had interacted little with Trentius since I'd joined the group in the swamp. The High Elves had kept themselves apart from those who weren't of their race, though Trentius had been an exception. Still, I'd realized quickly that he had more moss growing upstairs than good sense—unusual for that race—and I'd kept our discussions short.

"Why *don't* you look worried?" I retorted.

"Well," he said, focusing more on a cluster of debris he had to navigate than what he was saying. "For one, I don't believe Eryndra Tidebringer is evil. She has a tribal mindset and thinks elfendom plays a zero-sum game, so to improve the lot of Deara, she has to accomplish that at the expense of others. In my mind, that's a lot better than the leadership in Alenor, who think only of themselves and don't even realize how much they're hurting others. At least Eryndra is honest, even if she's wrong."

I stopped in my tracks.

Trentius took a few steps to notice I'd stopped, and I think he might only have noticed because Smoky stopped behind me.

"What did you say?" I asked, hurrying to catch up and keep everyone moving. His comment had been remarkably deep.

"What?" he asked.

"What did you say about Eryndra and her motivations?"

He scrunched his head up in concentration. "I don't know. What did I say?"

Grrr. "You said something about Eryndra being honest. But wrong. About what she thinks she has to accomplish and how. How did you know that? Are you using magic to read their minds?"

"Magic? No. I've always had a knack for understanding what's going on in people's heads. A lot more goes on in here," he tapped his head, "than people think. Hey, look at that!"

He was pointing at two storks on the pier, who looked almost as startled to be pointed out as I was by Trentius's excitement.

"What?" I was still reeling from his previous insight. I wasn't built for fighting—well, physically, I *was*, but I didn't think of myself that way—and surely they intended to recruit me, perhaps by force, into their ranks. They wanted to use my magic to help them fight. Did it matter if the taskmaster holding my chain was honest?

"Those two storks look exactly the same," Trentius declared.

We passed them and continued following Eryndra. "You mean the white one and the gray one? Those two look *exactly* the same?"

Trentius kept looking back over his shoulder. "Remarkable, really," he said. When he stumbled over a rope, he gave up on the storks.

Yes… remarkable was the right word.

Shortly, Eryndra stopped at the base of a formidable ship and began issuing orders to someone on the dock. The woodwork on the bow named the vessel—Dreadwake. Wonderful. Eryndra paused after some initial instructions and said, "Get on board," to the rest of us.

I didn't want to. For one, we'd just gotten off a ship. Second, she wanted me to fight something—I was certain. But I didn't see an option. Trentius started up the gangplank. Smoky tried to squeeze her feet together to fit on the plank behind Trentius.

"That dragon will not get in the way, will it?" Eryndra's question didn't sound like a question. It sounded like a threat.

But Trentius stopped, looking first at the dragon and then at the ship. He tilted his head at the ship, holding his hands close together, then far apart. "I don't see how," he commented with a smile and started back up. Eryndra's face hardened further—a seemingly impossible task—as she judged whether there was an insult to his words. Smoky's back feet didn't quite fit on the narrow plank, and he extended his wings and pushed on the air to right his tottering form. I laughed just a little, despite—or perhaps because of—the gravity of the situation. That earned me a squint-eyed look from Eryndra. Smoky continued up the plank behind Trentius, slowly, concentrating, with her wings extended. Why didn't she simply fly?

The guards waited for me, so I grimaced and followed Trentius and Smoky aboard. The guards were not far behind.

Aboard the Dreadwake, not only did the crew prepare for travel, but I spotted other ships preparing to leave as well. Trouble gathered on the wind.

"Welcome aboard the Dreadwake." A Salt in formal-looking leathers had halted barking orders in order to approach me and Trentius. "I'm

Captain Kael Tidebane. Tidebringer tells me you're going to keep our ship together while we hunt blues. What do you need?"

Hunt blues? Blue *dragons*? What did I need? "I need off this ship."

"Ha!" Captain Kael laughed, putting his hands on my shoulders. "I like you. 'Off this ship.' Ha!" He leaned in conspiratorially. "I wouldn't worry about your safety—we have a Warder aboard who's as beautiful as she is powerful. She'll hold the Dreadwake together."

"That's the theory anyway," he added, already turning away.

Trentius and I shared a look. Somehow, the word *theory* didn't especially reassure us.

"Stow your gear below," he said over his shoulder. "We'll get you billeted this evening. Let me know if you think of anything you need."

He thought I was powerful? I was scared to death!

Eryndra Tidebringer stepped off the gangplank, every man and woman on board stealing glances her way. She cast a stern eye over the proceedings, then marched toward Captain Kael. "You've secured the cargo?"

"Of course," he said, flashing an *I'm-not-an-idiot* grin—though it didn't stand a chance against Eryndra's withering stare.

"Well, mister insightful," I said to Trentius, trying not to think about the fact that hauling the gangplank in meant we were ready to go. "What do you think of our captain?"

"Oh, he's right," Trentius said as he stared out at the two storks, who were once again within sight on the dock from his perch on the ship. "You're much prettier than Eryndra. Cold beauty is death. Creative beauty is warm, sometimes cozy and sometimes *hot*."

"What are you *talking* about?" *Cold* beauty? *Creative* beauty?

My vehemence drew his attention from the storks. "What?" he asked. "What was I talking about?" He seemed genuinely confused, and he quickly changed the topic. "It isn't shaking."

By the boots and bogs! Why was I even talking to the half-wit?

"You're scared to death," Trentius said, "but the ship isn't shaking." Trentius smiled at me, then turned back to the docks, perhaps to look for more storks. To no one, he mumbled, "Mesmerizing Mage Maintains Magical Mastery."

And… he was right. As nervous as I was, I hadn't for even a moment lost control. It had not crossed my mind to focus on reining in my magic. And that realization was like a weight off my shoulders. I sighed, suddenly swimming in confidence. Unable to help myself, I laughed aloud, and Trentius joined in.

Wait, I hadn't said I was scared to death out loud, had I? How had Trentius known?

Elliah ~ 4

"Why did you bring that specific book?" I asked Janelle as we rode some sort of lifting platform up to the top of the cliffs. "Why *Talena Talonforged*?"

"Because I knew that you, knowing who the author was, would trust me for having a copy." She smiled knowingly, as to a co-conspirator in some grand mischief.

We'd crowded onto the lift, my personal bubble almost as squished as with the Alluvium in Cenaedth. My pack pressed awkwardly against my back, bumping into a merchant's satchel every time the lift jostled. I'd puzzled over the lift's mechanics while we waited in the short line of well-to-do Salts. A waterfall-powered system, most likely—wheels turning gears, gears shifting chains, all working together to raise and lower the lift. High Elves would admire it; the Luminarium would have benefitted from one.

"Who wrote it?" I asked.

"You don't know?" she asked.

"No."

The harbor below became a forest of masts, thin and sharp as spears. Falling from the lift would end in a very pokey death. How often did a gear snap?

"Well, if you'd known who wrote it," Janelle said, "you would already trust me. You're just going to have to trust me on that."

"Your logic is rather circular," I commented.

"Circles are the best," Janelle replied excitedly. "Perfect, endless. Then triangles. Triangles are where the real magic happens."

I really had no idea how to steer the conversation back onto the trail, so I hopped the fence altogether. "What convinced Drevin not to take me with him?"

"There's a book he's been after for a long time. Maelith Skywarden has it guarded so that only Maelith and his acolytes can get to it. I think you might be able to retrieve it for Drevin. Hence, our trip to the library."

"What book?"

We reached the top. The drop discomforted me despite a life spent in trees—no branches to slow a fall, no roots to cling to. Just air, waiting. The city before me reminded me more of Telloria'ahlia than anywhere else—a mix of wood and stone buildings. The styles were different. Deara looked more weather-worn, but housed a people who fought back with decoratively bright paints and cloth.

"*The Grimoire of the Thunderborn.*"

"Ah," I said. "That old thing." I was kidding, of course. I had no idea what it was. But the bubble of space around me and Janelle grew slightly larger as we exited the lift, expanding even more once the space allowed.

"Yes, that old thing."

She led me down streets carefully paved for smoothness—built to transport things much bigger than pedestrians—but only elves on foot used them at the moment.

"Why does Drevin want it?" I asked.

"For obvious reasons," Janelle said. "It predates the Breaking and is rumored to describe magic lost to the elves. That alone would make Drevin desperate to get his hands on it." She leaned in, her voice dropping to a conspiratorial whisper. "But some say it was written by dragons!"

"Written by dragons?" I said with a start.

"Hard to imagine, isn't it? Dragons, with their claws, daintily scratching letters into a book? Perhaps that rumor stretches the truth." She led me to a building decorated with statues of creatures reading books. Included among them was one, ironically, with a dragon holding a pen and writing in a tiny book. Another that caught my eye was a troll leaning on a war axe, reading a book. Ridiculous!

"You don't know? You haven't read it?" I asked. The library loomed before me, its stone facade weathered by time. I had arrived in Deara just that morning, and they had already dragged me—okay, companionably escorted me—into something beyond my understanding.

"I have not. When Maelith retrieved it from the cave where they found it, he locked it up immediately. Only he and his acolytes can get to it, and they're a tight-lipped crew." She laughed lightly. "Unlike the rest of Deara, who are *sooo* open with their knowledge."

"Deara keeps her secrets," I mumbled.

"That she does, my dear. That she does."

Janelle opened a door and ushered me in. The moment I stepped into the library, the air shifted, heavy with the scent of aged parchment and polished wood. A faint aroma of beeswax lingered, mingling with something sharper—ink, or the herbal tang of preservation oils. The floor beneath my boots was smooth, dark wood, worn down by centuries of restless pacing and careful footsteps. Overhead, a domed ceiling arched like the belly of a ship turned skyward, its beams painted with constellations I didn't recognize. At the very center of the room stood a circular countertop, its polished surface gleaming faintly in the light of hanging crystal lanterns.

Beyond the desk, the space sprawled outward, chaotic and unpredictable. Like the spokes of a ship's wheel, cleared walkways stretched out from the center, each leading to a set of double doors marked with symbols. Between those hallways lay the true chaos: towering shelves crammed with mismatched books, scrolls, and unidentifiable objects. Some shelves were organized with obsessive precision, their spines gleaming in neat rows. Others looked like they had been ransacked, with books stacked sideways, upside down, or leaning precariously like drunken sailors.

One section had ropes strung between the shelves, suspending books in nets as if the ground wasn't trustworthy. Another area boasted glass—glass!—cases filled with maps and charts. And then there were the personal touches—here, a table cluttered with half-finished experiments; there, a wall covered in scrawled notes pinned with rusty daggers.

The space thrummed with something restless, like the books it held weren't entirely content to stay shelved. A scroll fluttered in the corner of my eye. A book snapped shut on its own. Salts moved through the aisles, but I wasn't sure I could blame every shift and rustle on them.

And yet, despite the chaos, there was a strange order to it all. The walkways radiating from the desk were clean and well-maintained, their ends each marked with emblems I assumed meant *something*. One banner bore the outline of a ship, its sails edged with lightning; another showed a curling wave. They had to be sanctuaries of specific Salt mages or factions, the places where they hoarded their secrets and trained their minds.

But in the in-between spaces, the books told their own story. They existed on a battlefield of knowledge, a place where the past wrestled with the present, and order waged a losing war against chaos.

I tightened my grip on my satchel and followed Janelle to the counter.

"Tidekeeper," one man called, but Janelle ignored him. We kept walking toward that counter, where another woman sorted books onto a cart.

Boom!

I dropped to the floor, the weight of my pack knocking the breath from me as it slammed into my spine. Janelle startled, but kept walking.

Huh?

I stood and hurried to catch up, spotting a plume of smoke issuing from behind the doors of one corridor stretching from the spokes of the circular room.

"Can you go check on that, please, Naria?" The woman behind the desk looked up at Janelle's words. "I think someone stumbled onto one of Drevin's gadgets again." Naria nodded once, grabbed a metal can with some kind of gizmo on the top, and scooted out one of three archways in the circular countertop—very elegant woodwork that I expected to see in a Wood Elf town, but hadn't thought I would encounter among the Salts.

We entered the central area through a different archway than the one from which Naria exited. The interior of the round counter contained scattered stacks of books and scrolls, and carts for pushing them around. But it also had small statues, a box of rocks, an array of gemstones, a collection of springs and washers and more advanced doodads. They'd lined the space under the counter with drawers. Countless drawers.

"Set that down," Janelle said, waving at my pack. "Let's see. Where to start?"

She looked around at the contents of the various boxes and stacks and carts like she searched for inspiration. "Let's ignore politics for a moment and start from here, in the library."

Knowing little about politics, and wanting even less to be a part of them, I nodded my agreement while setting my pack by my feet. It looked safe enough, blending in with the other paraphernalia scattered about.

"Our library is the battleground for rival wizards."

To which I replied with all earnestness, "Come again?"

"In times past, we've had many wizards with great knowledge and power." She pursed her lips and looked up, testing her own statement for veracity. "Some with great knowledge but little power. Some with great power and little knowledge. Right now, we have two that have both. Drevin Cloudmuse is a genius—so clever with machines and devices that most forget how potent his magic is. The other is Maelith Skywarden, a wizard who constantly displays his magical prowess, to the extent that others forget how much he studied and learned to gain that power. They each have acolytes that train under them."

"Okay," I said. "Two main wizards, and most others train under them."

She pinched an eye closed. "More or less true. There are others. Most of the Peacekeepers train under Talyra Waveblade. Many of the merchant mages train under Keryn Seabroker. Oddly enough, though the political battles and potential long-term ramifications of the rift between the traders and the Peacekeepers are huge, those two StormWrights get along amicably, and share as many teachings as they do meals. But they will tell you that, even combined, they don't match up to either Drevin or Maelith, who cannot stand each other."

I nodded. Once again, the warning from the captain of the Salty Squirt came to my mind. "May I ask, why did you want me to trust you? Why not let me go with Drevin?"

Janelle reduced her voice to a whisper. "Drevin dissects things to understand them. Not everything can be put back together."

I looked around, suddenly aware that, though no one else was visible, we'd passed several people in aisles along our way. They were still there. I swallowed my next question—*why do you care?*

Naria returned, dangling two canisters, each looking much lighter than the one she'd left with. "We'll need more flame retardant," she said unceremoniously, setting the canisters on the counter. "No one injured, or at least no one around with injuries." She resumed organizing books.

"Perfect," Janelle said cheerily. "An opportunity to show you around."

She picked up the canisters and headed out the archway Naria had just come from. She stopped abruptly and spun. "Naria, this is Elliah. Elliah, Naria."

The Salt librarian looked up from her task and nodded at me, like it was perfectly normal to encounter a Wood Elf in her library, then went back to work. Janelle had already started away, heading toward the hallway next to the one with the thinning trail of smoke.

I'd always loved books, though chances to explore them had been rare. I'd craved more time in the library of Telloria'ahlia, longed to lose myself in Zoras's private collection. But the library of Deara was something else entirely—a living tapestry of knowledge and history. The Salt Library didn't merely hold secrets—it was built from them. Secrets too bold for Heartland scholars to even whisper.

The shoreline faded behind us as Pyrravyn led the way, his steps deliberate but unhurried. Bella skipped beside him, a bundle of energy and trust, while Gormar shuffled along at the rear, uncharacteristically quiet. A couple of guards trailed out of earshot. I followed Pyrravyn closely, my thoughts churning as I tried to make sense of everything I'd heard.

And, more than that, I kept thinking about the others.

Elliah, taken somewhere deeper into the island. My father and Illiara, off with the Wrasseguard, who appeared to be royal troops, on a mysterious quest that required Earth magic. Marinna, Trentius, and Smoky sent to the Peacekeepers—at least they had each other. I hated not knowing where everyone was—that we'd come there together, but they'd scattered us like pieces of a broken ship on the waves.

They had all come to help *me*.

"You've been thrown into the deep end, haven't you, cousin?" Pyrravyn said over his shoulder, his voice warm, almost too warm for our brief acquaintance. "I'm sorry for that. If I'd had more notice of your arrival, I'd have done more to ease the transition."

I kept my tone neutral. "We've managed before. We'll manage now."
Will we?

That woman, Janelle, had snatched Elliah from the clutches of Drevin, the experimenter Captain Striker had warned us about. But was she any safer? My father could take care of himself—I didn't worry as much about him. Marinna had looked ready to panic, and bad things happened when she lost control. And Gormar—*why was Gormar so quiet?*

"Of course you will," he replied with a soft chuckle. "A Warder never falters, or so I've heard. Still, I imagine it's strange—standing among us, stepping into a role you never chose, or even knew about."

He was baiting me, gently, but baiting me nonetheless. "You said there was work to do. Work I can help with?"

"That, there is." He sighed, the weight in his voice genuine. "The Peacekeepers, the traders, the Stormwrights—" Stormwrights? "Everyone is pulling in different directions. It's exhausting trying to hold it all together. And we always have Drevin and his... experiments to contend with."

The mention of Drevin piqued my interest. "Drevin? What about him?"

Pyrravyn glanced back at me, his face drawn into an expression of careful thoughtfulness. "Drevin has always been brilliant, but brilliance can blind a man to the cost of his pursuits. He's made strides with the power to reshape the world, but I fear the path ends in a cliff. Drevin is often late. I sent Trentius and his dragon to the Peacekeepers before he arrived on purpose. Not because I trust the Peacekeepers, but because I needed to control the situation—I needed time to think." He trailed off, shaking his head.

Trentius was with the Peacekeepers *because* of Pyrravyn. For safe-keeping?

Bella piped up, as if reciting a well-worn adage. "Whoever has what others covet steers the ship."

Pyrravyn smiled at her, a gentle, paternal smile. "Yes, sweet one. And it keeps the Peacekeepers distracted. They are like the tide—relentless, yes, but predictable."

That didn't sit right with me. "You think handing them a dragon will keep them distracted? It sounds more like arming them."

Pyrravyn stopped abruptly and turned to face me, his expression open and earnest. "You're right to question me. You should. But understand this: the Peacekeepers are like a fire. Feed it a little fuel, and you can control where it burns. Starve it, and it might consume everything out of desperation." He placed a hand on my shoulder, his touch heavy with unspoken expectations. "I need your help, cousin. Your name carries weight, even among those who might doubt you. Together, we can guide the fire, keep it from devouring what our family has worked so hard to build."

Gormar, who had been unusually silent, finally spoke up, his voice cutting through the moment. "You can guide fire, Lord Pyrravyn, but it burns as it pleases. Fire is never truly tamed."

Pyrravyn turned to Gormar, his smile patient, almost pitying. "That's why we need your wisdom, Prophet. To know where the flames might spread."

"And if it spreads to us?" I asked, my tone sharp.

Pyrravyn spread his hands in a gesture of surrender, the perfect picture of humility. "Then we'll fight it together. I have no illusions about the risks we face, Hughelas. But I also have no intention of letting the Peacekeepers or Drevin decide the fate of our people without a challenge. That's why you're here. To remind them that the Daughter of the Nine Winds sets our course, and our family is stronger when we stand united."

Bella looked up at me, her eyes wide and trusting. "Uncle Pyrravyn is smart. He'll keep us safe."

I studied Pyrravyn carefully, trying to read the man beneath the polished words and practiced gestures. I simply didn't know enough. Were the problems he worried about real? Was his concern for his niece just a show? Was speaking to me openly about maintaining control a genuine revelation of trust, or merely a gimmick to appear trustworthy?

We waited near the same lift I'd seen Elliah get on earlier, out of earshot of the other passengers. I looked up the wall and spotted my father among those climbing the stairs instead of riding. That told me much about the relative value in the Salt society of the librarian versus the Wrasseguard soldiers my father had left with. *I wish you were here, Father!*

I knew who my mother was to me, but she'd kept all of *this* a secret, from both my father and me. I needed to know why. "How are we related exactly?"

"You and I are cousins," Bella said. "My mother and your mother were sisters. Pyrravyn is our uncle, our mothers' brother. My mother, Selthira, was oldest, then Uncle Pyrravyn, then your mother, Lyrei."

"My mother didn't talk about her past," I said, frustrated and hating to display my ignorance, even though they already knew of it.

"She was considered 'a sail untrimmed'?" Bella said, looking at Pyrravyn to see if she'd gotten the phrasing right.

"Lyrei took after her grandmother more than her mother," Pyrravyn continued for Bella. "Jade Galefinger, founder of Deara."

In a conspiratorial whisper, Bella said, "Jade Galefinger was a *pirate*." Her face set with stern determination for a moment, but her gaze slipped back to the harbor, clouding with a wistfulness that softened her resolve.

Jade Galefinger? "When Captain Striker…" Kidnapped? "… escorted me away from Cenaedth, she used that name. She said I was wanted by Jade Galefinger."

"Our family has quite the dynamic range," Pyrravyn chuckled. "Miryndel, Bella's and your grandmother, transformed this island from a pirate's shelter to a civilized kingdom. We lost both Jade and Miryndel long ago, but to the outside world, we still behave as though Jade Galefinger rules Deara. Bella's mother, Selthira, tended along Miryndel's thoughtful and organized worldview. In fact, she was somewhat more passionate about it than Miryndel. Selthira founded the Peacekeepers and started them on the path you see before you. An armada ready to conquer the world."

"Mother was a big planner," Bella said.

"Indeed," Pyrravyn said, "but she also acted on her plans. She died in a Peacekeeper raid on the pirates of the Cur'matol islands, as a martyr, cementing her status as a symbol of peace through strength." Pyrravyn looked at me meaningfully. "The Peacekeepers gained much from her death."

Bella squinted at Pyrravyn, trying to puzzle out the undercurrent of his tone, but I knew what he meant: he implied the Peacekeepers might have been involved in Bella's mother's demise.

"I am led to believe you are studying magical theory," Pyrravyn said, changing the subject like a startled fish.

Since I'd spoken of it openly on the Salty Squirt, there was no point in denying it. "That's right."

"Like Drevin," he said. "Perhaps the two of you should compare notes."

I stiffened, an immediate reaction. *Wonderful. I had the same interests as the madman who wanted to experiment on my friends.*

"But in the meantime..." Pyrravyn continued, his voice taking on a calculated edge, "yes, I have a task for you. One that it would behoove us all for you to handle... quietly."

Here it comes.

He spoke in a whisper so quiet that I wondered if even Bella heard it. "I need you to locate the lair of a dragon."

There it was, the impossible demand I'd been waiting for. And the way he said it, I knew refusal wasn't an option.

"Who let you in here?" the angry wizard shouted. As he mouthed a spell, Beldroth took my hand and cast spells as well, locking the two of us in place.

Just in time.

A gust of wind tried to shove us out the only exit, and though Beldroth held us there, locked in place, the fierce wind howled, the vibrations coming up through the floor. Though the floor shook, the sound came from above—an open roof in the center of the cone.

There was little I could contribute, though I was prepared to Heal us if something struck because of the wind. My guess was that the spell, delivered by a mage whose sunken eyes promised quick fatigue, would die before it pushed Beldroth past his limit. But if he switched to lightning?

The wind abruptly ceased, causing Beldroth and me to pitch forward, feet pinned to the ground. Still, the tired mage glowered, and anger pumped adrenaline through his veins.

Beldroth took the opportunity. "Pyrravyn sent us!" he blurted. A quick glance behind revealed that the other Salts were gone, either hiding behind the wall of their own accord, or blown away. "He wants us to see a crown before sending us to help with some other dilemma."

The wizard panted, his fury undiminished despite his exhaustion. "He oversteps," the wizard said.

"Pyrravyn is regent of the Daughter of the Nine Winds," Feldryn shouted from outside the door.

"*I* defend Deara," the angry mage shouted. "*I* protect her secrets." A measure of his anger died and his shoulders sagged. "At great personal cost."

"I can take the next shift," the man guarding the door said, poking his head in cautiously.

"No," the mage said, putting his hands on his sides. "No, you're as tired as I am. With Juro incapacitated, we are too thin. I don't know how much longer we can keep this up." He closed his eyes hard for several seconds, then turned back to the pedestal.

The pedestal stood waist-high, carved from a seamless block of polished basalt, its edges softened by time or use. Like the one beneath Theopolis, metal runes traced paths between gems, suggesting some kind of magical map. No dark gem stood out—nothing like the previous one which had drained Elliah. No anchor for anti-magic—it was built to devour magic only. Atop the pedestal, instead of a mound of rock, crystals almost as tall as me reached for the circular opening at the top of the building.

"I was preparing anyway. We can't wait much longer." He turned to the doorway. "You swear Pyrravyn vouched for them? If I find out you've lied to me, I will push you into the Abyss myself."

Feldryn stuck his head into the doorway, then decided it was safe to proceed in. "I swear it," he said.

The mage returned to the pedestal, and with a final, weary sigh, launched some spell. Unsurprisingly, he placed a hand on a gem of the pedestal. I cast my spell to grant me the ability to see magic. As expected, the magic of the pedestal shined brightly under my spell. But the pedestal slurped up his mana, and as tired as he looked... like a sudden shift of the wind, his muscles went rigid.

"Oh no," the woman from the door said. Rushing over, she yelled at her fellow guard. "He's run dry!" She placed her hand over his, and from my experience underground in Theopolis, I knew what to expect—once she made contact, she would be stuck as well. His taut muscles relaxed, and for several seconds, it appeared everything might turn out okay.

Then both their muscles locked up.

I wondered if Beldroth's Earth magic—magic to bind, magic to break—would help. There were three likely outcomes. First, it wouldn't work at all. Second, it might bind him to the pedestal or backfire with tragic consequences. Third—and least likely—it would simply work.

But when the third mage hesitantly reached toward them, Beldroth stopped him.

"Let me try my magic," Beldroth told him. To me, he said, "Is this why they wanted me?"

"No," I answered, shaking my head. "This needs what I learned from the last pedestal. The spell I used in Cenaedth." I'd crafted it based on what my magic revealed at the last pedestal, and it worked with Marinna in Cenaedth, recharging her magic.

Reluctantly, he nodded.

It took a few tense seconds for me to weave my spell, targeting the tired, angry mage. I watched him closely with my magically enhanced sight, but my spell wasn't helping enough. I believed it was working, but it wasn't supplying him mana faster than the pedestal depleted it.

Beldroth prepared his spell.

"Wait," I said, stopping him. One other source of influence remained that wouldn't bring new dangers. I cast the same spell on the woman.

I waited and watched. It looked like a pretty even match... their mana together replenishing at a rate able to supply the pedestal. But time stretched on to the point where I worried Beldroth would have to try *his* method. Then, with another sudden shift, both of them relaxed at the same time.

The lead mage didn't let loose from the gem, and the woman was stuck to him, but thanks to my spells, their mana was recharging more rapidly than the pedestal. Just barely. They were able to supply the gems without completely draining their mana and killing themselves.

There was no stone to animate this time, only the crystal, and I wasn't sure what we would see as a result of charging it, but I had a strong suspicion.

A jolt of ozone scorched the air as a bolt of lightning shot from the crystal reaching up from the platform, through the open roof, and into the sky. A moment later, the thunder followed—deep and distant—as if the storm above had taken notice.

That was how they maintained the storm around Deara.

Marinna 4

Three ships. That's what went out from the harbor of Deara. Among them, only the Dreadwake had three masts, its sleek design suggesting speed. The other two ships had two masts and smaller crews. They lagged behind, but I think the only reason they kept up at all was because the Dreadwake let them.

We sailed straight for the opening in the ring of storms around the island, the gateway being more obvious from the inside than the outside.

"I've seen the way you look at rocks," Trentius said casually, watching Smoky, who'd spotted a school of fish and kept diving for them. Red dragons weren't built for the water—each time she dove, she entered the water with all the elegance of a stone. When she'd pop back up, empty-handed... empty-clawed, she would flap her wings furiously to clear herself, then flash bright red. Drying off? "You look for what's inside them, I think."

That was... accurate, to a degree. I looked for their potential. Had he watched me shape the rocks on our journey? I focused when scrutinizing rocks, and I must have missed his staring.

"Okay," I said. I remembered Taegen's hungry stare with a sickening concern about what it had meant—the thought of someone watching me like that while my attention was elsewhere made my hackles rise.

Trentius clapped when Smoky did its wing-flapping and red flash but came up with a fish in its talons. He cheered at her encouragingly as she came over to the ship and dropped the slightly charred fish on deck, a fish half my size. Smoky landed and batted the dead fish around playfully, perhaps hoping it would try to get away? "Don't play with your food, Smoky," Trentius chided, shaking a finger.

I relaxed. Trentius watching me stare at rocks wasn't the same as Taegen doing so.

"You're better with wood than Beldroth," Trentius remarked, watching Smoky get right down to eating the fish, biting off large chunks indiscriminately as the crew avoided the space. "Undoubtedly because of your Wood Elf heritage."

Trentius had said several intelligent things, or potentially intelligent things, over the past hour. But never when his attention was in tune with the topic. "He sure does like fish," I said, wondering if that would help or hurt the conversation.

"She," Trentius said. "Smoky tells me she will be a mother someday, a long time from now—if she lives long enough, of course. There are more dragons in the world now than there used to be, but they die younger, she says. It's conceivable you will see things in wood the way you see them in stone. But what if it's not wood specifically? What if you can see what's in other things than stone or wood?"

Smoky finished off the fish. Every piece. Afterward, she walked to the front of the ship and curled up for a nap. A Salt threw water from a bucket onto the drippings from the fish and pushed it off the ship with a broom.

See shapes in wood? I hadn't ever tried. Stone called to me. Wood never had. But he wasn't wrong—I'd held the Salty Squirt together when the blue dragon would have sliced through it with its saw-like plates. Beldroth had told me he didn't think he had the power to do the same. I frowned. That was probably why *I* was on this ship and not him. Someone on the crew had heard our conversation and reported it.

Yet that wasn't all Trentius had said. What other things might one carve or shape? Wood, stone. I looked around the ship. Bits of metal secured things here and there. My sword was metal. And jewelry. People shaped metal all the time.

Trentius's attention, with Smoky curled up, had turned to the rapidly approaching storm wall and its opening. Was there some point in pondering whether I might be able to see shapes in metal? Something he thought I was able to create that would help? Or was I reading too much into the words of an addled mind?

"I wonder if you can see the shapes in water," he said, holding out his arms and swaying like he was a dragon gliding on the winds. "My father was the engineer that designed the aqueducts in Alenor. Did you know that?" He lifted his left arm high and his right low and swayed to the right, toward the middle of the ship. "They thought I would follow in his footsteps." He lowered his arms and pointed at the storm wall. "There's no way that magic stops at the water. It keeps going. It has to." He raised his arms back up, swaying to the left. "Smoky is helping me to remember." He lowered his arms a final time, giving up his pantomime as he stared at the dragon. I stood behind him, but my angle revealed the side of his face. For the first time, Trentius wasn't smiling. "I don't enjoy remembering."

We entered the gateway, and the mist from the nearby storm engulfed us. Someone on the crew cast a spell, and the mist peeled back, creating a bubble of dry air around the ship. Thunder rumbled and lightning crisscrossed the opening. Smoky perked back up, puffed a pair of smoke rings out of her nostrils while staring suspiciously at the retreating fog, then put her head back down. But she didn't close her eyes.

For some reason, that made Trentius quietly laugh. The Dreadwake darted quickly between the walls of rain on either side, then cleared the gateway, returning to the semi-clear skies outside the storm wall.

We banked to the right... to port... and one schooner followed us, while the other remained just outside the gateway through the storm ring.

"Why does that one stop?" I wondered out loud.

"To go for help if needed," Eryndra said, startling me. Preoccupied with our surroundings, I hadn't heard her approach. "We're the bait. Stormrider there," she pointed at the ship following us, "will pull whoever they can from the brink should you not hold the Dreadwake together. If both ships are taken, the Azure Gale waits by the Crown's Corridor to get help. A bit of advice: if both ships go down, swim for the Tempest Ring. For reasons we don't understand, the blues don't cross it."

"Why are we going after a blue at all?" I asked. "Why would they target this ship?"

"They have something we want," Eryndra said, her words clipped, her gaze fixed ahead. "And we have something they want."

"See," Trentius muttered, his eyes on Eryndra. "Zero-sum game."

He'd said that before. *Zero-sum game.* I still wasn't sure what it meant, but it sounded like someone—possibly everyone—had to lose for the Salts to win.

"What things?" I asked, the wind making my words fragile, small. "What do you want? What do they want?"

Stones had given me more answers than Eryndra's icy silence.

The Dreadwake banked close to the wall of rain, the roaring tempest so near that the spray hit my face. The ship moved with unnerving precision, gliding swiftly along the storm's edge like it toyed with death. Behind us, the Stormrider hesitated, its bulk shrinking in the distance.

"Incoming!" A scout's voice pierced the air, taut with anticipation.

"Already?" I squeaked, gripping the nearest rope as though it tethered me to safety.

"I suggest you do what you did on the Squirt," Eryndra said, her words razor-sharp. "Quickly."

"No," I whispered, but the wind snatched the word away. I didn't want to fight. But this wasn't about fighting—it was about survival. Protect the ship, or die trying.

I glanced at Trentius, my closest semblance of an ally, but he was frozen, clutching the rail, his eyes fixed upward. Smoky had taken flight, a blip of red in the dark sky. Thunder mocked me in the magical wall of water we skirted. I was alone.

I centered myself, both physically on the deck and mentally.

Calm. Breathe. Cast.

I knelt, pressing my hands to the damp, creaking deck. My magic unfurled, sinking into the wood like roots into the soil. I bound the hull, tightening the connections, fusing the timbers until they acted like one, unyielding as stone.

The spell took over, drawing me deeper. My senses dimmed, my focus narrowing until the ship was my entire world. The hull sang to me, taut with power.

And, like on the Salty Squirt, I became lost in the spell. My reality became the hull, tightening the bonds between pieces of wood, making them strong as stone. Stronger.

Someone yelled, their cry tearing through my senses just as the impact came.

The beast hit us head on, a thunderous crash that reverberated through the hull, through me. The entire ship bucked under the force, the deck lurching hard to starboard. I braced myself, teeth clenched, my spell barely holding.

But then I was airborne.

My grip on the spell slipped as I tumbled toward the port-side rail. My stomach flipped, the world a mess of spinning wood and sky. I barely had a moment to think—let alone act—before the ship rolled, catching the edge of the storm, the rain wall slamming into the starboard side with crushing force. The mast groaned, sails whipping like panicked ghosts.

That sent me spinning head over heels back to starboard. I hit the rail hard, pain exploding in my side. A deluge of rain knocked me senseless and drove me into the ocean.

Beldroth : 3

Illiara used her magic to Heal the three mages, who sat on chairs made from sheets like sails that folded out from the walls. Ingenious little contraptions affixed by rigging to the walls, they could stretch out to become cots or behave in their present form like chairs for relaxation. Low cabinets kept all their goods safe inside, making me wonder how often they had to deal with Maelith's temper and the strong winds that ensued.

She didn't technically Heal them—there were no open wounds. She energized them, both in body and in mana.

"Sweet Mother of Storms," the woman said. "I can't remember the last time I felt this good. I just want to curl up and sleep now."

"The spells help," Illiara said, "but your body knows it has gone without sleep for too long."

Rhogar and Avanine, two of the Salt Peacekeepers, kept watch outside, giving the mages a chance to lower their guard. Maelith remained silent, chewing on his thoughts, glancing skeptically at the doorway, then turning his suspicious gaze toward us.

"Get some sleep," Maelith said. "You know the drill. We will have to do this again."

The woman hesitated, drawing a scowl and sharp words from him. "I said sleep."

She got up and pulled the end of the chair, stretching it out into a cot. After removing a blanket from the cabinets, then closing them up tightly again, she lay on the cot and closed her eyes.

"You've seen one of these before," Maelith accused, pointing at the pedestal but looking at us. He hadn't offered us a chair, but I'd made myself comfortable on the floor.

"Tch," Illiara said in response to his tone. She sat down beside me, irritated enough that she stopped casting.

"Yes," I said. "We've seen one before."

"Stop telling him things," Illiara said with irritation. "Too bad there isn't a spell to fix unpleasant personalities."

"Or one that grants people common sense," Maelith shot back. "You're not wanted here. You're not welcome here. Why would you come?"

"She just saved your life," the male mage said incredulously, bracing himself for a tirade.

"They're the reason I didn't have enough mana!" he barked. "Coming in and forcing me to use mana on a wind. It's their fault I nearly died."

Slate and shards!

"Do you know whether the High Elves have a spell that would help?" I asked Illiara. I made a face like I was mesmerized, enchanted by Illiara with a drooling fascination.

The woman under the blanket cracked an eye open and giggled. Illiara relaxed.

"How dare you!" Maelith said, and given that he'd already said it once before and how easily it slipped off his lips, he probably used that phrase a lot. What a pity. It was possible revitalizing him hadn't been the best idea—he'd been easier to deal with when exhausted.

"Look," I said, keeping my tone calm. "What you're doing is very impressive: using your magic—and I can see you are quite powerful—to keep your island safe."

Maelith squinted like he suspected some kind of trickery.

"Truly," I reassured him. "I mean that." Whether he needed to protect the island was another question. "Your power and dedication impress me."

Maelith unclenched his jaw a fraction.

"Think of how wonderful it would be," I said, "if you had the opportunity to focus more of that energy on solving other problems for the island instead of being stuck here all the time."

For just a moment, something other than anger passed behind his eyes. Oddly, it didn't look like excitement, which is what I hoped for. It looked like fear. Well, that changed things. If he wasn't angry because he was stuck, then anger masked his fear.

"This is where I belong," he said, still angry but not shouting. "I guard Deara. I protect her."

Time to abandon ship. I looked over at Feldryn. "Was there something else Pyrravyn wanted us for? I still don't understand his request."

"There was something else. He wanted you to see the Tempest Crown." Feldryn nodded to the pedestal. "Now we climb down into the old mines of the island."

"Yes," Maelith said, waving dismissively. "Get them out of here. Take them to the Abyss. I need rest."

I rose, pulling Illiara with me. "You understand," I said, "that Illiara's spell helped recharge your mana—and it worked better than you want to admit."

"I don't need help!" Maelith barked. The male mage coughed, and Maelith closed his eyes hard and said more gently. "I mean, I have the help I need."

The woman lying down cracked her eyes open again and mouthed the words, "Thank you," to Illiara, who nodded back to her.

Feldryn headed to the door, and we followed him out.

"Stay and guard the door so that the others can rest," Feldryn told his companions. "I'll see you get relieved. Or if he chases you off," he said with a nod into the building, "just go."

As we grabbed our supplies, Feldryn sighed heavily. "Okay, let's go fix the Abyss." Then he headed back the way we came.

Marinna 5

"Not much of a swimmer, are you?"

In fact, until that moment, I had been rather pleased with myself.

The cold torrent of rain from the magical storm had hit me like an icy rockfall, knocking the wind from me, not giving me a chance to breathe before plunging me into the thankfully warmer ocean. The relentless downpour churned the water, blurring the line between up and down in the dark abyss.

My left arm screamed with pain, making the pain in my hip almost bearable. I couldn't move my arm from the shoulder down. Even worse, I didn't know which way brought me back to the surface, and my lungs begged for air.

A flash of lightning showed me the way. Using only one arm and my feet, I swam in darkness toward where I'd seen the light.

It scarcely mattered when I broke the surface—I was still in the damned magical storm, and with every breath I sucked in rain. In a coughing, desperate mess, I kicked and dragged myself with my good arm in what I hoped wasn't circles, until the downpour abruptly ceased.

More time passed as I pulled myself farther from the wall of rain, the churn of waves blocking my view. I didn't know whether I was inside the circle or out. Every movement was agony on my shoulder—definitely dislocated or broken. I needed my working arm to keep me above water, so I didn't have the luxury of holding the bad arm in place.

Holy sweet freaking Mother of Trees. My curses didn't suffice, so I borrowed Illiara's. Exhaustion weighed on me, and the pain was unbearable. Death pressed in, close and certain, unless I acted quickly. Healing wasn't my strength, but a dislocated shoulder wasn't a wound—it was structural, like keeping a hull intact. I just needed to hold it together.

Fortunately, I could still wiggle my fingers. Desperate, I gathered my focus. It was a good thing Beldroth had forced me to practice so much. In a way, I struggled more than I had in the fight with the dragon—between the pain and the waves and my exhaustion, I barely managed the spell.

I let myself drop into the dark waters as the spell began. In my mind's eye, the ball of my shoulder sat outside the socket. Dislocated. All I had to do was push.

The ocean swallowed my scream.

But with two working arms, I followed the bubbles to the light.

Still exhausted, but in significantly less pain, I treaded water for several minutes, trying to catch my breath. If I let the waves take me along its highs and lows, it wasn't hard to keep my head above water. But as my desperation passed, my mind found other things to worry about. I didn't see any ships, and I didn't see the island. I was likely on the wrong side of the magical storm.

That mattered. Dragons on the outside. No dragons on the inside. I needed to know.

I wonder if you can see the shapes in water.

Trentius's words echoed through my mind. When I'd reinforced the Dreadwake's hull with my magic, I'd seen the trees the planks had once been a part of. The spell convinced them to cling together, as though they were one tree, to behave like something they *might have been, under different circumstances*. The first part of the spell helped me see both what they were *and* their potential.

Surely, water was too... flighty... to behave the same way.

But what did I have to lose?

So, bobbing on the waves, I turned to the wall of water and cast the spell.

Nothing.

I spat out the salty brine that had found its way into my mouth while I'd murmured the spell, and I continued to tread water. Minutes went by. No dragons, but no ships either. Of course, the water limited my visibility. There might have been a dragon swimming up from below at that very moment.

Curse it all!

I tried the spell again, focusing on the clouds above instead of the rain. Rain was just a byproduct, right? And... I actually thought I saw lines... shapes... hints of structure beneath the chaos. And a spot of red. It might have been lightning. Or Stormy. But whatever it was, it gave me no help.

But...

I spat out the salty water several times and prepared myself for one more casting.

Ducking my head underwater at the end of the casting, I searched down toward the ocean floor. To my shock, there was form beneath the water's motion. Not light, not color—just presence. It was more like seeing it in my mind's eye, like I saw the statues waiting to come from a rock, or what the ship's planks would look like if they worked together, or the bones of my shoulder. Something—or someone—was shaping the water with intent.

Unable to hold my breath any longer, I popped to the surface to suck down air. The Dreadwake had appeared out of nowhere, and the white hair of a Salt beelined to me through the water.

I gasped when Eryndra's frigid features came up for air. Without her leather jacket and the sword whose hilt usually poked from behind her back, she looked more approachable—her sharp features softened by the water, her shoulder length white hair slicked back.

And, unfairly, she still looked breathtaking.

But, with the precision of a blade, she'd cut down my efforts in one swift question. *Not much of a swimmer, are you?*

"I swim well enough," I spat. "I'm alive, aren't I?"

"The first goal of swimming, to be sure." A flash of lightning from behind me lit up her eyes. Was she smiling? Her lips weren't. Some trick of the light, gone in a flash.

"Yes, well…"

"Come on," she said. "Ship's this way." As though the ship's presence wasn't obvious *now*. Where had it been hiding?

"Which side of the wall are we on?" I asked, trying to gather the energy to swim to the ship after having declared my swimming prowess.

"The inside," she said, and once again, something in her eyes suggested a smile. "No dragons. Take your time. The Dreadwake isn't going anywhere quickly."

That made me look closer at the ship. The central mast was down, but caught up in the rigging of the other masts and consequently sticking out the far side of the ship at an awkward angle. Sailors crawled over the ship like ants on a kicked pile, trying to get things righted.

"Oh," I peeped. "I'm sorry I didn't hold the ship together."

"You did fine," she said, her words clipped despite being supportive. "The mast snapped when we pushed through the storm wall. You had already made your graceful exit by then." Her eyes were definitely laughing at me.

I was lucky I hadn't died!

"I saw something under the water," I said, hoping to change the topic.

"Hold that thought and be still," she said. Before I questioned it, she surged forward through the water with an ease of a fish. One second, she was treading beside me, the next, her arms were on me—strong hands wrapping something rough around my waist.

Her breath ghosted against my ear as she worked, her fingers moving with practiced efficiency, her body far too close in the water. The rope scratched against skin exposed by a tear in my shirt as she pulled it tight, but I barely noticed. She smelled like salt and steel, a frustratingly perfect match for her.

Rotting fungi!

"Almost done," she murmured, her fingers brushing against my ribs.

"Take your time," I blurted, horrified to hear the words leave my mouth.

Eryndra's gaze flicked to mine, something unreadable behind her storm-gray eyes. Then, she yanked the rope tight and swam back, shouting up to the ship, "Haul us up!"

Mercifully, the rope went taut, and they pulled me up the side of the Dreadwake, my mind still betraying me as I thought through my too-close encounter with Eryndra.

At the top, I tumbled over the rail onto the deck, sprawling unceremoniously onto my back. Sweet, solid wood.

Eryndra landed gracefully beside me, not even winded. Naturally.

"Marinna!" A familiar voice rang out, and before I had even sat up, Trentius knelt beside me, his eyes wide with concern. Smoky flapped down right behind him, snorting a little puff of smoke into my face.

"You're alive!" Trentius said, breathless. "I mean, of course you are, but that looked—well, I wasn't sure for a bit there." His hands hovered awkwardly near my shoulder, like he wanted to help but wasn't sure how.

"Ahhh, now that was exciting!" Captain Kael's voice rang out above me. He beamed down, a child who had just discovered a new game, and Trentius gave him room. Water dripped from his disheveled curls, and he clapped a hand against the nearest railing, utterly delighted by the destruction surrounding us, even as Smoky flapped up and perched beside his hand.

I should have found his enthusiasm insufferable. Instead, the steadiness of it—his ability to take chaos in stride—settled something in me. At least someone was enjoying themselves.

I groaned and sat up, pressing a hand to my aching hip. "Bog take you, Kael."

"I suspect it will," he replied, wiping water from his brow. "The damage was not as bad as I expected, if I'm being honest."

I shot him a glare that should have sent him running. He only grinned wider.

Eryndra, standing over me, shook out her arms like she was shrugging off the ocean itself. "You saw something under the water?"

I tensed. I'd behaved stupidly in the water. Surely, I'd created a problem. I nodded, unable to find words.

"The ocean holds *many* things." Her eyes laughed at me again.

My shoulders unknotted—she wasn't angry.

"The water, under the storm," I said. "It's doing… *something*." Oh yes, way to step up the explanation and impress her.

"Mmm," Eryndra responded, her eyes no longer laughing. "We've long suspected it must be. Why else would the dragons not swim through it?"

"You didn't attack the dragon," I noted.

"Attack a dragon?" Her eyes laughed again. "I suppose if one the size of your… Smoky… attempted to breach our ship, we might have a chance. Drevin," she uttered his name with disgust, "has even asked me to catch one for him. But I would sooner lop off my own arm."

That would be a shame—her arms were exquisite. Blushing at my thought, I tried to keep my focus. "But you said we were hunting for dragons."

"Yes, hunting *for* them. Not hunting them. Dragons are glorious creatures, even if they do cause trouble. It was Smoky and your High Elf friend who led us to you, by the way. We weren't even looking on the right side of the curtain."

I considered that for a bit. I had Trentius and Smoky to thank for saving my life. I needed to thank him. But why were we protecting ships if they weren't hunting dragons? They had a *fleet* of ships in their harbor. Fishing ships, trading vessels, but also ships that looked ready for war. If they didn't mean to fight the dragons, who did they mean to fight? And how was I important enough that they damaged their ship to get to me? Eryndra had personally jumped into the ocean for me. Why?

"I can only protect one ship at a time," I offered.

"I only need one ship protected," she replied.

"How can protecting one ship possibly help your efforts? You've got an entire armada of ships. You clearly have plans to take over the world." I'd probably gone too far. But I was in pain, about to drown out of sheer stubbornness, and I didn't want to be a part of any war, but most especially not a war against other elves.

Eryndra directed a piercing look at Captain Kael, who suddenly found he needed to direct his crew in getting the Dreadwake underway. She turned the look to Trentius, momentarily confusing him. But then he, and shortly thereafter Smoky, left us alone.

"Your actions today have earned you a secret," she whispered. She continued slowly, as though she measured each word to be sure it didn't reveal too much. "Deara was founded by pirates: the hideout of the great pirate Jade Galefinger. The original, self-declared Daughter of the Nine Winds. That was many centuries ago, and Deara… evolved… from a haven of safekeeping for criminals into a thriving island port, dependent on trade for survival." She paused. "A decade ago, a devastating hurricane struck the islands around Cur'matol. Cur'matol itself survived with the aid of its mages, holding off the worst, but many of the nearby island towns lost their ports and homes." I knew where Cur'matol was— the closest island range to the swamps where I grew up. "Relief ships never arrived. Too risky. Not 'profitable'." She sneered as she said the last, her eyes cold as ice. "These days, pirates hide in Baledor, where they're as likely to steal your goods as pay you for them, while Yselda holds to the naive belief that she can beat them through sanctions and tariffs."

"Once the Peacekeepers control key ports and trade routes, we can eliminate chaos and impose order, ensuring prosperity and safety for everyone." With that, she turned back around and left me alone.

Her words lingered, swirling in my mind like the currents beneath us.

Order. Safety. A world where no one had to fend off pirates or storms alone. Where no one had to run.

If someone had imposed order when I was a child, would my life have been different? Would the whispers about my magic have stopped? Would my father have been held accountable? Would I have felt safe enough to stay?

I didn't want to agree with her. I wanted to leave her vision behind the way I had abandoned my father's empty justifications and Fael Themar's hollow promises. But the part of me that still carried the scars of loneliness and mistrust swallowed the lure of her vision. Law and order. A promise of stability. Something I had never known.

To see the world as inherently broken was safer—easier than daring to imagine a version where it might be mended. I still didn't trust her. But shutting her out entirely piled rocks on something I'd long since buried. Something I wasn't sure I wanted to unearth… but wasn't ready to let go of either.

It came as a slight surprise that the Peacekeepers' main hall was down at the wharf. Their presence above the cliffs in the city proper was apparently a necessity for meetings with other leaders, but was not their preference—they stayed close to their ships.

I took the long stairs down, needing the time to think. It wove me into the press of those who couldn't afford the lifts: dockworkers, fishmongers, and the occasional group of children darting through the crowd like minnows avoiding nets. Unfortunately, I didn't go unnoticed; perhaps because I wore the wrong clothes or my skin was a little too dark—for the first time! But it might also have been my Wrasseguard escort, Kaelith, who never let me out of her sight. The scent of salt and seaweed thickened as I descended, and the cries of gulls grew sharper.

The wharf wasn't built to accommodate anything as grand as a headquarters. Instead, the Peacekeepers had claimed a string of wooden buildings indistinguishable from the bait and fish shops around them. No signs marked their purpose, but the people who came and went—hard-faced and heavily armed—made their function clear enough.

"You'll find her on the Dreadwake, *Scion*," an officer told me when I asked for Eryndra Tidebringer. He said my title—Scion—with a touch of scorn, and I didn't blame him. I hadn't earned authority; birthright had granted it. I thanked him, then chose to display my ignorance further by asking for directions.

Kaelith stopped me right after we left the Peacekeeper headquarters. "Why didn't you ask *me*?" Like all Salts, she had alabaster skin with white hair, but where she wasn't the tallest of Salts, she had more muscle than most. I wondered if she had Warder in her genealogy.

"An obvious spy for Pyrravyn?" I replied.

"What of it?" she responded with a shrug of her shoulders. "Would that have made the information less valid?"

She had a point. But I didn't like it.

"Look, you're my assignment," she said. "Yes, I'll report your comings and goings to Pyrravyn. That's not a totally ridiculous request for him to make." The way her eyes wandered when she said it made me wonder how many of his requests she deemed reasonable. "You might as well use me to your advantage." Her cheeks flushed slightly. "For information," she added hurriedly.

She was right. I nodded and waved for her to lead. I'd understood the directions, more or less, but the docks were a bit of a maze.

The Dreadwake stood out among the docked ships, though not for its grandeur. Its mainmast was missing, and its rigging hung in tatters, leaving it as noticeable as a missing front tooth. The red dragon perched on the foremast was another clue.

Kaelith paused to let me lead. As I approached, every eye landed on me. They knew who I was: the half-warder Scion, an outsider whose legacy didn't sit well in the shadow of the Peacekeepers' rigid ranks.

Eryndra Tidebringer stalked down the gangplank, her neck-length white hair whipping in the sea breeze like a banner. She stopped at the end of the plank, forcing me to remain on the pier.

"Son of Lyrei," she said in greeting, as warm as a glacier.

"Pyrravyn wants me to investigate something," I began. "He told me to be discreet, but he also said you are already aware of the problem." I lowered my voice. "A black dragon."

Her eyes narrowed, sharp as a harpoon. "I am aware. But you will not find help from the Peacekeepers."

I looked back at Kaelith for guidance, and she shrugged ever so slightly.

"Feel free to offer up helpful information without my asking," I told her, earning a look of surprise that transformed into consideration.

I spun back to Eryndra. "You despise my parentage more than you value the safety of your people?" I asked, fighting to keep my tone even. "Knowing where the dragon lives might at least enable a warning—"

"My refusal is *not* based on the identity of your mother," she interrupted, her voice colder than the wind. "It is the motives for finding the dragon that I question. Dragons are sacred. Once we find one, there are those who will try to capitalize on it, just as they did with the blues. My answer is no."

As if on cue, a familiar shadow passed overhead. Smoky flapped down to land beside me, his claws scraping the dock.

"Hughelas!" Trentius's voice rang out from the ship. He leaned over the rail, waving.

"Trentius!" I called back. "Are you faring well?" I willed him to read my expression: Tell me as much as you can.

"Well enough! We rammed into a dragon!"

I raised a brow at Eryndra, who returned my look with cool disinterest. So much for the sacrosanctity of dragons.

"Marinna held the ship together, but then she nearly drowned," Trentius continued, "and Smoky found her. Marinna's still resting, but I'm helping repair the Dreadwake! It's been quite an adventure, and I think we're doing it again! 'Dreadwake Dashes into Dragon-Driven Disaster!'"

Eryndra's lips pressed into a thin line. "The dragon rammed us," she corrected, as if that absolved the Peacekeepers of any blame. "And my answer stays the same. Smoky is safe with me, and no dragon will be harmed on my account."

I didn't argue with her. I had no way to convince her my motives were pure, nor any way to be sure Pyrravyn's motives were what he'd claimed. All I knew was that tracking the black dragon gave me the freedom to move and the chance to check on my friends.

In fact, Eryndra's resistance suited me just fine.

But merely pretending was dangerous—Pyrravyn would see through that in short order. After all, Kaelith was there to report my every move. So what was my next step? With dread, I realized my next move should be to seek Drevin.

"I can explain now," Feldryn said after we'd walked clear of the building. "Particularly since you've seen something like the Tempest Crown before."

"What makes you think we've seen one of those... things... before?" I asked. I didn't have to fake being confused, since I only had clues that made me think they were relics from before the Breaking.

"For one, you jumped to a lot of conclusions very quickly," Feldryn said. "Second, and I quote, 'This needs what I learned from the last pedestal. The spell I used in Cenaedth.' So, you've seen one before."

Feldryn hadn't been in the room earlier, which was probably for the best, yet he'd heard everything. At first glance, he looked like a brute—nearly as tall as Beldroth, broad-shouldered, with arms thick enough to twist the head off a small dragon. A ragged scar cut from his forehead to his cheek, long healed without magic, added to the impression. But that was just the packaging. I'd made the mistake of assuming his appearance reflected his intellect.

"I would have explained without making this trip to Maelith," he said, "if I'd known you knew about the Tempest Crown. That's the problem of the secrets of Deara—not knowing who knows what, and who might be *allowed* to know what—keeps everyone tight-lipped and slows advancement."

"That's an astute observation," Beldroth said. Another brute who was brighter than he looked, at least in some ways. "So why do it? Why keep secrets?"

"That's an important question, but one for another day." He said the latter with pinched lips. It was a discussion he'd had often enough that he was tired of it. "That pedestal, what we call the Tempest Crown, wasn't the only one we found. Just the first one we managed to activate. We moved it above ground—"

"They work after you move them?" I interrupted. It surprised me—I'd assumed they needed to stay where they were to function.

"We were worried it wouldn't, but it did us no good to create a storm underground. Quite a bit of harm, in fact. And we had no reasonable way to carve a hole straight down to the Tempest Crown. So we tried moving it. Fortunately, it worked. But you saw the struggle they're having—they have to keep feeding it every twelve hours, or the storm dies."

"Do you *need* a constant storm-ring around Deara?" I asked.

"That depends on who you ask," Feldryn said. "It does significantly cut down on dragon attacks. I don't know why. Both blues and blacks stay out, which are the only breeds we ever see in the Troll's Teeth islands."

"A storm keeps out storm dragons?" Beldroth asked, genuinely curious.

Feldryn shrugged. "I can't explain why. But defense from dragons is rarely the reasoning you'll hear used for why we need magical protection." He shook his head. "Again, a discussion for another time."

We turned off the main road and onto another, one that had once been wide and well-traveled, but brush had consumed its edges, and pockets of stone had disappeared here and there.

"We believe someone triggered another of the crowns... the pedestals." The road ended in an abandoned mineshaft. Like the road, it looked like it had once seen a great deal of activity, but a crude wooden facade with a worn door blocked the passage. "But unlike the Tempest Crown, it doesn't need to be re-triggered. We've tried waiting it out, mostly because we can't think of anything else to do, but that's proved fruitless."

Beldroth and I unslung our packs, taking a moment to roll our shoulders before descending into the narrow shaft. He probably didn't need it, but didn't want me to stand out. With a sigh, I hitched mine back up. No telling how long this would take.

Feldryn opened the door, summoned a magelight, and went in.

Beldroth followed, and the hackles on my neck rose as I entered, letting the door close behind me. I conjured my own light despite theirs being sufficient, revealing cobwebs and the dusty stillness of disuse—no one had ventured in there in a long time.

"So what is it?" I asked.

"We only have guesses," Feldryn answered. "We think it is Earth magic. Some kind of Shield. That's why Pyrravyn thought you, as a Warder, might help."

"Ahhh," Beldroth said, clearly relieved. "It makes sense now. There's a Shield and no one can get in to deactivate it, plus it's somehow replenishing its energy."

"That's the gist of it, sort of," Feldryn answered, leading us down a crude and worn stone stairway. As we began our descent, he said, "Don't worry, it isn't as far down as the stairs we climbed from the harbor—half that at most."

I wasn't worried. Not about the climbing anyway. I didn't like caves as much as my Warder did. A hollow might provide shelter from the rain, but I saw no reason to go deeper than that. Yet our journey had taken us under swamps, deep into the volcanic mountains of Cenaedth, and, apparently, into the Troll Teeth islands. It had been... I tried to do some calculations... a few months since I'd seen a silvervein. We'd had to run from town to town as Elliah grew up, but silverveins were still "home," and I missed them.

The air grew heavier as we descended. A faint hum, like the buzzing of far-off bees, reached my ears. I stopped, straining to listen. "Do you hear that?" I asked.

"It's the magic of the Shield stirring the air," Feldryn explained. "Like the crackling hum before a thunderstorm."

As we passed side tunnels branching off from the stairs, flickers of yellow light danced in the darkness. Not sparks, exactly—more like lightning trapped and writhing in the stone. I paused, turning my head to catch the faint gleam.

"And those sparks?" I asked. "They're some sort of byproduct of the magic?"

"Or something watching us," Feldryn replied, a grim edge to his voice. A shiver crawled down my spine. "Don't worry, though. It likes its distance."

I didn't find that reassuring. Still, curiosity got the better of me, and I sent my magelight chasing down one of the tunnels. Feldryn paused. "Gems," he said. "That's what we were mining. Peridot, quartz, zeolites, sometimes garnet." After a moment of quiet, he continued. "By chance, we stumbled upon existing caves."

"Natural caves?" Beldroth asked.

"No," our guide answered. "Carved. The crowns were an unexpected treasure. Someone had stashed them there—a vault, perhaps." He shrugged, like there was no value in guessing. "Many of the original tunnels had collapsed, and we hadn't yet found the proper entrance. We'd just chiseled into some random part of a previously established network of caves."

We descended in silence, but the hum grew louder, accompanied by the occasional flicker of yellow in the periphery of my vision. A gust of wind rushed past us, stirring the dust and setting the cobwebs quivering. It brought a faint metallic tang, like iron filings stirred into the air. I tensed, looking around.

"Wind," I murmured. "This deep underground?"

Feldryn shrugged, but looked equally ill at ease. Everything pointed to the place being long abandoned—yet the silence watched us.

"So what do you gain if I can remove this Shield?" Beldroth asked.

"We don't know, exactly," Feldryn said. "Well, obviously a Crown of Shielding, or whatever the powers-that-be decide to name it." He chuckled grimly. "But we had barely scratched the surface of our discovery when we got locked out from it. The Tempest Crown. A book. That's it. Who knows what other wonders might be down there?"

"And what would those wonders be worth to you?" Beldroth asked.

Feldryn smiled. "Now you're getting the hang of being Dearan. Unfortunately, I'm not the one you need to bargain with."

"So we need to talk to Pyrravyn?" I asked. For the first time, I found hope that we might get off of Deara.

The stairs ended in a mineshaft. They'd stopped going deeper once they'd uncovered the crowns.

"It's not far now," Feldryn said. The humming had grown from a whisper to a persistent vibration buzzing behind my ears.

"Dim your magelights," I said. "I think I see light ahead."

They obliged. I had to move cautiously in the relative darkness, and my discomfort grew. What if some creature lurked? Even though I knew no bear would live so deep in the ground, the idea persisted. There were worse things than bears. I drew my knife, the weight of it reassuring in my hand.

I took us to the corner and looked around it. A wall of light blocked us from going further. Dark red, like molten iron, atypical of a Shield, and flecked with bolts of yellow tearing through it like chained lightning. It looked… angry.

"Don't get too close," Feldryn warned. "Don't touch it."

"Why not?" I asked.

"It's a one-way Shield," he answered. "Once you touch it, you can't pull away. You can only go in."

"An inverted one-way Shield?" Beldroth murmured, his voice tinged with awe. "That's new to me."

"That's a fearsome trap," I said.

"Guarding a powerful treasure," Feldryn replied.

The hum that had whispered at the edges of my hearing roared like an angry swarm. My skin prickled as if the air itself crawled, alive with unseen energy. I tightened my grip on my knife, finding comfort in it while recognizing its inadequacy against magic.

Beldroth stood beside me, his magelight dimmed but still casting faint shadows against the jagged walls. Feldryn had pulled ahead, moving quickly and deliberately, his face drawn and tense.

I opened my mouth to speak, to ask what was wrong, when the first bolt of lightning struck.

It wasn't like lightning I'd seen in the sky—this was golden, jagged, and alive, lancing down the tunnel and exploding against the stone with a deafening crack. The flash left me blinking away bright spots, my ears ringing as the air filled with the acrid scent of storm-scorched air.

"Run!" Feldryn shouted, his voice sharp and panicked.

"What is it?" Beldroth demanded, even as we stumbled, shielding our eyes from another blinding strike.

"Storm elemental," Feldryn snapped, already sprinting toward the Shield. "It doesn't like us here!"

I wanted to question him further, but there was no time. The surrounding air shimmered and sparked, and another bolt of golden light slammed into the ground, sending shards of rock flying. One grazed my arm, the sting sharp and immediate.

Then I saw it.

The storm elemental was not a creature in the conventional sense—no solid form, no flesh. It was the storm itself—a writhing, roiling mass of wind and crackling energy, its presence filling the tunnel with a terrible, oppressive weight. The yellow light we'd seen earlier wasn't just sparks or resonance—it was this thing's essence, its warning.

It surged forward, its lightning limbs reaching, striking the walls and floor with relentless fury.

"Move!" I screamed, grabbing Beldroth's arm and yanking him toward the passage ahead. My pack thudded against my back with every stride, throwing me off balance and slowing me just enough. I would have abandoned it, but to unclip it would cost precious seconds. Feldryn, unburdened, widened the distance between us, while Beldroth remained by my side.

The elemental roared—a thunderous cry that pulsed through my bones more than passing through my ears. A rush of wind tore through the tunnel, driving me forward against my will.

"Feldryn!" I called, but he didn't look back. He disappeared into a side passage just as another bolt of lightning struck, this one so close the heat licked my face.

The moment I reached the side passage, another gust of wind hurled me forward, forcing me past our only chance at escape.

I barely had time to register the red glow ahead before we were upon it—the one-way Shield, its angry light flecked with yellow.

"Don't touch it!" I yelled, but the elemental's thunderclap drowned out my warning.

We had our backs to the Shield, facing the strange creature that had slowed when we stopped running.

A bolt of lightning struck the ground directly at my feet, and the force of it hurled me backward. My shoulder hit the Shield, and for one terrible moment, its pull seized me—a searing, magnetic force that dragged me in.

"Illiara!" Beldroth's voice was distant, muffled, as if coming through water. I twisted, reaching for him, but the Shield's grip was too strong.

He stumbled in after me, his face pale but determined, and I knew he'd chosen to follow rather than leave me alone.

The last thing I saw before the Shield's glow enveloped us was the storm elemental, its form surging toward the side passage, and Feldryn's shadow slipping deeper into the tunnels.

And then we were through.

Elliah ~ 5

The library's spoke-ended aisle led to a closed door, its frame blending seamlessly into the curve of the circular room. Behind the wooden door rested stairs going down into a corridor lined with closed doors, lit by occasional openings at the tops of the walls to the sunlight above.

"This hallway suffers from the elements coming in through the windows," Janelle said, "so we store nothing perishable here." She walked down to the third door on the left, and using a key, opened it. She summoned a magelight and sent it into the dark room. It had many canisters, similar to the ones Janelle carried. She put hers down with a small collection of empties and picked up two seemingly heavier ones.

I'd expected her to ask me to carry one or both. Insist on it. But she didn't.

"Can I take that for you?" I asked.

She smiled and let me carry one. It was heavy, but not as bad as the hammer, whose weight I hardly noticed on my back anymore. And somehow, the weight sat easier because I'd chosen to bear it.

We left the room, and she locked it back up.

"Fire retardant," she explained. "Drevin invented it. Of necessity." She shook her head. "His acolytes restock it for us." She pointed at other doors in the hall. "Cleaning supplies and solvents. Bandages and salves. Ink. Scrolls are elsewhere, in a less damp area, which is a nuisance but necessary. Towels."

"Towels?"

"Oh, yes. Towels aplenty." She stopped at another door, unlocked it and grabbed towels from inside, putting them under the arm she used to carry the canister. She locked it up and continued on her way. "The ones with the blue squares are magical. You could stop the Stormshroud Falls—the waterfall that powers the lift—with one of those. For a time."

"Why would you want to do that?" I asked, trying to picture a towel sopping up a whole river.

"To halt the lift, I suppose."

"Has anyone ever done that?"

"Not to my knowledge. Which means probably not. Did you want to?" She looked at me with raised eyebrows.

"No!" I said, perhaps a bit too forcefully. "You brought it up." While trapped on the island, the last thing I needed was more trouble.

We'd walked deeper into the corridor, but she stopped and looked at me curiously. "You have to understand—Salts are experimentalist. They

92

can be cautious, but typically you'll find their curiosity overwhelms their restraint. Now that you've brought it up, someone will try it."

I looked around the empty hall, slightly irritated. "I didn't bring it up. You did. And there's no one here to hear."

"No one?" she said, sighing heavily. Then she resumed her walk. "Be careful speaking of your ideas in Deara."

But it wasn't my idea! Her statement, a forced manipulation of the conversation, hinted at a buried lesson, that she meant me to hear something deeper. Survival in Deara meant watching your tongue, even when you weren't at fault? And, like her rescue at the beach, I sensed she was trying to prepare and protect me.

The long, straight hall ended abruptly, with passages going to the right and left. No light filtered into the halls. She paused, setting down her canister, and created a magelight. She turned to the left, where a double door blocked our passage after a short distance. "This will connect with the hall where the accident occurred. We will drop one of these off there." She pushed the door open, and I followed her through it.

The corridor had a gentle bend to the left, and it had no natural lighting, which prevented me from seeing all the way to the end. Bricks lined the walls, and the air was both more dry and chillier than the hall we'd just traveled.

"It can get cold down here. Colder than it should. Some of the Drevin's experiments—or his acolytes' experiments—drain heat instead of generating it. There are a few labs in this stretch, but I wouldn't go in them. These connecting corridors are a no-man's-land. There's no telling what you'll find."

We passed two such doors on our left and three on our right before connecting back to what appeared to be another spokeway hall that would shoot us back to the library. I mapped out the tunnels in my mind— spokes radiating from the library like arrows, linked by concentric rings. A system, not chaos.

"This way," Janelle said, heading to the left, back toward the library, but she placed her canister on a shelf-nook carved into the corner. The spokeway we entered continued to the right, going deeper than the one where the supplies were kept. The chill from the previous circular passage faded. The rooms along the hall had no doors. "This is one of Drevin's halls. His acolytes—his Driftlings, to be specific—train here. Driftlings, Wavebinders, Currentweavers, Tidewardens—those are the levels of acolytes, and they train under Stormwrights, like Drevin and Maelith. You'll find beginners' books here in these rooms, but also their experiments. And to the extent Driftlings are able, they'll have... guarded... their secrets."

"That's what happened earlier?" I asked. "The explosion was

someone protecting their secrets?"

"Lethal traps are discouraged. But young snakes can be more dangerous than adults, lacking the ability to regulate their venom, and this is a beginners' hallway." We approached a door that was lit from inside. Janelle stopped at the door and waved. "Everything okay, Urella?"

A woman in light blue robes stood at a table cluttered with vials and candles, scrolls on the floor at her feet, and a book open before her. "Hi, Janelle. Yes, everything's fine here. The explosion was a few doors down." She pointed with a vial in her hand, spilling a few drops of glowing green goop onto the table. "Oh, shoot."

Janelle hastened on as smoke issued from the spill.

The room two doors down was a mess. Similar to the occupied one, except the table was on its side, the floor littered with broken vials and their spilled contents, glowing embers of books, and no sign of any other papers at all.

"Hmph," Janelle said. "Might not have been one of Maelith's acolytes at all. One of Drevin's could have done something wrong… or something right."

"Is it…" I began, but trailed off. Janelle was tiptoeing around the debris.

"Yes, dear?"

"Is it your job to figure out what happened?" I asked.

"No," she said, poking at the charred bits of the book. She stopped and smiled up at me. "But I like to know."

"Is that blood?" I asked, pointing at a smattering of dark spots near the wall.

Janelle's magelight flitted over the stain. Blood—fresh—and a scrap of cloth.

She tiptoed back out of the mess and we completed the walk up the corridor. "It was one of Maelith's students," she said. "That fabric— Drevin's students wear light-blue colors, with white patterns as they advance. Maelith's wear white, with some darker blue patterns as they gain skill. The cloth was pure white, so a beginner trying to prove something. I bet we'll find the bandage and salve room is missing a bit of its supply tomorrow."

I was surprised she divulged the information. Deara keeps its secrets, right? Just not the gossip about beginners burning their hands?

"You should be wary of the information I'm sharing," Janelle said, reading my mind. "Careless quips sink ships."

Then why tell me? At the surface, Janelle appeared flighty, but she'd pulled me out from under the looming threat of a fight for survival at the beach. Janelle wielded information like a blade, and yet she appeared uncut by the pointy bit when she tossed it around. That… appealed.

We climbed stairs to re-enter the library. I was quite happy to deposit

94

the canister back at the counter. Though it was not as heavy as the hammer, I was ready to put it down.

"Jaylyn, is Elliah's badge ready?" Janelle asked a shy elf behind the counter who, like me, hadn't quite reached the ageless look of an adult.

"Badge?" I wondered, but quietly.

Jaylyn handed her a medallion akin to the one Janelle had used to open the doors to the wizards' private training areas. Janelle, in turn, handed it to me. It came complete with a string to loop it around my neck, so I put it on. It looked to be made of copper, in the shape of a compass, with a small gem at the end of each compass rose, and more gems sprinkled in the middle.

"I imagine you'll have to hold that well out at arm's length to get it to work, but you'll be able to get to the supply rooms with it."

The medallion, cool and weighty, carried a silent warning. A tool, a token, a tether.

Maybe she meant it as a kindness. Maybe it was a way to keep me moving where she wanted. But it unlocked things—maybe even a way forward.

The library was not what I expected. From outside, though decorated with statues, it was an unassuming structure, but as I stepped through the threshold, the scale of it opened up around me. A vast dome stretched overhead, painted with constellations I didn't recognize, their unfamiliar patterns tugging at the edges of memory. There was an elegance to the architecture, but the space itself was almost defiant in its chaos.

Bookshelves leaned and loomed, some meticulously ordered while others seemed to be waging an active rebellion against structure. Nets suspended tomes as if to keep them afloat in a storm, while glass cases offered tantalizing glimpses of maps and charts I would have given weeks of my time to study. The air carried a weight of old ink and varnished wood, the kind of smell that promised secrets but gave no guarantees of answers.

I forced myself not to linger on the details. The place wasn't meant to be understood at a glance; it would take years to fully unravel its logic— or lack thereof. Still, my mind catalogued everything it saw. Symbols above the doorways—some nautical, others elemental—hinted at organization, or perhaps isolation, a way to protect the most guarded knowledge. The banners they bore were warnings, not invitations.

The centerpiece of it all was a circular desk, polished to a gleam, as though to suggest a focal point amidst the clutter. It was an anchor holding the chaos in place. The entire building pulsed with its own rhythm, as if the library itself were alive and restless, and the desk held its beating heart.

I wasn't there for its wonders, though they tempted me. I had come to check on Elliah, under the guise of searching for Drevin. That thought sobered me. As much as I wanted to lose myself in the library's depths, such indulgence was more than I could afford.

Still, I hesitated, letting my gaze linger on the strange, beautiful chaos around me. It wasn't the kind of place you simply entered. You committed to it, like a voyage with no clear destination.

When Elliah walked out from between two shelves into the aisle right in front of me, a couple of books in her hands, all thoughts of the library fled. She was looking at the shelves and didn't notice me. She moved slowly, rolling her shoulders before she disappeared back into the shelves across from where she'd emerged.

"Elliah!" I called, hastening forward just in time to collide with her as she spun back. Her tired eyes nonetheless smiled up at me. She rested the books on an adjacent shelf as I glanced back to make sure my Wrasseguard escort kept her distance. Kaelith's expression flickered with something I couldn't quite place—a quiet curiosity. Then Elliah wrapped her arms around my neck. I hugged her tight, my body lighting up with desire at her touch. When she pulled her head back and looked up, I lifted her for a long kiss.

"You and libraries," she finally said, pulling away with a smile.

Telloria'ahlia. We'd had a moment there. My interest and desire had only grown since that time, and yet my analytical mind forged ahead. "You didn't take my mana."

She rested her head against my chest. "I'm just tired. Worried. Not drained of my resistance. Plus, I'm carrying the hammer."

All very logical. It was part of why I loved her—she would be analytical with me when I needed it.

A cough behind me caused Elliah to jerk her hand away from my ear and put an almost-respectful gap between us.

I didn't turn around... watching Elliah blush was more precious to me than whatever reprimand the library had to offer.

"Sorry," a woman said, her voice familiar from the beach. "Book dust. Carry on."

Elliah blushed even more, a memory I tried to burn into my brain.

"Janelle," Elliah said, grabbing the books she'd set down, "I was just—"

"I saw what you were justing," Janelle said with a sultry chuckle. "My sources failed me. I didn't realize you two were... justing. I'm happy for you. If I may, the Thaldrak Curnshaw Collection of Arcane Regulations is ideal for privacy."

"Thank you," I said, partially turning to see the woman behind me. It was the same woman who'd gone down to the beach and cleverly rescued Elliah from Drevin's clutches, still wearing her belt with pouches of books. Kaelith, Pyrravyn's Wrasseguard spy, eyed Janelle warily with a hand on her sheathed sword, but stayed back.

"No—" Elliah protested, blushing as her eyes darted between the two of us, then over to Kaelith, who hadn't retreated from the awkward encounter the way a normal person would.

"This is Kaelith," I told Elliah. "A Wrasseguard spy for Pyrravyn. She reports my movements back to him. But she also helped me find the library."

Kaelith nodded at Elliah, who squinted back at Kaelith suspiciously. "I report what I choose to report," Kaelith said smoothly, with a faint trace of amusement.

Elliah's brow furrowed as she took in Kaelith's athletic build, slightly short for a Salt, but still much taller than Elliah.

"Elliah," Janelle said, calmly, interrupting an unnecessarily tense moment—I didn't *want* Kaelith there after all. "I have five children. You're very unlikely to be disturbed in the Arcane Regulations, and the chance someone will catch you makes things more interesting."

I liked Janelle already.

We'd had no time alone in Cenaedth after Elliah had drained me of my mana. No privacy on the Salty Squirt. Then they'd separated us upon arrival in Deara. We'd just learned we could kiss without Elliah draining me, though things might get a little awkward with a magical war-hammer involved. But I was ready to figure it out.

"Why are you here?" Elliah asked, her cheeks as red as blood, while her hand on the side far from Janelle snaked up under my sleeve to caress my skin.

I hesitated. To reveal the real reason I'd shown up, in front of Janelle and Kaelith, risked too much. My cover story would have to do. "I need to talk to Drevin."

Elliah's hand pulled away as she stepped back. Curse it all! "Drevin?" she asked. "Why?"

I tried to tell her with my eyes that I was lying, that I didn't care about Drevin at all, that I was there to check on her. But my eyes failed to say everything behind them, and my silence drew a pinched look of suspicion from her.

Kaelith sighed behind me—I'd asked her to show me the library, not how to find Drevin. She undoubtedly would have saved me time if I'd said that up front. But since I really wanted to check on Elliah, asking for Drevin's whereabouts directly would have backfired. I didn't mind looking slightly foolish for the chance to see that Elliah was safe.

"Pyrravyn has me on a mission I'm not allowed to speak about," I said in response. "I spoke with Trentius," I said, trying to convey what I knew about the others. "He and Marinna are… surviving. Pyrravyn keeps Gormar close—he seems fascinated with prophecy. I haven't heard from our parents since they left."

"Drevin rarely comes into the library himself anymore," Janelle said, her voice more formal and less playful than it had been. "He sends his minions if he needs anything. But I can get him a message."

"Thank you," I said, my eyes still pleading with an unseeing Elliah. "Tell him I'd like to speak with him, please."

Elliah clutched her books to her chest and spun away.

"Elliah!" I pleaded.

"I have books to shelve," she muttered, walking away like she'd taken a beating.

I tried to follow, but Janelle was suddenly in front of me. "Why do you need to talk to Drevin?" she asked in a whisper.

I shook my head, refusing to speak of it. The last thing I needed was Pyrravyn knowing I couldn't keep the family secrets.

Janelle shook her head, sighing. "Dragons will wait," she said, earning a chuckle from Kaelith. *She already knew about my mission!* "A woman's heart won't."

Trentius *1

Drevin tapped his quill against the side of his notebook, eyes sharp and hungry, as though waiting for me to hand him a revelation wrapped in silk. I wished I had one to give him, just to make him go away.

"Go on," he prompted, flipping the page, already preparing for the next thing to pry out of me.

Marinna stood nearby, leaning against one of the masts not under repair, and Captain Kael stood at the helm, watching from above. No one else was on board, as we were there for Marinna to practice her spells on the Dreadwake.

"I don't know," I said honestly.

"You must know something," he countered, his voice acerbic. "The spell you cast, however mangled, did something no High Elf in recorded history has achieved. It doesn't matter if you don't understand it entirely. Tell me what you *think* you remember."

I didn't like that he called it *mangled*. Or that he was right.

"I didn't cast a spell," I said. "I... *was* the spell."

Drevin paused, his quill hovering mid-air. Marinna, leaning against the railing with her arms crossed, let out a snort of laughter. My eyes flicked her way, and she smiled—she wasn't laughing at me; she laughed at Drevin's attempt to get information.

Smoky, perched beside me on the rail of the Dreadwake, her tail curled around a post, let out a low rumble, her fiery breath curling from her nostrils. Skepticism came through our bond; she didn't like Drevin.

"Explain," Drevin ordered, quill poised again.

I sighed and ran a hand through my wind-tangled hair. "It wasn't... exactly... like casting. I didn't shape the magic. I mean, I *did*. Once upon a time, I knew how to Compel. That's what I wanted to cast. Simply to stop Smoky." Smoky put her head on my shoulder. "But it wasn't like I cast the spell." I didn't repeat that I *was* the spell—he hadn't liked that answer. "And when it happened, I wasn't thinking about *binding* her. I wanted her to empathize with our plight. I was just... there. And then *we* were... just there."

Drevin's eyes gleamed. "Fascinating. So, it was a resonance. A natural attunement. Not Compulsion, then." He scribbled furiously in his notebook, muttering to himself as he did. "And the elements? Were you using only Air?"

I hesitated. "Perhaps Fire?" We'd been in Cenaedth. Fire was everywhere. And Smoky, after all, was a red dragon. I thought I remembered weaving some Fire in with Air. I just hadn't really *cast* it, per se.

That made him *really* interested.

He stepped closer, studying me with unsettling intensity. "Have you noticed any… *changes* in yourself since the bonding?"

Yes.

But I wasn't going to tell him that.

I wasn't going to tell him how, lately, things had been *sharper*. How my mind, once fogged and pleasant, had begun to clear in ways that made me uncomfortable. How memories I had long accepted as lost had crept back, and how those memories weren't all good.

Some were *horrifying*.

I swallowed, pushing those thoughts aside. "Nothing significant," I lied.

Drevin didn't believe me. The way his fingers tightened around his quill, the way his mouth quirked in amusement—he thought I was a particularly *fun* puzzle.

"I see," he murmured. "I think it is time for some experiments."

Before I could react, he flicked his fingers.

Water surged from the air itself, wrapping around my arms and legs like liquid chains. I gasped as the spell solidified, locking me in place.

"Stormwright Drevin," Captain Kael called lazily from the helm. He hadn't moved much since the conversation started. "What're you doing with my crewmate?"

"He's not your crewmate," Drevin replied smoothly. "He's a *foreigner,* and I'm taking him."

Marinna's boots thudded against the deck as she pushed off the railing. "I'll rot in the reeds first."

Drevin sighed. "I don't have time for this." He flicked his fingers again, and a wave of force sent Marinna skidding backward, her feet scrambling for purchase. She tried to get a spell out to lock herself in place, but Drevin interfered with her mnemonics, messing it up. Kael half-drew his sword but didn't move forward, weighing his options. I knew Captain Kael enjoyed a good risk, but he clearly didn't want to confront Drevin head-on.

I already knew the answer.

Smoky growled, her body tensing, ready to fight. But she wasn't big, and I worried about her taking on someone like Drevin. If I wanted to get out of this, I had to be the one to do it.

I tested the bonds. The water held, solid as steel, cold against my skin. My magic was useless against it—I had no training for that kind of thing.

But Drevin had made a mistake.

As my memories had reassembled since bonding with Smoky, physics had proven among the safest ideas to consider—predictable, logical, solid. A few months ago, I wouldn't have thought about physics at all, and for the briefest moment, something close to pride bubbled up. Then unease crept in. Other memories awaited me, and the more they reassembled, the harder they were to ignore.

As the idea clicked in my mind, Smoky stirred—already reacting, like the thought had jumped from me to her through the bond. Then, a flicker of understanding—the moment she connected the idea to action. Not just my plan. Ours. I hadn't trained her for what she was about to do, but she had learned from me the same way I was learning from her.

A second later, facing me so that Drevin would not become suspicious, she exhaled. Not fire, which would have burned me, but a rush of nearly scalding, dry heat.

The moment it hit the water bindings, the surface tension broke. Water was *not* unshakable. Heat *evaporated* water.

And in the instant Drevin realized his spell was failing, I *moved*.

I lunged forward, shoving him backward with all the force I could muster. He staggered, slipping on the now-wet deck. Marinna was on him in an instant, her knee pressing into his back as she twisted his arm behind him and cast a spell to pin him down.

Marinna had no reason to fight for me. A few months before, I'd been nothing more than a well-meaning fool playing at quests, barely worth a second thought. Yet there she was, throwing herself into the fight to keep Drevin's hands off me. The realization settled in my chest—not loud, but solid. Unfamiliar, like the weight of loyalty, or possibly friendship. Whether I had earned it or not, I wouldn't take it for granted. I would have done the same for her—but this was different. A foundation had been laid, the first stone set in place, and though I didn't yet know what we were building, I welcomed its construction.

Captain Kael, still looking *entirely* too amused, finally came down from the helm. "Well," he said, "you two know how to make an impression."

Drevin hissed, actually *hissed*, as he twisted his head toward me. "How did you—"

I shrugged. "You were trying to pull apart my mind, Drevin. You should've known by now—I don't *think* about magic; I *am* the magic." I didn't mean anything by it—I knew I wasn't the magic. But anything to keep him off-balance.

Drevin didn't laugh. He just stared, mapping out the best place to insert a scalpel.

Smoky hopped up onto the Dreadwake's railing, letting out a satisfied puff of smoke.

Drevin scowled at both of us. "You have *no* idea what you are."

"Maybe not," I said, stretching out my now-free arms. "But I know enough to know you're not the one who's going to figure it out."

Captain Kael clapped his hands together. "Well, that was entertaining. Now, Drevin, kindly get off my ship."

Drevin's eyes flashed with frustration, but he didn't resist as Marinna let him loose, lifted him up, and shoved him toward the gangplank.

He took several steps, stopping abruptly. Marinna readied a spell. But he didn't try anything. He looked thoughtful. Then, as though he'd forgotten about us entirely, he pulled out his notebook and his self-inking stylus and scribbled a quick note.

"Believe it or not," Drevin said, slipping his notebook into a pocket, "That may have been enough."

Those words should have comforted me—knowing he might be done with trying to learn what made me tick. But they didn't.

Because he didn't look at me as he uttered them.

He looked at Smoky.

Elliah ~ 6

My conversation with Hughelas lingered—heavy and unfinished—as Janelle approached me where I'd retreated behind the counter. I'd hoped he'd come for me. But he'd sought information, and that stung.

"Come," Janelle said, going out a different arch in the countertop and marching down another spokeway aisle.

I followed, my thoughts snagged on Hughelas. But the air ahead pulled me back—thick with secrets that didn't want to be found.

"Another damp hall?" I asked, attempting to sound casual despite the hackles rising on my neck.

"No," she answered as we approached it, and I realized the door was not just a door—mist curled from the edges, clinging tightly. "This is for Maelith's most advanced students. It's closed to protect neophytes from harming themselves."

"Wait, we're not going after—"

"Shh!" Janelle hushed me. But surely we weren't going after the Omnibus of Thunder—or whatever it was—right then!

When we were close enough to touch the door, Janelle pulled out a charm on a necklace she'd tucked into her robe, much like the one she'd given me, but with even more gems. She held it in front of a plate on the door, and with a click, the door on the left opened a crack. After summoning another magelight, she went in, the mist dissipating into nothing as she passed. She waved for me to follow.

"Every part of the library needs staff services from time to time," she said as she closed the door behind us. It clicked into place with a deadly finality. "So librarians have a pass."

The mist reformed around the door's edge. A very tiny part of me wanted to touch it and see what would happen.

The space behind the door was much like the other hall. She walked me down the hall, each room bearing a door that looked threateningly closed.

"Best to hold your tongue a bit longer," Janelle said. "Even though the halls appear empty. There will be a place where we can talk."

We marched purposefully on, eventually reaching the intersection that seemed to connect the spoke-like hallways. Each side had doors wrapped with mist.

"Can I ask what the mist does?" I ventured.

"It carries an electrical charge. Strong enough to drop you where you stand. We keep the doors locked, but the mist serves as a reminder—for those foolish enough to test it. "

"How does it stay there? How do you keep a spell on an object like that?" The High Elves didn't have that knowledge... though I'd encountered something similar in the gateway to the silvervein that housed the Mother of Trees.

She gave me a look that said, do you really think I'm going to answer that?

"Deara keeps her secrets," I acknowledged. So did the High Elves. But the spell around the Mother of Trees hadn't worked on me. Would the mist?

She nodded. The door before us, that went deeper into the spoke, had a similar mist and metal plate. She brought us into a short hallway before yet another door.

Sighing, she shut the door behind us. When she did, lightning danced around the inner door with a quiet buzzing. At first, only a few sparks, but they increased until the hallway was bright and the door swimming in lightning.

"You're hoping that won't affect me?" I asked. I suspected the lightning was the output of some other magic, and not itself magical. Still, the deathfire in Cenaedth hadn't killed me—I wouldn't know if the lightning were magical unless I tried.

When I moved forward, she grabbed my arm. She shook her head no.

So I waited. The mist around the inner door darkened and spread over the door, the lightning still engulfing it. Then the dark cloud and lightning moved away from the door.

I stepped backward, but Janelle held my arm firmly. She lightly patted it, as if that would somehow make the elf-sized lightning storm less alarming.

The storm stirred something hauntingly familiar. Fragments of memories from the Mother of Trees flitted through my mind—had I seen the creature before?

"You're alive?" I asked it.

Janelle cocked her head at me. "You've encountered one of these before?"

With a shake of my head, I said, "I must have heard about them somewhere." I tugged at the memory, but it was pointless—too much of what I'd seen from the Mother of Trees was completely alien to me.

The storm had stopped, and we stared at it, while it—if it was alive—did the same to us.

"Are we meant to do something?" I asked.

"It's guarding the door, which presumably holds the Grimoire of the Thunderborn," Janelle said. "If you try to pass it, it shivers your timbers and then some. I have it on good authority that Maelith summoned the creature using a spell in the Grimoire. And that Maelith talks with the creature."

"And does it talk back?" No mouth. But also, no eyes, yet it knew we stood before it.

"That's less clear."

"Seems like a pretty dismal existence," I said. "Stuck guarding a door, with only a wizard and his acolytes for company."

"Funny, that's what I said, too. But it has its perks, I suppose. Zapping folks that aren't supposed to be here might be interesting."

I nodded. "Yeah, okay. We're the entertainment. So... you stopped me from approaching it. Was there something else you wanted me to try?"

"No," she said. "I just wanted you to know what you were up against. My last visit, I peed myself."

"Ah, most undignified."

"You get used to it around here. Lots of zapping. And I brought towels."

"Let's say I succeed in getting past." The small, living storm rumbled with laughter. "Anyway, let's say I do. That gets me in the good graces of Drevin? But makes this Maelith person, who controls whatever-this-is, angry with me?"

"I have a remedy for the latter. And to be fair, being in Drevin's good graces is only slightly better than being on his shit-list. What you really want is to be ignored by Drevin. But that's not going to happen. You're Bereft, and that's far too interesting for him to ignore."

"Wonderful. And why are you helping me at all?"

"If you knew who wrote that book you're hauling around, you'd know."

I cocked my head at her. "Why don't you tell me then?"

"What's the fun in that?" she responded.

Strange woman.

Sighing, I tried to go around the storm to the door. It didn't move so much as expand, reaching out to cover me.

For the briefest of moments, I thought I was safe. No bolts of lightning. Nothing but the slight dampness of the cloud.

Zzaap!

Not just pain—raw, crackling force lit every nerve on fire, my body a conduit for searing energy. I flailed, half-blind, my vision swallowed in white. My knees buckled, but the storm's magic held me upright, rigid, while my brain boiled.

And then, amid the chaos in my body, something else seeped in.

An image. A storm, writhing, bound by sparking chains of light fastened to... a book. My skull pounded as the vision sharpened, pulling me closer. A trap, a cage.

I tried to move, to pull free of the creature's grip, but my muscles didn't respond. The electricity locked me in place, forced to endure the crackling energy while more images flashed behind my eyelids: the living cloud spinning endlessly in a storm that held it, each move against its bonds met with a surge of unbearable force.

Then came a memory—or an impression of one. Someone had tried to break the chains, to free the storm from its prison. But instead of unraveling, the bonds had constricted, pulling tighter with every touch of magic.

Maelith?

He'd tried to help it. He'd failed.

I opened my mouth to shout, to scream, but no sound came out. I thrashed uselessly against the storm's power.

A blast threw me against the doors through which we had entered. The surge vanished as suddenly as it came, and I crumpled to the floor, a puppet with its strings severed. My limbs twitched uncontrollably, the storm's energy still buzzing faintly in my veins.

The cloud hovered, flickering, watching. Deciding. My breath came in ragged gasps. My limbs twitched. But my mind—my mind seized the vision, turned it over, examined its edges.

It wasn't just guarding the book—it was chained to it. Bound.

But what power did I have to help? My whole body buzzed, crackling and useless.

I remained where I'd fallen, trembling and staring, too overwhelmed to move.

The towel Janelle tossed over me offered little comfort—like trying to patch a sinking ship with a scrap of sailcloth.

My head exploded with pain. Deafening sound wailed in my ears, in my head. I crashed to the ground, but the pain of that was nothing compared to the one in my head. Spellcasting was impossible. Thought, unreachable. But some primal part of me knew to move away from the noise.

Beldroth!

That was my first coherent thought.

I looked for him, disoriented, the painful wailing in my ears bearable when my hands covered them. I'd gone further down the passage, though I had no idea how I'd gotten there. Ancient packs lay scattered along the hall, and I'd stumbled on one. A red glow blocked the hall on the other side of Beldroth. He inched his way toward me on elbows and knees, his hands over his ears. I tried to think how to help, but the screeching and pressure were too much. I scooted further away, and the noise and pain eased—enough for my thoughts to return. Enough to cast. I tried Healing Beldroth, and I knew for sure that the spell landed, but it didn't do any good. He continued to crawl forward, like a bug that knew nothing except that the fire behind it was hot. In the end, it was his own persistence that got him out of range, and nothing to do with me. Once he was close enough, I risked darting forward and pulling him to his feet, hoping it would speed his retreat. It wasn't clear I sped things up at all—he was a mountain of a man, and in his confusion, he resisted me.

In the end, we found ourselves around a corner and out of sight of the barrier, leaning against a wall with ears ringing, panting like we'd sprinted. The red light from the Shield dimly illuminated the one wall where we'd turned the corner, so I cast a magelight for us to see better.

"Well," Beldroth probably said, though I only suspected that. No sound reached my ears, and I relied on reading his lips. "That was a meal I'm eating."

"What?" I shouted.

"I said, 'That was you meditating.'"

I shook my head.

"That was humiliating!"

Ah, yes. Yes, it was. At least the creature born of storms hadn't followed us in—it would have killed us for sure.

I took his hand and pulled him farther down the passage. It was just a normal mine shaft, rough-hewn rock around us, but ahead, it took a few carved steps down and opened up into a room.

A tomb or mausoleum, perhaps. The difference between the irregular walls of the mine and the once-strict lines of the room were obvious, though any elegance in the carvings of its walls had long decayed into the sands of time.

I Healed myself, and the ringing diminished, but didn't disappear. I tried experimenting with a basic calming spell I'd learned in my tenure with the High Elves. That also helped. I repeated the former on Beldroth, but I didn't know how to cast the calming spell on someone else. Spells that influenced others went much deeper into High Elf specialties and were beyond me.

"Basalt," Beldroth said, and I heard him clearly, partly because he spoke too loudly. "Between geological shifts, moisture and humidity, and limited but unignorable interaction with elves…" He fingered the lettering carved from a discarded dagger on the wall to our right that read, *Welcome to the Abyss*, "…there's little left of the original decorations."

He pointed across the room. "Now that's interesting," he said. An exit led out of the room, and next to it, someone had chiseled a map into the wall. We walked over for a closer look. It showed an array of rooms, connected by corridors, some of which had X's in them. One of the rooms in the middle had a six-sided star. Another small room at the edge of the map had a small six-sided star and a long, trailing shaft leading from it, with a line cutting across the hallway at the bottom of the map. "That's where we are," he said, pointing to the small room with the tiny star. "And I guess that's where we're headed," he said, poking the larger star. "But not now. We rest first."

I nodded my head. We'd walked all day, climbed up and down countless stairways, and while it had been tiring with our packs, I was glad that we'd brought them. Beldroth began rummaging through his.

"It looks like this is where past sojourners set up camp," he observed, loudly enough that I knew his hearing wasn't right yet. "Close to the entrance. Space for sleeping mats. Two ways in, which isn't great for defense, but those same passages can be used as exits, which is good when the unexpected happens."

"Unexpected?" I asked. "Like walking through a one-way Shield into certain death?"

"Yes, like that. Doorways are tricky devils—half the time I walk through one I can't remember why I did so." Like it was the worst problem ever, he exclaimed, "And now we have two!"

"Tch!" I answered, unable to contain a smirk—he was at least *trying* to be lighthearted. I leaned into him, letting my deeper concerns pop their ugly heads out. "What are we going to do? How do we keep the others from following us in? I don't want our children to die here." I squeezed a hand between us to put on my belly and made another noise of irritation. "It's likely Elliah could walk in and out the actual Shield without a problem, but I'm not sure about that noise. I wouldn't care to risk it." After a moment's thought, I added. "They knew she was Bereft. But they may not have understood the implications: magic sometimes—lately often—fails to work on her."

"We can figure this out, my love," he said. "You saw how insular this island is. All Salts. Between my Earth magic and your Healing, we're bringing in something different from those who came before us. But we've had a long day. Let's get some sleep and explore tomorrow. I'll set up trip wires for the tricksome exits. Find us a nice spot with a bit of privacy." He added a wink for good measure.

"Oh, sweet Mother of Trees," I said, though I was sure he was teasing. While he went to work on the trip wires, I cleaned up the debris in a nook where someone had moved square-cut stones to create a small, barricaded sleeping area. "You get in a cave and you can't think of anything else."

"That Shield was powerful," he said. "The Tempest Crown had to be recharged constantly. The effort wore out its caretakers. If there's an artifact down here creating the Shield, how does it maintain power indefinitely?"

I didn't answer. I had no idea.

"Do you think this is Fumaro?" he asked.

"What?" He'd thrown me off with that question.

"Remember? That poem Elliah and Hughelas knew. In the swamps, they thought they'd discovered Stellaris. And Fumaro had been destroyed. Those were the two ancient civilizations mentioned in the poem."

"I remember. You just surprised me with... you surprise me... my love." I said the last like I was trying on a new outfit, deciding whether it fit. "Yes, supposedly, Fumaro was destroyed."

"This is basalt," he said again. "That's volcanic."

Volcanic. He was trying to make a point, so I pried at childhood memories. "Well, I learned of those ancient cities when I was young. Oddly, a mix of stories from High Elf and Wood Elf legends. Stories of places from before the Breaking. Fumaro was supposed to be where the Alluvium lived. It was believed to be volcanic, like Cenaedth I suppose. Stellaris was supposed to have been populated by High Elves. The legend is that the volcano Fumaro was built around erupted, utterly destroying it. Stellaris was buried by the explosion."

"But if Fumero was built around a volcano," he said, "they might have had outposts. Or tombs that were more distant."

"Might have," I agreed. "It's possible this is some remnant."

Quietly, we settled onto our blankets.

"We'll have no way of washing our clothes," I said, noticing we already weren't the freshest.

"We might find an underground lake or river," he offered. "Perhaps that's what the star is marking."

"Or possibly everyone before us died from their own stench," I suggested.

"Mmm. I'll bet the Salts' magic works wonders with washing clothes."

"Unless there's too much salt in the water," I responded.

"Glad you were listening. It's that sharp intelligence and attention to detail that will get us out of here. You know, if you're truly worried about your clothes getting dirty, we should probably remove them." He pulled me close and inhaled deeply while working to pull a decorative string loose on my blouse. "I want to remember how you smell on our first night… just in case it gets worse."

I laughed. "Anything might be down here… my love. Listening." But I didn't stop him. There was a high likelihood we would die in the near future. He wasn't the worst distraction in the world.

"If anyone is listening out there," he said even more loudly, "you might want to take notes."

I didn't expect Drevin to respond immediately—if at all. Janelle had promised to pass my message along, but she hadn't speculated on when I might hear back. I wasn't sure I wanted to actually meet with him. While a part of me, a very noisy part, just wanted time alone with Elliah, another part of me continued to dwell on our larger dilemma. My father and Elliah's mother had not returned. Pyrravyn assured me they were working on the problem he'd assigned them, urging me to focus on locating the dragon. But of everyone, I was the only one permitted to roam "freely," so it fell to me to ensure they were all okay.

I lay in my luxurious bed, alternating between fantasies of having Elliah there and worrying about where she was instead.

The bed was too soft. Too quiet. I shifted, unable to settle—alone in such comfort while everyone else was scattered, supervised, siloed. My father and Illiara would be fine—they'd navigated the roughest of terrains in their lives. Gormar had beamed with pleasure at his invitation to the royal quarters—no worries there. But Marinna and Trentius? And, most especially, Elliah. Kaelith assured the library staff had found room for her. Kaelith's dismissive lack of concern was oddly reassuring—the topic apparently too trivial for lies.

I wasn't afraid for Elliah exactly—she handled herself better than most of us—but I hated not knowing where she was. Hated that she didn't know where I was. That first night dragged me into a hole I failed to crawl out of.

As I flopped about, sleepless, a slim, folded note appeared with a scrape under my door. The script on the outside was precise, almost mechanical in its neatness, and bore my name.

The Skyward Spire. Come at dawn. Come alone.

The brevity left much to the imagination.

One nice thing about the royal mansion—someone was always awake. I searched out a Wrasseguard to get more information. I learned the Spire was a relic of the past, left to crumble into obscurity once the Tempest Crown made celestial observations all but impossible by obscuring the view with a ring of storm clouds. It was also well away from prying eyes, outside of the town on the west side of the island.

As we arrived at the edge of town, I stopped and turned to Kaelith. The first light of dawn illuminated the neglected cobblestone path ahead, and the Skyward Spire loomed nearby, its silhouette sharp against the orange-pink sky. Kaelith looked at me expectantly, her hand resting casually on the pommel of her sword.

"I'll take it from here," I said.

Kaelith raised a brow, her expression skeptical. "Take it from here? I'm under orders to stick with you. Where you go, I go."

"I know," I said, pulling the folded note from my pocket. "But this time, I really do need to go alone." I handed her the note. "Here."

Kaelith unfolded the paper and scanned it quickly, her sharp eyes narrowing as she read. "*Come alone,*" she repeated flatly. "Sounds more like a trap than an invitation."

"It's from Drevin," Hughelas said, his voice low. "You know him better than I do. Will he meet with me if you're there?"

Kaelith folded her arms, holding the note loosely in one hand.

I sighed, rubbing the back of my neck. "If something happens, you'll know where I went and why. You can follow up if I'm not back quickly."

"That's assuming I don't just follow you now," Kaelith said, her tone cool. "Why are you even doing this? Your search for Drevin was obviously a ruse to visit your lover, even if it didn't pan out for you." I nearly choked. *Lover?* "Why follow through?"

"She's not—" I began, but her raised eyebrow stopped me. I spent increasingly unproductive amounts of time fantasizing about Elliah. Even if Kaelith was wrong, she wasn't off target on my motives. And Kaelith had seen through my ruse.

I met her gaze steadily. I'd dragged her to the docks, then back up to the library, and she'd barely shared a word with me. Janelle had made her uncomfortable, probably because Janelle knew more than she should have. I didn't know what to think of my guard. "Kaelith, I need him to trust me. If you follow, I might as well not bother going. Right?"

Still, she hesitated, her eyes flicking between me and the spire. "And what if you don't come back?" she asked again, softer this time.

"I will," I reassured her. "But if I don't, you know where I'll be. And honestly, if anyone can drag me out of trouble, it's you, right?"

Kaelith allowed a small smirk to tug at the corner of her mouth. "Flattery isn't going to change my orders."

"I'm not asking you to break them," I said. "Just... bend them a little. Wait here, or somewhere nearby. Give me a little time. If I'm not back in, say, an hour, come after me. Deal?"

Kaelith exhaled slowly, nodding once. "Fine. One hour. If you're not back by then, I'm coming in after you, Drevin's trust be damned."

"Fair enough," I said, smiling faintly. "Thank you, Kaelith."

"Don't thank me yet," she muttered, stepping back to lean against a tree at the edge of the path. "I'll be right here, counting the minutes. Don't make me come after you."

"I'll do my best," I replied, turning toward the spire.

I paused, a question born of worry bubbling up. "What," I asked her, facing away in a whisper, "did you tell Pyrravyn about me and Elliah?"

Her ears were sharp.

"Nothing," she whispered back. In a normal voice, she continued. "I like that you're checking on your friends. That you *care*. I know you asked Pyrravyn about your father and the Wood Elf mother of your *lover*." She jabbed the last word at me with a snorting laugh. "They left with Feldryn. Feldryn's a good man, once you get past his bravado. The quest Pyrravyn sent them on had real import. It wasn't a trick. They made it to Maelith and the Tempest Crown safely. There are any number of innocuous reasons their efforts may have slowed—at least one of which is progress on their mission. I'll let you know when I hear more."

I nodded. It was more answer than I expected. "Thank you," I said. As I walked away, Kaelith's sharp gaze on my back prickled until the path curved and took me out of sight.

The Spire loomed above me, a solitary tower clinging to the edge of the cliffs like a forgotten sentinel. Its stonework was weathered, the once-sharp edges softened by centuries of storms. A rusted brass door stood at its base, and I hesitated only briefly before pushing it open.

Inside, the air was cooler, tinged with the faint, metallic tang of disuse. The room at the base was circular and empty, save for a spiral staircase that wound upward.

Drevin was waiting at the top, or at least he seemed to be. When I reached the summit, he was muttering to himself, pacing in an erratic circle as a magelight hovered behind him. He clutched a thick, leather-bound notebook in one hand, and his other hand gestured absently in the air as though sketching invisible diagrams.

"Oh, there you are," he said abruptly, as though we'd already started the conversation. "I was considering the effects of sustained storm energy on the seabed. The blond-haired elf said she saw something." Great. Even my friends were talking to him more than they were telling me. "It got me thinking. Fascinating problem. Completely unrelated to why you're here, of course." He paused mid-stride, eyes narrowing as he examined me like I was a puzzle piece that didn't fit.

"You've come alone. Sensible. Or stupid. Possibly both," he added, already turning to fiddle with the broken remnants of the telescope near the open dome. "This telescope—once upon a time it was a wonder, but utterly useless now. Like so many things."

He waved a hand vaguely at a piece of stone at the base of the telescope, where one might sit, though he didn't sit himself. "Go on, sit. Or don't. It's no concern of mine."

I remained standing, my anxiety high.

Drevin turned back to face me, his gaze flitting briefly across me before it darted to the magelight, which he adjusted with a flick of his fingers. "I hear you're smart," he said, his tone flat but curious. "But you grew up among Warders. Your access to knowledge must have been…

pedestrian."

I bit back the urge to bristle at his condescension. "I hear you'd disassemble your own mother just to see what made her think she cared about you." Yeah, okay, I bristled a little.

That got his attention. He froze for a beat, then let out a sharp laugh. "Bold. Reckless. Predictable." He tapped his notebook with a finger. "Now, why are you here? Spare me the theatrics; I've little patience for them, though infinite patience for real questions." His tone implied I was unlikely to have any of the latter.

"I need information," I said evenly. "About the black dragon. Its location."

Drevin hummed, half-listening, his attention wandering to the corroded telescope again. "I might be able to point you in the right direction, but I have questions of my own. I'm curious about your friend. Elliah, is it? Bereft. Resistant to magic. A fascinating anomaly."

"No," I said firmly.

He blinked, unbothered. "Ah. Protective. Admirable, if tediously uncooperative. What about Trentius and the red dragon? Now that is a puzzle worth solving. How does one leash a creature like that?"

I hesitated. I needed information, but sharing too much with Drevin was handing a knife to a man who'd already measured my back. Still, I gave him something. "Trentius had... problems. Mental ones. He tried to Compel the dragon, and his condition made the bond... unusual. Unrepeatable."

"Nonsense," Drevin said after a pause, his tone clipped. "Anything is repeatable with the right experiment."

"The dragon," I reminded him.

"Black dragon... yes, storms, altered fishing patterns. Old records might suggest something useful. Or just old knowledge. You should talk to fisherfolk! Dreadful conversations, I imagine. Smell like fish, too. Always do." He glanced back at me, his expression suddenly sharp. "Did you know the blue dragons don't come inside the waters created by the storm circle? We had an incident recently. The magical storm came down. That's when the black flew over the island. Haven't seen it before or since. Not sure it even lives nearby—its visit might have been coincidence. The people who reported it said it was enormous—but that was fisherfolk, happy to exaggerate about the one that got away. When the storm came down, the blues swarmed. Maelith had the storm back up again in minutes, before the blues reached the port. Now he refuses to turn off the storm again to test what would happen."

The fact that Maelith refused an experiment seemed more offensive to Drevin than the idea of being swarmed by blue dragons.

From his robe, Drevin pulled out a book and whatever contraption he'd come up with for writing, muttering, "Compulsion..." while drawing something. I wanted to look over his shoulder. I wanted to know how much of Drevin's theories on magic aligned with the journal Felaern had sent with me. The journal I'd lost when the Dearans kidnapped me. But I didn't want to give him the pleasure or leverage of knowing I was interested. So I turned and walked back down the stairs.

Talk to those who fished the ocean about changes in fishing patterns or, perhaps, weather anomalies. I hated to admit it, but it was a pretty good lead.

Elliah ~ 7

Janelle's den smelled like old ink, dust, and dry sarcasm—the place you end up in when nobody knows where to put you. Her home was a warren of books and quiet shadows, a forgotten annex tucked beside the library.

"You'll stay here tonight," she'd said, nudging a pile of journals off the couch with one foot. "You need rest more than pride, and I doubt anyone's handing out room keys. Except to the Scion, of course."

I'd snorted, but the word had caught something in my chest. The Scion. He'd hurt my feelings, but I still worried about him. Was he okay? Had they really handed him a room?

I hadn't argued. Not because she was right—though she was—but because the idea of sleeping alone, in an unfamiliar city, after everything we'd been through... I wasn't ready for that. I didn't know where Hughelas was, or my mother. To stay with Janelle wasn't simply practical—it anchored me.

She left me to rest, and not long after, she returned and quietly set my pack beside the couch. I hadn't moved. Only breathed and tried to relax, allowing the occasional twitching to fade. The sight of my bag—dirt-smeared, weather-worn, but familiar—hit me harder than I expected. It tethered me to the life that Deara attempted to pull away. And Janelle had brought it to me, not kept it elsewhere.

My body had calmed, but the static still clung to my skin, a ghost of the storm's touch. Janelle's old couch cradled me, surrounded by shadows and stories, yet my unease remained. Whatever that thing was—whatever it *wanted*—it had chosen not to destroy me. And that demanded answers.

Janelle appeared with a bottle of wine and two glasses. I wanted to sleep. But I had to ask—because if I didn't, the questions would keep me awake anyway.

"How do you think Maelith and his acolytes get by it?" I asked, my voice low, almost hesitant. "The creature—why doesn't it stop them?"

"I suspect their magic is strong enough to contain the creature," Janelle said.

"And Drevin's is not? You said he was powerful too."

"Drevin's magic is strong, but he tends towards esoteric magic. I have no doubt he is capable of mastering the storm, but it would take him away from his other... passions."

The idea had gnawed at me since the thing had touched me. "I don't think Maelith summoned it," I said slowly.

"In my head, I've been calling it an elemental," Janelle said. "It's better than 'thing' or 'whatever-that-was.' Can we agree to call it an elemental?"

I nodded, sipping a glass of white wine Janelle had proffered. The warmth of the wine didn't immediately loosen the knot in my stomach. I'd only ever shared wine with my mother, and every sip reminded me of her. Where was she? Was she okay? Wood Elves were stronger while pregnant—energized, casting harder spells, solving problems faster—but that didn't make her invulnerable. What if there were more of those *elementals* around?

"So why don't you think Maelith summoned the elemental?" she asked, looking askance at a teetering stack of books and deciding to drink her wine instead of right the pile.

"Did the elemental try to communicate with you?" I asked, testing how far out on the limb I perched.

"Honestly, it might have. I saw images of storms and a book. Obvious stuff, given, you know... the storm and the Grimoire." After a sip, she added, quietly, "More or less the same every time."

"Wait, how many times have you tried to get past it?"

"Personally," she said with a sigh, "five. Counting today, six."

"You've let it shock the crap out of you five times?" I stared at her, waiting for the punchline. When none came, I set my glass down. To go through that ordeal four more times *voluntarily*—I struggled to imagine.

"Well, *that* only happened once. But I knew to bring towels. I didn't mention this before, but the ones with a green border can handle... messes."

"Glad we didn't need them."

"Is that what you saw?" she asked. "The elemental and the book?"

"At first," I answered. "The elemental and some kind of binding, like light, to a book."

"Already more distinct than what I saw."

"Wonderful. I'm more attuned to dark, brooding storms than you."

"Carry on. Elemental. Book. Binding..."

"And I saw someone trying to free the elemental. I've never met your Maelith—"

"White hair. Tall. Alabaster skin."

I laughed at her joke—there wasn't a Salt in Deara who that didn't describe, including Hughelas's personal guard, Kaelith. *She'd better keep her hands to herself!* "Honestly, the imagery wasn't that clear. It might have been you for all I could tell, but I'm thinking it was Maelith. Only his attempt to free the elemental made things worse. The elemental is tied to the Grimoire, but I think trying to free it tightens the bonds for the elemental, like pulling the ends of a knotted rope." I retrieved my glass and sipped my wine. I wished I had Hughelas there with me instead of Janelle. He would understand it all. And he would look at me the way he always did, calming my anxiety while riling up something else entirely. "I don't know." The ceiling held no answers, but I stared at it anyway. "I think he was asking me not to make things worse. But I'm not sure."

"Is it possible it sensed you were Bereft?" Janelle asked. "That it was hoping you provided a different option?"

"I… I didn't really think so. That final shove was definitely a 'now, go away' type message."

"I suppose it was. I've heard it often enough."

"Five times," I reminded her.

"Indeed."

"Then I guess I can handle it at least once more. But… not today."

Janelle smiled. "And I'll bring the green-edged towels. Just in case."

I swirled the wine in my glass, watching the liquid catch the light. "You ever get tired of it?"

She raised an eyebrow. "Tired of getting zapped? Or failing spectacularly?"

"No," I said, exhaling. "Of never really steering anything. All I ever do is… react. Always moving because I have to, not because I choose to." I hesitated, then pushed forward, the words spilling out. "I want to be in control for once. Not just running, not just surviving—actually making a choice that sticks."

Janelle studied me for a moment, then leaned back against the arm of the couch. "Control is an illusion, Elliah. But knowing the rules? That's power."

I frowned. "So you're saying control isn't real?"

Janelle smirked. "No. I'm saying it isn't what people think it is."

She gestured vaguely at the piles of books around us. "People like Drevin and Maelith—powerful as they are—don't actually control anything. Not really. Maelith is a slave to the Tempest Crown. Drevin though? He watches the winds. He knows when to set his sail, when to tack, when to wait." She tapped her temple. "That's why he wins. Not because he steers the storm, but because he doesn't fight it head-on."

I considered that, rolling the words around in my head. "So power isn't steering the ship—it's knowing which way the wind is blowing?" The words tasted bitter on my tongue.

Janelle smiled faintly, raising her glass. "Something like that. If you fight the storm, you sink. But if you read the winds—"

I interrupted, shaking my head. "So what, we're just supposed to drift wherever the wind takes us?"

Janelle chuckled. "No, you can set your course. But if you don't learn how to sail, the storm makes your choices for you."

Beldroth : 4

When I awoke, nothing had changed. None of the trip wire alarms had gone off. But some stirring of the air or vibration in the stone beneath us roused me. I reached out to place a hand on the wall, regretting that I'd muted my connection to the earth with a blanket. *Something* had pulled me from slumber, yet nothing came through the stone. The ringing in my ears had passed, but was I really hearing correctly?

It was impossible to know the hour, but my limbs moved easily, steady and light. A day. In just a single day on Deara, I'd managed to get trapped inside a magical cage the locals had named the Abyss. At least the sleep had done me good. I summoned a small magelight, but the spell seemed sluggish, like it had caught in molasses. I put a finger to my lips when Illiara's eyes flipped open. She tensed when she saw my caution. I ran the magelight down her form, enjoying her shape.

"Ass," she said. "That's no way to wake a woman."

"Ah, but it woke me," I said, rolling on top of her.

"Oh, get off, you big lunk. I'm trapped in a cave already. You think I want to be trapped under you."

So I rolled us over with her on top.

"Oh, sweet Mother of Trees," she said. "We're not lounging in a forest glade. We are trapped and going to die!"

"What better way to meet our Maker?"

"We've already met Her," she snapped, standing up, summoning her own magelight. She frowned at the light like it disappointed her and started putting her clothes on.

I sighed and began dressing, my thoughts tangled. We *had* met the Mother of Trees, and I had tried to pretend everything was fine, even as the weight of everything that was terribly wrong had pressed down on me. Comatose. Deranged. Broken. And then we had stumbled upon an ancient artifact beneath Theopolis—perhaps in what was once Stellaris—only to be told that for her creations to survive, the Mother of Trees would have to die. Was it a trick? I'd wanted so desperately for it to be a trick. Some cruel scheme devised by the Father of Stones. After all, there had been a troll in that magical memory. A minion of the Father. Yet doubt had taken root in me. My faith had wavered, and I'd found myself avoiding Hughelas's research into a magical cage—not because it didn't make sense, but because it made *too much* sense. And I didn't want it to.

"I'll go retrieve those old packs. Feldryn may have tossed in more," she said, exiting through the passage by which we'd entered. "Besides, I want to try some spells to see if I can overcome the noise and pain."

She didn't like caves—but *hated* giving in to fear. That direction should have been safe from anything but the Shield itself, so I let her exert her independence even though I still worried about her safety. Since we would likely be there for some time, I didn't completely remove the wires I'd set up, but I moved them enough to get through the passage that led deeper into the catacombs. A few feet beyond the room, the passage ended in a wall with halls going to the right and left. The two of us would fit side by side, but it was too thin for a third. Stone-cut bricks lined the wall, with patchy holes that revealed the rock behind it. Someone had cleared the crumbling bricks from the middle of the passage and stacked them along the walls. Of course, we already knew others had been down there, but the confirming evidence reassured me. People had tidied up.

I stood at the intersection, sending my light one way and then the other, when Illiara returned.

"Nothing," she said. "He better come back with some food and water."

"Or you'll do what to him?" I asked with a mischievous poke.

She snarled. "I'll haunt him mercilessly."

"Unfortunately, no one is afraid of an attractive ghost. You can haunt me anytime. It will be torture not to touch those beautiful—"

"Enough, Warder!" She took the bite out of her words with a quick kiss. "Concentrate on getting us out of here with the focus you apply to sex, and we will be free before we need any supplies." With more seriousness, she added. "Something is off with my magic."

"I feel it too," I said. "Like it is dragging its feet."

"And my mana isn't recharging the way it should," she added. She squinted at me. "Be more careful than usual. I'm not sure how effective my Healing will be."

"Yes, ma'am." I stole one more kiss before turning back to the branching hallways. "Would you like to pick the path?"

"This is your Earth magic at work? Lucky guesses?"

Grinning, I said, "Let's call it strategic intuition. Besides, we'll probably be wandering for a while—I'm saving the big magic for when it really counts."

She pursed her lips at me in exaggerated disbelief.

"Let's go this way," I said, turning into the left-hand passage—the one I'd half-memorized from the map chiseled into the wall.

Nothing significant had changed relative to the map—at least not that I noticed. Warders were supposed to have an unerring sense of direction, a trait tied to their connection to the physical world. But for me, that connection had always been... abstract. My Warder peers instinctively navigated forests and followed the faintest of trails, while I had once led a hunting party in circles for half a day before realizing my mistake. I sought truths of a different kind, and sometimes the practicalities—like finding the right turn—eluded me. If we'd had parchment, I would have copied the map outright, but I'd had to settle for memorizing it as best as possible. The etching wasn't exactly to scale, and I wasn't completely confident we'd reached the "big-star room" on the map. Still, I liked my odds. To hedge my bets, I'd dropped small markers from my pack at every fork and exit we passed. Even if I was wrong, at least our return would be simple.

A pool of water occupied the center of the large room, the width of the pool about three times my height. Columns decorated the room in a regular pattern, but several had collapsed, and all had lost their decor. A ring of phosphorescent fungi, reminiscent of those in Cenaedth, surrounded the water. We'd seen their faint purple glow when we'd first sent our magelights to the far side of the chamber to explore the room. The floor was damp, suggesting water had seeped in somewhere, though it wasn't obvious where.

"This hole is exceptionally deep," I told Illiara after I finished casting, fighting the sluggish effects of magic inside the Shield. I didn't see any significant stalactites or water dripping from the ceiling. It didn't smell stagnant. Knowing Illiara would Heal me—assuming her magic didn't fail—if I was wrong, I touched the water and dabbed it on my tongue. "Not salty."

"Hm," she answered. "Help me understand how you know the depth of the pool from your spell. All I've ever heard about is Warder combat spells, and that's all I've seen you teach Marinna."

"Not true," I said. "I've even taught you one."

"The sound amplification," she said. "Fair enough. So one non-combat spell, though Marinna found a good use for it during combat."

"Yes, yelling commands to troops is a common use for it in battle. But, in fact, it is a variant of that spell which I used here." I put my hands on the rock of the floor, nodding for her to do the same. Then I cast the simple spell, noting how little mana I had to work with. I exaggerated the finger motions so she might note the similarity to the spell I'd taught her. The rock below us vibrated as the spell traveled through it. She raised an eyebrow. "The spell creates a low-frequency pulse, and its echo tells me what lies beyond the immediate stone."

"Tells you?"

"You learn to interpret the way the rock responds. It doesn't speak to me in words. And in this case, it tells me there's a lot more water below."

She nodded, accepting my answer. "So, we walk around with you talking to walls until we find something interesting?"

I smirked at her deliberate facetiousness. "That's one option. There's another similar spell that might be faster. But you're probably going to have to leave for me to cast it."

Her brows lowered. "I'm too distracting?"

"Yes, my love."

"Well, I'll just go over here then," she said, walking around one of the columns, swaying her hips saucily as she departed.

"Suit yourself," I said, "but try not to make any noise."

"Tch."

I sat on the floor, slowed my breathing, then, taking and holding my breath, I cast the spell. I mentally frowned—my mana had not really recharged at all.

The quiet grew louder. I knew what would happen, so I covered my ears. A rustle echoed and grew, crescendoing into a *boom!* Then everything went quiet.

"Holy Mother of Rutting Trees!" Illiara exclaimed, hands over her ears as she marched back around the rubble. "What in the fiery pits of Cenaedth was that?"

"Amplifies ambient sound," I said. "Unfortunately, it goes out of control very quickly. You really must be much quieter."

She kept rubbing her ears. "You root-rotting twig-snapper. Why didn't you warn me?"

"It turns me on when you rub your ears." Truth was, I knew it would cause no lasting harm, and it was how we always taught the importance of being quiet while we cast the spell. She'd made some noise that had caused the spell to explode.

She froze. "Freaking men," she said as she walked out the entrance we'd come in through.

"You'll still need to be quiet!" I shouted. The spell would amplify even distant sounds, which was part of its beauty. I waited until her curses died away and slowed my breathing again.

I recast the spell and listened. *Drip.* So there was water coming in somewhere, though I hadn't spotted it. Illiara's breathing, though distant, grew louder. My own heartbeat became audible. I put my hands over my ears—if Illiara was still muttering curses, they would come through in a blast, destroying the spell and leaving my ears ringing. Then, I heard it: a rhythmic sound… a deep vibration, followed by many small taps of stone on stone… and something dragging or scraping almost silently. Stone on stone… claw on stone.

I dropped the spell and lunged to my feet. "Illiara! Come back!" I ran toward her. Panic gripped me. Her footsteps echoed down the corridor as she ran toward me.

"What is it?" she shouted.

I dashed into the corridor and pushed through the sluggish magic to create a bubble Shield over us both as soon as she was close enough.

Wham! We tumbled end-over-end inside the ball I'd created, flying back into the room—something had slammed into the bubble.

As we bounced off walls and rolled slowly to a stop, I stated the obvious: "Dragon."

"You know," I said as we righted ourselves in the bubble Shield, drawing our hopelessly useless weapons, "before I met you, I'd never encountered a dragon." The white dragon, almost too large to fit in the hallway, took its time stalking into the room. It was considerably smaller than the enormous red beast Beldroth had fought in Cenaedth, but much larger than Smoky. Its head was as big as Beldroth's chest and flat like a viper. No spikes ran down its spine the way they did on the red in Cenaedth. I tried to remember—did the blacks that attacked us on the river have spikes? I thought they had. And the greens in the forest? They'd darted back and forth so quickly, I wasn't sure. "Felaern claimed to have talked to one, and it wasn't that I thought he was lying, but they somehow remained unreal." The dragon stretched its wings out, then shook like a wolf shedding water, though it wasn't wet. Just cramped in the hallway? "How many have we fought now?"

"I don't know how many reds there were in Cenaedth," Beldroth said. "I think there were three blacks on the river. Two greens in Alenor." He looked from side to side and had us roll the bubble to the corner farthest from the young white. "You weren't with me when I killed the white in Bellon. I'm going to drop the Shield," he said as he sheathed his sword, "and use these boulders."

The dragon, moving faster than seemed possible, loomed before us.

"Scratch that plan," Beldroth squeaked out, drawing his sword slowly, like someone trying not to startle prey.

The dragon reached out a front leg toward the bubble Shield, then one claw. It touched the Shield like a test.

The Shield dissolved.

"Run," Beldroth said, swinging toward the claw.

I backed up, but I didn't run. Yes, there were passageways that would allow me to flee and some halls we'd already traveled had collapsed enough that the dragon would not have fit. But, ultimately, there was nowhere to go. We were sealed in. I would only prolong the inevitable.

The dragon pulled its arm back, out of range, and growled. A sound that came up through the stone at my feet. *Okay, prolonging the inevitable isn't all bad.* Beldroth murmured something, and I cast a spell to recharge his mana. The magic oozed like molasses, but my spell helped.

"*You* killed my mother, elf?"

We froze. Like the enormous red dragon we'd heard before, its voice contained multiple pitches that took on an eerie resonance, like two voices speaking at once. Only this one's pitch was higher. Because it was smaller?

Beldroth looked askance at me, not sure what to do, but I was as confused as he.

"I slew a white dragon much larger than you," Beldroth declared, then looked at me with wide eyes. Could we bluff our way out? Or would the dragon want revenge? Was the dragon Beldroth killed truly the mother of the one before us?

The seconds dragged out, growing awkward.

"Why don't you fight?" the dragon growled. "Bind me with magic, beat me to death with a hammer you crafted from the bone of my mother."

Startled, I blurted, "But Elliah has the hammer."

The dragon's eyes pierced me. I hadn't realized its attention had been so focused on Beldroth until it landed on me. Silver pupils housed knowledge vast and profound, wise beyond time. "The hammer formed from my mother's bone is not here?"

My gut told me lying was a death sentence—the dragon would know and slay me for an untruth. However, answering truthfully was also a noose around the neck. The dragon knew of the hammer. It expected Beldroth to fight, and win, with the hammer. Without it, we were not a threat. In the end, I found those eyes impossible to lie to. "The hammer is not here."

The dragon roared, a dis-harmonic echoing sound that rattled my very bones.

"Someone has used True Sight," the dragon said. "Let us hope they have not pushed the future out of the path my grandmother intended. But you must kill me for this cage to be broken. It is your... lesson."

The dragon had directed that message to Beldroth. His lesson. Cages and death. Again, cages and death.

Beldroth calmly and solemnly told the dragon what he'd informed me of long ago, on our travels down the Flawless River, "I intend to inter her bones, should I ever make it back. I don't know why she attacked us. She was already wounded when she arrived." He grimaced like he'd said something he hadn't meant to. "I will inter her bones when I make it back."

"That," the dragon said, looking surprised, "would be a kindness." Then its expression soured. "Though a pointless one while the Mother yet lives. Also moot for me, since you need to kill me to get out. I am too young to have children, so none would profit from your goodwill. Even if we had a thousand years to wait for me to come of age, which we do not, you would still have to slay me to escape."

The dragon crouched like a tiger to leap, while I tried desperately to sort through what she had just said. If I understood correctly, the only way out of the one-way Shield was to kill the dragon. Or at least the dragon believed that to be true.

126

Beldroth cast spells, readying himself to fight.

"Why?" he shouted, as the dragon launched itself at him. Good, he was thinking about what the dragon said too, and not rushing in. He jumped aside, dodging her teeth, but not quickly enough to avoid getting hit, and while his Shield protected him from the sudden impact, it dissolved before he hit the wall. "Why does killing you end the spell?" he croaked out as he pulled himself together.

I Healed his battered body as he recast his Shield, just before the dragon's claw slapped him across the room and into another wall. His Shield broke earlier, and with it, an arm.

"Fight me!" the dragon roared.

"Why does killing you end the spell?" Beldroth shouted back as I magically repaired his arm. Though it pleased me the spell worked, I wouldn't have mana much longer.

The dragon noticed the Healing. She turned her attention to me.

"I think you need more incentive to kill me," the dragon said, stalking me, but talking to Beldroth. The dragon's pursuit of Beldroth had put some distance between us. Like before, the dragon's stare had power to it. Its eyes saw through me, laying my hopes and fears bare. It was beyond unsettling.

"Why does killing you end the spell?" I shouted, trying to shake the mesmerism of those eyes and edge toward an exit. Though we were ultimately trapped, I would buy Beldroth time.

"It's the way the pedestal works!" the dragon snarled. "Unless you've brought a troll, we cannot end it except through the death of the one who activated it. Me."

I was ready to bolt out of the passageway, even while doubting my ability to outrun the dragon, but her words froze me. And the dragon saw through me—recognized in me *why* I froze—and she halted her lunge.

In the strange, dual-voice sound of a dragon speaking, with eyes so wide as to be comical, she asked, "You've brought a troll?"

We left our room and crossed the open space between buildings, shaded by a thick canvas sheet—perhaps an old sail. The morning air was cool, but mid-summer on Deara would be suffocating. Like the entire sky pressed down on you.

We entered the library, and I was once again assaulted by the smell of the books, oiled wood, and something more biting, but it had become more familiar. "Salt libraries are chaos," Janelle explained, sweeping her arms. "Writers hoard books that inspire them, so the library is a maze of private collections. Organized insanity." She pointed at the section with books in netting as we passed it. "Corlan Tidehook writes about fishing. But he collects books about fish." She waved at the maps in the glass cases. "Mira Driftline makes the best maps in the world. You'll find a wealth of maps created by others in her section." She spun in a circle. "Tarys Tidestone has the most pristine collection—each shelf in her area is organized by the shape and color of the books."

"How do you find anything?" I asked.

"Great question," she replied. She pulled me behind the circular counter in the center, then pointed at it. "This is the big difference between our library and other Salt libraries. We've devised a way to rein the chaos in. Or possibly a way to enable the chaos to grow. Hard to say."

She opened one of the hundreds of drawers, and inside was an array of tiny crystals stuck to pieces of paper with what appeared to be book titles written on them. *Tides and Trophies: The Art of Fishing Across the Nine Winds, Casting Shadows: Fishing Lore of the Open Seas,* and *Secrets of Deepwater Fishing.*

She pulled one out and cast a tiny magelight on the crystal, directing my attention back along the path we had taken. A dim light flickered in the section of the library we'd passed that had all the nets.

"So you can find books," I said, impressed.

"Over short distances," Janelle said. "When acolytes—or even leaders like Drevin and Maelith—take them into the tunnels, they're harder to track down. One has to go wandering up and down all the alcoves." She sighed. "Naturally, those are the books most requested."

On another part of the counter, a librarian was standing with a mage who was looking through a similar drawer of labeled books. While I watched, the librarian pulled out a second drawer for the customer. "That's Kaelith Oreharbor. He's probably read every book we have on mining, but he keeps searching for hidden gems. Ha!"

"Unfortunately," she continued, "this doesn't stop the hoarding and fighting over books. People still grab what they want and bring it to their own section. Most folks put in requests for us to find books, and we do our best, holding them up here for a reader. But many still enjoy the old ways of knowing who reads what, hunting on their own, and nabbing the books they want."

"You embed a piece of crystal in the covers? What stops someone from pulling that out?"

"That's right, and nothing stops them. We occasionally light up all the books at once and look for dark spots in the room. It helps us find books that need crystals. It's a mess, but it's much better than it was a century ago."

"Okay," I said, rubbing my eyes. "How do I actually help when I can't cast a magelight?" I'd grown long accustomed to lacking even the simplest spells other elves learned when young, yet the tiny reminder still prickled.

"I think you'll be able to help more than you realize," Janelle said with a mischievous grin. "Jaylyn?"

"Reader needs *Bridging Currents: Tidal Structures of the Stormbound Isles.*" The young elf looked worried, though the title sounded... well, boring.

Janelle raised an eyebrow at me. "Think you're up for your first fetch?"

"I'm not exactly lit up with magelight," I muttered, but I stepped forward anyway.

Jaylyn held up a slip with a tiny sliver of crystal pressed into its top. With her tongue sticking out the side of her mouth in concentration, she cast a magelight right on top of it. A dull glow flared in the direction of a row of shelves toward the western wall. I wove through the maze of alcoves, nets brushing my arms, walls of books narrowing unexpectedly. The light sat amidst a tightly-packed shelf—some titles legible, others worn down to sea-rubbed leather. I found the book sandwiched between two massive volumes about anchor-forging techniques. The moment I touched the cover, the light winked out.

Back at the counter, Janelle took the book with quiet approval, smirking, while Jaylyn breathed out a sigh of relief. "See," she said to Jaylyn, "I told you the trap wouldn't activate on her. Keep this at the front desk. I have a feeling her boyfriend might come looking for it.

"Trap?" I asked. Boyfriend? Hughelas would want a book about tides?

"You're officially a Library Runner," Janelle said. "Keep that up, and they'll start calling you something impressive—like Assistant to the Deputy of Retrieval." She nodded at Jaylyn, who blushed deeply.

"Sounds like a promotion," I said, peeved about how she'd used me, yet also… just a touch proud that I was able to do something easily that others found difficult. "Better than being a lightning rod," I muttered. Finally.

Beldroth : 5

"We have to tell Feldryn," I said. The thought leapt out before reality caught it—we had no way to reach him.

"The elf with a scar across his eye?" the dragon asked in its bivocal way.

I nodded, though I'd spoken to Illiara, not the dragon. Or possibly I'd been thinking out loud. Then I realized the dragon wasn't looking in my direction and wouldn't see my nod. "That's the one," I said.

The dragon rumbled, settling her belly down on the ground. She didn't seem concerned about me having my sword drawn, standing near her haunches. I wondered, would she wrap her tail around me, like her mother had done with Lyrei's corpse, like the skeleton wrapped the pedestal under Theopolis? I moved out of range as the tail swept past. While keeping stone columns between us, I worked my way around to Illiara.

"Are you aware that white dragons can See?" the dragon asked.

"No," Illiara said. "Is that like what the Mother of Trees does when she Blesses quests?"

"It is," the dragon said. "I am of an age where I would be able to do it, if I had the knowledge. But I have no one to train me." Her head swiveled around to look at me. I didn't understand her next words, but my throat tightened anyway, like I'd been handed something sacred I wasn't ready to carry. "And I am not who I am supposed to be."

The dragon tested me, but I did not understand how. I stopped moving, pinned down by her gaze, but I only offered confusion.

The dragon closed her eyes, and the spell broke. When she opened them, they were once again merely silver eyes. "Nevertheless, I have had dreams. I suspect they are related to Seeing. The elf with the scar across his eye is in them."

Lacking other context, I asked, "What does he do in your dreams?"

The dragon was slow in answering. "Brings something. Takes something. Or someone. I am not sure." She blinked once and then pinned Illiara with her gaze. "Tell me of this troll you bring. Did the elves get their message out? They gave up long ago, but you suggest it worked."

"I..." Illiara stammered. "I don't know what message you're talking about. And it isn't *exactly* a troll that came with us." The dragon bristled, her claws scratching the rock as they tightened, and her tail slamming against the floor. Illiara held up her arms. "But she's *like* a troll. She has activated one of these pedestals before. Where we found the remains of another dragon. It can't be—"

"What?" roared the dragon, jumping back up. I moved between her and Illiara, bringing up a Shield, not that it had done much good thus far—a waste of the tiny mana I had remaining. The dragon before me broke them faster than the mighty red had done in Cenaedth, despite being a fraction of the red's size.

"We found dragon bones under Theopolis," I said. "I am sure it was also a white. That cannot be coincidence." The words tumbled out, desperate and raw. I needed the events of my life to mean something—to prove there was more than chaos behind everything.

The dragon huffed a few breaths, her eyes glimmering like silver fire. Then she closed them, and, sighing, she lay back down. "Indeed," she said. "Theopolis." With her eyes still closed, she said. "You will take me to my mother's bones? Jenat, the First of the Lost? And my grandmother is under Theopolis. What torment that will be."

Torment? I didn't understand.

"If you wish," I said, unsure whether my offer was a help or a burden.

"But first we must get your not-a-troll in here," the dragon said.

"She may come on her own," Illiara said. "Once she learns we are trapped. Though I must admit, I hope she does not." The dragon narrowed its eyes. "What if it doesn't work? She will also be trapped."

"Then you will have to kill me to escape," the dragon said. "It is little risk to her. Come," the dragon said, rising again, "we will discuss with the others." She turned and walked back to the pool in the center of the room.

"Others?" Illiara called out, following the dragon.

"The other elves," she said, not turning around. "Just swim down there," she said, nodding to the pool. "It connects to a pool in another room."

I'd already used my magic to plumb the depths of the pool. "It is too deep for us."

The dragon cocked its head curiously. "Wait here," she said, then looked around the room and laughed quietly to itself, the sound reverberating through the chamber like the closing of a tomb. Where would we go? With a soft *sloosh*, she slipped into the pool, disturbing the water surprisingly little for such a large creature, and vanished.

Illiara - 6

We waited near the pool, sitting on one of the spilled columns, eating dustmeal, the summoned paste mixed with the freshwater. Though we'd brought our packs, we'd depleted them of foodstuffs on the journey to Deara. We hadn't restocked them before our inland journey.

"Should we go look to see if Feldryn threw in any supplies?" Beldroth asked, as he pushed the paste around with a spoon.

"Do you really want the dragon to think we tried to run off?" I asked, smacking my lips to get the pasty sensation out of my mouth.

"No," he answered, still playing with his food.

"Just eat it, you big baby," I said.

He stuck a spoonful in his mouth and tried to swallow it down without letting it linger, resulting in a coughing fit. I rolled my eyes, working my way through the last of my bowl.

The food summoning spell was actually a piece of the basis for the spell I'd concocted to recharge mana. Along with what I'd learned from years of effort to write the spell that enabled me to see magic and the absorption of magic. The transformation and packaging of mana: how else might that be used?

Bubbles breaking the surface of the pool stirred me from my pondering. Soon after, someone's head popped from the water. She spotted us and moved to the edge to pull herself out. I'd never seen anyone like her. Salt, certainly, with her white hair. But she was wrinkled, like the garonaut from the swamps. She was... old. *But elves don't get old!*

"I suppose I am a sight," the woman said, dripping water as Beldroth gave her a hand getting out of the pool. "It's part of the trap that holds the dragon. It drains us as it does the dragon, using our magic to lock us in. Because of that, we age."

"Well," Beldroth said, searching for words. "It's... becoming."

"Becoming a pain in my ass," she said, holding out an arm where skin dangled loosely underneath. She pushed it and it rocked back and forth. We all stared, transfixed.

"Yes," Beldroth finally said, "okay. Well, I'm Beldroth."

"And I'm Illiara."

"Jade," the woman said. "Flurry sent me to bring you back."

"Flurry?" I asked.

"Arsyli is her proper name. Much more pronounceable than her grandmother's name—Kryhryzar. Nevertheless, we've taken to calling her Flurry. She hasn't eaten any of us for saying it, so she must be okay with it."

Flurry. It seemed too soft a name for a creature of wings and teeth and raw magic. But maybe that was the trick of it—hiding danger behind something that sounded harmless.

"Used to be," Jade said, glancing back at the passage we'd come through to reach the chamber, "you'd never get close to the edge of the Shield. There was something out there—a creature made of pure electrical storm. It attacked anything that came near it. But it never strayed far—seemed stuck to the Shield. Bound to it." She looked around the crumbling room. "Nobody comes here much anymore, but Flurry says she hasn't seen the creature since the day the magic flickered."

Beldroth shuddered beside me. "It was outside the Shield, and it attacked us. We only escaped it by diving straight through the Shield. It was right behind us."

"Interesting," Jade said. She smiled. "And hopeful. If it was on the other side, then at least *something* can get out of the Abyss. Too bad we didn't send it with a message." She turned back to the pool. "Well, come on."

After directing her attention to a small boulder on the edge of the pool, she cast a spell. She took a deep breath and repeated the exercise. "Give these a shove into the water, big guy. Don't use any magic."

Beldroth looked at her questionably, but did as she'd asked. When the first one went in, it bobbed across the surface, creating strange indentations in the water. Beldroth smiled and rolled the other one in, to the same effect.

"That's your air supply," Jade explained. "I've bound the air to the rocks using water. Not so much that they'll keep you from sinking, but enough for you to have air for your journey. I'm all out of mana. One of you is going to have to attach a magelight to me so you can see where you're going."

"Where's your rock?" Beldroth asked.

"Ha! The day I can't swim that far in one breath is the day I die." She dived into the water, avoiding the floating boulders and popping her head back above the surface.

"Well?" she said.

I cast a magelight and latched it to Jade's feet.

Beldroth took off his boots and socks and stuffed them into his pack, which I didn't think would keep them any more dry.

Unless we left them. I set my pack down. He sighed and did the same. I walked to the edge of the pool, then stepped off it, dropping into the cool water. My head popped up to see Beldroth, like a child, take a running leap and curl into a ball, creating a tremendous splash.

Jade looked at me and shook her head. "Men," she said, and I nodded my agreement and understanding. When he bobbed back up, he smiled like we were on some grand adventure rather than locked in a magical underground trap. "I'm going to like you," Jade said.

I grabbed one of the bobbing rocks, marveling at its strange enchantment. The water didn't touch the stone—a thin sheen of water held a bubble of air to the stone. My grabbing it pulled it under, but the air stayed attached. There was about a hand's breadth of air all around it. My holding the rock didn't push the air away. Quite the spell!

"While the hole is deep, we're not following it down," Jade said, calm as the water we swam in. "There are tunnels and more rooms like this one, but filled with water. Just follow me and breathe from that air, and you should be fine."

I nodded my head, trying not to worry, but failing.

"Ready?" Jade asked.

"Ready," Beldroth and I both answered, holding our air support like lifelines. Which they were.

"Then follow me," she said, and swam down, the magelight clinging to her feet.

I went under, glancing back to be sure Beldroth was right behind me. Then I focused on the light. The faint glow faded as Jade descended, and a sharp twinge of anxiety clawed at my chest. Yet turning back was no real option—the only way out was forward.

I chased the light.

The enchanted air clinging to the rock was miraculous, but using it came with its own challenges. I had to hold the stone so close to my face that it blocked most of my forward vision, forcing me to rely on the faint flicker of Jade's magelight to guide me. I would occasionally bump against stone I hadn't seen—which scared me—and, once, banging my head painfully. The longer we swam, the more disorienting the water became. The vastness of the submerged tunnel was a dark void that seemed to stretch endlessly in every direction. My sense of up and down wavered, and I worried I was following my imagination instead of Jade.

Anxiety tightened in my chest, and my instincts screamed at me to hold my breath, even though the air was right there. With each breath, my lungs ached from the strain of keeping it in, but I feared something might go wrong if I let out too soon. Each time, desperation forced me to press my lips to the edge of the rock and inhale. The air was crisp, tinged with a faint metallic tang, but it filled my lungs and eased the burning.

The magelight shifted ahead, darting upward, and relief swept over me as I followed, pushing myself harder now that the surface was near. As my head broke free of the water, I gasped loudly, even though I'd been breathing the entire way. The instinct was primal, impossible to shake.

Around me, the water rippled gently in a wide alcove, the sound amplified by the cavernous space. I wiped my face and blinked, trying to make sense of the scene before me. The walls were black stone, lit faintly from somewhere behind me. I spun around and froze in awe.

Buildings. Entire structures carved directly into the stone walls of a massive cave stretched out to the left and right, their sharp edges gleaming faintly in the dim light. Pools of water dotted the cavern floor, their surfaces broken by the occasional ripple as currents moved unseen beneath them. Narrow walkways connected the pools, winding between the stone buildings like veins through a living organism.

Movement drew my eye, and my heart skipped a beat. Salts. They moved with purpose, their lithe forms weaving through the cavern like shadows, strange purple light following them about.

A loud splash behind me stopped my gawking. I turned to see Beldroth's head emerge from the water, his broad shoulders glistening as he sucked in air and blinked up at the cavern in wide-eyed amazement.

Our escort, already standing on one of the stone walkways, looked back at us with a small, knowing smile. "Welcome to the Abyss," she said, her voice echoing off the walls like a ripple in still water.

Beldroth : 6

The underground city reminded me of Cenaedth, but without the heat and magma. I wondered if the tiny rivulet that ran lengthwise through the city had once carried lava. The pool where we'd emerged sat on one side of the trickle of a river. Dim purple bioluminescence provided some sense of the boundaries of the cavern, without providing enough light for detail. The dragon, Flurry, was nowhere to be seen.

Aged elves waited with towels, and one used her magic to pull the bulk of the water from our clothes. I understood her reluctance to do more—if using magic caused one to age faster, then mundane tasks were best done in mundane ways. The cavern, though large, was not densely populated, with sporadic stone and brick homes nearly as decrepit as its few citizens. When I heard a child's giggle, my eyes whipped toward the sound. He hid behind a rock, getting shooed away by one of the older elves. The sight made me smile. Something about the idea that, even trapped in an underground prison, a child might explore and laugh brought joy to my heart.

An elf who wasn't old approached. She didn't have the same youthful look as Illiara, but she wasn't as old as Jade. All Salts looked something alike—white skin and hair, tall and lanky by nature—but the one who walked up to us reminded me enough of my lost Lyrei that my heart skipped a beat.

"Welcome," she said. "My name is Miryndel. Welcome to the Abyss."

"Deara really does keep its secrets," Illiara mumbled, trying unsuccessfully to tame her wild brown hair after the brisk magical drying caused it to poof in alarming ways. "Gah!" she complained, stooping to scoop water back onto hair that reminded me of the thistle in Themopolis.

"Ironically," Miryndel said, grinning at Illiara's predicament, "we've given up all pretense of secrets down here." A brief frown crossed her face. "The cage we're in keeps them for us well enough."

"Let me jump right to the point," she said, "and then we can circle back to your questions, okay?"

I nodded my head. Illiara was too busy taming her hair to do the same.

"We were expecting to be freed today. Arsyli sensed when you entered the Abyss yesterday and went to fight you, but claimed you weren't ready—whatever that means." The thought of a dragon leaving Illiara and me alone for our lovemaking made my face heat. "She returned to face you today, ready to fight and die, but came back again, saying you didn't have her mother's bone to slay her. That detail seemed to upset her quite a bit."

One of the older women helped Illiara, producing a fish-bone comb from a bag and wrangling her hair using bindings of long, thin leaves of some water-plant.

"We actually care a great deal for Arsyli," Miryndel continued, "and I am glad she remains alive, yet that leaves us in the predicament of still being trapped. There is a Shield around this city, activated by Arsyli centuries ago. It was, quite literally, designed to trap a dragon. It uses the dragon's magic to feed the cage that holds it. Arsyli says it was created for another, but even she knows little about it. The field it creates affects elves inside it: causes us to age, causes our mana to recharge at a trickle. It is also harder to have children."

Illiara's hand went to her belly.

I reached for my mana, though I already knew what she said to be true. I wanted to see just how slowly my mana trickled in. It was bad—at the rate my mana grew, a simple spell or two a day would be all I could manage. Illiara shared a look with me—how much would her ability to speed up mana recharging help? We would have to experiment later.

Miryndel raised an eyebrow, saying, "Flurry told us to ask you about a troll? Did Lyrei bring us a troll?"

Her gaze was on me, and I froze under it.

"Lyrei?" Illiara asked.

"My daughter," she said, blushing. "We were never sure whether it worked, but I tried to get a message to her to return with a troll."

"Lyrei?" I asked, stupidly. Lyrei?

"I'm sorry," she said, still blushing, "I just thought, since you're a Warder, it was possible you'd helped her bring a troll. It was silly. We gave up hope that she'd gotten the message decades ago. Your showing up... well, never mind. Why did Flurry tell us to ask you about a troll?"

"Lyrei was my wife."

We stared at each other, mutually frozen.

Lyrei had come to Bellon from over the mountains. She'd come from troll territory. She was secretive—only after years of being together had she confided that she'd arrived by ship at the bay on the far side. Troll territory. She'd lost her ship. Her crew. She'd never explained more. Deara keeps its secrets, but I didn't know Lyrei was from Deara.

"I think she was trying to bring you a troll," I said. But she'd failed with her crew. Then she met me. I fought trolls. We'd fought them together. She'd tried many ways to capture one. Constrain or contain one. But their protection from magic and insane strength made that impossible.

The old woman from the pool slapped Miryndel on the shoulder. "Married to a Warder. I told you she was crazy enough to try anything." She let out one cackling laugh, then asked, "Is she here too?"

I swallowed the sudden ball in my throat. "She died. A decade ago. Killed..." I looked around. "Killed by Krygr... Kgryhr... Flurry's mother, if I'm understanding correctly."

Both women froze at my news. Then Jade, hand still on Miryndel's back, gave her shoulder a comforting squeeze. "It has to mean *something*. Newcomers, with a troll, and Flurry doesn't have to die for us to be free."

Jade's eyes pinched in a half-hearted smile as she turned her attention from Miryndel to me. "We've grown fond of Flurry. Though she's ultimately the cause of our being trapped, she's a good kid. She's as much a victim of her mother's plan as Lyrei was. Tell us about the troll you've brought."

"Flurry's mother," Miryndel muttered, "killed my Lyrei?" She was still digesting the grim news.

"She was a white," Jade said, gently shaking Miryndel. "Jenat, First of the Lost, daughter of Kryhryzar, was a white. She had the power to See." With her other hand, she gestured toward me. "It's led to the salvation of her daughter—and us."

Miryndel pulled her shoulder out from Jade's grasp. "You'll be so casual about my death, I suppose." Her tone had some bite, but not a lot. She was more sad than angry.

"Everyone dies," Jade whispered. "Everyone. Look at me, Miry." Jade forcibly turned Miryndel. "Look at me. I'm sailing straight for the final harbor. Everyone dies. It's how you live that matters. She went after a troll, Miry! She and this yummy *beast* of a man swabbed each other's decks." Jade elbowed the blushing Miryndel in the ribs.

"We have a son," I offered.

"See, Miry," Jade said. "A Scion. Our sure-footed Selthira's at the helm, and wild Lyrei turned the tides."

"Selthira?" Illiara asked, diverting the Salt's attention to her. Their pinched eyes made even Illiara take a step back. "I'm sorry, I just hadn't heard that name."

"Who's leading Deara?" Miryndel asked.

"And where's this troll?" Jade added.

"Pyrravyn leads Deara, as regent to a girl named Bella," Beldroth answered, diverting the attention back to him.

The two Salts exchanged a look. "A daughter of Selthira?" Jade asked her, an eyebrow raised. Miryndel shifted her weight, glancing away.

"And we don't have a troll, per se," Beldroth continued, earning another scowl. "But we *do* have one who can activate the magic of these artifacts as though she was a troll."

"How can that be?" Miryndel asked, clearly the skeptic of the two.

"She is Bereft," Illiara said, and the eyes of both Salts widened. "She absorbs magic like a troll. And she will undoubtedly come looking for us eventually, if they let her. And she might even if they do not. But if you communicated to Lyrei to send her hunting for a troll, we should use the same technique to get a message to Elliah. My daughter. The Bereft girl… the Bereft woman, Elliah, is my daughter."

Life in the Abyss looked simple but precarious. The space enclosed was quite vast. One pond, saltwater, brought fish from outside. Once in, the fish, like everything else, had no way to escape. Fish and cave mushrooms supplied the primary staples for the elves and dragon, though, incredibly, we passed a garden with sparse vegetables and tiny trees.

"How do plants grow underground?" I asked. "Without sunlight?"

Jade reached into the dirt and came back up with a couple of worms that glowed green before fading. "They thrive near us. Flurry explained it to me once. Something about their needing an environment with 'bad air.'" She dropped the now-pink worms to the ground. "They come out of the ground when Flurry turns off her light." She waved at the magical light overhead. "That's when they glow." She scooped a couple of handfuls of dirt into a container of glass and stone, then carted it along. "The plants came from vegetables thrown to Miryndel's team through the barrier, back when we still pretended we might find a way out. A real game changer, those vegetables. They threw us some mutton once—as good as it was, I wish I could've grown a sheep from it. Ha!"

Jade was a character. I hadn't heard her personal story, but she talked like she predated Miryndel, from the references she made and her appearance. Yet she made jokes quickly.

"How many people do you have to feed here?" Beldroth asked, a roundabout way of asking how many people the magical barrier held captive.

"Eighty-seven," Miryndel answered swiftly, the words slipping out as effortlessly as a well-worn melody stuck in her head.

"Ninety-one," Jade contended, pointing at the two of us.

My hand instinctively went to my belly. "I'm not having twins." The thought of having my baby in a magical cage sent a surge of determination through me—we had to get out.

"She's counting Flurry," Miryndel said, irritated. "She always counts Flurry."

"Flurry's a good kid," Jade insisted. "Her only mistake was listening to her mother, and don't tell me you fared any better *ignoring* yours. Ha!"

I didn't know what that meant, but Miryndel turned red again. Jade had her number for sure.

Eventually we made it to a small alcove off the main chamber. Jade untied a vial from her waist and poured its contents on the dirt she'd collected. The worms inside the dirt glowed green, creating enough light to see a room of collected rocks and gems atop boulders carved flat like tabletops. "Magelight is too expensive to use casually down here. Fish oil creates smoke that is hard to get rid of. We can't make enough vegetable oil. The worms suit our needs."

Miryndel brought us to a boulder whose only immediately unique feature was that atop it, unlike the others, only two stones occupied the surface.

"That's how you got the message out?" Beldroth asked, his skepticism founded. Two geodes the size of my head lay split in half on the table before us, one with purple crystals inside and the other citrine, both looking rather unremarkable in the dim green lighting.

"That's the transmitting side of an echo stone," Jade said, pointing at the purple. "It's one of the secrets of Deara. We use them on our ships to communicate over distances. The other is a receiver."

"Like a communication crystal," I said.

"No," Jade said, shaking her head. "Communication crystals are expensive to make. They require a High Elf to own one end. They allow two-way communication, and they bond two specific people. Echo stones communicate in only one direction, only through pulses of light, but anyone can use them, and the magic to create them is much simpler. Some geodes have water in them, water that's been trapped inside for thousands or millions of years. The ones here are not so old, but old enough. We have a relatively simple spell that bonds the water before we split a geode open, but when we split it, the pair polarizes, like a magnet that has only one partner."

"And the other end is outside of the cage?" Beldroth asked.

"It is," Miryndel said.

"Who has it?" he asked.

"Selthira had it," Jade said. "Lyrei's sister. Miry's daughter."

"But we decided no one had it or it just didn't work," Miryndel said. "We haven't tried sending messages for at least a hundred years. We've never received any messages at all." She stared at the geode. "But you say Lyrei was trying to capture a troll."

"She never talked much about her past." Beldroth looked at the geode as he spoke, like it contained some secret. "But over the years, I learned that she and her crew took a ship into the bay in the back of the mountain range that lies to the east of the Two Fangs. She claimed it was simply 'to explore.' Trolls attacked and destroyed her ship. They killed her crew, but she got away. She traveled through the mountains on her own, a remarkable feat, and I found her while I was on a mission scouting the Witless Tarn. She was delirious, starving, nearly dead. Yet, even at death's door, she attacked me. She told me later, after a forced rest, that she'd thought I was a troll. She joined me on my missions to clear trolls out of the Blasted Lands. Yes, she helped me chase off the occasional dragon that came over the mountains, but she was always trying new ways to *catch* a troll. She'd claimed she wanted to study how they resisted magic, to learn how to better fight them." He shrugged—that explanation had been enough for him. I suspected it hurt him that Lyrei had not shared the truth.

"Well," Jade said after a long pause. "We've lost Selthira, but... but we can hope someone still watches on the far end."

"How did it get here?" Beldroth asked.

"I brought them in," Miryndel said. "But like I said, nothing ever came of our requests, so we decided either something had gone wrong with the owner of the receiving echo stone, or the magic cannot work through the barrier."

"So," Beldroth said, peeling his eyes off the crystal. "Do we try again?" He was asking me, not them. I knew what he was truly asking: do we risk bringing Elliah in and trapping her?

The morning's visit to Drevin still lingered in my thoughts, but there was no time to dwell on it. It was my second day on Deara, and my second trip to the wharf—already too much time lost chasing answers. The scent of salt and fish hung thick in the air, mingling with the rasp of ropes against wood and the clamor of merchants unloading wares. A cluster of fisherfolk stood near the edge of the docks, their clothes battered by the elements, their faces unreadable. Boats swayed gently in the tide, their hulls patched but sturdy, nets draped across them like discarded cobwebs.

Kaelith followed a few steps behind me, her boots barely a whisper on the worn wooden planks. She was an obvious presence despite her silence—her gaze swept over every face and movement with the intensity of someone who saw more than she let on. She'd been the perfect shadow during our walk there, but she scrutinized me as much as the fisherfolk.

I lingered at the edge of their gathering, wondering how to approach. The fisherfolk spoke in low tones, trading words with the same efficiency as they'd handle a line. My arrival turned a few heads, but they quickly resumed their work. It wasn't indifference; it was caution. They'd undoubtedly heard rumors of a new Scion, and the Wrasseguard at my back confirmed my identity. Those men and women likely wanted nothing to do with the politics looming over the island.

Finally, I cleared my throat. "Excuse me. I'm looking for information."

A few exchanged glances, wary. One man, his hair bristly as a worn broom, spoke up. "We're busy," he said. His tone wasn't unkind, but it left no room for pleasantries.

"Understood," I replied, keeping my voice steady. "This won't take long. Has anyone noticed unusual changes in fishing patterns? Or anything strange happening with the weather around other islands?"

That earned me a few raised brows. One woman holding a long knife, with the other hand in the gills of a fish as long as her arm, tilted her head. "What's your stake in it?"

Before I could respond, Kaelith's low voice cut in, smooth but edged with amusement. "The Scion's asking questions, not giving orders. That should count for something."

I glanced at her, surprised. Her tone wasn't mocking but carried a weight of sincerity that caught me off guard. She nodded for me to continue. I hesitated, though I'd already thought through my response. "Pyrravyn tasked me with understanding how the weather created by the

Tempest Crown might affect fishing and even other islands."

Her gaze lingered on me, sharp and appraising. "You're that new Scion. Lyrei's son. She was good people. Used to fish with us from time to time." Her statement took some of the tension out of the group, making me a little more one of them than one of the nobility. She slapped the fish on a metal plate by the docks and sliced into it. Just as I thought she had nothing more to say, she spoke again. "The storm wall has decimated some of the best fishing spots around Deara. Either the storm itself, or the amount of dragons waiting to eat outside it. On the other hand, some spots close to the island, inside the storm, fish better than they used to. Overall, we have to fish other islands more often than we did before the Tempest Crown."

Her openness got the others started. As the fisherfolk shared stories of storms and strange weather patterns, Kaelith took it all in, her expression unreadable. But her eyes flicked toward me when I asked questions that revealed my knowledge of fishing—all learned from my mother. I wasn't there to complete an assignment; I was trying to understand their lives, their risks, and their struggles. They weren't part of the politics of Deara and its secrets—they deserved better.

Eventually, one of the men chimed in, his voice gravelly. "Been more storms than normal out at Shattercove to my mind. It was always dangerous to fish there—if a storm trapped you, you'd be likely as not to see your ship dashed against the cliffs. But boy, the angelheads you'd catch there—"

"You're not lying," another man said, elbowing him. "Did I ever tell you about the angelhead I caught out there what almost capsized my ship?"

The first man laughed, shaking his head at the looming story. "Anyway, been more sudden storms there lately, and the fish won't bite. Is that the kind of thing you'd want to study?"

"That's exactly the information I need," I said. "Shattercove." I didn't have money, and I should have asked Pyrravyn how to fund an excursion. "What would it cost to get someone to take me to Shattercove... to study the fish?"

The man with the fish story grunted and shook his head. He looked at his more talkative friend, who also shook his head. Finally, it was the woman who answered. "You're not going to find a fishing vessel that will take you there. No fish means no money, and even if you paid one of us, it's still an unnecessary risk to our ships. We can't see the storms out that way until we get past our own, so we can't watch for a safe time to plan a trip. It's just not worth it."

I clenched my fists, but kept my tone calm. "I understand. Thank you for speaking with me."

She wiped her knife clean on her apron, her expression softening ever so slightly. "A fool's task for a Scion, searching out weather patterns and fish. Study the fish here. Our real danger is the Tempest Crown, if you ask me. Of course, no one does. You should have seen the blue dragons storm in the time the Crown failed. And that black dragon that flew overhead." She whistled between her teeth. "Biggest beast I've ever seen. *That's* what you should be looking for. Not some silly fish. Leave the fishing to us."

I stood there with my mouth hanging open.

"If you haven't seen the Crown yet, you should," she said. "Once upon a time, they let us. Now, Maelith Skywarden barks at anyone who comes close. Chases us off. But he can't chase off a Scion. Worth seeing, the Tempest Crown, even if it is a danger. Ask him about the dragon too—like I said, that's what you should look for."

I closed my mouth and nodded.

"Come out with us some time," she said, a smile on her face. "Like your mother used to."

"I would like that." And I would, but I still had my assignment that I had to at least look like I was pursuing. As I turned to leave, my gaze drifted to the traders and Peacekeepers further down the docks. Their ships were larger, sturdier, built to withstand harsher conditions.

Kaelith stepped closer as the fisherfolk resumed their work, lowering her voice so only I would be able to hear. "You could've pushed harder," she said, her tone oddly approving. "You could've used your clout, or reminded them that Pyrravyn wanted this done. Why didn't you?"

I stopped, meeting her gaze. "Because I'm not doing this for him. This is about my family." And by family, I didn't mean Pyrravyn and Bella. Neither did I mean just my father—Illiara and Elliah both meant the world to me. "My father and friends," I clarified, "who risked everything for my safety." Elliah crossed my mind, fierce and unwavering, throwing herself into danger for all of us. I hadn't seen her in two days, though I'd attempted to catch her at the library. She'd left a book for me—one eerily on point for my assignment. It detailed the usual tide flows and weather patterns around Deara, giving me the baseline I needed. But books alone wouldn't show me what was wrong. For that, I needed the people who lived the sea every day. How had Elliah known I would need that book? She was undoubtedly neck-deep in something reckless, despite my hope that she was just shelving books. "My mother's memory. Her people." With a falter, I added. "My people." Because the group of fisherfolk had, in their odd way, welcomed me more than my cousin. "They can't afford for me to make this about power games."

For a moment, her expression softened, the faintest smile tugging at the corner of her lips. "That might be why you'll succeed," she said, her voice barely above a whisper. Then, with a flick of her braid over her shoulder, she added, "Or why you'll fail. Either way, you're worth following."

Which is a good thing, I thought, *since that's your assignment.*

The fisherfolk had given me a lead, but if I wanted to pursue it, I'd need someone with the courage—and the resources—to take me into unsafe waters. Eryndra Tidebringer knew what I was about and wouldn't let the Peacekeepers get involved. The traders, the people who kidnapped me in the first place... I sighed at the irony of who I would need to approach next.

Five days. I'd waited five days with Janelle, recovering, restless, knowing the world outside the library hadn't paused just because I had. But I couldn't put off a second attempt forever. Five days was long enough for Hughelas to visit once and then disappear again. Long enough to drift farther from my mother and the rest of my crew.

"I want to help you," I told the elemental, though doubt gnawed at me. Would my anti-magic, if it worked, break the chains? Or would it break the elemental? What if I made things worse? Still, I did *want* to help.

"I'm not convinced it understands words," Janelle said. "Then again, it may simply be ignoring you."

The elemental hadn't done more than coalesce and approach us, the same as the previous time.

"You've got the towels ready?"

"And the salves," she answered.

I hesitated, breath catching in my throat. The thought of trying again sent a slow ache through my chest—not just from the memory of pain, but from everything else pressing in from beyond the chamber.

My mother and Beldroth—somewhere out there, fighting their own battles. I pictured them: stubborn, precise, powerful. I didn't need to worry about them, not really. But I did. Not the panicked, breathless worry that left you paralyzed, but the deep kind—the kind that settled in your bones and waited for news.

Marinna and Trentius—with the Peacekeepers. She'd been on the run when we met her, heading into isolation, so I doubted the separation from us concerned her. Plus, she'd taken out a gargantuan red dragon! She would be okay. And Trentius seemed happy anywhere he went. My worry for them wasn't fear—just that quiet unease that creeps in when you can't see the road ahead.

Hughelas, whom we'd sought to rescue but who ended up moving the most freely, at least according to how many times I'd missed his visits. We hadn't crossed paths since the day we'd arrived. I'd sent messages and tried to catch him in the common spaces of the city— Janelle had warned me not to enter the royal grounds or I might get scooped up and kept somewhere much less accommodating than her rooms—but either he never received them or something prevented him from responding. Janelle swore she passed my messages along, but I wasn't sure I believed her. Hughelas had disappeared into meetings and politics, and I'd buried myself in the tasks set forth by Janelle. That was the safe way, the smart way. But I missed him. Missed what it was like to move through a storm beside someone who didn't try to calm it—just kept walking with you, even when the thunder got loud.

Even Janelle, who masked the burdens of her knowledge with humor, far too willingly placed herself in danger's way. Likely she didn't know how to stop—she would do the same if I weren't there. But my being there meant she took risks for me.

I clenched my fists. Everyone I cared about was out there—doing, moving... presumably paying their dues and earning their way forward in order to reunite us. It was time I did the same.

"How is it..." I began, stalling because *still* I hesitated to get the daylight beat out of me again. "How is it we haven't run into Maelith nor his acolytes down here? Or Drevin's acolytes trying to steal the Grimoire?"

"Maelith is an ass... it takes real fortitude to train under him, which is why there aren't many volunteers. Plus, there's something brewing at the Tempest Crown. That's Maelith's mess to handle." She tapped a finger to her lips. Another secret. A carefully dropped one. "Drevin's acolytes wouldn't attempt this often, so no surprise there, and as you can imagine, they rarely try twice. Plus, I think Drevin has them pretty busy." Another finger to her lips.

I sighed. Deara was built on secrets. But, one thing had become clear—Janelle had an ear to most of them. That brought my thoughts circling back to my friends and family—the more I knew of the secrets of Deara, the better chance we had of getting away.

"And what about Hughelas?" I asked. "You told me you passed along my messages."

Janelle didn't flinch. "I did. But I didn't deliver them quickly. And I didn't follow up."

My eyes narrowed. "Why?"

"Because he's being watched. And because if he came down here—into this part of the library—he might bring those eyes with him. Some things are safer apart."

"For me or for him?"

"For both of you," she said. Then, after a pause, she added almost absently, "Storms don't tether well."

I frowned, but she just shook her head, as if brushing the thought away.

"I need him to know I'm okay," I said. "And I need to know that he is."

Janelle looked at me with a small, sad squint. "Neither of you is okay, Elliah. You're trapped on an island wrapped so tightly in its own secrets that it's on the verge of self-destruction. Or destruction of the world." She huffed out a breath. "I'm doing my best to keep you alive and to unravel the knots."

I stiffened. She was manipulating me! Keeping me separated from Hughelas on purpose. Damned if I would help her unravel *this* one.

Janelle noticed. "You don't have to help me," she said. "You don't have to *believe* me. I'm not asking for your trust." She looked up at the ceiling and mumbled. "I wish you knew who wrote *Talonforged*."

What?

I wanted to snap back. Tell her she didn't get to make that choice for me. But something in her tone gave me pause. She wasn't just scheming—she was afraid. Maybe she wasn't trying to control me so much as protect a secret bigger than either of us.

Plus, striking back out of spite wouldn't free me—it would only scatter the pieces further.

Regardless, she didn't pause, snapping her eyes back to mine. "You lack *options*, Elliah. You can't deny that I'm creating them for you. For now, let that be enough."

And… she was right. I'd seen enough to believe that storming onto the royal grounds would land me in a less hospitable cage. Drevin saw me as an experiment, and Janelle had saved me from his hands. At least temporarily. She hadn't steered me off a cliff. Yet.

"Well, here goes nothing," I muttered, reconciling myself to my path. For now.

"I'm hoping *nothing* is what you ate and drank." She waved a towel meaningfully.

If nothing else, Janelle was at least entertaining.

I stepped forward, not even trying to go around the elemental. I had my moment of calm, and even hoped that it might allow me to go past it.

Like before, the jolt slammed through me—expected, but impossible to brace for. Fire raced through my veins, my limbs alternately locking up or twitching, my mind frying. Once more, a picture formed—swirling dark clouds shackled by light to a book.

Then I did what I'd come for: I pushed back, altering the image in my head, showing the shackles breaking.

The image of shackles reformed, and once more the elemental showed me someone attempting to untie the knots of the shackles, and the bonds constricting, pulling tighter.

I changed it again—me, reaching for the Grimoire. The chains breaking.

The elemental snapped the image back. My fingers brushing the book. The bonds flaring. Tightening.

I tried again, but with a twist. I shifted my image, presenting myself as a troll. Whether the elemental would grasp the intended message, I doubted, but I pursued it anyway. A troll grabbing the book, and the bonds breaking… the storm set free.

Then, to be honest about the possibility, I showed the same thing again, but with the storm fading with the bonds. I didn't know—what I intended might destroy the elemental.

The elemental took control of the image again—not yanking it away, but shifting it gradually. It didn't repeat what it had shown me before. A shape formed within the haze—the impression of motion, of reaching. Not toward me, but outward, toward something else.

Another storm. A presence just beyond the edges of the vision. And suddenly I understood—whatever had bound the elemental had also kept it apart from something. Not some *thing*—someone. Whatever else the elemental was, it was not alone. Or at least, it hadn't always been.

Once more, a blast of electricity flung me against the door. As I lay there, panting and disoriented, I waited to be draped with a comforting towel.

It never came.

Frowning, I cracked open an eye.

Janelle waved from the far side of the elemental.

I pushed myself upright, my back against the doors to the next room, knees drawn in. The hammer got in the way, so my head couldn't rest against the door as I wanted, but I was too wrecked to do anything about it—I let my head flop forward, boneless with exhaustion.

"It looks like you convinced it," Janelle said, wincing at my pain. Holy Mother of Trees, electrocution was *brutal*.

"Just… give me… a minute." I held up my fingers and watched smoke waft from the tips. Had the lightning been cooking me? Where was my mother's Healing when I needed it? Where was my mother?

Groaning, I considered how to get to my feet. It had been easier with Janelle's help. I started by removing my hammer from its sling and setting it aside. Besides, for any chance of my anti-magic to break the bonds holding the elemental, I probably needed to leave the hammer behind. I used the hammer's handle as a crutch to get my feet under me, then leaned against the door.

"You're doing *amazing*, sweetie," Janelle quipped. "Holding up that door like a true champion."

Yeah, yeah… absolutely smashing.

With my sleeve, I wiped the drool from my chin and stretched my arms and legs, one at a time. It hurt worse than training with Beldroth.

More like a beating from Beldroth.

Mother of Trees—what if Beldroth and my mother were worse off than me?

And Hughelas—was he okay? I hadn't seen him in days, not since that first night, and not for lack of trying. Janelle's evasions still prickled. There may have been wisdom in keeping us apart, but that didn't stop me from wondering whether Hughelas was somewhere above, watching the clouds, thinking of me too. Wondering if I avoided him?

Groaning again, I tried standing without a crutch or the support of the door. Still shaky, I leaned into the door once more, but I put a hand on the handle and pulled.

"Can you send a magelight in?" I asked. It would have been smart to arrive better prepared. At least a candle. Though flames and grimoires didn't play well together.

Janelle sent her light ahead and brightened a room barely larger than the antechamber. It contained a simple table, a couple of chairs, and a black-covered book. She stood on her tiptoes to see over me, and I scooted aside, leaning against the door to let her look.

"I expected something bigger," she said.

It was a normal-sized book. What was she expecting, something as big as my chest? I was too achy to shrug.

I shuffled into the room, getting a hand on the table for support as quickly as possible, then shuffled around it to get to the chair on the other side. If my anti-magic was going to work, it could do it from a chair.

After a couple of deep breaths, I said, "Okay, I'm going to try it."

It was hard to see Janelle from that angle, but I imagined she was smiling encouragement.

I exhaled, shutting out the bone-deep ache and the lingering hum of electricity in my nerves. In my mind's eye, the glowing bonds pulsed, anchoring the elemental to the book. My fingers brushed the cover—dry, solid, real. Then, with a deep breath, I pressed down.

Nothing happened.

I wasn't sure what I had expected, but after getting electrocuted, I'd assumed something bad. The image of the bonds breaking, releasing the elemental, played over and over in my mind. With my head resting against the book, the thought became a mantra: Break the bonds. Break the bonds. Break the bonds...

"Elliah?" Janelle's hand settled cool against my neck. "Are you—are you drooling on the Grimoire of the Thunderborn?"

"No," I said, not opening my eyes.

Janelle's fingers brushed my shoulders. "The elemental is gone."

"Yay," I mumbled, swallowing hard. Then—*slurp*. Ugh. Great. I had definitely drooled on the Grimoire of the Thunderborn.

"You did it," she said, rubbing my shoulders. Relief crept in, quiet but steady.

"Yay," I mumbled again, followed by a groan. I pushed my head up, opening my eyes. The elemental *was* gone. "Did I kill it or free it?"

"I don't know," she said. "The lightning stopped, and the clouds expanded until they faded. I really don't know."

"Damn," I said. I really hoped I hadn't killed it.

"When you're ready, let's get you back to my couch," Janelle said.

"Yeah, that sounds good," I said, looking more closely at the book. Black cover, it looked like leather, but leather would have degraded. Perhaps unsurprisingly, the cover had an imprint of a cloud, obviously dark.

Janelle helped me up, then slipped the Grimoire into her bag of towels. She took my hammer as we exited the room. "Heavy," she said.

"I'll take it." I was at least used to it.

"Uh-huh," Janelle murmured, adjusting her grip. She cradled the hammer's head like a particularly inconvenient baby, the handle sticking awkwardly up. "Okay. I've got it. Let's leave before I drop something—or someone. If we can get out of here on our own, I'll call for help." She closed the door to the small room. "It would be better if no one knows you've got the Grimoire just yet." Clutching the hammer and bag with one hand, she put an arm around my waist to help me across the relatively short antechamber.

It was a long trip. One I'd traveled much more quickly when an elemental flung me across it. Somehow, thinking of that made my aches even worse.

When we got out, and Janelle had locked the magical door behind us, she called for help. "Oh, Calidor—I'm glad it's you on duty. Did Mirielle's date go well? That Rivian is one handsome Peacekeeper." While Calidor helped gather us—and what remained of my dignity—back to Janelle's rooms, the two of them carried on about stolen glances, bad wine, and how Rivian apparently had two left feet on the dance floor.

Marinna 6

It took many days to repair the Dreadwake, the ship Eryndra was dead-set on using despite other frigates being berthed in Deara's harbor. Six days of work, of waiting, of being tested. Every morning, I practiced my spell under Eryndra's watchful eye—first in quiet repetition, then with the crew moving around me, and finally while the ship rocked beneath my feet. Controlled, but with increased distractions. Preparing me.

Thinking about how the collision with the dragon had pitched me overboard, I practiced adding a spell to bind myself to the deck I held together. It surprised me to find I did it better with boots off. Beldroth always wore boots. Did he know something I didn't?

The routine should have numbed me, but the more I trained, the closer the Peacekeepers watched me—evaluating. They'd folded Trentius and me into their daily life, yet I wasn't sure if we were guests or prisoners. Our belongings were brought from the ship to the Peacekeeper barracks, stashed beside bunks in narrow, single-person rooms. My pack sat in the corner, my boots beside it. Not much—but enough to make the room feel less like a cell.

We slept in their barracks. We ate with them. After a few days, we drank with them. The tension never vanished, but it softened, shifting from suspicion to something closer to wary camaraderie.

Still, some things gnawed at me. The Dearans kept Trentius and me apart from the others. I wanted to ask Beldroth why he always wore boots. I wanted Hughelas to check on us again—I thought I spotted him on the docks more than once, but he never came aboard. Had the Dearans stopped him? Or was he choosing to stay away?

Then, finally, Eryndra set her plan in motion.

"Well," Trentius remarked, "*this* looks like an easy way to die."

We'd made way from Deara for a day, bearing east, deeper into the Trolls' Teeth islands. No dragons had attacked, and despite their having assimilated us into the crew, they hadn't shared our goal, nor why the dragons didn't pounce on the ship as soon as we left the magical curtain wall.

"Is the ocean boiling?" I asked, confused. The water around the island looked like it bubbled.

"Those are dragons," Trentius said. "Mostly little ones, chasing memories, but some bigger ones."

I looked for Smoky, but didn't spot him on board nor flying over the approaching island, though the latter would have been hard to see.

"Chasing memories?" I asked.

"I don't know," Trentius said with a shrug. "Not everything Smoky says in my head makes sense. He says it's something younger dragons do. I think it's something like looking for wisdom or teachers. Life lessons?"

"We're going *there*?" I asked more loudly. It hardly seemed worth their concealing any longer, if that was our target.

"Going in isn't dangerous," Eryndra said.

"And getting out again?" I asked, but my gut told me the answer.

"You've got this," she said, solid as a block of ice, but I swore her eyes sparkled with laughter.

Lovely. "What are we taking from them? What do they care about so much? Are we hurting them?"

She stared stoically at the island, which took up more and more of the horizon. A natural harbor seethed with the writhing of elf-sized dragons. "Rocks," she finally said. "Geodes, specifically. We need them, and the blue dragons collect them. We can sometimes get away with one. They don't always care if you take just one. But sometimes they do, and a ship is a high price to pay for one geode. Our plan today is to gather enough that we don't have to do this again. No, it doesn't hurt them. We don't know why they collect them from around these islands. Mating rituals?"

"Definitely not mating rituals," Trentius scoffed.

"And why do *we* need them?" I purposefully included myself as part of the team—part of *we*—hoping it would lower her defenses on that secret.

"We use the geodes to communicate over distances, to coordinate our ships," she said. Her voice carried a steady conviction. "It's the key to securing our hold on the seas. A fleet united in purpose, able to call its sister-ships for aid. Imagine being able to call for help from a pirate attack, or to bring hope to a devastated village after a storm." She paused, her eyes, for once, burning with passion. "These stones are all that stand between us and the peace this world has never known."

Communicate over distances... that would obviously be an advantage in naval warfare. And I did find the mission of the Peacekeepers appealing. Keeping the seas safe and helping those in need. But I also wasn't so naive as to think the power that gave the Dearans wouldn't be abused.

"And if I refuse to help?" I asked.

The fire faded from Eryndra's eyes, but her resolve didn't falter. "If you refuse, we'll keep going as we always have. Slowly, carefully, one geode at a time. And the cost will be more lives—our people's and others'—lost to chaos on the seas. Piracy. The vagaries of nature. I'll accept that choice, if it's the one you make."

We'd danced around this conversation for days. I'd dodged the subject every time it crept too close, and Eryndra, for all her intensity, hadn't pressed—until now.

She stepped closer, her tone lowering. "But Marinna, you *know* this isn't just about us. There's more at stake than you and me. I've watched you—you've seen what unchecked power can do. Surely you understand why we need to protect people before someone else seizes control. Every day we wait, more lives are in jeopardy."

"So what's it going to be?" she asked, her voice warmer and more quiet than I had yet heard it. Eryndra's cold resolve covered a tenderness I doubted many had the opportunity to witness. "Will you help us secure the geodes and take a step toward the future I know we both want to see? Or will we keep limping along, letting others pay the price for our hesitation?"

The ship had undergone some complicated maneuvers as we'd talked, tacking the sails to slide backwards into the natural harbor, banking to follow the inlet that protected the island from the beating of the sea. Unlike Deara, the island before us had a long section of sandy beaches. Blue dragons—small things, like Smoky—splashed and undulated, bumping harmlessly against our hull.

I nodded. I didn't have the power to stop Eryndra from achieving her goals. My denial would just slow her down, creating a higher price. For the first time in my brief time with her, the smile in Eryndra's eyes reached her lips.

But before she'd even turned away, it was gone. "I'm diving," she declared, already stripping off her sword. She handed the sword and jacket to Captain Kael, who looked like he wanted to protest, but kept his mouth shut. She took a cloth bag and joined others who stood poised along a line of ropes on the port side of the ship. The sailors readied the sails for a quick exit.

I ran over to Eryndra. "When do I need to be ready?"

"We will clear the harbor before anything big reaches us. That's when you'll need to hold her together."

And the more pressing question: "Is the Dreadwake faster than a blue dragon?"

"Ask Captain Kael," she said. "I need to go." She joined the other divers, climbing on the rail, and with a shout from one of them, they all jumped.

"Captain?" I asked.

"At their top speed, no," he said. That wasn't the answer I wanted to hear. "But they can't maintain that speed. Even dragons get tired."

"You've seen dragons tire? Or is that more of a *theory*? How long until they get tired?"

"Don't know. I've never withstood a hit from one before." He smiled with genuine excitement. "Let's find out!"

He marched up and down the deck, encouraging his crew, spreading his excitement.

Smoky had returned, circling once overhead before descending onto the rear deck with a gust of hot wind. Her claws clicked against the boards as she approached slowly, her wings folding in with careful grace as sailors worked around her.

Trentius looked up at her and gave a weak smile. "You don't have to stay close just for me," he murmured, but Smoky only lowered her head and bumped it gently against his leg.

"She misses something," he said quietly, laying a hand against her warm scales. "Or she wants a geode too."

I watched the way she leaned into him—protective, almost mournful. It wasn't only Trentius who was changing. They looked calm, oddly inward-facing, while the rest of the ship buzzed with urgency.

I turned to see Kael grinning at the chaos like it was a festival.

Salts are out of their minds!

Too many days.

In that time, I'd walked the same streets so often I could've mapped them blindfolded—looping past the library where Elliah always seemed to have just left, checking the wharf where Marinna was always busy, scanning every shop for someone who might give me a real answer. Deara had grown smaller, somehow, even as it refused to open up.

Every path I took curved back on itself. Every door closed. Every face politely unreadable.

I paced. Waited. Fished with the harbor folk. Questioned Kaelith too often. Tried to push past her to Pyrravyn on the second night. Nothing worked. Even sleep had failed me—except for one night, when I'd returned so drained that even my frustrations hadn't kept me awake.

Deara was a labyrinth of power struggles, secrets, and factions. And I was the outsider, walking a maze where every path led to another dead end.

One thing I had accomplished—Yselda Coldwind, the head of the Dearan trade community, had agreed to check out Shattercove. The day before, I'd joined the crew of the Salty Squirt, to check out the island that the fisherfolk had hinted might suffer from stranger weather patterns than usual.

It was something.

But it wasn't enough.

I'd asked about my father and Illiara more than once over the previous few days, but all I had gotten were polite evasions or vague reassurances. Kaelith had said they were still on the mission with Feldryn. That it wasn't unusual. Except, she didn't believe it either. Her eyes held something back. Kaelith had surprised me with the truth upon our return from Shattercove—a quiet gesture of trust I hadn't expected. If she hadn't told me, would Pyrravyn have bothered at all?

I climbed the stairs to Pyrravyn's study, my boots striking the stone harder than necessary. Seven days, and still no news of my father and Illiara. The Wrasseguard outside the door didn't stop me; they, at least, no longer hindered me. Kaelith's doing?

Inside, voices murmured—not about my father, not about the search, but about prophecy.

I stopped short, frustration curling hot in my chest. Seven days, and he wasted time on riddles?

The study smelled of ink, old parchment, and the faint tang of sea salt carried in by the open window. Shelves lined the walls, brimming with books bound in leather, their spines gilded with titles I longed to peruse. At the center of the room, Bella sat at a long table, her small hands clasped as she leaned forward, her gaze transfixed by the strands of hair in Gormar's palm.

The Alluvium Red Prophet murmured softly, his voice steady and deliberate, as fire burst to life in his hands, flames consuming the hair and swirling between his fingers. A fiery vision twisted and reformed—a lone figure standing atop a desolate mountain, framed by swirling storm clouds. The figure's features were elusive in the flames, yet I had no doubt about the woman's identity—Bella, grown to an adult.

Around her, the horizon stretched vast and empty, the shadows deepening with every flicker of Gormar's flame.

The wiry, gray-haired tutor hovered nearby, wringing his hands. He glanced at Gormar nervously, clearly uncertain whether he should intervene.

"This is you, child," Gormar said, his tone low and reverent. "The mountain represents the weight you will bear. The storm? Your power to command. But even at the peak…" His voice faltered for a moment. "You will stand alone."

Bella's expression tightened, her small face trying to mask the flicker of fear that passed through her eyes.

I paused in the doorway, my presence unnoticed for the moment. My heart ached at the sight of her—so young, yet already burdened with expectations. I'd lived with the weight of prophecy on Elliah for some time, and my chest tightened at the idea of imposing the future on another. Yet, I let the situation play out, unwilling to interrupt whatever lesson Pyrravyn thought the young leader needed.

The vision dissolved as Gormar lowered his hand, the fire vanishing with a final, crackling sigh. He turned to Bella, his lined face softening. "Prophecies are meant to guide us, to ease the weight of heavy decisions."

"And what if I don't wish that to be the future?" Bella whispered.

Gormar smiled faintly. "Then your very resistance is what will make it happen."

"That's enough," I said, stepping into the room at last.

Gormar turned sharply, his brow furrowing. The tutor jumped, nearly dropping the stack of books he was holding. Bella looked at me, her eyes wide and uncertain, but the hint of a smile tugged at the corners of her lips.

"Hughelas," Gormar greeted, inclining his head. "I didn't hear you come in."

"I imagine not," I replied coolly, crossing the room. "I'm sure prophecies can be… consuming."

Bella's gaze darted between us, her small hands folding over each other. Her smile faltered at my expression.

"Can we speak privately?" I asked Pyrravyn, my tone measured but lacking the firmness I'd intended to muster. The request came easily enough—it wasn't a command, not quite—but I knew it revealed my unfamiliarity with their norms.

The tutor paused, looking uncertain, and turned to Pyrravyn for direction.

Pyrravyn arched a brow but gave a slight nod. "That will be all for now. Bella and I can continue her lessons later."

The tutor and Gormar bowed slightly to Pyrravyn. The tutor gathered his notes while Gormar shot me a look of quiet disdain before they exited together. Bella's gaze shifted with a mix of nervousness and eagerness between me and Pyrravyn, her quill forgotten on the table.

I'd expected the room to clear entirely, as would have been customary in my homeland, but Bella's presence didn't bother me. It was her home, after all. Yet, I'd assumed the conversation would be between just Pyrravyn and me.

I stepped forward, my voice tight. "What's happened to my father and Illiara?"

Pyrravyn leaned back in his chair, his fingers laced together. "Straight to the point, as always," he said with a sigh. "From my perspective, Bella can stay, but—" He raised an eyebrow, as if waiting for me to object.

I met his gaze, my tone even. "I don't mind."

Pyrravyn studied me for a moment, then nodded, satisfied. "Very well." He gestured for me to sit, but I remained standing.

"I wish to congratulate you on your efforts at locating the dragon. I hear Yselda supported your quest." Of course he knew already. I'd barely returned. He hadn't heard it from Kaelith—she'd been with me the whole time, right until I'd entered the royal quarters minutes before. But it didn't shock me that Pyrravyn had multiple sets of eyes and ears. "Shattercove?"

It had been quite the trek. We never saw the dragon, but Shattercove's jagged cliffs rose like broken teeth from the churning sea, waves crashing with violent futility—except in one cove calm enough for approach. The signs were unmistakable: deep gouges in the rock, lightning scorches on the cliffs, storm clouds nesting over the island like the magic of the storm wall. That was enough for Captain Striker and her crew. And I didn't need their confirmation. My gut had twisted the moment we entered the cove. Something lived there—something ancient and powerful.

"I hear they're missing," I said evenly, steering back to the topic for which I'd interrupted Bella's lesson, but careful not to betray the source of my information. I was glad Kaelith hadn't followed me into the royal quarters, because I probably would have glanced at her and exposed my source.

"They were safe," he replied evenly, though his tone carried a hint of irritation. "Until they weren't."

"What does that even mean?" I demanded, slamming my hands onto the table. Bella flinched; Pyrravyn didn't.

He sighed again, rubbing the bridge of his nose. "Beldroth, Illiara, and Feldryn all disappeared. There was some issue at the Tempest Crown, and two of my Wrasseguard stayed behind. Feldryn took your father and Illiara to the Abyss alone. I didn't expect them to return quickly, but... we never heard back at all."

Too neat. Too packaged. I narrowed my eyes.

He held up a hand, forestalling my next outburst. "You understand what the Abyss is?"

I frowned but said nothing, and he continued.

"The Abyss is a pocket inside a magical Shield, which is why we thought your father, a Warder who knows Shields better than any, might dismantle it." His expression darkened. "But the Shield covering the Abyss is unique—it allows passage in one direction but not the other. Once something or someone goes in, it doesn't return. If your father and Illiara went in..." He trailed off, the implication heavy.

"Then they're not just 'caught'!" I snapped. "They're *gone* because of you!"

Pyrravyn stood abruptly, the chair scraping against the floor. "And do you think that was my intention?" His tone wasn't anger, wasn't regret— it was measured. It wasn't an apology or excuse—it was a deflection. "Do you think I want to lose resources—"

"They're not *resources*!" I roared.

Bella gasped, her eyes wide and brimming with tears. I hadn't even realized how loud I'd gotten. Pyrravyn glanced at her, his expression softening slightly before returning to me, hard as steel. For half a second, I regretted my outburst—but not enough to take the words back.

"I've sent scouts," he said, his voice quieter but no less firm. "Every available one of them." Kaelith had told me the same. "They're searching as we speak."

I wanted to go search too, but I didn't know the island. I desperately needed to do *something*. "You knew the risks, and you sent them anyway."

"I sent them with protection," he countered. "I cannot hold every hand. Truly, I'd believed your father would prove superior to the magic of the Abyss."

Bella spoke then, her voice small but piercing. "It's possible they are still alive, hiding in the old mining tunnels."

Her words were so simple, so innocent, that they stung more than Pyrravyn's sharpest rebuke. Pyrravyn's gaze flicked to her, his expression unreadable, before he nodded.

"That's why we're doing everything we can, little one." His eyes looked pained as he encouraged her. He stood, his expression sharp but controlled. "We found Feldryn's body in the mines near the Abyss. It was burned as though by lightning—believe me, we see that often enough to know—even though he was deep underground." Pyrravyn pursed his lips in irritation. "There are creatures, embodiments of storms. Elementals. One attacked whenever our scouts approached the Abyss. That slowed our search." He shifted slightly. "It no longer attacks. In fact, scouts now report seeing two of them hovering near the Shield. Always together— watching and waiting. Regardless, there was no sign of your father or Illiara. That means there's still hope."

I hesitated, his words cutting through my anger, though I wouldn't let it show.

Pyrravyn pressed on, his voice softer now. "Plus, your father is a Warder. Even if they crossed into the Abyss, he may discover how to counter its magic. Frankly, as long as they're not found, there's a chance."

Bella spoke again, this time with a quiet conviction. "He wouldn't stop fighting for you. So... don't stop fighting for him."

She knew what it was to be left behind. Yet, she still believed. I wanted to believe too. Slate and shards, but I wanted to. Her innocent sincerity frustrated me—there was nothing tangible to fight. No one to take my anger out on except Pyrravyn, her uncle, the man she clearly trusted and adored. I'd spent days pushing for answers, and I had nothing. A stretch of silence, of dead ends. Seven days of standing in Pyrravyn's shadow, chasing after the scraps he chose to drop.

My attempts to meet with Elliah had also been thwarted. I'd checked the library at least a dozen times, but I'd always missed her. I'd begun to wonder whether she was avoiding me. Even so, my worry gnawed at me. Not only because she wouldn't let anyone see when she was hurting— but also because she was dangerous when cornered. And how that might escalate.

I turned toward the door, my chest tight. As I reached for the handle, Pyrravyn's voice stopped me one last time.

"Hughelas."

I paused, forcing myself not to clench my fists.

"I've called a council meeting in two hours to discuss the next steps regarding the dragon. You must attend." After a pause, he added, "If they're alive, we'll find them," his voice low but steady.

I almost laughed. If they were alive, *I'd* find them. Not him. Not his scouts. But, I didn't answer. The door clicked shut behind me, leaving his promise and Bella's faith behind.

Marinna 7

"Catch the wind! Trim the sails!" the captain shouted, pulling his head back from looking over the rail, even before all the divers had climbed aboard. Presumably, they were at least scaling the side.

The sails unfurled with a sharp snap, filling with wind as the ship surged ahead, a wolf unleashed. I kept watching the rails, even as a magical wind sped us along. Eryndra vaulted from over the side, dripping with equal parts confidence and seawater. She dropped her bag of geodes in a wooden crate alongside the others and donned her jacket and sword.

We shot out of the harbor and heeled starboard, the deck tilting beneath us, and I wondered whether the bumpy ride was waves or middling-sized dragons trying to reach the geodes from beneath. Smoky climbed on a rail, wrapping her tail around a post for added security on her perch, as she alternated between watching the water below and looking at the crate full of sacks of geodes.

"Port side," shouted a lookout. "She'll be on us in short order."

"Time to test your magic," Eryndra said, looking genuinely cold as the wind whipped her short, wet hair about.

I was as ready as I could be. I cast my spell and looked into the very familiar form of the Dreadwake, and it responded like an old friend picking up a conversation. The boards of the hull worked together out of practice and familiarity into a seemingly solid piece. For the first time, I saw my imprint on that form, and realized that I'd helped shape that through daily iterations. As a secondary thought, also from practice, I bound my feet to the deck.

As I awaited the impact of a dragon, I considered all the things that might go wrong. My magic might not be strong enough to withstand the blow. Dragons had magic, but the bigger ones also had a level of immunity. What if one of the dragons nullified my spell? At the more mundane end of my concerns, what if a mast snapped and hit me, with my feet bound to the deck? And finally, would I ever get the chance to sculpt again?

I sensed the dragon before it hit. My eyes were closed, focused on the unified hull. Yet I *perceived* it, determined to slice the ship in half. In response, I borrowed strength from the starboard to strengthen the port. The Dreadwake hummed with the cadence of the dragon's sawtooth scales rattling off the hull, vibrating the ship like a tuning fork. I felt it as much as I heard it, but in the span of a breath, it was gone.

"Two more incoming!" the scout yelled.

Eryndra's voice carried no urgency, only an easy amusement. "Full sail, Captain. Hold the wind abeam," she requested. "If it's not too much trouble."

"Aye!" the Captain called back, the grin evident in his voice. He was in his element. The ship's timbers shuddered as the crew relayed their orders, the ship groaning under the shift in wind and strain.

But the dragons came at us from the prow—with my eyes closed, I *sensed* them, though likely they wouldn't be visible to Eryndra from the deck. More speed would only have brought us to them faster. I encouraged the ship to tighten the bones of its bow.

Then, the dragons struck.

A bone-deep crack shuddered through the hull as their bodies slammed into us, the force splitting the air with a sound like a breaking mast. The ship's stem lifted sharply, timbers groaning, ropes snapping taut with a sharp twang as the mast bent under the strain.

For a split second, everything hung in eerie silence—then we crashed back down.

The impact boomed through the deck, jarring my knees so badly I might have fared better falling, untethered from the ship. The hollow thud of something shifting below deck echoed through the hull, followed by the sharp whine of protesting wood. Salt water sprayed over me, the waves slapping the deck, but the magical wind urged us forward.

I groaned with pain, even as the ship sped away and the dragons turned to give chase.

"Rest yourself a moment," Eryndra breathed in my ear. "Recover mana while they turn about."

She was right, but I didn't completely let go. I kept a loose hold, worried that eyes above the ocean wouldn't be enough. I needed the special sight the spell provided. But with a light touch on the spell, I burned less mana. Why hadn't they shared their plan with me before we left Deara? The thought nagged at me, along with a growing fear that I would wish we'd brought Illiara along—her ability to boost mana recovery might make the difference between sailing triumphantly back into Deara or being digested by dragons. I opened my eyes for the first time since I'd cast.

"Spread them out!" Trentius shouted, surprising me. "They're louder together." He stared at the crate of geodes, then looked meaningfully at Smoky, who had moved from the rail to stand by the crate, lashing her tail to nearby tack.

"What?" Eryndra shouted back, but not for lack of hearing. Trentius had surprised me over our days together—his sprinkled moments of insight into the ocean of absurdity were worth catching. I gathered Eryndra had decided the same, as she gave him her attention.

"Get them out of the crate! But not below deck." He looked around madly. "Not below deck. That will be worse."

Eryndra looked up. She grabbed a sack of geodes from the crate and scrambled up the mainmast. I'd seen her swim, but I hadn't expected her to climb like a squirrel. Ironically, I had yet to see her swing the intimidating sword she carried on her back. But I supposed the scarier the weapon, the less one had to use it. She tied the sack off and hurried down for another.

The crew was busy. I was busy. The first dragon who had hit us had almost caught up, and the other two bigger dragons, though farther behind, shot through the water even faster. That left only Eryndra and Trentius, who each pulled more sacks from the crate and ran to the other masts.

"It's coming from underneath us!" I shouted, realizing I was the only one able to sense it. Other than me, all anyone could do was brace themselves, but that was doubly important for Trentius and Eryndra, who scurried about the ropes like spiders. I had no authority, but I shouted the command anyway. "Hard a-port!"

I braced the ship for impact, as though the captain would ignore me. Which was good—no one heeded the warning. When the dragon hit, we bucked out of the water, tilting ominously to starboard, but we hit the water before we were too far gone. Then the ship over-corrected with a lurch that I imagined might've tossed some of the crew overboard.

"The next one is going to be worse," I shouted. The other two dragons were bigger. It wouldn't matter whether the hull held—the entire ship would flip.

I loosened my hold on the spell while the dragons closed in because I needed to conserve mana… I'd depleted a lot. After a quick check to be sure Eryndra and Trentius still clung to the ship—Smoky defied the winds and flew a sack up to Trentius!—I closed my eyes again. It was easier to see the dragons that way.

"Give me as much warning as you can about the ones coming from below," Captain Kain shouted in my ear, startling me because I was focused on the ocean beneath us. My eyes flipped open involuntarily, and I lost track of the dragons.

"What do you mean?" I yelled back, shutting my eyes hard even as I answered. "They're already getting ahead and under us. But if you turn now, they will have enough warning to follow."

"Light the charges!" he shouted. "Fire!"

As I sunk back into my spell, I saw or sensed—I wasn't sure which—coiled springs release at the bow. Captain Kain had something more planned than just strengthening the hull and running fast.

But I quickly found the dragons. One had pulled ahead of the other.

"Hard to port!" I shouted.

"Hard to port!" Captain Kael echoed. "Bring the bow around!"

166

I strengthened the starboard side and the dragon hit, its momentum pushing us even more port-side. A spray of water startled my eyes open in time to see the dragon's head above water, housing a circle of teeth like a monstrous lamprey. The front of the dragon rose above the deck then arced back to the water, and though we sped past quickly, the dragon's long, snake-like body whizzed by, with its tail flinging a spout of water high in the air.

I had no time to admire it, as the second dragon was not far behind. I slammed my eyes shut and refocused. A deep thrum vibrated through the hull—once, then again, closer to starboard. Water fountained up in two great plumes. Between the first dragon and the exploding devices launched from the ship, I'd lost the second dragon!

I strengthened the hull all around, not knowing where to focus, but it cost me mana. Smoky had abandoned her efforts to ferry geodes and perched mid-ship on a spar, staring at something beyond the ship. I followed her gaze out, hoping for a clue. The dragon shot from the water right where Smoky had been watching—between the charges and the ship. The blasts must have thrown the giant blue dragon off course! Because it missed us entirely, it went higher than the other, climbing well above the deck of the ship. That's when I realized it had never intended to hit the ship from beneath. It intended to crush us.

Marinna 8

I quickly shifted the focus of my spell amidst shouted orders from the captain that I didn't have time for. I was busy convincing the deck and the masts that they were all part of the same tree as the hull. In a way, it was easy. My feet were already bound to the deck. I'd worked through the wood touched by my bare feet in order to get to the hull. The bond with the deck was ready and almost eager to join in. In another way, it was excruciatingly difficult. I hadn't practiced with the deck or masts. The masts had all the pride of trunks, but so did the deck.

It was possible the Salt-crafted explosive devices *had* thrown off the dragon, but its bulk was on a trajectory to hit between the mainmast and the mizzen. In the end, it was the skill of the captain and crew more than any magic of mine that averted total disaster. The helmsman wrenched the wheel, and the rudder groaned as the ship heeled sharply starboard. He steered *toward* the dragon, zipping past the monstrous length of blue scales and serrated fins so that the bulk of the dragon grazed the stern of the ship, tearing wood that had no magical strength to pieces, and sending braces flying into the ocean.

Several seconds passed while I scanned the water beneath the ship with my eyes closed. The dragons had disappeared. I looked behind… in front. No dragons approached. I peeked through my tightly shut lids to look around. Sacks of geodes dangled from the ends of the yards like ugly ornaments, separated as much as possible from each other and away from the water. The captain traded looks between me and a lookout on the upper yard of the foremast. Salts scrambled to secure what remained after the dragon's impact.

"All clear!" shouted the lookout.

I closed my eyes and searched the ocean once more.

"The geodes are quieter," Trentius said, his voice a mix of hope and sadness.

I kept looking, praying I wouldn't find anything. I didn't think I had the mana to withstand another hit. To use my remaining magic to search, when there might be another dragon coming, would have been the wrong move.

But the dragons had lost interest, their distance from the Dreadwake and whatever call they heard from the geodes becoming too great. "All clear," I sighed.

A cheer went through the ship, and I let go of my hold on her, tumbling to my knees. *Oh, how I ache!*

"Do you have a Healer?" Trentius shouted.

I tried to tell him I didn't need one. I was merely tired. But when I tried to speak, I coughed, and goopy blood spilled forth from my mouth. I looked for a wound, but my eyes were heavy. *Later. I will look later.* I lay down on the deck, closing my eyes, needing just a moment of rest.

"Stay with me, Marinna!" Trentius said, crouched beside me, his hand gripping mine tightly. A shadow passed over us, and I realized Eryndra had joined him, speaking quickly to a Salt nearby—something about a Healer and warm water. Her voice was cool, level. Like nothing could shake her. "Thank you, Smoky." Trentius's gratitude drifted down as warmth enveloped me like a toasty blanket as hard scales pressed gently against my side, inviting me to sleep.

Somewhere in the haze before slumber, I listened to their voices— Trentius frantic, Eryndra steady—and realized how differently I reacted to each of them. Unlike Eryndra, Trentius had no use for me, no agenda, yet his concern for my safety came unfiltered and raw.

Eryndra had rattled me once, even tempted me. But it wasn't purely physical attraction—it was how she tamed chaos. She made the storm manageable, and I hadn't known how badly I wanted that until then. But her control wasn't the kind that made space for others. It was the kind you fell under. The kind that decided where you stood, whether you liked it or not.

I still didn't trust men. Not completely. I probably never would. But whatever had drawn me to Eryndra had passed. It was her steadiness I'd craved, not her. And her beauty and steadiness had a price.

And… hadn't Trentius proved just as steady? Only softer. Real.

When next I opened my eyes, it was to the sight of Janelle curled up in a big chair, her legs tucked beneath her, a wine glass in one hand and the *Grimoire of the Thunderborn* open in her lap. Stars glimmered through the window, though dimly, making me think it wasn't long until morning. It looked like Janelle had stayed up all night.

Seven days. Had it really been that long since I'd last seen Hughelas? Heard anything from my mother and Beldroth? No update from Marinna or Trentius. Janelle had told me Hughelas had come by, and I believed her—it wasn't like he'd vanished. But that didn't stop the gnawing sense of distance. Seven days, and we hadn't spoken once. Seven days of just missing him, of never crossing paths, of always being a step too far away. Of course, I'd discovered why, but it didn't make me miss him less.

"You're holding wine over a sacred text?" My voice came out as a croak, each word dragging itself from my throat like a reluctant child from bed. Every muscle in my body protested as I stretched, a wave of stiffness rolling through me. My shoulders carried the weight of a mountain, and my legs ached as though I'd run to the horizon and back.

"Who said it was sacred?" Janelle quipped without looking up. "Just prized. A little splash of wine might add to the mystique."

With a groan, I sat up, each movement a minor battle against my body's insistence that I lie back down. I rubbed my eyes, willing myself not to ask Janelle again if she'd heard anything new about my mother or whether Hughelas had come by. "Learn anything good?" I muttered, latching onto the easiest way forward. Every step of my slow shuffle to her chair reminded me of the night's ordeal—lightning, being tossed around like a rag doll, using my anti-magic. I leaned over her shoulder, half for curiosity, half because I didn't trust my legs to hold me upright much longer.

Janelle flipped through some pages, displaying unreadable text and intricate charts which I had no hope of understanding, especially in my current state. "This writing is from before the Breaking," she said. "A form we jokingly call Dragonese, though I doubt dragons used pens. I've seen it before, but it's not like I can translate it on the spot. Our own common elvish is derived from it, so it isn't wickedly difficult. Undoubtedly, Maelith has worked some or all of it out."

"So… nothing good?" I pressed, my voice dull. Even speaking proved to be heavy labor.

"Well, some figures suggest it's about how magic works," she admitted, "which would make it dragon-informed knowledge—highly valuable. Particularly to Drevin. That's why you need it. Oh, and this drawing in the back..." She flipped to a page and held it up, her grin wicked. "Do you think this is two elementals having sex?"

The drawing was a tangle of clouds and lightning bolts, but when she turned it sideways... I blushed, caught off-guard by its suggestive shapes. "Surely not."

"Dragons are mysterious beings," she teased. "Who's to say?"

My thoughts tripped over themselves as the picture made me think, embarrassingly, of Hughelas. Was he safe? He was as bright as he was kind, but I worried about his ability to navigate the secretive Dearans. And what of my mother? I knew she could take care of herself, but it didn't stop me from worrying. Surely, Hughelas would have an update the next time he showed up. Which, I had to admit, I hoped would be soon, despite our last parting. I swallowed hard, pulling myself back into the moment.

"So, what now? I just hand this over to Drevin?" I asked, hoping to steer the conversation away from elemental erotica and searching for the simplest way forward.

Janelle set her glass down and stood, stretching languidly. "Not yet. Don't forget, handing that to Drevin will send hot-headed Stormwright Maelith Skywarden into a full-blown tantrum."

"Okay," I said slowly, bracing for whatever convoluted scheme Janelle had in mind. "So what's the plan?"

"You need something Maelith wants," she said, swirling the last of her wine like a scheming noblewoman.

I frowned. "That sounds... manipulative."

Janelle smirked. "That sounds smart."

"Perhaps some of that wine you prescribe for electrocution?" I suggested weakly.

Her laugh was rich and warm. "If only it were that simple. Maelith oversees the Tempest Crown—an ancient artifact from before the Breaking. It's this kind of pedestal with gems and metal etching all over it. It's what powers the storm that shields this island. Drevin has devised a way to recharge it with less effort, but he's keeping it to himself."

I rubbed my temple, her words only half sinking in. My thoughts strayed again. Hughelas would understand the Grimoire better than I ever could. My mother, given time, would optimize its spells. Together, they'd do something smart with it. Together. A word that had meant something before Deara. They'd do *something* that wasn't playing games with Maelith and Drevin like Janelle wanted me to do. I forced myself to focus on Janelle. "Believe it or not," I said slowly, "I've seen a pedestal like that before."

"You what?" Janelle nearly dropped her wineglass. Then she leaned in, eyes alight with the thrill of a fresh secret. "Elliah, my dear, you cannot dangle a revelation like that and expect me to move on. Spill."

Her enthusiasm caught me off-guard. Despite the weight dragging at my every limb, a smile snuck in. "Well... it was in the caves under Theopolis..."

Janelle was relentless. Her questions came fast, her wonder genuine, and before I realized it, I was swept into the memory, recounting details I didn't even know I'd noticed. Her laughter rang out often, a balm to my frayed nerves, and she kept the conversation light, teasing me when I stumbled over words or offered clumsy explanations. For a while, I forgot about the ache of separation from my family and friends.

"Wait, wait," she said, interrupting me with a raised hand. "You're telling me the magical statue of a troll, from thousands of years in the past, preserved a *joke*?"

"Pretty sure," I said, stifling a laugh. "Though the punchline got clipped."

"Gods, and I thought my family heirlooms were weird." She grinned, shaking her head, and waved her hand for me to continue.

It was a long, meandering conversation in which I lost all track of time. Worries about my mother and Hughelas still lingered, but Janelle's warmth was a welcome distraction, like a fire warding off the night's chill. It might have been because we'd survived something together. Accomplished something. Or maybe because I'd never gone so long without my mother, and I needed to talk. But my reticence cracked. And once it did...

Janelle had a way of making me feel like every word I spoke was a rare artifact she'd spent years searching for. It was dangerously easy to get swept along with her. And somehow, between her jokes and questions, she wove in little bits of her own stories—short, tantalizing glimpses that made me want to hear more.

Before I knew it, the sun had risen, we'd talked throughout making and eating breakfast, and I'd laid out more about the caves under Theopolis—and myself—than I'd ever intended.

"Oh, but what happened next?" she asked, her tone equal parts curiosity and mischief.

I blinked, trying to retrace my own steps. "Wait. What was I saying?"

"You were saying you attacked an Alluvium warrior in a ring of deadly magical fire," she reminded me, her smile widening as she leaned back in her chair.

I groaned and rubbed my forehead. "How did we even get here?"

Her laugh was warm, filling the room like sunlight. "Elliah, my dear, you're the one who started this whole fascinating tangent. I'm just an innocent bystander."

"Innocent, my ass," I muttered, though the corners of my mouth betrayed me with a smile.

She drained the last of her morning tea and stood, brushing crumbs off her hands. "Well, much as I'd love to hear more, I've got some things to take care of in the library. You coming, or are you going to sit here and try to remember where the conversation went off the rails?"

The mention of the library reminded me of my exhaustion. Rest sounded heavenly. But she deserved my help after how much she'd helped me. "Oh, yes, please. Take me with you." My mind finally latched onto the start of the conversation. "You were telling me about the Tempest Crown."

She turned, her grin a blend of mischief and calculation, and tossed me a conspiratorial wink. "We'll talk more once we're out of earshot, but I already told you the gist of it: Drevin—or one of his little protégés—has a formula for a spell to recharge the Tempest Crown without draining as much mana."

"That's great!" I said, though my enthusiasm quickly faltered. "And also terrible. Why would he keep that to himself if the Tempest Crown protects the entire island?"

Janelle headed toward the door, her movements light despite the seriousness of the topic. "Because, Elliah, Drevin likes to keep people like Maelith busy. Idle hands and all that."

I followed her, every step reminding me of my aching muscles, but her energy was magnetic. As she held the door open, her voice dropped to a playful whisper. "Now, let's see if we can steal a little knowledge of our own."

Her grin widened as I stepped past her, and, despite myself, I smiled back. Whatever tangled web of secrets we were about to step into, Janelle would make sure I played my part. Whether I wanted to or not.

I found Kaelith outside the council chamber, leaning against the stone wall, her arms crossed. Her eyes flicked to me, but she didn't move, as though she'd expected this conversation before I'd even sought her out.

"You've been avoiding me," I said, keeping my voice low.

A corner of her mouth twitched. "Have I? Or have you been avoiding the truth?"

I exhaled sharply. "Don't do that. If you have something to say, say it."

She studied me for a moment, then pushed off the wall with a sigh. "You shouldn't go in there blind."

A prickle of unease crawled up my spine. "Meaning?"

Kaelith's expression was unreadable, but something in her stance had changed—more rigid than usual, like she was weighing the risks of speaking at all.

Part of me wished Elliah was there. She would've already stormed the room, torn the truth out of someone, and started flipping chairs if she didn't like the answers. And I needed that. I needed her clarity of action more than I realized.

"I doubt I'm telling you anything new," Kaelith mumbled, justifying her actions, presumably to herself. "Pyrravyn doesn't present problems. He presents solutions. Solutions that he's already made sure are the *only* option."

A cold weight settled in my gut. "So he's already decided what's going to happen."

She rolled her eyes, but it didn't appear directed at me—something internal. "I bet he decided before you ever set foot on this island." Her gaze flicked past me, to the doors of the council chamber. "What he needs now is your compliance."

I clenched my jaw. "And what if I refuse?"

Kaelith hesitated. For the first time since I'd met her, I saw something flicker across her face—uncertainty. Regret? Then, just as quickly, it was gone. She gave me a slow, considering look. "That depends," she murmured. "Do you know what you'd be refusing?"

Something in her tone made my breath hitch. "Do you?" I countered.

She didn't answer right away. The pause stretched too long. Then, with quiet finality, she said, "Tread carefully, Hughelas."

She turned to leave, but I stepped in her path. "Kaelith." My voice was firm now. "Is my father alive?"

A flicker of something—guilt?—crossed her expression before she schooled it back into neutrality. "If I knew, I shouldn't tell you."

Not *yes*. Not *no*. Just another carefully constructed answer that gave me nothing.

I stared at her, frustration and a rising sense of dread colliding in my chest. "Pyrravyn's using him against me, isn't he?"

Kaelith exhaled through her nose, then met my gaze with something softer than her usual sharp-edged amusement. "Be careful in there, Scion."

With those words of wisdom, she stepped around me and disappeared into the room.

The council chamber was more of a battlefield than a place of diplomacy. Tension rippled through the air, unspoken but heavy, like the charge before a storm. The room itself reflected that sense of strain: the walls of the square room were carved from smooth black basalt, their surfaces veined with shimmering silver runes like bands that held the tension in place. A high, arched ceiling loomed overhead, its intricate mosaic depicting the Daughters of the Nine Winds soaring against a tempestuous sky.

The circular table at the center sat in stark contrast, its polished, light-color wood worn smooth by centuries of debates, betrayals, and uneasy alliances. Chairs of dark oak lined its perimeter, each bearing the sigil of a faction or house, though many were empty, their occupants lost or absent. Flickering braziers in the corners cast shifting shadows, the smoky tang of their burning oil clinging to the back of my throat.

I adjusted my chair at the table, fighting the urge to fidget, and it creaked ominously over the faint crackle of the braziers. Across from me, Pyrravyn lounged, though less like someone at ease and more like someone holding themselves together through sheer force of will. He sat with his eyes closed, but they darted around behind his lids in thought, belying his relaxed pose. Without even having known him for long, I sensed that meant trouble.

To his left, Maelith was anything but casual. His hands gripped the edge of the table so tightly that I half-expected the wood to splinter. Shadows etched deep lines under his eyes, and the slight twitch in his jaw gave away his barely controlled temper. I hadn't met him yet, but it wasn't hard to figure out from the description of an angry master wizard who spent all his time and energy preserving a magical storm to protect Deara. Drevin sat beside him, eerily composed compared to my previous encounter with him, the flickering lamplight casting sharp lines on his face as he paged through a leather-bound notebook. I wondered if he ever truly stopped thinking, or if every quiet moment was just another opportunity for him to calculate. Was that how my companions saw me?

To my right, Eryndra Tidebringer exuded an air of quiet command. Her steel-gray eyes flicked around the table, measuring each of us in turn. The leader of the Peacekeepers was a picture of controlled strength, her presence as steady and unyielding as the cliffs that surrounded Deara. Did her silence mean she was biding her time or was she simply unimpressed? Either way, I didn't find it comforting.

Yselda, seated next to Eryndra, leaned forward with her hands clasped on the table. The head of trade carried a veneer of politeness, but the tight set of her mouth betrayed her irritation. From what I'd seen, she was a woman of numbers and logistics, and meetings like this one—brimming with unknowns and egos—were probably her idea of hell.

Notably missing? Bella. Apparently, her training to lead Deara had not reached the level of joining closed-door council meetings.

"I'd like to get this over with before the Crown fails again," Maelith snapped, his voice hoarse. "Speak your piece, Pyrravyn."

Pyrravyn straightened, then leaned forward, his elbows resting on the polished wood. "Fine," he said, his voice quieter than I'd expected. "Let's talk about the Crown. It's breaking. You're breaking, Maelith. And if we don't do something soon, we're all going to pay the price."

"You think I don't know that?" Maelith bristled, though there was no real venom in his voice—only weariness. "If you have a plan, then out with it."

Pyrravyn nodded, his tone more measured than usual. "We need a solution that doesn't depend on you and your acolytes bleeding yourselves dry day after day." He looked around the room, meeting each person's eyes in turn. "I won't pretend this is easy, or that I like what I'm about to propose. But we're running out of time."

Kaelith had cautioned me when I'd sought her out after my semi-private meeting with Pyrravyn. She'd prepared me, hesitantly, for what a council meeting might look like. "Pyrravyn's charm is his sharpest blade," she'd warned me. As he spoke to the room, his words reasonable, even sympathetic, I couldn't help but admire his skill, even as I sensed the trap being set.

"What's your plan?" I asked, pushing past the rising dread in my chest.

Pyrravyn turned to Drevin, giving him the floor. "Drevin?"

The tinker adjusted his spectacles, his voice smooth and detached. "With the information brought back by Marinna..." At least he'd learned her name. "I believe I understand better how the Tempest Crown works. It uses, and creates, two types of magical energy—one related to black dragon magic, which is what we see as the manifestation of protective storms, and the other is blue dragon magic, which is less visible under the water and feeding back into the Tempest Crown from under Deara. Dragons created it, and dragon magic was meant to recharge it, not elf magic. What we do—what Maelith and his acolytes do—isn't enough. The efficacy of the artifact is diminishing. It will ultimately break down, and as we saw from the recent failure, the blue dragons will rush in when that happens."

Maelith's jaw clenched like he attempted to chew through a tree branch, but I also saw the wheels spinning in his head as he assimilated the information.

"So, patching it isn't enough," Pyrravyn cut in. "We need something... transformative. Something permanent. And we may have the solution."

"Send in the prophet!" Pyrravyn commanded the guard who stood at the door that led to the halls which the hereditary leadership called home, where Pyrravyn and Bella stayed, and where they'd provided me a room. The guard opened the door and Gormar Blackfoot walked in. The self-satisfied smile in his eyes made me think he'd spent time with Pyrravyn while I'd trooped around on Pyrravyn's fools' errands.

Yselda raised an eyebrow, her voice sharp. "Spare us the theatrics, Pyrravyn. If you have a solution, state it clearly."

Gormar scowled at the denigration of his efforts as theatrics, but Pyrravyn ignored her insult more easily. "Call forth your prophecy," Pyrravyn told him.

Gormar stepped forward, drawing a small, ornate bowl etched with jagged, flame-like designs from within his robes. "The fire has shown me what is to come," he said, his voice low and resonant. "Allow me to share it with you."

He placed the bowl on the table, ensuring everyone had a clear view of its contents—a braid of stark white hair, carefully twisted together. Had it come from a willing participant, or had Gormar experimented with multiple strands, seeking the vision he wanted? The thought of Gormar skulking about, collecting random hair, or nabbing it from specific people, unsettled me, but before the idea fully took hold, he poured a handful of fine red powder into the bowl, instantly drawing everyone's attention. Even Drevin paused, setting down his pen to watch.

With a snap of Gormar's fingers, the powder ignited, a swirling column of fire rising from the bowl. His theatrics had certainly improved since the prophecy aboard the Salty Squirt. The flames coalesced into shapes—first amorphous, then forming distinct images.

I watched, transfixed, as the vision unfolded. Pyrravyn stood holding an egg, its shell shot through with glowing veins of fire. He strode through a storm, the winds parting before him, until he reached what I presumed was the Tempest Crown. There, he raised the egg high. The vision lingered on Pyrravyn, resolute amidst the howling winds, before the flames dissipated into smoke.

The vision quickly shifted. The flames blurred and reformed into a fleet of ships. One ship, bearing the flag of the Peacekeepers, cut through calm waters, its passage serene and unchallenged. Around it, other vessels burned, their crews consumed by fire and chaos.

Once more the flames shifted and created an image. The Tempest Crown again, with a small dragon standing on its rear legs while the front rested on the gems that controlled the crown. Then, with a whoosh, the flames went out.

"We need a dragon," Pyrravyn said, his voice low and deliberate. "Not just any dragon. A black one."

Maelith's head snapped to Pyrravyn, his eyes narrowing. "Are you out of your mind? What do you want to do, turn off the Tempest Crown and hope that a black dragon shows up with a beneficent mindset before the blues swarm us?"

"If you'll excuse us," Pyrravyn said to Gormar, dismissing him. Gormar's jaw clenched, and he looked my way for help.

"He should stay," I said. "We have had many debates on the interpretation of prophecy. I would like to question him on yours." Gormar's lip twitched in a snarl. It wasn't the help he'd hoped for, but it kept him in the room. Meanwhile, Pyrravyn's ready acceptance unsettled me—had I just done what he'd wanted me to do?

Maelith hadn't calmed down. "What do you expect us to do? Summon a black dragon?"

"Not summon." Pyrravyn grinned. "Hatch."

The room fell into stunned silence. Even Eryndra, unshakable Eryndra, tilted her head slightly, weighing just how mad the scheme and the council had become.

"Explain," Eryndra said, her voice as cold and precise as the steel she wore.

"We have our new Scion to thank for our solution," Pyrravyn said smoothly, and the smile he cast my way felt like a noose tightening around my neck. "He's located the habitat of the black dragon some reported when the Tempest Crown came down several months ago." He'd made it sound to me like I was helping Deara by locating a threat. Yet, as I feared all along, the real threat had never been the dragon.

I'd convinced Yselda to get me close to the island the fisherfolk had described. Sure enough, the weather turned foul as we approached the island, and a roar more resonant than thunder had warned us to turn back, which we'd promptly done.

"Yes, he found the dragon's lair," Yselda said. "And its behavior suggests it was guarding eggs." Her eyes squint in calculation, weighing the risk versus reward.

Eryndra slammed a fist on the table, her cold demeanor cracking like ice, though her voice remained cool. "Dragons are sacred. You can't be seriously considering—"

"What of your *peace*, Tidebringer?" Pyrravyn interrupted, for the first time letting heat into his voice. "If the Tempest Crown goes down, your *sacred* dragons will swarm the harbor, and your fleet will be destroyed.

All your hopes of bringing peace to the world will end." His tone turned slightly condescending. "And don't get all self-righteous with me. I know what you steal from the blues."

"What I take from under their noses is but a prized bauble for them. They don't eat them, drink them—their lives don't depend on them. They create a challenge we've paid for in ships and lives. You go too far. There must be another way than stealing an egg from its mother," Eryndra protested.

My own feelings were not as strong as Eryndra, though I agreed with her. Growing up next to the Dragonlands, we'd had to fight dragons that came over the mountains. It was fight or die. I did not hold dragons sacred. But stealing an egg?

"I suppose you have a plan for how to retrieve this egg?" Eryndra said into the growing silence.

"I do," Pyrravyn said with a grimace, betraying misgivings. "I don't like this any more than you do, but survival demands sacrifice."

"It will not include Peacekeepers," Eryndra responded coldly.

"It need not," Pyrravyn allowed. But then he slid in a verbal blade. "Of course, history will remember that the Peacekeepers had no part in saving Deara. That you refused to act."

The faint narrowing of her eyes was the only sign the jab had landed. She turned to me, her expression hard. "You are a Scion, too, Hughelas." Her words struck like the crack of a gauntlet against stone. "Do not permit this."

I froze.

Permit this? Pyrravyn played me like a lute, and she expected me to stop him? She was handing me power. But how was I supposed to wield something I didn't even understand?

I flicked a glance at Pyrravyn, but he was unreadable. He wasn't worried.

Because he didn't believe I could use it either.

My stomach clenched. A Scion. I had to try. "Gormar," I said. "It was *your* prophecy. Do you interpret it the same way?"

Gormar's jaw tightened, his voice measured as he replied. "Get the egg. Hatch the dragon. The Peacekeepers will win the battle that will come."

"And what might go wrong if the egg is lost?" I pressed, careful to keep my voice neutral. "What if we don't, in fact, succeed?"

Gormar met my gaze, his words weighted with finality. "The fire speaks in certainty. To act against it is to invite ruin."

Pyrravyn's eyes met mine, unflinching. "I understand all of your doubts." He turned from me to look upon each person at the table. "But I've seen the stakes. This isn't about ambition or conquest. It's about survival—ours, and everyone who depends on the storm shield to hold."

Eryndra's icy gaze never left mine. She was still counting on me. Did I even have the authority to stop what was happening?

"Which brings me to a sore point," Pyrravyn said, turning his gaze to me. "I have learned with certainty what has happened to your father, Hughelas." I *knew* what he was doing, saw it coming like a wave on the horizon. And still, it hit. "Sadly," Pyrravyn continued, with the perfect measure of regret, "it is as I feared—he and the Wood Elf have become trapped in the Abyss, the same cage we sent your father to dismantle."

My chest tightened. My father—trapped. And Illiara too. A cold ache spread through me, threatening to swallow me whole.

Pyrravyn let the silence settle. Let me swim in it. Then, at just the right moment, he offered me the rope he'd intended all along.

"But there is hope," Pyrravyn said, his tone softening, almost tender. "There is reason to believe Elliah will be able to free them. I can show you."

My breath caught—hope flaring, just for an instant—and then he cut it off at the knees. "But I cannot risk letting her try until we first have the egg we need to save Deara."

The words *slammed* into me. I saw the trap—*saw* it—but I was already ensnared. My father's fate dangled before me like bait, but it wasn't just him, was it? It was Illiara, too. Elliah. Every thread I cared about, knotted into a net meant to keep me right where Pyrravyn wanted me.

I clenched my jaw, *hard*. I wanted to fight him, to throw his words back in his face, but what was the alternative? If I refused, did that mean I was the one abandoning my father? If I walked away, did I lose whatever fragile chance I had to save him?

Pyrravyn had backed me into a corner so tight, I wasn't sure there was a way out. Eryndra's barely audible sigh of resignation settled over me like a verdict, a quiet confirmation of my failure.

The proceedings continued with more questions and answers, and I heard some of it, but my mind was elsewhere. The worry about my father warred with anger over how Pyrravyn had played me. Though he gave a legitimate explanation for the need to capture an egg, I distrusted everything he said.

Maelith looked relieved that something was being done. Yselda, puffed with self-importance at her role in finding the dragon. Eryndra reluctantly let herself be involved. Pyrravyn danced around everyone's concerns and calmed or cajoled the council into a path. He played us all.

My mind kept returning to Gormar's prophecy, a compelling picture. The egg, the dragon, the Peacekeepers. And Gormar's words echoed in my mind: *The fire speaks in certainty*. Yet, it reminded me of Wynruil saying the opposite: *Fire lies*.

The cave whispered with the restless echoes of children. Stale air hung close, thickened by the damp stone, and though no wind stirred, the space never seemed still. Shadows curled along the jagged walls, pulsing slowly in the light of the bioluminescent glow-worm lanterns that clung like pale stars. Their faint purple radiance gleamed on the damp walls of the cave without the caustic burn of smoke or the strain of magic. A nearby shallow freshwater pool reflected the shimmer, catching the faint ripples from unseen droplets that fell from above.

Distant shouts of fisher-folk reached us in distorted fragments, caught in the twisting acoustics of the cave as they nabbed the small fish which the sea brought in through an underwater passage. The Abyss held the fish as it held its people, unwilling to release the lives it claimed. Yet the salt water itself escaped, pulsing in time with the distant tide. The gentle surge echoed with the rhythms of the world beyond—a world that still danced with sunlit waves and shifting clouds. But there, the water's whispers reached us like forgotten promises, stirring memories of freedom out of our grasp. Each distant pulse seemed both a comfort and a cruel reminder that the sea moved on, untethered, while we remained bound within the Abyss.

I sat with my back against a cool outcropping, my hands resting protectively over the slight swell of my stomach. The knowledge of my child within me stirred an ache I could not name. Fear, perhaps. Hope. Or something heavier—the weight of uncertainty.

Laughter rippled through the cave, soft but vibrant. I followed the sound to where Beldroth stood, crouched low with his hands raised like a great monster. Children squealed and scattered, giggling as they darted around him. He gave chase, roaring in mock ferocity, only to let them dodge and tumble away. Alrenna's daughter, the girl I'd just Healed, discarded her hesitancy and sprinted in. She shrieked with delight, ducking beneath the Beldroth-monster's grasp as he made a dramatic show of nearly catching her.

It suited him—the joy, the unguarded playfulness. Beldroth had a gentleness I hadn't fully understood when we first met. I wondered what kind of father he would become. He hadn't spoken of it much, beyond the fleeting mentions of possibility. Perhaps he feared it as much as I did. After all, with Elliah born Bereft, chances were…

Alrenna's voice pulled me back. "They're resilient." The words came low and even. I'd only just met Alrenna, when she'd approached me with a daughter whose wrist twisted at an unnatural angle. An accident while climbing rocks with the other children. Alrenna's voice had been steady, though there had been no mistaking the fear in her eyes. I'd Healed the girl without hesitation, knitting bone and soothing pain, though it had cost me all my mana for the day. Since then, Alrenna had remained near, a quiet presence amid the uncertainty.

Her daughter—a girl of perhaps fifty—no longer sat back in cautious observation. With a triumphant grin, she launched herself at Beldroth's back, but didn't quite make it. Alrenna tensed, her knuckles whitening, but as her daughter sprang up from her small tumble and resumed her attack, a flicker of relief softened her features. She exhaled quietly, the kind of breath that carried the weight of constant worry and the fleeting joy of seeing it momentarily lifted.

"You mean they endure." My voice sounded rougher than I intended.

Alrenna shook her head. "No. I mean resilient. More so than us." She studied me with the steady patience of someone who had measured time by the slow erosion of stone. "The Abyss changes them. But not like it changes us."

"How do you mean?"

Her gaze flickered toward the children. "Every child born here carries magic. None are Bereft."

The words struck with the force of a rockslide.

"None?" I pressed.

"None." She paused, her fingers tracing the fraying hem of her tunic. "The bounds of magic down here…" She absently held an imaginary ball in her hands. "It constrains them, too. They're born weak. Weak enough that you will fear for your child's life. But not Bereft."

A pulse of nausea twisted through me. The memory of Elliah's birth flared sharp—her frailty, the heavy silence that followed before her first cry broke free. Even then, I had sensed something was wrong. And later, the truth had come. My daughter—my beautiful, stubborn Elliah—arrived Bereft. Stripped of magic. Just as Zoras had warned.

Another burst of laughter drew my gaze. "I've got you now, monster!" Alrenna's daughter crowed, somehow having scaled the Beldroth-beast.

Beldroth roared in mock defeat, staggering as though overcome. "Oh no! The brave warrior has bested me!" He stumbled to his knees, feigning collapse as the children cheered in triumph. Alrenna's daughter lifted her arms in victory, her laughter echoing through the cave. Alrenna's shoulders relaxed as she sighed softly, one hand absently smoothing the folds of her tunic. Despite the gravity of our situation, a small smile tugged at my lips. It was absurd how natural Beldroth made it seem. Was this a moment of genuine ease, or did he play the monster to mask his own worries? I wondered if the laughter of children offered him some solace, a reminder of simpler times. Or perhaps he simply held tight to fleeting joys, unwilling to let the Abyss steal every piece of himself. Even with the shadows of the Abyss pressing in, Beldroth spun laughter from the gloom, like a wave breaking free of the tide's pull. For a moment, it almost felt like hope.

The warmth of laughter lingered, and my thoughts slipped away… back to my first night with Beldroth. How easily I'd fallen into his arms. There had been no careful dance of courtship, no whispered promises beneath starlight. Just heat, desire, and reckless abandon. And somehow, absurdly, it had turned out well. *The relationship,* I amended to myself, *not the insane progression of life-threatening adventures that followed.*

How jealous I'd been when I thought his attentions had turned to Marinna. It was almost laughable now, thinking of how I'd fumed in silence. Marinna, with all her strength and Warder magic—it had been easy to think I would never compare. But Beldroth hadn't been hers to lose. In hindsight, he'd never even looked at her that way. With our future locked away, the jealousy I'd once carried felt like a stranger's dream.

But perhaps that was Beldroth's true strength. He held the shadows at bay, not with magic or force, but with faith and laughter. Even now, in the depths of the Abyss, he found light and made others see it too. It was as though, in questioning his faith, he had uncovered a strength that had always waited beneath it. But for how long could anyone manage that? When the shadows pressed harder, what then?

A ruckus ensued as Alrenna's daughter defended the fallen corpse of the Beldroth-monster with a roar of her own. Alrenna smiled. "But they grow stronger for it. Who knows what their magic would be like if they escaped?"

"You think it shields them?" My voice trembled. The lack of Bereft children might have been pure coincidence.

Alrenna shook her head. "The Abyss feeds off of us. It is no kindness. But in this one thing, it gives something in return."

A part of me recoiled. The Abyss twisted all it touched, locking us in. It stole our magic and subjected us to the ravages of time, like other creatures. Yet, even as the thought rose, another lingered close—the possibility. Would a child of mine, born here, be spared the curse that had marked Elliah? Even entertaining the thought twisted my stomach—like I was turning my back on Elliah's suffering and the amazing woman crafted from it.

I traced the curve of my belly, my fingertips lingering as though they might summon answers. The warmth of my skin provided little comfort, and I struggled against the urge to press harder, to coax reassurance from within. The memory of Elliah's first stirrings lingered—delicate flutters that had filled me with awe. But fear tainted even that memory—fear that my unborn child might share Elliah's fate. It was too tiny to kick, yet I imagined a faint flutter against my palm. Was it wrong to consider what might be gained? To wonder if the Abyss might offer what the Mother had denied?

I looked one more time at the children. They spoke softly once more, giggling over some imagined game or plot against the Beldroth-monster. Resilient, Alrenna had said. And they were. But at such cost!

"Do you think it changes them forever?" I asked, my voice little more than a whisper.

Alrenna's eyes softened, though her answer was no comfort.

"It changes everything."

The silence between us thickened. The shadows pressed close once again. I traced the curve of my belly. If I had any magic to spare, I would have cast it to feel the rhythm of my child's heartbeat. And yet the thought lingered, trapped in the Abyss with me: if this place held even a faint promise of sparing my next child the fate Elliah bore… was captivity a price worth paying?

Elliah ~ 12

The next morning, Janelle had me back at the front desk. Whatever tentative warmth had passed between us during our long talk, it hadn't translated into leniency. I was still her best Library Runner, still expected to pull my weight.

"Grenthis!" Janelle barked. The librarian helping a customer startled. He quickly wrapped up what he was saying and hurried over.

"Yes?" he asked, a nervous grin on his face.

"I assume you've heard of our newest Library Runner," Janelle said dryly, gesturing toward me.

Grenthis's eyes narrowed. "Of course I have. The whole floor's buzzing about the hammer-wielding elf who retrieves books like they're just... well, books."

He looked at me, unimpressed. "You don't look like much."

"Neither do you," I muttered. His white hair and skin were unremarkable on Deara, and his scholarly stoop and twitchy fingers transferred anxiety to me. He wore layered robes the color of sand-washed parchment, and his belt carried as many pens as scrolls. Despite his bluster, he didn't meet my eyes.

"It's time for you to go back on retrieval," Janelle said.

"But—" Salts didn't exactly pale when shocked. They turned a sort of light blue, like their blood had stopped circulating. Hughelas hadn't inherited that, or I'd never seen him shocked, which seemed unlikely given our past.

"Relax, you're not going alone," she said. "Elliah's going with you."

Grenthis scowled. "So she can watch me get eaten by a book?"

"You've got to move on, Grenthis," Janelle said, a touch of understanding infusing her tone. "Face your fears." She patted my back, or, more specifically, the hammer on my back. "She'll keep you safe."

"Who's going to keep *her* safe?" Grenthis grumbled.

"Go!" Janelle said, her voice hard again. Then, after just a moment, "Wait, I haven't told you which books." She went to a set of drawers, opened one, and cast a magelight. Sparks lit around the vast library. She ran her light up the length of the drawer, creating a symphony of light dancing around the room. Twice more, she repeated the motion, her gaze scanning the room with intent. At last, she retrieved a few cards, bringing her light near them with no echo in the room.

"These," she said. "Go find them. Try the Hall for Drevin's Tidewardens. Elliah..." Her look was full of meaning: keep my eyes open for Drevin's notes.

She deposited the cards with their glued-on crystals in Grenthis's hands, then she went to help the mage Grenthis had been talking to when we arrived.

It seemed my time to rest had ended, and I was being sent back into the minefield. The weariness of the previous day's adventure, combined with talking all night, came back to hit me. I wasn't just tired—I was drained. The last time I'd felt that way was in Cenaedth, and Hughelas had paid the price for it. I would need to be careful not to steal Grenthis's mana, even though I hadn't really understood how it happened before. I would be vigilant.

"The other librarians do this all the time," Grenthis said to himself more than me. With a grunt, he set off through one of the counter's archways. I hurried to catch up.

We marched down one of the straight paths between the counter and the outer wall, Grenthis alternating mumbles of encouragement and dismay.

"What happened?" I asked, when he stopped before the double-doors, staring at the cards in his hands. I removed the badge from my neck, holding the band of the necklace high and dangling the key against the lock-plate. The door clicked open. My odd maneuver—one no one else had to do—rattled Grenthis out of his internal battle. He cocked his head inquisitively.

Since I had his attention... "What happened to you?" I asked. "I get that retrieving these books can be hazardous—"

"Can be?" he said with a snort. He shook his head. "Ink of the Deep," he said, as if that would explain it all.

I walked through the door, shrugging that I didn't know what he meant.

"Really?" he said, following me, flabbergasted at my lack of knowledge. "Janelle didn't even *warn* you?"

I almost laughed at the depth of his concern, but I kept it bottled up and pointed at the location circlets in his hands.

"Oh," he said, casting a magelight. "Ink of the Deep is the most common trap in the library," he said, using the magelight to light our way and holding the gems on an outstretched arm to be near his light. "It's simple but nasty because it hides in scrolls and pages. All it takes is a breath of air to activate."

"I thought scrolls required fire to activate," I said. My mother had worked with scrolls for a long time. They needed fire.

"There are materials that ignite when exposed to air. We've created an ink—you use it to write a scroll, then you coat it with a special dust and cover it. The ink and the dust react in a way that the next time air hits the scroll, the ink ignites, activating the spell. You'll find them all over

186

the place in labs and training rooms. Ironically, the really dangerous ones are in the Driftling's Halls. Have you ever heard that some baby snakes are more dangerous than their parents because they don't understand how to regulate their venom?"

I nodded my head—a well-known fact among Wood Elves.

"It's that kind of idea. The beginners, Driftlings, might make a spell that doesn't fire, or might create one with far too much... venom." He shook his head. "I got snagged by such a one. Ink of the Deep, as a spell, is nasty. It blinds you, muffles sounds, mutes your senses, so that you become trapped in a cave of nothingness."

The corridor was busier than the ones Janelle had taken me down. Light emanated from many of the doorways, and I leaned into the rooms on the right side of the hall to look for the glowing of the books we hunted, while he leaned into the doors on the left. A mage or two would look up questioningly, but I just nodded to them, looking for the telltale glow from a book, and then moved on.

When I didn't muster the dismay Grenthis wanted, he added, "People have died! Falling, burning themselves, drowning."

"Okay," I said, "that sounds horrible. You were trapped in one?"

"Yes, for days." His voice dipped lower, almost a whisper. "Parched. Starving. Nothing but blackness pressing in. Every second stretching forever."

Ouch. I imagined how frightening that would have been. And thirst? I licked my lips, thinking about the mana walking right next to me. *Get it together, Elliah!*

My shiver somewhat mollified Grenthis. "So why did Janelle think pairing me up with you would solve the problem?" he asked. "You are clearly unprepared for encountering such traps."

"Well, I can imagine having a second person around helps immensely, doesn't it?" I asked. "If nothing else, I can scream for help."

Grenthis frowned. "I suppose," he said. I knew Janelle thought I was safer than Grenthis knew, but I was reluctant to share why.

"What made you want to become a librarian?" I asked. A mage worked with beakers and tubes and open flames in the next room, not looking up as I peeked in.

"I actually started off as a student of Marodus Tideforge." He looked askance at me, but I shrugged. "He was a visionary, intent on harnessing the raw power of undersea magma vents. Alchemy, pyromancy—truly remarkable. He died a decade ago in one of his experiments, and several of his Tidewardens along with him. I was only a Wavebinder at the time, so I would have had to join with either Drevin or Maelith to move up. Neither appealed to me, so I became a librarian."

"Tidewardens? Wavebinders?" I asked. I'd heard the terms often enough on Deara to have a sense of the titles, but I wanted to keep

Grenthis thinking about other topics.

"Rankings of study. Driftlings, Wavebinders, Currentweavers, Tidewardens, Stormwrights." He shrugged. "They're just levels of expertise. Drevin and Maelith are Stormwrights. Obviously a fitting title for Maelith, but it is just a title of expertise, and Drevin wears it as well. Along with Keryn and Talyra, but I didn't want to become a Peacekeeper or go into trade either."

We approached a darkened room on the left—a faint glow emanated from it. "I think we've found one of our books," Grenthis said. I followed him cautiously, my limbs heavy and my vision slightly blurred from fatigue. His magelight revealed a table set up like a desk, and on it rested small stacks of books. A faintly glowing cover caught my eye.

Grenthis leaned over the book. "Key Elements of a Storm," he read aloud, then crouched to examine it from the side. "See all these bookmarks? Any one of those might hold a trap." He gestured at the table. "Sealed-off ink pot," he added, his tone full of suspicion. "Pens are clean." His voice dipped lower, conspiratorial. "Definitely a trap."

I pressed my palms against the table to steady myself and bit my lip. His careful inspection gave me a moment to breathe. My exhaustion buzzed at the edges of my thoughts, but I forced myself to take in the scene. Titles about storm magic dominated the room, but others stood out: *Magical Biases of Gemstones, Mana Conductivity, Geometric Theorems and Their Magical Applications.* Hughelas would have loved that one. My gaze lingered on an open book on the desk—one page with meticulous handwritten notes and the other blank, waiting for me. Was that the information Janelle wanted? My fingers itched to grab it, though my body screamed to just sit down.

Hughelas knew magical theory—pulling meaning from tangled words the way a fisherman sorted his best catch. If he were there, he'd have already worked out whether the journal was worth taking. Guilt twisted in my chest at the thought of our last encounter. I'd lashed out at him because he mattered to me, because his cold logic had stung more than it should have. Because I cared when I wasn't sure he did. I missed him, and I owed him more than just an apology. I owed him honesty—not just about what had happened, but about how I felt.

Yet while Hughelas had been granted more freedom of movement than the rest of us, it came with strings. Kaelith, Hughelas's shadow. Janelle had taken care to keep those eyes off me, but that meant Hughelas wasn't there. He wouldn't sort this out. That left it to me. I made my decision.

I reached for the journal, intent on slipping away with it.

"What are you doing?" a sharp voice interrupted, making both Grenthis and me jump.

A Salt in pale-blue robes, complicated patterns of white tracing the fabric, glared at us from the doorway. Sudden guilt swept over me—I'd been about to nab that journal. My shoulders sagged, the idea of explaining myself too exhausting to contemplate.

"One of your books is overdue," Grenthis said, pointing at the faint light on it.

"Ah," the newcomer said. "Do you know who requested it?"

"I didn't check," Grenthis replied. "But you know the rules. I wouldn't tell you if I knew."

"No matter," the Tidewarden said, walking around his desk and sitting. "If it's one of Maelith's cronies, I'll have it back before morning." His condescending smirk spoke volumes. He cast a spell, then slipped each of the bookmarks from the book in question to the back of another.

"I told you," Grenthis whispered.

"All clear," the Tidewarden said. Grenthis picked up the book like it might bite him, but when nothing happened, he tucked it under his arm.

The Tidewarden leaned back in his seat, considering me. His smirk didn't fade. "You're fitting in well here, aren't you? Learning our ways, making yourself comfortable."

I frowned. His shift in tone threw me off. Was that a compliment? A question? A warning? "I suppose?"

He hummed in mock thoughtfulness, drumming his fingers against the desk. "Funny thing about outsiders. Some learn fast. Some never do. The ones who last?" He smiled, all teeth. "They stop pretending this place belongs to them."

A test. A baited hook, waiting for me to bite.

I stiffened. "I'm not pretending."

"Aren't you?" His voice was soft, knowing. "Tell me, outsider—what do you think gives someone the right to knowledge?"

I hesitated. This was exactly the kind of conversation Janelle had warned me about—recognize the trap, shift the footing, never let them dictate the terms. I should have redirected, dodged, stayed in control. Instead, I did the one thing she told me not to do.

I let him lead.

"I came to help Hughelas," I said, too defensive, too reactive.

The shift in his posture was subtle, effortless, like a net tightening around its prey. "And yet, here you are, rooting through our knowledge like a thief in the dark." He tilted his head, his smirk widening. "How very fitting."

I hesitated. Janelle would have already found her way out—flipped the conversation, redirected the insult, made him lose ground even as he thought he gained it. I scrambled for footing, but the words weren't there.

No, I could still turn this. Janelle had prepared me—one slip didn't have to mean a fall. Redirect. Control the pace. "I'm not—"

"Aren't you?" His voice was soft, knowing.

The conversation slipped further from my grasp.

"You arrived with the High Elf that has a dragon, did you not?" He shifted the conversation before I recovered, guiding me from one trap straight into the next. I'd lost control, and now I was chasing after it, a step behind, scrambling to catch up.

I nodded, too drained to offer more.

"Drevin asked me to learn more about that, but the Peacekeepers have him and the blond-haired Wood Elf on ships. What can you tell me?" He leaned back in his chair, exuding an air of effortless confidence.

A trap.

I knew it was a trap. But even that knowledge rattled me. I was still *losing*. I needed to steer the conversation back to solid ground. "Trentius is nice," I said, forcing a light tone. "A little addled—"

"The dragon's name is Trentius?" the mage interrupted, his scorn clear. The disdain in his voice was almost funny—he clearly hadn't paid attention to the new arrivals of Deara until Drevin handed him homework.

"No, the High Elf," I corrected, my irritation flaring briefly before exhaustion snuffed it out.

"I'm more interested in the dragon and the bond between it and the High Elf," the mage said, his focus sharp as a blade.

My attempt at deflection had failed.

He wasn't listening to me—he was controlling the conversation.

My teeth clenched. "Trentius," I repeated, forcing the words out. "The High Elf's name is Trentius. Try to keep up."

Grenthis elbowed me in the ribs, a silent warning. But I was too angry to care.

The Salt's nostrils flared. "Drevin is also interested in you." He let the words settle, like a net tightening. Then, softer, almost amused—"Elliah."

My pulse hammered. I had lost—not the fight, but the battle of words, the one Janelle had tried to prepare me for. And the worst part? I hadn't even realized when it happened. Like a fool, I'd let him pull me under.

As he rose, slow and deliberate, I matched his pace, pulling out my hammer with a weary inevitability.

"There's no fighting allowed in the library," Grenthis hissed, backing toward the door. "Let's just go."

"Hold this," I said, holding the hammer out to him. Grenthis grabbed the head and nearly dropped it, his startled curse barely registering.

The Tidewarden, whose name I had yet to learn, had lightning bolts dancing between his fingertips. I was still unclear on what my resistance to magic would do and what it wouldn't. The lightning from the elemental had hit me. I suspected it had to do with whether the lightning carried magic within it, or magic had created natural lightning. The death flames were magic, so I resisted them. The elemental's lightning was still just

190

lightning—natural in its effect, even if summoned by magic—so it shocked me.

With no energy for experiments, I went with what I knew. A sharp twist, a low sweep—Beldroth's lessons snapped into place and I took the acolyte's legs out from under him. No fighting? Well, I wasn't just going to let him fry me.

To my surprise, knocking him on his ass didn't break his focus. He barely had to move—a flick of his fingers—and lightning shot through me!

The jolt wasn't unbearable, but it was enough to knock me off balance, sending me sprawling—on top of him. His spell fizzled out on impact. For a moment, I just lay there, my head swimming, every muscle in my body aching. His magic pulsed beneath my skin, abundant and vibrant, and I craved it with a desperation that startled me. I was so sore and so tired, and he had an abundance…

"Okay," Grenthis said, his voice high-pitched with disbelief. "That just got *really* weird." Grenthis took a slow step back. "Should I be worried?"

Horror snapped me back—right as I realized my lips were on his. His pale skin had gone ashen, his breath shallow. Energy pulsed through me, warm and intoxicating, sinking into my aching limbs like rain into parched earth. For the briefest moment, I craved more. What must that have looked like to Grenthis? My first thought was, *don't tell Hughelas!* My next was: *What is wrong with me?* But as the mage slumped into unconsciousness, my final thought wasn't victory or regret—it was: *I guess you won't be needing those journals after all.*

The council doors had barely closed before Pyrravyn was already on the move, leading me through a series of dimly lit corridors. I hesitated, glancing at Bella—had she been waiting for us, or had Pyrravyn sent for her in advance? Either way, she trailed behind, small and determined, as if she already knew she was meant to be there. The air was thick, heavy with unsaid things. I'd barely gotten out a demand for answers before Pyrravyn had cut me off with something unexpected: *This is important for Bella too.*

I wasn't sure if that made me more, or less, willing to follow. Once more, I wondered what Elliah would have done in my situation. She would have demanded answers. It might have resulted in reckless destruction, but she wouldn't have tried to navigate the situation so much as push the rocks out of the way. She must have been avoiding me, or someone strategically kept us apart—my many visits to the library had only frustrated me.

As we walked, my thoughts briefly flickered to Kaelith. We were in the private halls of the royal family, where she didn't follow, but the weight of her steady gaze came with me. Was she playing a long game, or had her recent candid moments been genuine? I wasn't sure, but the memory of her voice—when she spoke on my behalf to the fisherfolk, when she'd told me of my father being lost, when she'd advised me before the council meeting—comforted me in an otherwise fraught situation.

The chamber was smaller than I expected, the air thick with the faint scent of oil and parchment. A polished obsidian table reflected the magelights that Pyrravyn and I brought in, and at its center sat two geodes—one citrine, the other amethyst. A scroll lay unfurled beside them, its edges curling slightly. My eyes flicked to Pyrravyn. Another stage, another performance.

He gestured for us to sit. I hesitated. Bella, however, took the seat immediately, her gaze locked on the crystals with wide-eyed curiosity.

"These are from the ships, aren't they?" she asked, biting her lip with interest.

Pyrravyn's face lit up with playful surprise. "And how does the wise Bella of the Nine Winds know such a secret?"

"You know it's Bella, Daughter of the Nine Winds," Bella said with the scowl of a child trying to be serious. Then, sticking her nose in the air, "A girl never reveals her sources."

Pyrravyn chuckled. To my ears he sounded genuinely pleased. I struggled to reconcile his manipulative maneuvering of the council meeting with the apparent sincerity of raising Bella.

"As she says," Pyrravyn said to me, "these are used for communication. They're the key to Eryndra's big plans for the Peacekeepers. Worldwide instant communication. It truly would be a game changer." He sounded bored by the idea. "Unfortunately, they're very hard to obtain. Do you recall, in the council meeting, the one time the Tidebringer was willing to push the limits of her sacred standards for dragons?" He said the latter with an eye-roll.

"She steals these," I concluded.

"They're stolen from blue dragons!" Bella said in awe, reaching her hand out to the geode, but stopping short of touching it.

Pyrravyn tsked. "You shall have to guard that secret carefully, Bella of the Nine Winds."

Bella nodded, not concerned about her misused title in light of such a fine secret.

"What ship has the other half?" she asked.

After a hesitant pause, Pyrravyn said, "The other end of this one isn't on board a ship. It's here, on Deara."

"Well, that's a waste, isn't it?" Bella said. "Why not just go talk with someone if they're on the island?"

"The other one is inside the Abyss," I concluded. "Where you sent my father."

Pyrravyn's expression softened, his eyes meeting mine with something close to sorrow. "It hasn't lit up in a century," he said, his voice quiet. "I assumed everyone inside had perished. Perhaps they have. It might be just the Warder or Wood Elf sending out a message."

"How would they know the language?" Bella asked.

Pyrravyn unrolled the scroll. "Perhaps instructions like these still exist down there," he said, then casually nudged the amethyst geode a few inches closer to me with one fingertip, like moving a game piece into play. "Now wait."

He fixed his gaze on the purple gem. Bella, wide-eyed, mirrored him. I followed their lead, bracing for whatever came next.

A light shone forth from the purple depths of the geode. It cut off quickly, then lit again, a little longer.

"Short-long," he said, then pointed to a place on the scroll. "See, the light patterns translate to letters."

"Well, what does it say?" Bella said, her childlike excitement barely contained.

"You can translate it yourself. In fact, I encourage you to, but it says, 'Trapped. Elliah can free us.' Once a day at the same time, we get the message, the same as it used to happen a century before. That gives me pause."

"When?" I asked. "When did you start receiving messages?"

Pyrravyn held out his hands defensively. "I believe this is day three, but it is possible I missed earlier messages." We'd been on the island for at least seven, maybe eight days? How had I lost track? My father and Illiara had gone missing on day one! "No messages have come through those geodes in decades," Pyrravyn explained. "And knowledge of this communication isn't something we share, so it had to be *me* checking. Because of the situation, I've looked in on them, but one has to be here at the right time to see the message."

"Why wait three days to tell me?" I asked, scowling.

Pyrravyn scowled back. "I only saw the lights three days ago. I'd missed the message. Yesterday was the first day I saw the message and translated it. Today, I brought you. If I'd told you yesterday, before you saw it for yourself..." He held his hands out like it was a foregone conclusion that I wouldn't have trusted him. He was right.

"Let's send a message back!" I said. I would think of some way to confirm it was actually my father and not some elf in the next room sending messages.

"It only works in one direction with each pair of geodes." Pyrravyn explained. His faintly apologetic smile returned. "They can only send messages to us with this one, not the other way around. This other one, the amethyst, is meant for us to send messages, but they never respond when we do. I don't know if the other end got damaged, or if something about the trap prevents the message from getting through." He scratched his cheek, frowning slightly.

My mind spun with magical postulates and theorems. But what Pyrravyn suggested was essentially the same thing Drevin had proposed with the Tempest Crown. Polarized magic would not be symmetrical.

"You said it hadn't lit up in a century," Bella said. "What did it say back then?" Good question.

"Back then, the geodes were in your mother's possession, not mine," Pyrravyn said. "But she let me see the message. It was very similar. Something like, 'Trapped. A troll can free us.'"

Chills ran down my spine. *A troll can free us. Elliah can free us.* The messages were consistent. But Pyrravyn might have entirely invented his story. A cruel manipulation. I'd witnessed his ability to play people like pieces on a board. Yet even as I questioned him, another part of me recognized that much of what Pyrravyn did seemed to come from a genuine concern in a legitimately complex situation. A voice in my head whispered, *What if it's true?*

"It's why Lyrei left Deara," Pyrravyn said. "Presumably, the whole reason you exist is because of the message from this geode. She went searching for a troll to bring back. To free..." He trailed off like he'd said too much.

"To free who, Cousin?" Bella pleaded.

"To free your grandmother," he said with a rush. "Miryndel, my mother." He turned to me. "Lyrei's mother too." He sighed and rubbed his eyes. "The original trap sprang long ago, before I was born. When Selthira was old enough to rule, my mother took a force into the trap to attempt its destruction. She took the other halves of these geodes with her. That was a century ago, and to some extent, she succeeded—she may not have escaped or brought down the trap, but she got out the message to send a troll in. Lyrei took on the challenge."

"Why are you showing me this when you don't want to let Elliah rescue them?" I asked. He already had the high ground.

"I need you to understand—I do want your father out of there." I tried not to let my doubt show.

"You don't have to believe my altruism," he said. "Believe that we think there are treasures down there from before the Breaking. Things that would help the world."

"Things that would help *you*," I retorted.

"Things that would help Deara," he consented. "And, possibly, my mother."

I said nothing, wary of where he led me. Pyrravyn watched me, then shifted tactics with practiced ease.

"Trolls." He grimaced. "Elliah." He held out hands, balancing imaginary scales. "Her resistance to magic makes her uniquely suited. But, by the same token, she is also uniquely suited to saving Deara from the failure of the Tempest Crown."

Bella gasped.

"I'm sorry," Pyrravyn said, putting a hand on her shoulder. "I'd wanted to tell you later, in private. We have a plan to save Deara, but it requires Elliah's help."

I wanted to argue, to claw my way past Pyrravyn's cold logic, but Bella's trembling voice rooted me in place. "If we don't protect Deara," she whispered, "they'll die anyway." She put her tiny hand over mine on the scroll that held the key to the messages.

The words weighed heavier than I'd expected. Pyrravyn leaned closer, his voice soft but no less cutting. "I want your father out of there, Hughelas. I want my mother out of there. But not at the cost of everything."

I met his gaze, searching for a crack, a weakness, some hint that he was lying. I found none. The trap wasn't just beneath the island—it was there, surrounding me.

"Then let's hope Deara is worth saving," I said, pulling away from Bella's hand and turning toward the door.

Neither of them followed me.

I'd been there before. Too many times in the past days, always just missing her, always finding some excuse to come back. Kaelith had made a joke about it. I hadn't laughed. But now, standing there with no excuse left, I hesitated.

She hadn't seen me yet. For a moment, I let myself take her in—the way her brow furrowed over whatever she was writing, the smudge of ink on her wrist, the way her braid had come half undone, stray wisps catching the lantern light.

Ten days.

And now I had to be the one to break her world apart.

Kaelith trailed behind me, casting a glance around the towering shelves. A flicker of a smirk—brief, knowing—pulled at her lips, but it faded just as quickly. She knew how many times I'd looked for Elliah. How many times I'd come back, circling the library like a man caught in his own orbit.

I gave her a look, a bit of a plea.

Kaelith's amusement dimmed, replaced by something quieter, something almost... pity? Sympathy? "Sure," she murmured, her voice softer than I expected. "I'll leave you to your little reunion." No judgment in her tone, just a careful neutrality. Then, a flicker of her usual edge: "I'll be near the main counter, far from the Thaldrak Curnshaw Collection, in case you need anything—or don't."

She hesitated—a fraction of a second—then turned on her heel, her braid swishing behind her as she disappeared into the labyrinth of shelves.

When I looked back, Elliah was watching us, frowning at Kaelith's departing form. Her brown eyes locked on mine. A flicker of hesitation— like she wasn't sure what expression she *should* wear. Then a smile, quick but uncertain, chased by the flush of color on her cheeks. A test. Was I still angry? Had I given up on her? Was I still *there*?

"I need to talk to you." The words came out rougher than I intended. I cleared my throat, shifting on my feet, resisting the urge to rub the back of my neck. She wasn't going to like this.

Her posture softened, and the corners of her mouth twitched as if suppressing a smile. "You do?"

There was a lightness in her voice, tentative but unmistakable. I pulled out the chair opposite her, the scrape of wood on stone loud in the quiet space.

I opened my mouth. Shut it again. What if I started with something else? Asked how she was. Commented on the ink stain on her wrist. Anything.

But there wasn't time. There was never time for *us*.

"It's about our parents," I said.

Her expression froze, the softness replaced by something far sharper. "What about them?"

"They're in trouble," I said, the words falling heavy between us.

Elliah stared at me, unblinking. For a moment, I thought she hadn't heard me. Then she leaned forward, her voice low and tight. "What's happened?"

"They're trapped. Some kind of ancient magic, like what we encountered in the swamps of Fael Themar. They call it the Abyss."

Her eyes narrowed, as if assembling puzzle pieces.

"They're sending messages from inside the Abyss," I said. "Specifically, they say to send you in."

Her breath caught, and for just a heartbeat, she looked at me—*really* looked at me. A flicker of something deep, unreadable. Ten days of near-misses, of silence, of not knowing where we stood.

Then she swallowed, forcing something down. The set of her shoulders tightened. A sharp inhale—resolve. "It must be like the artifact we found before. They think I can deactivate it. Let's go." She closed her two books and gathered them, turning to head out.

I rose to follow her, keeping my voice calm. This would be the hard part. "We can't act yet."

She whirled to face me. "What?"

"There's a risk," I said, struggling to keep my voice steady against the weight of her anger. "If you go in to rescue them now and something goes wrong—if you get trapped—then it's all over. I lose you, and..." I swallowed hard. "And we lose any chance of saving Deara."

"We're doing this for Deara now?" she said, her voice low and tired. "The same place that kidnapped you, kept us apart, and has tangled us in messes since we got here?"

Frustration bubbled up inside me. She wasn't wrong. "The Tempest Crown is failing, Elliah. The device that creates the ring of storms. If that collapses, the blue dragons will pour in. Everyone will die—everyone, including us, including our parents."

Her laugh was short and bitter. "What does that have to do with my going into this Abyss or not?"

"To fix the Tempest Crown, we need to stabilize its magic, and that means stealing a black dragon's egg."

She stared at me, her face a storm of disbelief and fury. "You're serious."

I nodded. "I wish I wasn't."

She set the books back on the table, gripping its edge so tightly her knuckles went white. "So what's the plan?"

"They'll need your anti-magic to steal the egg," I admitted. "But if something happens to you..." My voice faltered. "I don't know how I would ever—"

Her expression softened, just a fraction, but her words were still cold. "You're worried about me."

"Yes," I whispered. "But I don't see another path forward."

She looked down at the table, her fingers tracing the edge of the journal she'd set aside. When she finally spoke, her voice was quieter. "Maybe there's another way." She slid the journal toward me. "Take a look at this."

I took the journal, its worn leather cover cool against my palms. "What is this?"

"From one of Drevin's acolytes," she said flatly.

"Drevin's?" I echoed, my stomach sinking.

"Yes," she snapped. "I stole it." She blushed so deeply that I had a sinking sensation in my stomach about what she might have done to obtain it. She wasn't just embarrassed about stealing it. I... didn't want to know. "You think Pyrravyn's the only one playing games? Drevin knows things he's not telling anyone—about the Crown, about the dragons, about everything."

I looked down at the journal, my thoughts spinning. The idea of Elliah stealing didn't surprise me as much as it probably should have. The idea of what she might have done to make her blush the way she had when Janelle caught us kissing?

"Elliah," I said carefully, "this is dangerous."

"No more dangerous than stealing a dragon's egg," she shot back.

She wasn't wrong.

I set the journal on the table and flipped it open.

"Drevin knows a more efficient way to recharge the Tempest Crown," Elliah said as I thumbed through, "but he's not sharing it with Maelith. I was making a copy." She thumped the book she'd kept.

I sat down in the chair before me. "I... I don't think so."

"What?" she said, her voice taking a dangerous edge.

"This isn't about the Tempest Crown or storm magic." I gestured at the charts and formulas. "These are about leylines and tying magic to physical locations."

"What?" she repeated, color returning to her cheeks. It wasn't the same blush—she was just embarrassed she might have the wrong information.

"Is it possible he's trying to find a more optimal position for the Tempest Crown?" I suggested, trying to connect the dots. "A place that would allow it to charge more easily?"

Her blush let up as she digested that she hadn't stolen a book from someone for no reason.

"Can I take it back and study it?" I asked.

"I got most of it copied," she said, sliding the other book my way. "I'd intended to give it to you when I finished. And return that one before its absence caused trouble. More trouble."

I flipped to the end of the original version, and it looked like notes on failed experiments. Elliah's copy had the theory. That was all I needed. I swapped with her.

"But if this doesn't pan out?" I asked her.

"Yes." She sighed, watching me carefully. "I'll help with the egg." A pause—just long enough for me to wonder if she wanted me to talk her out of it. Then, with forced lightness, she added, "But if I die trying to get it, I *will* haunt you."

"Wouldn't have it any other way," I said, a small grin creeping on my face. "Besides, I'll be right there dying alongside you. But together we can haunt Pyravyn, Drevin, Maelith... pretty much every leader on this island."

My grin faded. The humor barely lasted before the weight of what I had to say settled back over me. "Elliah," I said, quieter, "when I saw you last, I came here to check on you. My search for Drevin was just a cover. I wanted to be sure *you* were okay."

Her smile faltered. "I know," she said softly.

I blinked. "You do?"

"I got your messages." She looked away. "Not all of them, and not right away. It was safer to keep us apart, just for a bit."

My breath caught. "Safer?" That didn't sound like Elliah. "Was that *your* decision?"

She didn't meet my eyes at first. "I didn't fight it." Her gaze met mine again, steady now. "But I missed you. Every day."

I walked around the table, irritated that it kept us apart, but she'd also taken a step back, hiding behind a chair. "Wanting to be sure I'm okay and sending me into a dragon's lair don't fit well together."

The emotional turmoil of missing her, worrying about her, having her say she missed me, but still placing a barrier between us... a bite crept into my voice. "I'm not *sending* you," I said. "We can try to come up with another plan. Right now, I don't see another way to keep our parents safe." My failure pained me—I understood why she would see me as the culprit. "You're right," I said, defeated. "I am the bad guy in this story."

"I'm sorry," she said suddenly, breaking through my thoughts. "You're not the bad guy. Your father is trapped too."

She stepped around the chair, her hand hovering near mine before she wrapped it around my wrist. Her touch was warm, grounding me in the moment.

Then she hugged me, and I regretted that I still held the journal between us, its edges digging awkwardly into my ribs.

When she pulled back, her blush deepened, but she didn't retreat. I set the journal down, the motion automatic, as her gaze stayed locked on mine. Everything we'd been holding back—fear, frustration, and something unspoken—rushed forward all at once. I reached for her, but for just a breath, she stilled—caught between the past and the present. Between Deara and the life we'd had before.

Then she closed the distance—a choice, deliberate and fierce—meeting me with something fierce and aching, both of us trying to steal back the time we'd lost.

When we finally broke apart, breathless, she whispered, "The Thaldrak Curnshaw Collection of Arcane Regulations. I found it."

She slid her fingers through mine, firm and steady, then nodded toward the table. I grabbed the book she'd copied for me, clutching it tightly as we moved deeper into the library.

Elliah ~ 13

Hughelas had left hours before, yet his voice still echoed in my ears. *We can try to come up with another plan.*

Try.

But I wasn't waiting. Not anymore. Not for someone else to make my choices for me, forced to react while the leaders of Deara played their games. Hughelas had come looking for me—not as a tool to wield, but as myself. He'd reminded me who I was. Not something to be used. Not something to be controlled.

And if I was going to walk into the fire, I'd do it on my own terms.

Drevin entered like a man who had already won, his mind two steps ahead of the rest of us. He barely registered the grand chamber or the people within it—only the prize he had come to claim. His eyes flicked past me, past Janelle, scanning the shelves and boxes behind the counter as if the grimoire might present itself without delay. Whatever pleasantries or formalities existed in the space between arrival and acquisition, Drevin had no use for them.

"Elliah." His voice curled at the edges with amusement, though his sharp eyes skimmed past me, still searching. "I am told you've got something for me?"

Janelle had sent word ahead, letting him believe he would collect the Grimoire of the Thunderborn without fuss. But I wasn't about to let him pluck it from my hands like a ripe fruit. We stood in the library's heart, Janelle inside the opposite end of the circular counter, watching from a distance, giving me room. No other librarians were there, but prying eyes peeked from behind the shelves that marked the aisles of the library's wheel-like floor-plan.

Yet, it felt like a battlefield.

And the last time I'd tried to fight with words, I'd lost. The acolyte in the tunnels had toyed with me, steering the conversation where he wanted it, and I'd let him. I hadn't even realized I was losing until he'd trapped me. What if Drevin did the same? What if I walked straight into another verbal ambush? I'd been exhausted then—too drained, too slow. But if I failed with Drevin, what excuse would I have?

Then I remembered—and not just the kiss. A flush crept up my cheeks as I thought of everything that had come after. Not just that, but how much I'd *needed* it. Needed him. Because Hughelas hadn't come to outmaneuver me. He hadn't tried to pull me into someone else's war. He'd come to remind me I was more than a piece on a board.

And I wasn't going to let Drevin, or anyone else, forget that again.

Had my mother been there, Drevin wouldn't have made it five steps before she had a blade to his throat. No hesitation. No patience. If you couldn't run, then initiate the fight—that was her way. But Janelle had spent days grafting her own lessons onto me, pruning my wild instinct to strike first, replacing it with something more subtle. The hardest part wasn't the restraint—it was convincing myself that words could hit as hard as a hammer.

I took a measured breath and held my ground. "Before I give it to you, I want to know what you plan to do with it."

Drevin stopped, tilting his head like I was a specimen under glass. His ever-present quill hovered in his hand, poised to dissect my words the way a butcher separates flesh from bone. "That's a bold demand for someone with no leverage."

I shrugged, feigning indifference, though inside, I bristled. I'd slipped the hammer off when Janelle had nudged me, pointing out Drevin's entrance to the library. If I needed to fight, my ability to neutralize magic provided more power than the strength of the hammer. "Maybe. But Maelith locked the grimoire away for a reason." In fact, I suspected Maelith had locked it away because he didn't want anyone else harmed by—or harming—the elemental bound to it, rather than trying to keep hidden the knowledge contained therein. But I didn't know that for certain.

His lips curved in something resembling amusement. "Caution, how novel. What exactly do you think I'll do with it?"

"Storm magic," I said. "You'll harness it, shape it. You'll use it to turn the sky itself into a weapon. If that wasn't the case, you wouldn't be so interested."

He exhaled a quiet chuckle. "Less novel. What if I told you the Tempest Crown is failing? That without new knowledge, its magic will unravel and take Deara with it?"

I folded my arms. "How lucky for you that Deara's fate happens to align with your personal ambitions. Besides, Maelith keeps the Tempest Crown running—if there were knowledge in the grimoire worth using, he would have done so already."

"Maelith is good with storm magic. I will concede that. But he doesn't understand the underpinnings of magic the way I do. I believe I will find something where he hasn't. Now hand it over."

His attitude, his tone, his presumption—they set my teeth on edge, tension coiling in my shoulders. I wanted to leap over the counter—I pictured it vividly, imagined the precise angle of my bone knife against the exposed skin of his neck. A warning. A lesson. But Janelle's voice echoed in my mind: *Diplomacy is how you win the wars you can't afford to fight.*

Fighting Drevin wouldn't serve me. But winning didn't have to mean drawing blood.

I pulled the grimoire from under the counter and held it out to him. "This is what you came for," I said, keeping my tone neutral. "Just remember who made it possible."

Drevin took the book with eager anticipation, running his fingers over the ancient binding. His gray eyes flicked back to me, considering. "You're proving more... interesting than I anticipated, Elliah."

I forced myself not to stiffen. The last thing I wanted was to be interesting to Drevin. "I'd rather be forgettable," I said flatly.

"I have a parting question for you," he said as he petted the book like a prized cat. "Tell me, Elliah—why do dragons collect their dead?"

I blinked. What? That had nothing to do with storm magic. With the grimoire. With—anything. Or did it? A flicker of a memory from the Salty Squirt—Trentius having to tell Smoky repeatedly to ignore my hammer which the captain had locked away. Later, Trentius saying something about the ocean around Deara "swimming with memories."

I opened my mouth, but no answer came. Drevin's smirk sharpened—like he knew I grasped at something just outside my reach.

"Think on it," he murmured, turning away, his focus already shifting to the prize in his hands.

And I did. Even after he disappeared into the tunnels, his question clung to me like damp clothes after a rain.

I barely had time to exhale before the next storm arrived.

The library doors slammed open with a force that rattled the shelves. The scent of storm-scorched air curled through the aisles, sharp and acrid, raising the hairs on my arms. Tiny sparks of lightning jumped from Maelith's white and silver-streaked hair, flickering down to his fingertips like impatient predators.

At least he wasn't throwing water around—that would have earned him the wrath of every librarian in Deara. Though starting a fire would be even worse. I glanced back and noticed that Janelle had a canister of the fire retardant parked next to her, but she stayed back.

The storm-wizard strode forward, his expression thunderous, his gaze locked on me.

"You," he snarled, his voice the promise of a coming storm.

Every muscle in my body coiled, every instinct screaming: Move. My nerves still remembered the storm elemental's fury, still expected to be flung backward, burning, broken.

But I forced my feet to stay planted. Forced my voice to stay level.

"Me," I said.

"You stole from me," he seethed, stopping only when the counter forced him to. The surrounding air crackled dangerously. "Do you have any idea what you've done?"

"I recovered something lost," I corrected, channeling Janelle's lesson. "And if I hadn't, Drevin would have found another way to take it." Maelith opened his mouth to yell, but I kept going. "Only he wouldn't have freed its guardian."

That gave him pause. He shut his mouth, but his storm-gray eyes narrowed, distrust sharpening his expression. "And what exactly did *we* get, girl?"

I reached into my coat and pulled out the second journal—the one I had taken from Drevin's acolyte.

Maelith raised an eyebrow.

"I thought you might want this," I said. "To even the scales."

He didn't move to take it right away. Suspicion warred with curiosity in his gaze.

"I won't pretend to understand it," I said, "But if you want answers about what Drevin's been up to, this is your best chance."

A long, tense silence stretched between us. Finally, Maelith reached out and took the journal. His fingers curled around it like he was afraid it might vanish.

He exhaled sharply. "You're reckless," he muttered, tucking the book away. "But not as big of a fool as I assumed."

I took that as the closest thing to a compliment I was ever going to get from him.

With a final glare, Maelith turned on his heel and strode away, the acrid smell of burned air receding with him.

I let out a slow breath and turned toward the person who had stayed silent through the entire ordeal.

Janelle watched me with a small, knowing smile. "That went better than I expected."

I scowled. I hadn't wanted to deal with either of the Stormwrights, but Janelle had refused to do the trades for me. "You thought I would fail?"

"I thought you'd lose your temper," she said. "I'm impressed you didn't."

I leaned against the counter, scrubbing a hand over my face. "I still don't see why it was necessary." Janelle would have sent both men away smiling, each thinking they'd landed the better end of the deal.

Janelle walked over and took my hands, her touch gentle, grounding. "Because you're learning to wield something more than your hammer, Eliah. You're training to fight using words. Power isn't only about what you can break—it's about what you can build."

I frowned. "I don't build things." It came out almost like a reflex, a knee-jerk denial. But something in me hesitated.

Magic failed before me. Cenaedth had nearly collapsed because of me. Alenor's government overturned. Destruction sought me, a parched root probing for water. But... hadn't I shaped something here?

Redirected something instead of breaking it?

Janelle smirked. "You just did. And one day, you'll realize just how much." She let go of my hands and went back to the other side of the counter, sorting through books like it was an ordinary day at the library.

For a long moment, I stood there in silence, mulling over her words.

The version of me from weeks ago would have fought. Would have leapt over the counter and pressed my knife to Drevin's throat just to prove I could. And I might have won.

But winning a fight wasn't the point. It wasn't about proving my strength—it was about deciding where to use it.

Hughelas didn't see me as a weapon to be wielded. He didn't love me for the power I lacked or wielded—he loved me for who I was. Janelle hadn't forced me to abandon my instincts—only to sharpen them into something stronger.

Diplomacy wasn't strength as I knew it—it wasn't battle or force.

But for the first time, I chose it for myself. And for the first time, I understood why it mattered.

A legitimate storm roared threateningly as Kaelith led me down the path to the Tempest Crown. It was odd in a way—the constant presence of the storm wall on the horizon acclimated one to the noise and visuals. An actual storm had snuck in and loomed overhead.

The upcoming mission loomed as much as the storm—undeniable, inescapable. If the Tempest Crown failed, dragons would destroy us all. So I wanted to see the thing that dictated our choices, the thing we would steal a dragon's child to fix. I needed to see the Tempest Crown for myself.

The wind whipped at my cloak, tugging it like some impatient child, eager for my attention. I tightened my grip on the journal Elliah had given me, its weight a steadying presence in my arms. The diagrams and notes inside spoke of limits and power, of ancient magic tied to place, and as I walked, I wondered what truths might lie hidden in the artifact that guarded the island.

I'd intended to give it to you when I finished. And return that one before its absence caused trouble. More trouble. Elliah had risked much to get me the information in that book. But every time my thoughts turned to Elliah, the passion that started from our kiss flared hot, blinding me for a moment before the weight of everything returned.

But if I die trying to get it, I will haunt you. That sobered me—was I forcing us down a path that would damn us both? And so my thoughts circled on the long walk. Curiosity, passion, dread. Curiosity, passion, dread. The cycle ground against me like river stones trapped in a current, tumbling endlessly, wearing me down with each turn.

When I reached the small building, the understated accommodations of an artifact that predated the Breaking surprised me. The building was simple, almost disappointingly so. A squat, whitewashed structure, it stood in stark contrast to the raging storm that surrounded the island and lingered overhead. There were no carvings, no grandiose embellishments, only smooth stone walls weathered by centuries of wind and salt. A single set of double doors, reinforced with tarnished metal bands, marked the entrance. They seemed mundane, almost out of place for something so critical to the island's survival. A mage in white robes with dark blue markings pushed himself tiredly away from the wall as we approached. He didn't try to stop us.

Inside, the air shifted immediately—calmer, heavier. The room was circular and stark, its walls unadorned save for faint scorch marks that hinted at the artifact's volatile nature and the cabinetry and contraptions built for sitting or resting. At the center, the Tempest Crown stood atop a dais of black stone, the base very much like the one under Fael Themar, lined with metal symbols and decorated with gems. Atop the pedestal, unlike the one I'd seen before, crystal spires reached upward like jagged teeth toward a circular opening at the top of the building. Each shard crackled faintly with contained lightning, a pale glow pulsing from their cores like a heartbeat. Above the crystals, a swirling vortex of energy hovered, casting fractured light and shadow across the room. It felt alive, impossibly old and impossibly dangerous, and yet the surrounding space remained quiet, holding its breath.

Its power was undeniable, and the part of me that loved magic and history wanted to understand it, know its story. It was what we were risking everything for. But I had to clamp down my curiosity about it to ask the more relevant question—was it really our only choice?

Maelith stood at the edge of the Crown, his back to me. His long white robes, etched with elaborate dark blue patterns, hung as still as death. His posture was rigid, his shoulders set with a tension that spoke of weariness. As I drew closer, he turned, his face sharp with irritation, which didn't lessen when he recognized me.

"Hughelas," he said, his voice clipped. "Scion of the lost daughter. What brings you to this place? I trust it's important." His tone suggested it wasn't.

"I wanted to see it for myself," I said, nodding at the Tempest Crown. "To understand what it takes to keep it going, the burden you bear."

Maelith let out a sharp, humorless laugh, his expression darkening. "You want to know how long I can hold it together, and whether there is another path we can choose." A flicker of hope sparked in me—if even Maelith, the one who bore the burden of the Tempest Crown every day, doubted Pyrravyn's plan, then maybe another path existed. I had to find it. Before it was too late.

He turned his gaze from me, his face becoming less harsh as he looked at the pedestal. "It failed once already. A momentary lapse. And yes, I've heard the stories—how the winds broke, how the sea trembled. Dragons in the ocean and sky." He looked up toward the swirling vortex above the crystalline spires, his gaze distant. "The Tempest Crown is a relic of the time before the Breaking, a work of dragons and elves. Together, we shaped it—woven with magic far beyond what remains in our diminished world."

He gestured faintly at the base of the artifact. "Those symbols you see, those gemstones embedded in the stone, were carved and placed by hands that no longer exist. Dragon claws, elven tools, crafting something that bound storms and kept even dragons away. But magic like that requires more than just power. It requires sacrifice. Constant vigilance." He glanced at me, his eyes shadowed. "It was not meant for one person to carry."

I studied the Tempest Crown as lightning coursed through jagged crystals reaching from the pedestal. While the details differed from the artifact under the swamps, the similarities were unmistakable. Lines of and swirls of metal presented symbols of magic that tugged at familiarity without being the ones used in our modern era. Gems dotted a pedestal, much like the other one I'd seen. But instead of an amorphous blob of rock atop it, yellow crystals jutted from the surface. "This plan of Pyrravyn's…" I began, but hesitated at that point.

"Dragons changed after the Breaking," Maelith said. "Or so I understand. What we have now are mere scraps—fragments of something far greater. I shoulder the burden of keeping this artifact going because no one else can. Because if I don't, we all die." Maelith mimicked my voice then. "This plan of Pyrravyn's…" He puffed out a breath. "I don't know."

He paused, his gaze flickering toward the lightning at the center of the Crown. For a moment, his expression softened, and he sighed. "Beldroth and Illiara came to me not long ago. Illiara's magic was… surprisingly effective at replenishing my strength. I was rude to her, of course." He waved a hand dismissively, though there was a hint of regret in his voice. "Her magic helped. It might have been another way."

Could that have been another way? Use Illiara's magic to replenish mana and keep using the Tempest Crown as they had been? But that would tether Illiara to the artifact as surely as it tethered Maelith. That was no long-term solution, even if we pitted Elliah against the Abyss to rescue Illiara.

"They disappeared shortly after they left you," I said, watching his reaction carefully. "No one knows what became of them." That was a lie, of course. Pyrravyn and Bella knew. I knew. Elliah knew. But I wanted to see what Maelith suspected.

His eyes pinched, then darted to Kaelith. He knew, or at least suspected, *something*. "Foolish," Maelith muttered, shaking his head. "They didn't understand the dangers of this island."

My jaw tightened. *Didn't understand?* No one had warned them. And now Elliah was being asked to throw herself into harm's way to save them. Which begged the question: what wasn't Pyrravyn telling me?

I had one more wild goose to chase. "This journal," I said, holding it up for him to see. "It's a copy of work from one of Drevin's acolytes. It might reduce the magic needed to recharge the Tempest Crown." It didn't read that way to me, but… no stone unturned. I wouldn't let Deara's secrets strangle Elliah.

Maelith shook his head. "Drevin and I don't get along." Maelith's lip twitched in a snarl for a moment. "But we discussed his research on that topic. We even tried a few things. It addled poor Rymalie's wits so badly that I've lost her as one of the few Tidewardens who can help with recharging the Crown. Though she recovers, her absence is part of why we are so badly stressed now."

So our only options were to risk Elliah in pulling our parents out of the Abyss, or risk her in retrieving a dragon's egg. Could I sneak Elliah out of Deara to search for the entrance to the Abyss? Would Kaelith show me the way? But even if we did reach the Abyss, what would happen when Elliah reached the artifact? The last time she forced an artifact to shut down with her resistance, it nearly killed her. Her resistance worked—but it had nearly destroyed her. What if the Abyss was worse? What if ancient dragons and elves built it to resist her as much as it resisted magic?

No. I wouldn't risk that.

But while I'd wrestled with my doubts, Maelith's patience wore thin, like a cloud bank unraveling before the wind. His expression hardened, irritation sharpening back into its usual edge. "If you've no more questions, leave me. The Crown requires constant attention, and I don't have time for idle chatter."

The weight of Maelith's weariness hung heavy in the air. Pressing him further seemed pointless.

"I'll leave you to your work," I said, inclining my head. "Thank you for your time."

As I walked back down the long road, the storm threatening me, I couldn't shake the image of Maelith standing alone within the Tempest Crown, holding back chaos by sheer force of will. For all his crankiness, he was one of the more open Dearans I had encountered, even if it did all spill out in fits of nastiness. For all his bitterness, there was something tragic in his isolation—a man tethered to an ancient artifact that demanded everything and gave nothing in return.

It reminded me of Elliah. Of the weight already pressing down on her shoulders like the storm above us. I'd told her we would find another plan. But with every step, I feared I had lied. And that might have been the answer I'd come looking for. If Maelith had known another way—if there had been any other path—he would have taken it.

Maybe Pyrravyn was right.

Maybe the egg was the only way.

The Dreadwake creaked and groaned as it cut through the waves, like it might shudder apart at any moment. I stood at the prow, staring at the jagged silhouette of the island rising ahead of us, its black peaks wreathed in a haze that seemed to cling to the dark stone like a curse.

The air clung heavier near the island, charged. Shattercove. Every breath tasted of salt and ash, like the very earth was warning us to turn back, while the island itself watched us, waiting for us to come closer.

Four days. That's how long it had been since Maelith confirmed what I already suspected—there wasn't another way. Or maybe there was, but not one with any less risk to Elliah. In the end, *she'd* made the call. I'd laid out both paths as evenly as possible—rescuing our parents from the Abyss, or taking the dragon's egg—but I knew the moment her gaze lingered on me which way it would go. She'd watched me too carefully, her gaze steady while her hands curled into her sleeves. Too careful. Measured. The way she gets when she's trying not to let me see how much something hurts. I told myself I hadn't influenced her—but what if I had? My fear of watching her die in the Abyss might have been too easy to read.

And yet, my gut told me I'd lied to both of us. Standing on the Dreadwake, approaching the looming cliffs, with sudden gusts of wind howling against the island and ship, I realized I'd pushed Elliah toward the path that would keep her alive just a little longer. Because I couldn't bear to lose her.

Nagging thoughts of Gormar crept in on top of my fears for Elliah. I'd told him—firmly, even a little harshly—that he needed to stay behind. That he had nothing to contribute to this mission. And I'd believed it. He wasn't a fighter. He wasn't stealthy or subtle. But part of me also hadn't wanted his dramatics, or his know-it-all attitude. Now I wondered if that had been a mistake. Not because he might've helped, but because it had cost something. Maybe him. Maybe me.

Kaelith leaned casually against the railing nearby, her sharp eyes fixed on the island. She had said little since we'd set sail hours before, passing through the storm shield and out to sea in silence, though her presence felt as deliberate as ever. "Charming," she said dryly. Elliah, who stood next to me, squinted at her as though Kaelith had kicked a squirrel.

Marinna stood in the center of the ship, eyes closed and casting, but not so deep in a spell that she was unable to find a time to speak. "No blues in the water," she reported, "but there are plenty of rocks."

The captain of the ship, Kael, smiled like he was enjoying himself. "Those who fish this island say that's always been the danger here. Sudden storms dash their ships against hidden rocks."

"Why can't you use your magic to chase away the storms?" I asked, genuinely curious, but also apprehensive.

"While fisherfolk are critical to our existence," Pyrravyn answered, instead of the captain, "those with enough power to chase away a storm are typically recruited into other areas—trade, research, Peacekeepers. The crew of the Dreadwake have the power to clear this weather up—if it's an ordinary storm."

"But the Scion here has forbidden us from doing so," the captain added. "We are to... sneak... in."

We were near enough to the island that one of the ship's rowboats could get us the rest of the way, but the Dreadwake continued, as fat drops of rain began to splatter around us.

"There's a cove right up under that cliff," Captain Kael said. "It provides some protection. We will anchor there and prepare for a quick departure."

"I assume there are caves we should target?" Elliah said, raising her voice as the rain added its thrum to the noise of waves crashing on the island and the creaking of the ship. "How do we get to them?"

"No," Pyrravyn said. "There are no caves that I know of. Black dragons don't burrow. Their nests are out in the open, in the storm. You just have to go... up."

"Just climb up that wet cliff in the wind?" Elliah asked, her voice thick with sarcasm. "That's all?"

"Wood Elves are good climbers," Pyrravyn said, his tone dripping with feigned patience.

"Not in a gale while being struck by lightning!" Elliah protested. "That's insane."

"I can do it," Marinna said, her determination evident as she spoke. "With the tiniest of magical bindings, and yes, being a Wood Elf, I can get up there. Once I'm up, I'll lower a rope."

We'd made it into the cove, and the Dreadwake weighed anchor, shuddering as it came to rest in the relative calm of the sheltered waters. Water still pelted us from above. "Are you sure you want to attempt that?" I asked Marinna quietly. I knew how to cast the same binding spell, but her ability far exceeded mine. If I had to bet on one of us, it would be her.

"No," she said, letting her spell on the Dreadwake go. "Like you, I'm just trying to hold things together. Well," she added with a grin, "maybe slightly more literally than you." At least she managed a sense of humor. "But," and her smile stretched thin, "I don't want to do this forever. I joined because it would have been unbearable to let your father lose you like that. It means a lot to me to see a father care for his son. But *you* have to figure out a way to get us all off this island. Well, not *this* island. Deara. Well, this one too, please."

While she joked, it was actually the deepest conversation about her motives she'd ever had with me. I didn't know what made Marinna tick. She'd joined up to escape her home—I'd gathered that much. And my father had taken her on as a kind of pet project, as he'd done from time to time with missionaries who'd come to Bellon to train. It was so normal to me, I'd practically ignored the interaction. I learned she'd joined the expedition to retrieve the geodes. I'd assumed it was a Peacekeeper assignment, something Pyrravyn or Eryndra had assigned her. But she'd done it for her own reasons. She'd stepped up in Cenaedth and saved us all. And she was doing it again.

I regretted how little I'd given her in return. The least I could do was try to understand her better, and she seemed anxious, eager to talk. "And what is it you will do with your time once we are free of all this?" I asked her.

She looked at me and hesitated. "Sculpt," she said, her eyes downcast and her shoulders drawn in, like she was afraid of being laughed at. After everything brave she'd done, and everything she'd offered to do, simply being known scared her more.

"That's wonderful, Marinna. And a very natural pastime for Warders." Possibly, the Wood Elves in Fael Themar *had* laughed at her, but in the Contentious Mountains, the home country of the Warders, it was non-sculpting elves like me who were the odd ones. "I hope you make it to Aendolin one day and can see the treasures there."

She raised her head back up. When she realized I was completely serious, she bit her lip and puffed a breath out of her nose. Then, just as she nodded her head and prepared to say more, Captain Kael interrupted us by handing Marinna a rope with a grappling hook on the end.

"Smoky can fly it up," Trentius offered, appearing out of nowhere.

Smoky! Of course. I should have thought of that. Trentius had insisted on going with us. Going with Marinna, specifically. He'd done it with a quiet determination that brooked no quarter, and with none of his usual pithy alliterations. At that moment, I was grateful—no one needed to risk climbing the cliff without a rope. It wouldn't just be faster; it would be safer.

"The sooner we're out of here, the better," the captain said, handing the rope and hook over to Trentius.

Trentius hesitated, turning the hook in his hands like it might betray him. "You're sure your ribs are healed?" he asked quietly.

Marinna blinked, surprised. "You remembered?"

"You nearly coughed up a lung. Hard to forget."

I didn't know what injury they were referencing, but I understood

Marinna's observation—it wasn't hard for Trentius to forget things. At least that used to be true. I couldn't remember the last time he'd uttered something absurd.

She gave a faint smile, one hand brushing her side. "Hurts less every day. Healing's done. I just keep telling the ache that."

He nodded once, then looked away. "Good. Don't let it happen again."

The High Elf walked to a relatively clear space between rigging on the deck and held the rope and hook aloft. Smoky hopped off a spar and flapped his wings, reaching out his claws to take the grappling hook, letting the rope drop and dangle behind. With jerks and spurts, the rope uncoiled as Stormy disappeared into the rain, the wind swallowing the beat of his wings.

Elliah and I clambered into the rowboat they'd lowered, the rain driving against us in sharp bursts as we prepared to make our way to the cliff wall. One of the Dreadwake's crew joined us, a burly sailor for a Salt, with hands calloused from years at sea. Kaelith climbed in next, her gaze flicking briefly to Elliah's daggered glare before settling back to the cliff, her composure unshaken and her purpose clear.

Marinna dropped in with us. "I'm going with you. I can see things," she said in a tone of frustration. "Even in the dark. I think you're going to need me."

I didn't know what that meant, exactly—we needed a longer conversation—but it sounded like some of the older Warders back in Aendolin. While I hated putting Marinna in more danger, she seemed willing, and we probably did need the help.

When Trentius climbed over the railing, Marinna shouted up. "Stay on the Dreadwake, Trentius! Protect the ship." I agreed with her. Of all of us, he had the least business scaling a cliff. High Elves weren't known for their strength, and Trentius, for all his heart, wasn't exactly strong or clever—his presence might slow us. But he gave a little wave before disappearing from sight, leaving Smoky to do a lazy fly-by of the rowboat. Trentius would keep an eye on both us *and* the ship.

The boat rocked as we shoved off, the Dreadwake's lanterns fading behind us as we entered the swirling storm. The cliff was not far at all— a running jump from the lowest spar would have gotten me there—but in the storm, that would have landed me in the drink.

"Let me lead," Marinna said. "My magic can keep the rope secured."

I knew the same spells, but didn't have Marinna's raw power. We let her go first.

The trek up the cliffside quickly became grueling. The rope held firm under the weight of each of us, but every gust of wind threatened to hurl us back into the roiling sea. My fingers, numb from the chilly rain, fumbled against the wet, knotted rope, and the rough hemp bit into my palms. The slick rock face loomed inches from my nose, its surface streaked with rivulets of water that shimmered like molten silver in the dim light. Occasionally, Smoky would swoop in and disappear just as quickly, startling more than comforting me with her presence.

The storm wasn't merely above us; it was alive all around, pressing in like a living thing. Rain pelted my skin in stinging needles, and the wind howled through the crevices in the rock, a feral cry that sent shivers down my spine. The air felt different—thicker, as if laden with invisible threads of tension that clung to my chest, making every breath an effort.

If we fell, if the storm took us, what would it matter? I'd thrown Elliah into the maelstrom. I'd told myself it was the better path, the safer path, but was it really? Or had I just chosen the one that let me cling to the illusion that I was protecting her?

Elliah climbed ahead of me, her brown hair plastered to her back with rain, her muscles straining. She didn't hesitate. I wanted to borrow a dash of her certainty—or at least some of her resolve.

I glanced down briefly, to ensure Kaelith followed. She climbed a little below me, her movements calculated and efficient, as if she were scouting even while ascending. "You've got to hand it to Pyrravyn," she said between breaths, her voice steady despite the storm, and loud enough to be heard over it. "He's found plenty of opportunity to return to his status as last Scion."

I nearly slipped. She wasn't wrong. Was it possible the whole adventure was a ruse to rid himself of troublemakers? If we turned around, would the Dreadwake even be there? I tried to see out into the storm, but the gloom had swallowed the ship's lanterns long before.

Kaelith chuckled humorlessly. Surely, Pyrravyn wouldn't sacrifice his Wrasseguard. Would he? I suddenly felt better about Trentius remaining behind—he would find a way to warn us somehow via Smoky.

Far above me, Marinna chanted, a spell to steady her footing or anchor the rope further. The sound of her voice over the storm and winds comforted me.

When I reached a narrow ledge, I paused to steady myself. The rock beneath my boots was slippery, but it gave me a moment's reprieve from the strain in my arms. The world tilted slightly as the wind shoved me sideways, and I pressed against the cliff to avoid being torn from the rope.

Marinna's voice came from above. "Keep going—we're close!" She sounded more determined than tired, but I heard the strain creeping into her words. The storm seemed to sense it too, its gusts growing fiercer as we climbed higher.

The rope tugged hard as Marinna reached the top and pulled herself free. Her voice came again, faint but encouraging. "It's safe! Come on!"

I had thought the mission to retrieve the dragon's egg would be safer for Elliah than jumping headlong into the Abyss. But what if it was no safer, no better—just slower? Wouldn't we still have to face the Abyss? Had I simply postponed the inevitable?

I reached for the next handhold, my arms burning with the effort. Mist shrouded the top of the cliff, but the storm's energy buzzed against my skin like a warning. Whatever was up there, it was waiting. And I'd brought Elliah right to it.

"There's *nothing* up here," Marinna said, her voice cutting through the howling wind.

"There has to be," I responded, whisper-shouting against the storm.

Hughelas had laid it all out for me—calm, measured, careful. Rescuing our parents from the Abyss, or taking the dragon's egg. He hadn't pushed me toward either one, but I knew which path he was hoping for. He tried to hide it—he was good at that—but I saw the way his shoulders tensed when he talked about the Abyss. The way his eyes darkened, haunted by the idea of me stepping into it. He was more afraid of that. Afraid of losing me.

And I feared losing more too.

So I'd chosen the egg—but not because it was safer. He was trying to protect me, but what he hadn't realized was that I wasn't trying to protect myself.

I was trying to protect him.

If I led him into something that had trapped our parents, even if I could get out, he might be stuck there. That thought was unbearable.

Marinna's eyes were shut tight. How could she possibly know there was nothing there if she wasn't even looking?

Kaelith stayed close but quiet, keeping watch as the storm pressed in around us. Her sharp eyes darted to every shadow and crevice, as though expecting the island itself to strike at any moment. It probably would. I didn't take the same comfort from her presence as Hughelas did, with her Salt height and silky white braids that swayed about, waving for attention.

During a slow dance of heat lightning from the south, a shadow flickered across the ground. I glanced up in time to see Smoky darting between storm clouds, his small red form barely visible. I took that to mean the Dreadwake awaited us. If Smoky spotted a dragon, would he consider that something worth warning us about?

"No," Marinna said again, her tone sharper now, as if addressing the storm itself. "They were here, but they're not now. What if... the eggs hatched?"

"No!" The word escaped me as a roar of frustration. We'd committed ourselves—made the climb, braved the storm, risked everything. I was freezing, soaked to the bone, every muscle aching from the effort. "No, they have to be here." Struck by a sudden thought, I shouted, "If they're gone, why is the storm still here?"

Marinna hesitated, her brow furrowing as she considered my words. Then, slowly, she nodded. "I'm looking," she said, stretching out a hand as if to touch something invisible. Her eyes remained closed, her breathing shallow, deliberate.

The wind drove freezing rain into my face no matter which way I turned, its icy sting biting into my skin. I closed my own eyes for a moment, futilely trying to imagine what Marinna might be seeing.

"There's something that way," she said suddenly, pointing ahead into the storm. "Come on."

The wind fought us every step, but we pressed forward, climbing over jagged rocks slick with rain. Kaelith kept to the rear, her hand resting on the hilt of her sword. She didn't say a word, but her presence was a constant reminder that we weren't just there for the egg—we were trespassers on land that didn't belong to us, and the storm wasn't our only enemy.We hadn't gone far before we found it—nestled in a hollow formed by the rocks. An egg, black as midnight. Sparks of energy crackled across its surface, like lightning tethered to the storm. The storm didn't just surround it—it seemed to radiate from it.

"It looks like part of the storm," Marinna said, her eyes closed once again. "It's very hard to see at all." Strange statement, given it was quite easy to see, but it was obvious she meant something else.

Kaelith circled the hollow, her gaze shifting between the egg and the surrounding rocks. "One egg," she said. "This feels wrong."

"It's the size of my torso," I said, awe mingling with dread.

"That's small for a dragon egg," Hughelas said, raising his voice over a burst of howling wind. "There should be others. Dragons don't lay just one egg."

"They were here," Marinna murmured, repeating herself and shaking her head. "But they're gone now."

Not just gone, but no sign of them remained. No shards of midnight shells. No gooey mess.

"Do dragons have runts?" I asked, the words spilling forth without real thought.

"I don't think so," Hughelas replied, though he sounded uncertain. "I've read nothing suggesting that. But maybe the runts get left behind and destroyed."

"All we need is an egg, right?" I asked. "No one said it couldn't be a runt."

Hughelas exhaled, relieved. "Its mother left it."

"Or something took the others and left this," Kaelith said, her voice edged with steel, her hand tightening on her sword as she scanned the rocks again.

I agreed with her. It didn't feel right. The storm still raged—was that from the egg or the mother? The question gnawed at me, but there was no time to linger. We had to take it. And that was my job.

I reached out tentatively, expecting a shock the moment my fingers brushed the surface. Instead, a pulse—not quite warmth, not quite energy—ran through me. It was as though the egg saw me, recognized me. The surrounding air hummed, the storm curling inward as if drawn to the shell itself. I hesitated, then pressed my palm against its surface, surprised by the warmth that radiated from it through the cold storm.

"It's alive," I murmured, the words clumsy and inadequate, struggling to capture something more profound.

The bag I had brought would have fit the larger egg we'd expected, so it was more than enough for the one before me. I crouched down, working quickly to maneuver the egg into it. The shell was thick, more like a rock than a shell. With a careful tilt, I rolled the egg to the bottom and cinched the bag shut. The lightning licked at the edges of the fabric as I pulled it closed, but it didn't harm me.

"Okay," I said, standing and hefting it over my shoulder. The egg was heavier than I expected, reminding me of the enormity of what we were stealing. Marinna's eyes were open, though she squinted against the rain. Kaelith doggedly scanned our surroundings.

"I should carry it," Hughelas offered. "You've got the hammer already. I wouldn't be touching the egg itself."

The logic was sound, but I shook my head, remembering the sensation when I touched it. "Try," I said. "Just to be sure. Carefully."

He reached out hesitantly, but the moment his fingers brushed the bag, he yanked his hand back with a sharp gasp. "It—it burns," he stammered, shaking his hand as if trying to rid himself of the lingering sensation.

I nodded grimly. "It has to be me then."

"Can you carry the hammer and the egg?" Hughelas asked.

"I don't have a choice," I said, adjusting the bag's strap over my shoulder. I tried to sound calm, but my voice wavered. "We're going down the cliff instead of up. Should be easier this time."

Hughelas gave a weak grin. "Nothing about this has been easy, but I'll take 'less deadly.'"

As we turned back toward the edge, Marinna froze. I followed her gaze up into the clouds. Smoky flew south, breathing his tiny flame in puffs as he left us. That wasn't the direction of the ship. Marinna cocked her head slightly, her eyes narrowing, then she closed them altogether.

"What is it?" I asked, the words catching in my throat.

"She's coming back," Marinna whispered, her voice tinged with fear.

The world shrank to the weight on my shoulder and the sudden, terrible understanding that we had stolen something that was never meant to be taken.

The wind shifted then, carrying with it a low, resonant sound—a sound like far off thunder, but with the dual tones of a dragon's call.

"Move!" Kaelith shouted, and urgency jolted me forward. The bag dug into my shoulder as I scrambled over the rocks, every step toward the cliff's edge feeling like a lifetime.

Behind us, the storm seemed to gather strength, as though it too anticipated the mother dragon's arrival.

The rope strained under my weight as I descended, the storm howling in my ears and battering my body with stinging rain. The bag dangled off my shoulder, the straps tied securely to the sling for my hammer. Shifting winds pushed it against my back from time to time, the warmth of the creature inside it a momentary balm. When I finally saw the lanterns of the Dreadwake swaying in the chaos, an anchor of light in the storm's dark heart, I enjoyed a moment of relief.

"Move faster!" Hughelas's voice barely reached me from above over the roar of the wind, distant and urgent. We descended in the reverse order of how we climbed. Marinna went first, and she kept slowing to wait for me. I was the bottleneck, and I knew it, but I couldn't drop the hammer or the egg.

I gritted my teeth and forced myself downward, sliding hand over hand. Every muscle in my arms burned, and I struggled to find purchase for my feet against the slick cliffside.

A sharp crack of thunder startled me, and for a heart-stopping moment, the rope swung wildly to one side. My stomach lurched as I slammed against the cliff, jagged rock scraping my shoulder and tearing through my soaked coat. I bit back a curse and pressed myself against the stone, clinging tightly until the rope steadied again.

"Elliah, hurry!" Marinna called up. "She's coming!"

I didn't need her to explain who *she* was. The low, resonant roar that had shaken the cliffs earlier was growing louder, closer. My pulse quickened as I imagined the dragon's enormous wings tearing through the storm clouds, the fury of a mother who had sensed her stolen treasure.

I forced my arms to move faster, ignoring the strain in my muscles and the searing ache in my shoulder. Finally, my boots hit the wet surface of the rowboat. I quickly sat, exhausted and unstable from the trek. Marinna held the rope, chanting reinforcing spells into it.

"Almost there!" I shouted, though the wind likely carried my words away.

When Hughelas finally landed beside me, his knees buckling slightly, I reached out to steady him. He gave me a shaky nod, wiping rain from his eyes, and readied the second set of oars.

Kaelith slid down seconds later, pushing the boat away from the rock with experienced precision.

The short journey to the Dreadwake took an eternity.

Once more I had to hold a rope as the crew pulled us aboard, the ship lurching forward as they weighed anchor and unfurled the sails, abandoning the rowboat like we'd abandoned the rope.

And then I heard it—a piercing, guttural shriek that cut through the storm like a blade. The dragon.

The crew turned as one, our eyes scanning the swirling clouds. There—a massive, serpentine shadow broke through the mist, its wings unfurling with a crack that seemed to split the air itself. Lightning arced around its body, drawn to it like iron to a lodestone.

"She's here," Marinna whispered, her voice barely audible. She closed her eyes and whispered spells, crouching to put her hands on the deck. Hughelas stood over her, urging me with a jerk of his head to come closer as he cast a Shield above them. Kaelith stood with sword drawn in front of Hughelas.

A blinding flash of lightning split the sky in two—for a moment, I saw nothing but white.

Then pain.

It didn't just hit me—it took me, every nerve ablaze, every muscle betraying me. My limbs spasmed as I hit the deck, my body convulsing like a marionette with its strings tangled in a storm. The sensation was regrettably familiar.

Through the blinding agony, I caught flickers of movement—the bag sliding away, the hammer clattering out of reach. I couldn't move. I barely held on to consciousness.

Not again.

Pyrravyn lunged for the bag—but his hand never touched it. He yanked back, like the air itself had bitten him. His breath hitched. For the briefest second, even he hesitated. Then, swallowing whatever unease had stopped him, he stomped on the straps instead. Marinna still crouched on the deck, undisturbed—the dragon had targeted me. Lucky me. Hughelas ran toward me and Kaelith moved to defend him. I turned my eyes upward, expecting the ship to be pummeled at any moment, only to find the dragon had halted its dive, hovering in the storm just off the ship's port side. I had seen a big dragon before, in the caves of Cenaedth. I had thought I understood big dragons. I had been wrong.

It should not have been able to fly. Its sheer mass defied the sky itself, a force that should have crashed to earth like a falling mountain, yet it hovered, wings shifting lazily against the storm as if gravity did not apply to it.

My chest clenched. It wasn't just big. It was impossible.

Casually, it shot more lightning at the ship, hitting the masts, causing some to splinter, and creating massive holes in sails, which caught fire even in the rain. The ship lurched, dead in the water, as the dragon settled onto the ocean, or possibly the rocks beneath the surface—no way would that beast float.

As I recovered, Pyrravyn fumbled with a bag at his waist, pouring its contents into his hand and casting a spell. The complicated magic took time and many gestures, and while he performed it, I pulled myself together and sat up, watching the dragon watch us. Marinna continued to hold the ship together, while Hughelas helped me to my feet.

Kaelith's voice cut through the chaos—sharp, urgent. "Pyrravyn— what are you doing?"

Pyrravyn's incantation rose above the storm, his voice wrapping around the wind, swallowing the thunder, drowning out everything else. He slammed his palm onto the bag.

A blinding flash. A sound like the world itself drawing breath—

And then—nothing.

When my vision cleared, Pyrravyn was gone.

So was the egg.

Elliah ~ 16

The dragon floated on the dark, rolling ocean, a mountain of shadow broken only by flashes of lightning. Her wings, like massive black curtains, folded in as she settled, their tips trailing in the churning waves. Beneath her, I imagined unseen claws digging into undersea rocks, anchoring her colossal form as she *watched*. The storm, as though mindful of her presence, parted around the Dreadwake, leaving it in a brief, rainless hollow. She didn't rage, didn't roar—she *watched*—still and predatory, like a panther's unblinking stare from a low branch.

Around me, the crew of the Dreadwake sprinted, their movements frantic against the pull of inevitability. Shouts mixed with the hiss of steam as Water spells met stubborn flames. Wet canvas slapped as the crew hoisted new sails, white against black—until the dragon stirred. A flicker of light gathered in her throat, a warning glow like a smoldering ember buried deep.

Then lightning cracked.

It struck with the sound of splitting stone, the sail shriveling into blackened threads before the clap of thunder even ended. My ears rang with it, the echo rolling outward, swallowed by the rain. A sharp acrid scent—like singed hair and burning copper—filled my nose as flames flared in the rigging. For all the crew's shouting and scrabbling, they were ants rebuilding a broken hill under the eye of something far larger.

And still, the mother dragon watched. Her eyes—black, yet deep, shimmering with threads of starlight—remained fixed on us. A cat stalking mice. Waiting. Deciding.

Kaelith hovered near Hughelas, her sharp gaze constantly flickering between the dragon and the crew. She stayed close to him, her usual composure tinged with tension. She held her sword toward the midnight dragon, though what she expected to do against a creature capable of swallowing us all whole was beyond me. Still, her presence was steadying—not comforting, exactly, but grounding.

Smaller dragons began to land on her, little black silhouettes against the bruised sky. They perched and shifted like restless crows atop her colossal back. One even settled on her horned head, its wings awkwardly folding as it peered down at us, curious and toothy.

On the Dreadwake's railing, Smoky sat like a puffed-up king, little wisps of smoke curling from his nostrils. He faced the massive black dragon and huffed small clouds of defiance. A pup confronting a wolf.

The dragon remained motionless, her breathing slow and deliberate, but every exhale rocked the ship as if the sea itself heaved beneath us. When the crew finally got another sail aloft, the dragon moved. Not much. Just a narrowing of her eyes, a faint flicker of her throat, and—crack.

Lightning lashed through the air, splitting the night open. My vision burned white-hot, then dimmed as I blinked rapidly to recover. The new sail dissolved into flame and ash, cascading in fiery scraps to the soaked deck. For a moment, there was silence, save for the creak of the ship and the hiss of rain.

The dragon snorted, and the sound vibrated in my chest, deep and oddly mirthful.

"Enough!" Captain Kael's voice boomed over the chaos, raw and edged with helplessness. He waved the crew to halt, their shoulders sagging in defeat. Only the Water spells continued, the hiss of extinguished flames making a mockery of progress.

"What happened to Pyrravyn?" I muttered to no one in particular. He was gone. Nowhere to be seen. Somehow fled or magically hid with the egg. He'd left the rest of us to pay the price.

Kaelith's voice cut through my thoughts, sharp and low. "He's doing what he thinks is best for Deara." Her words carried both irritation and a reluctant admiration, like someone acknowledging a rival's skill even while cursing their existence. "I *knew* we would pay the price."

Not again. How many times?

How many times was I going to watch someone else take the reins while I scrambled in the wake of their choices? My gut twisted, my jaw clenched. Pyrravyn had played us. Played me. And now we were the ones left to face the consequences.

I hastened over and scooped up my hammer, grounding myself in its familiar weight, in the solidity of something I could hold. *No more watching from the wreckage.* But, what good was resolve without a move to make? I gritted my teeth. I wanted to act, to take control—but how? Fear and frustration mingled, foxes in the same den.

The ship creaked under the weight of silence.

The dragon did not strike. Did not roar. Did not move. She only watched.

And then, finally, she spoke.

"Interesting." The word rumbled through the air, felt more than heard, in the now-familiar dual-tone voice of a dragon. One of its voices was so deep as to make the Dreadwake vibrate. "I did not think to see anything… interesting… before I died. Ancient location magic uncovered. An elf bonded with a dragon—I haven't seen that since the Breaking. A troll in elf's clothing." Her voice quivered with something like amusement, dark and unfathomable. A sound like stones grinding together emerged from her throat—a *laugh*.

Her eyes bore into me, so dark and vast that the cosmos swirled within them. "What dragon is that from?" she asked, and this time the voice sounded deeper—like a part of it rang from *inside my head*.

It took me a moment to realize she was referring to my hammer. The weight of her attention was too much—like staring into the void and feeling the void stare back. I tried to speak, my tongue like dry sand.

"A white dragon," Hughelas said hoarsely, drawing her attention. "I did not know its name."

"*Her* name," the mother dragon corrected, her voice snapping like a whip, the wind jolting around us.

Kaelith tensed beside Hughelas, her sword raised like a shield before them. Hughelas paled, his wide eyes reflecting both terror and awe. I couldn't blame him. Her eyes bore down with a weight that made breathing feel like defiance.

"You don't *chance* upon the bone of a white, even since the Breaking," she murmured. Somewhere far off, thunder rolled across the sea, low and resonant. "I'd decided ages ago that Kryhryzar had given up."

"Kryhryzar," I whispered, my voice barely audible. I glanced at Hughelas. The magical images on the pedestal under Fael Themar had mentioned Kryhryzar several times. Had implied Kryhryzar was the dragon that kept them from being overrun by lava, and as a result, became the bones whose tail wrapped the pedestal.

The mother dragon's eyes snapped back to me, her enormous head jutting closer. My breath hitched as her hot, storm-charged exhale blasted against my face, crisp and metallic.

"You know what became of Kryhryzar?" the dragon demanded. In a shockingly insane moment, I noticed that the rain had stopped falling. Along with the observation that, if the dragon bit me, I would only take up about two of her teeth—if she turned me sideways, I might span four or five. Oh, and the baby black dragon on her head had fallen onto the ship and squared off against Smoky after an awkward recovery from the spill.

"We do," Hughelas said, with more confidence than I felt. "She died saving an artifact from before the Breaking."

The mother dragon slowly retracted her head, her sharp gaze narrowing.

"The fact that you know where Kryhryzar is means *something* is in play," she said, her voice dripping with grim understanding. Then, she lifted her head and crooned—a sound so loud and alien it rattled my bones. It was horns and whale song and wind all at once. Her children joined in, their smaller voices weaving through hers. Even Smoky accompanied them, harmonizing in his own way, and for a moment, the sound surrounded us—a chorus of dragons, vibrating through the storm-torn night.

For the first time since re-boarding the ship, I spotted Trentius. He came from nowhere to stand beside Smoky, squaring off in some odd way against the baby black.

"Now," the mother dragon said, her voice slicing back into us like a blade. She turned her night-filled eyes to Hughelas, who shrank under her gaze. "If there's still a play to be made, it is imperative I have my egg. Where..." and the dragon moved its head closer. "... is..." She reached a claw out and tilted the ship slightly toward her, making all of us fall a step closer. "... my..." Lightning danced from her eyes, nose, and mouth. "...egg?"

"I don't know," Hughelas squeaked. "But I can guess where Pyrravyn took it!"

"Took *her*," the dragon corrected.

Hughelas paled at the correction, but mustered the bravery to speak. "But you would have to stop lighting our sails on fire."

"I have a better idea," the dragon said. The behemoth focused its attention, for the first time, on Trentius. "Take care of my children," she commanded him, and Trentius froze like a statue, then nodded vigorously.

With a speed that defied her size, the dragon's neck shot forward, her maw opening wide. I felt a rush of air as the world tilted—her massive teeth framed the last image I saw before darkness closed in. She scooped us up—me, Hughelas, and Kaelith—into the cavern of her mouth.

I didn't span even two of her massive teeth.

Beldroth : 7

Days blurred in the cave's darkness, but I thought it had been fourteen. Or fifteen. I battled an unusual fatigue—Jade, with her casual flippancy, had laughed and welcomed me to "old age." But it wasn't merely exhaustion. It was like my body was forgetting what it meant to feel normal—the Abyss sapped not only mana but memory, definition, edges. Sometimes I closed my eyes and the memory of sunlight on stone eluded me. Or the smell of wind. It had to be all in my head—plenty of Salts had lived in the Abyss for years, some for close to a century, if the stories were true. It was too uncomfortable to fathom. I reminded myself that playing with the children brought a taste of joy to each day, but carrying on forever in this cage?

"You know that Earth magic is about Binding," I told Illiara. Despite the reprimand I suspected Illiara to deliver, I marched forward with my idea.

She lay next to me in the dark cave, murmuring something that made me think she wasn't really listening. Even after days and days sealed up in those caves, waking up with so little mana made it feel like you might still be sleeping. And the closer you were to the center—closer to the artifact and the dragon—the slower your mana recovered. The message we sent out once a day—holding a magelight and using a cloth to block its light from the geode to create the patterns—drained what little mana recharged in a day.

We had food, though none of it appealed to me. Mushrooms, worms, even some fish, but I'd never *really* enjoyed fish. The dustmeal was the worst—I'd always hated the taste, or lack thereof. Unfortunately, it helped. Illiara had discovered it seemed to restore mana faster than the other food. She was playing a delicate game: casting her spell to boost mana recovery, then using that precious mana to summon more dustmeal, which in turn accelerated the effect. It left her tired, and the loop was fragile—too easy to break. I took over handling the magelights to send our daily signal so she could focus on the other spellwork.

I sent prayers to the Mother that someone was watching for our signals. That someone watched the flickers from the geode and knew we were here. But something inside me, something quieter and crueler, whispered that no one did. That the world had moved on. That we were already ghosts—trapped in a place the living forgot. Oddly, prayers came easier of late. The Mother *was* dying, but too many things had lined up for me to think her hand was completely off the wheel.

It was Flurry who kept track of the time—she told us when to send our message. I wondered, did she sense the sunlight above the Abyss? Was that how she knew the time? If so, what torture!

Illiara's hand had drifted to her abdomen as I spoke. She probably didn't even realize she did it anymore. She didn't fear for the baby's health, or giving birth, but the idea of raising a child, locked in the Abyss? That fear clung to her—and no matter how often I tried to convince her otherwise, I knew it clung to me too. She told me we didn't need to worry about our baby being Bereft, and I tried to take solace in that—but the cost...

I'd never thought about being a father this way—not in a cave, not in near-darkness, not where your first lullaby might be silence and stone. I wanted to believe there was still a world waiting above. A place where laughter wasn't rationed, where light didn't come from lanterns of worms and fungi.

"I said, 'Earth magic is about Binding.'" She was going to kill me.

She roused from whatever deep and depressing thoughts she'd wandered into.

"Yes," she said, dully. "Earth magic is about Binding."

"But we also use it to shatter bonds," I continued, having gained her attention. "Like the stalactites Marinna pulled down on the dragon, or her threat to break up the Salty Squirt." The little Wood Elf was crazy powerful in Earth magic. If the Alluvium were correct—and I suspected they were—Marinna would not be able to have children that weren't Bereft. Hughelas had explained a theory on the Salty Squirt, and I understood the concept in his simple presentation.

"You... have some idea how to shatter the trap we're in?" she asked, propping herself up on an elbow to look at me. The dim light of the glow worms in the lantern behind her let me see her silhouette. "Or the artifact that creates the Shield?"

"Not exactly," I said. "I can't get close to the Shield. The noise hurts too much." *Hurts too much* was an understatement. The sound clawed into my skull—like glass being ground to powder behind my eyes. It wasn't just sound; it was pressure, memory, a kind of wrongness that turned my thoughts sideways. "I already tried to break the artifact. But I think dragons built that thing. It resists magic. If Flurry didn't have the power to break it, I never stood a chance. But the barrier affected Flurry even more than it affected us. I can get closer to it than she can. If I can just get close enough..."

"You think, if you can get close enough, you can break a hole in it?" she asked.

"Maybe," I said.

"But that's not a new thought. You've got something else in mind."

"Well, if Earth magic binds and breaks bindings, it's possible your

Healing magic can be turned on its head too." It was a nasty thought.

"What?"

"What if I couldn't *hear* the painful sounds that keep us from getting to the Shield?"

She laid her hand on my chest, her touch light but grounding—holding me in place with something gentler than words. "You want me to use my magic to *damage* your hearing? You're a fool," she said softly, sweetly. But beneath the sweetness, there was something harder. Fear. I knew the thought of losing anyone—even a part of someone—clawed at her. She'd lost so much already. And with a child growing inside her, that fear had only grown sharper. "If it didn't work, and we were still stuck, it's likely I wouldn't have the mana to Heal you completely. By the time I recovered enough, your situation might become permanent."

"If we're stuck, it might be a blessing to lose my hearing." I hoped to earn a laugh. "Won't have to hear you whine about the lack of trees."

Her eyes flashed. "Stop it."

"It's true. I'll sleep soundly through the baby crying, too."

She slapped my chest, not in anger—just enough to silence me. No laugh, not even a smile.

I was glad it was too dark for her to see the look on my face. If I lost my hearing, half my spells would be useless. But, worst of all, I would never again experience Illiara's laugh. Or the baby's first cry.

The Abyss was already so silent. The echoes of laughter and distant voices shimmered through the dark—fragile proof that we yet lived. Without sound, even that would be gone.

Hours before, the cave had echoed with the laughter of children, their joy rippling through the dark like light on water. But even that sound felt distant now, like a dream slipping out of reach—already half-swallowed by the Abyss.

The world was thunder and shadow, the air sharp with the scent of sundered sky.

The dragon's mouth, large enough that I could have stood upright in it, and warmer than the deepest forge, tilted, and we rose. My hands clawed at the slick, ridged surface of her tongue as the pressure shifted. Elliah pressed against me on one side, the handle of her hammer jabbing me in the ribs, while Kaelith kept a steadying hand on me from the other side. Everything vibrated, the sound more felt than heard: a deep, resonant hum that rattled my bones and curled around my thoughts.

We were flying.

The darkness inside the dragon's mouth was near-absolute, save for occasional flashes of light through the gaps in her teeth or from deeper in her throat—lightning from either side. I couldn't get stable enough to create a magelight. My ears popped, and a moment later, the vibrations intensified into a disorienting rush.

Magic. A shift in the world's fabric.

I had no idea what the dragon might be doing, but it thrilled me that chewing wasn't involved.

There was a terrible lurch, as though the dragon had punched a hole through the sky, dragging us with her. My stomach flipped. The hum stopped.

A long, rattling exhale swept over us. Then light—blinding—spilled in as the dragon opened her mouth.

I squinted against the sudden glare, my senses a blur. I thought I heard Elliah curse softly beside me. The dragon's tongue tilted, and we slid, ungainly and unprepared, onto the curve of her massive palm.

The air hit me like a slap—salty, chill—I hadn't realized how much I'd warmed in the dragon's mouth. My boots scrambled for purchase as I steadied myself, blinking furiously. And then I saw it.

"Deara," Kaelith said. "In the blink of an eye." Even Kaelith couldn't keep the awe out of her voice. "Dragon magic."

We looked down upon the harbor, floating like gods over the clustered ships. The city sprawled at the top of the cliffs we hovered over, its towers sharp against a roiling gray sky. The storm shield, which had been ever-present around the island like a dome of rage and lightning, crackled uneasily.

High above us, at the end of its long neck, the dragon's galactic eyes scanned the landscape below. "Where?" she demanded, her voice a rumble that made my chest vibrate.

I'd traveled to the Tempest Crown by foot, but from our vantage, it only took a few seconds to figure out which road exited the city toward the artifact. "That way," I croaked, barely trusting my voice. I had a moment of curiosity about the storm shield: we were inside it. It hadn't stopped the dragon at all.

The dragon turned her enormous head, narrowing her eyes against the wind. Her claws curled slightly to steady us, and Kaelith, having sheathed her sword at some point without me noticing, grabbed our arms and pulled us down into a crouch. Then the dragon banked, and the world dropped out beneath us. Far below, sailors scattered like ants, pointing up at the impossible sight of a black dragon flying inside the storm shield. The harbor looked less crowded than I remembered, and I wondered if that was a trick of perspective caused by looking down on it from above. We cleared the harbor in no time, and then it was the denizens of the city proper who froze in awe.

Elliah knelt beside me, one hand braced on the dragon's claw. "I haven't been this far inland before. Have you?"

I nodded my head yes, my throat dry.

We neared a building fed by a single road, surrounded by fields with scattered sheep. A group of mages argued outside the simple structure with an opening in its roof, their robes flapping wildly in the wind.

"There!" I shouted to the dragon. "That building."

As the dragon turned, I caught a flash of movement—crimson cloth whipping in the wind at the Crown's edge. Someone sprinted toward the structure, arms pumping.

Gormar.

Stone blind fool. What was he doing?

We'd left him behind. I'd seen him in the city. He wasn't supposed to be anywhere near the artifact, and yet there he was—running headlong toward the very place where everything was about to collapse.

No one had asked him to come. No one had told him. But clearly no one needed to.

He'd read the signs—a prophecy he believed in too literally, too completely. He must have seen the threads pulling tight around the Crown and come running, determined to play his part. Whether we wanted him to or not.

The dragon closed her claws around us, keeping us from falling when she banked hard, diving. The mages scattered, and I recognized Maelith among them.

The dragon spread her wings wide, making another wild turn as she descended. Her claws opened just enough to allow us to glimpse the ground rushing toward us before she landed with a jarring thud on three legs and her tail, keeping us safe in the other. The impact sent a ripple through the earth, scattering the mages like windblown leaves.

She lowered her claw, dumping us to the ground in a heap. Gormar had already moved clear of the dragon's landing, crouched low near a cluster of mages. He wasn't shouting—but his hands moved, tracing symbols in the air. Fire flickered faintly in his palm, barely controlled. We scrambled to our feet as the air hummed with tension, a pressure that built in my ears and chest.

"Maelith!" I shouted, moving toward the wizard who stood, frozen in shock, eyes locked onto the enormous black dragon that crooned with a bellow that might have reached all the way to its children back at Shattercove Island.

"It's inside," he squeaked, his voice thin and strained, his eyes darting between the artifact he had sworn to protect and the enormous dragon watching us.

"What's inside?" I demanded, but I was already moving, already running toward the building, where the ornate door hung slightly ajar. Beyond them, shadows flickered, illuminated by erratic flashes of blue light.

Gormar shouted something—maybe a warning, maybe a spell—but the wind tore his words away.

Maelith's next yell barely reached me over the roaring wind. "The hatchling!"

I lurched to a stop at the broken doorway to the chamber where a crackling burst of blue light coursing with energy stopped me in my tracks. Elliah and Kaelith pounded to a halt on either side of me.

Pyrravyn stood in the center of the room, his body rigid, his fingers half-curled in a spell that would never be completed. Blue lightning wrapped around him like living chains, binding his limbs, searing his fine clothes to his skin. His mouth was open in a silent scream, his muscles locked in agony.

The hatchling crouched before him, its sleek, black-scaled body wreathed in arcs of lightning. Shards of its black shell lay scattered around the room, but the biggest piece lay right at the base of the Tempest Crown. The hatchling was small, barely the size of a wolf, but in that moment, it was as terrifying as its full-grown mother. Its glowing blue eyes narrowed as it bared its fangs, a snarl crackling through the air.

Pyrravyn struggled, his eyes flicking to us in the doorway. For the first time, I saw desperation in them. No smug calculation, no practiced arrogance—just the raw, awful realization that he was about to die.

Something in me clenched.

He'd betrayed us. Lied to us. Used us like pawns. But he had done nothing for apparent self-gain. He'd done bad things for what he believed to be the greater good. I hesitated, my body rigid with indecision.

Elliah looked to me, reading the moment, ready to help if I was. But I didn't move.

A part of me wanted to save him. A part didn't. A part of me wanted the hatchling to finish what Pyrravyn had started. The dragon was so small—no bigger than a cat. What had Pyrravyn seen from the hatchling that frightened him so?

Lightning flared, a single, focused arc that lanced through Pyrravyn's chest. His back arched violently, and a strangled, guttural sound tore from his throat. The electricity danced through his limbs, locking them in place before—suddenly—releasing.

Pyrravyn collapsed onto his knees, his fingers twitching, smoke rising from the burned fabric of his clothes.

I took a step forward. Just one.

I could have called to the hatchling, struck at it, reached for Pyrravyn—done *something*. Elliah would have followed. Maybe the baby would have stopped.

But I didn't.

I let the silence stretch. And in that silence, the hatchling moved.

A single, savage bite.

The sound of tearing flesh.

Pyrravyn toppled, his lifeless body hitting the stone floor with a dull finality.

For a breath, none of us moved. The only sound was the residual hum of electricity, flickering through the air like an afterthought. The hatchling lifted its head, blood staining its snout, and let out a sharp, piercing cry.

A deep growl rumbled in response. The mother dragon.

The baby stilled, its head snapping toward the doorway and the sound of its mother on the other side. Lightning crackled along its small frame, vibrating with barely contained power. It hesitated, caught between rage and recognition.

Then, slowly, it turned and took a hesitant step toward its mother.

We backed out, clearing the way. The hatchling paused, cocking its head at Elliah.

"Go!" Elliah urged Maelith, stepping back with her hammer raised, as if to lead the hatchling away. Oddly, it followed.

Kaelith silently placed herself between Elliah and the hatchling, sword still sheathed, earning a grunt of irritation from Elliah. The baby dragon pinched its nose at her, and its eyes... *her* eyes... flared with blue light.

The mother dragon had crouched, lowering her massive head, her eyes locked on the miniature version of herself. The giant dragon crooned, her head low, a deep harmonic rumble aimed at her child, and the hatchling lifted her head and crooned back.

Behind us, Gormar edged closer to the building, his gaze locked on the Crown as if still trying to divine something from it.

The hatchling gave a final snarl at Kaelith, ignoring Maelith, who sprinted through the vacated doorway. Then the baby leapt forward, bounding into the shadow of her mother's massive form.

Relief surged through me, but it was short-lived.

A sharp shout drew my attention—Gormar, off to the side, one hand raised toward the artifact, the other clutched around a flame that danced wildly in his palm. He was saying something—trying to read it, maybe—even while danger surrounded him.

"Gormar, get back!" I shouted. He didn't seem to hear. Or wouldn't listen.

The hum in the air turned sharp, its pitch rising like a blade slicing through my skull. I winced, clutching my ears, just as Maelith shouted something incoherent over the piercing sound. My head snapped toward the building that held Tempest Crown.

The first crack came like the report of a thunderclap, a jagged line of light splitting the air above the building. I stared in disbelief as that line fractured outward, spider-webbing lines of lightning coursing throughout the translucent shield that surrounded the island.

And then, it shattered.

The web of lightning burst apart with a cataclysmic roar, shards of light peeling away into the storm-churned sky. The fragments dissolved as they drifted down in the distance, leaving the air eerily quiet for half a breath.

But the reprieve didn't last.

A low, ominous groan rippled through the earth, and the island buckled beneath us. I stumbled, and Kaelith grabbed my arms—and Elliah's—once again, pulling us away from the Tempest Crown as the ground rocked. With a tiny rumble, the walls of the building collapsed outward, giving me a clear view of the ancient relic.

I got the briefest of looks.

A deafening boom echoed across the island as the earth itself split open. A massive fissure tore across the landscape, jagged and raw, and the Tempest Crown disappeared into the new expanse of stone and shadow.

I caught a glimpse of red fabric where I'd last seen Gormar, flung like a puppet by the shockwave, then nothing. He was gone, swallowed by smoke and debris. A pang of guilt twisted in my gut. For all his arrogance, Gormar had come trying to help, believing in something greater. And we'd left him behind—I'd left him behind—again.

The mother dragon reared back, her wings spreading wide as she let out a roar that shook the very air, the sound raw with fury and desperation. Clutching her baby tightly in her claw, she whipped her head toward the fissure, her nostrils flaring as if drawing in the scent of something unseen. Her tail lashed violently, cracking against the ground with a force that sent shards of stone flying. Then she crouched low, her immense body coiled with tension, every muscle poised to strike or leap.

"She senses something," I muttered, half to myself, though I didn't know what it might be. Only that it had shifted her focus like a lodestone swinging north.

Elliah shot me a sharp look. "What does that mean?"

Before I could respond—though I had no answer to provide—a rush of air hit us as the black dragon surged forward, her bulk barely squeezing through the jagged opening. She was heading deeper into the island, toward something we couldn't see—and every instinct told me we had to follow.

On the horizon, the skies over Deara opened, a vast and unguarded expanse... and that meant the waters around Deara, swarming with blue dragons, lay unprotected as well.

Elliah ~ 17

The ground hadn't stopped shaking since the storm shield broke. It still thrummed through my boots, a relentless reminder that the world was cracking apart beneath us.

Below us, the black dragon crouched in the fissure, its claws gouging deep furrows into the rock. Her wings spread wide as she pushed herself forward, but the crevice had become too thin for her to keep going. Even her immense strength wasn't enough to force her bulk through.

"She's stuck," I muttered.

The dragon thrashed, her tail carving deep gouges in the rock, her wings beating in futile rage. The sound that tore from her throat was not just a roar—it was a wail, a mother trying to dig through the world itself to reach her child. Her baby had slipped through the gap moments before, vanishing into the shimmering barrier far below. Now, the dragon's focus oscillated between the impassable crevice and the glowing expanse of magic.

Kaelith's voice cut through the chaos, steady but laced with urgency. "She's not just stuck. She's panicking." Kaelith stood close to Hughelas, her sharp eyes darting between the dragon and the growing Shield-like magic below.

I followed her gaze. The shimmering wall wasn't just holding steady— it was *moving*. Expanding. Its faint ripples had grown into jagged surges, bright flares of light that devoured the distance between it and the dragon's outstretched claws. My chest tightened as the Shield advanced toward us, its light pulsing brighter with each surge.

"What's happening?" Hughelas's voice cut through the roar of shifting stone.

I hoped his question was rhetorical, because I had no idea. No idea what magic was approaching. No idea why the black dragon dug for it. But my leap of intuition said that my mother and Hughelas's father were trapped on the other side of that magic. It was the one I was supposed to free them from. It didn't look like I would have to seek it out—it seemed to be coming for me.

The black dragon slammed her claw down, her talons scraping against the edge of the crevice. She bellowed, a sound so raw and full of anguish it made my chest ache.

Did she want her baby or the Shield?

Another surge. The light rippled outward, brighter, faster. My breath caught as the shimmering edge shot forward and brushed against the dragon's outstretched claw.

The reaction was instantaneous.

A flare of brilliance erupted from the Shield, a blinding wave of energy that crackled like a thousand lightning strikes. The black dragon roared again as the light surged outward, expanding in an explosion of power that sent a shock-wave rippling across the island. Wind or magic screeched as the wave of light flew past me, like a sharp blow to the head that faded as quickly as it struck.

"Elliah!" Hughelas shouted, grabbing for my arm as the ground again buckled beneath us, throwing me forward.

I was falling.

The edge rushed toward me, my limbs grappling for anything—and then, fingers locked around my wrist. A sharp yank—my breath punched out of me as he hauled me back from oblivion. My arms wrapped around him, gripping tight, my heart hammering. Too close. Too damn close.

And then I felt it—the shape was wrong.

Not Hughelas.

Kaelith.

Of course. Kaelith. Always one step ahead. Always knowing what to do while I stumbled through the wreckage.

A fresh wave of frustration burned through me as she steadied me. I'd been wrong about her, hadn't I? I'd suspected she wanted Hughelas, that she was waiting for me to slip up. But when she could have let me fall, she'd caught me.

That stung.

Pyrravyn was gone, but the wake of his choices remained. The ground still shook beneath us. The Tempest Crown had fallen and some new, unknown magic forced its way in. And I stayed one step behind, scrambling to react while the world spun out of control. How many times? How many times would I be the one left to deal with the wreckage?

Next time... next time, I wouldn't be the one waiting for someone else to catch me.

As I disengaged, blushing, my head craned upward, my stomach dropped.

The Shield had spread, its shimmering dome of light towering over us, reaching up toward the sky and out across the island. The air felt heavy, charged, as if the magic itself suffocated everything it touched.

The black dragon's desperate clawing stopped. She looked up, narrowing her eyes in anger like a woman betrayed by a lover. The Shield pulsed, bright and hungry, and I knew deep in my bones—if I didn't stop it, it wouldn't stop at all.

The ground beneath my feet rumbled on without pause, a deep and angry growl that had started suddenly, rousing us all to meet up in the main chamber. Dust rained from the ceiling, coating everything in a gritty film. The air reeked of damp stone, fear, and the bite of thunder's breath.

"Dragons!" someone yelled from the direction of Saltreach Lake.

I turned, catching a glimpse of Beldroth struggling to follow the sound. His steps faltered as he glanced around, confusion clouding his face.

"Beldroth!" I reached for him, gripping his arm tightly and shouting. "Saltreach Lake! Do you see them?" He towered over me, turning in the right direction.

He nodded, his lips pressed into a grim line. His hearing was all but gone. Then he took off at a run, drawing his sword. I chased after him.

We found a crowd gathering at the lake, glowworms in lanterns lighting the shore in small purple dots. Water rippled and the distinctive blades of a blue dragon's fins showed briefly, then disappeared. Everyone took a collective step backward.

Flurry appeared, towering over us, growling first at the water, then at the cavern above. What did she see?

"Maybe we won't have to fight," Beldroth said, too loudly. "Blues rarely come out of the water."

The spray of water hit a large swath of elves, but the blue dragon that caused it hit only one, knocking the older man to the floor and landing atop him. It was small compared to the one that had attacked us when we were aboard the Salty Squirt, only as long as a couple of elves were tall, and no thicker than the man's head, which the dragon targeted.

Beldroth was on it, stabbing into its swirling maw of teeth with his sword.

"Go right for their mouths," he shouted, not aware of how loud he was, though he spoke calmly. He once again reminded me that he had trained people to fight for a long time. "Their bodies are too tough to penetrate." Blood poured from the blue dragon he'd stabbed as he pulled his sword from its thrashing body. He kicked it off the poor man, who scrambled backward out from underneath it.

Flurry glared at Beldroth, who noticed and turned to the much bigger white dragon.

"What?" Beldroth said. "I'm to let them eat us?"

Before the white could answer, Beldroth was knocked forward by a blue dragon big enough to bite his head off. Beldroth rolled, trying to get his sword pointed back toward the blue's mouth, but even if he stabbed it, the sword wouldn't have the impact it had on the smaller one.

Another small one popped out, as the crowd slowly reformed so that fighters, with weapons drawn, stood closest to the shore, and onlookers backed away to give them space. With just my dagger, I relegated myself to the irritating role of an onlooker. Was there some way to use my crumb of mana to help?

Beldroth didn't have time to get up, but rolled and folded his legs as the dragon struck again and again. It finally managed to get its mouth over one of Beldroth's legs. He yowled as the curved teeth sunk into his calf.

As quickly as it had grabbed him, it released him again. The much larger Flurry had pinned the blue down in its middle, making it let go of Beldroth to strike at its attacker.

"Save your Heal!" Beldroth shouted, as he got up onto his one good leg, favoring the leg with the rapidly growing blood stain. "We may need it more later, and you might only get one Heal."

And then the ground heaved beneath us.

I stumbled, my hands slamming against the cavern floor. Flurry roared, her tail lashing as she steadied herself, but even she was caught off guard by the violence of the quake. A deafening crack split the air, and a jagged fissure opened in the ceiling above.

Light poured in.

Sunlight!

I stared, momentarily stunned. It had been quite a few days since I'd last seen it, and the golden rays felt almost alien in the dark and suffocating cavern. How hard must it have hit the elves who had been down there for decades?

But its beauty was fleeting. Through the widening crack, the shimmering dome of the Shield that caged us glimmered and glowed with an eerie brilliance. It was expanding, leaping outward in bursts of energy that made my skin crawl.

"What in the Mother's name is it doing?" I whispered, though no one was close enough to answer.

Then, beyond the Shield, something worse appeared.

An enormous black dragon.

Even distorted through the magical barrier, its size was staggering, casting a massive shadow that seemed to stretch endlessly. Its head loomed over the fissure, eyes locked on the trap. On us.

A cold dread settled over me. The blues were bad enough, but if that monster broke through…

"Illy!"

Beldroth's shout snapped me back to the present. I turned to see him pointing toward a baby black dragon. A hatchling. Where had it come from? Above?

239

It was perched near Flurry, watching the battle between the white and the blue with a curious tilt of its head. One of the blue dragons lunged toward it, but Flurry intercepted the attack with a ferocity I hadn't seen before. She roared, her claws raking deep gashes into the intruder's flank.

The hatchling let out a sound—a high-pitched, almost musical trill that seemed completely out of place amidst the chaos. It darted forward, weaving between Flurry's legs, and snapped at the blue dragon with its tiny jaws from behind its shelter.

I couldn't help it. Despite the dire circumstances, a laugh escaped me. "Bold little thing."

The ground trembled again, and the fissure widened. The Shield's light flared brighter, pulsing with an intensity that made me wince. Above, the black dragon roared—a sound so deep it pressed into my chest, the toll of some ancient, inescapable bell.

"Illy," Beldroth said softly, his voice almost lost in the noise. "We can't win this."

I didn't want to agree, but he was right. The blue dragons kept coming, and the black dragon above was a harbinger of doom we had no means to fight.

Yet we couldn't give up. Not while Flurry fought. Not while the Salts fought. Not while that little hatchling nipped at its enemies with more courage than sense.

The sunlight above grew brighter, spilling across the cavern floor like a spotlight. And in its glow, I saw not just despair, but the faintest glimmer of hope.

Beldroth : 8

The screech barely reached me—distant, distorted, like it came through water or from a memory I'd rather forget. My hearing had never fully come back after the last push toward the Shield, but I felt the sound more than heard it. The air shifted, sharp and sour, and the vibration rattled through my ribs.

Not Flurry. Not Smoky. No, the sound had a different pitch—higher, laced with terror and fury and something deeper that didn't belong in my world. The cave walls caught the noise and stretched it, rebounding it in broken pieces until it came from everywhere. I'd never heard a blue dragon before, and I imagined the same noise sounded quite different under water, but in the cave, it haunted.

I limped forward, my right calf still bleeding from the last engagement, sword gripped tight in one hand. Every step was a jolt of pain, and I had to grit my teeth to keep moving. The wound had stiffened, and the uneven stone beneath my boots made balance a constant battle. Illiara moved beside me, pale in the flickering torch-light we'd resorted to for lack of glow worms, her face set in that distant calm that only appeared when she was in extreme danger. I wanted to reach for her, say something brave or comforting. But words caught in my throat, drowned out by the wet rush of wind ahead.

Then came the blue.

It burst from the chamber's far tunnel with the same piercing cry as before, scales wet and glistening, its long, sinuous body coiling unnaturally as it heaved itself onto the stone. We'd collapsed the larger tunnel we'd fled to after we'd retreated from the salt-water lake to the deeper hollows. Flurry had held the blues at bay to give us time to set off explosives the Salts kept handy for mining. That limited the dragons' approaches. But our refuge had many passages. Now the blues came in waves—smaller blues, as round as large plates and as long as three wagons, sleek and eel-like, gliding across the ragged stone with unsettling grace. They didn't need wings. They were water-born hunters, all muscle and malice, but they moved well enough on land. Luckily, the Abyss drained their mana as readily as it did ours, and that hurt them, maybe more than us.

But the newest one was larger, the size of my chest, and behind it, more followed.

Elves screamed. Children scattered toward the deeper bolt-holes. I wish they'd stayed—encountering even a small blue on their own would not end well for the children. I shouted something to Illiara—not a spell, not a plan, just a warning. She was already moving, her mana flickering weakly around her hands.

I tried to cast and failed. Not enough. Not even for a push. The Abyss drank mana faster than I could pull it or Illiara could boost it. But someone tossed a flaming flask at the entrance they came through, and it exploded in fire and rock. At least that cut off the flow. Hopefully.

"Get behind me!" I shouted, swinging my sword as the dragon struck. We held. For a time.

How long? Minutes? Hours? Time bled differently down there, mixed into the screams and the fire and the rock dust. Many Salts fought alongside me. Perhaps some had once been warriors. But the Abyss hadn't kept those particular skills sharp, and the dragons, even weakened from the pull of the Abyss, had thick hides and sharp teeth. I concentrated on the biggest one.

The largest of them slithered forward with a hiss caused by its scales dragging across the stone. My leg slowed me more than I wanted to admit; every shift of weight stabbed at me. I couldn't pivot fast enough, couldn't dodge without risking collapse. But the dragon wasn't moving quite right either—it was sluggish, and its swipes missed by just enough to matter. The Abyss dulled it. Drained it, possibly more than it did us. Or maybe it was simply unused to fighting on land.

I aimed low, jabbing at the inside of its mouth, trying to keep it back rather than take it down. It was all about survival.

I heard explosions, saw someone's hair catch fire. Illiara gasped, her hand pressed to her ribs. *So, this is how it ends*, I thought.

We couldn't hold that chamber forever. Illiara's face tightened, her eyes flicking toward the tunnels—her calculation confirmed my perspective. We needed to fall back. But leading them back to the main vault was like marching in reverse toward defeat. We'd already fled that place once, carving a path through blood and flame to reach what we hoped was safety. Now we returned, wounded and fewer in number. We could repeat the maneuver again, holding another small section of the Abyss for a time. But I needed to see whether more blues were coming in to formulate a plan.

"Pull them toward the main vault!" I shouted to anyone in earshot. "Retreat! Slow and controlled!"

We backed through one of the side passages, ducking low under overhangs slick with moisture, protecting those who had no battle training as best we could. Illiara half-dragged a limping Salt who refused to drop an iron skillet. I carried a child who clung to my neck with bloodied fingers. The large blue didn't follow immediately. It paused at the tunnel mouth, its sinuous body twitching like it was deciding whether to commit. The space was narrow—low ceiling, jagged walls. *Good*, I thought to myself. *Let it think. Let it wait.*

The tunnels narrowed, then widened again. I rushed forward, not wanting to send the non-fighters into a trap. They waited in the shadow where once-familiar sunlight touched the tunnel entrance. The light glinted off the saltwater lake as it sloshed with nervous energy, spitting more blue dragons ashore while waiting to see who would live through the next minute. I didn't see any really large ones, the biggest about the size of the one I'd just fought. But they replenished their numbers while ours dwindled. We would ultimately lose.

That's when I felt it—no, heard it.

The song.

It rose over the chaos, brazen and wild, a shanty I couldn't make out, yet it sounded familiar all the same. The dragons turned. We all did. Through the smoke and ruin at the far side of the main vault, I saw her.

Jade.

Riding Flurry.

She stood astride Flurry's back, balanced as though born to ride dragons into battle, her coat flaring behind her like a storm banner, her white hair wild. Her sword flashed in the sunlight while her voice carried a rhythm that made the Abyss itself hold still for one impossible moment.

Like the stories of Jade Galefinger.

Jade Galefinger!

I knew the name. Everyone did. Pirate queen. Storm-chantress. The kind of legend you didn't expect to bleed in the same dirt as you.

She bellowed curses like the blue owed her money, then flung a small, oddly round object that bounced off its nose with a hollow thunk, and Flurry launched herself forward with a roar.

It wasn't over. Not by a long stretch.

But for the first time since the battle began, I thought we might survive. At least for one more round.

Beneath me, the ground still rumbled faintly, the aftershocks of the earthquake making every step treacherous. The sky above shimmered with the expanding Shield, a barrier of light and sound that pulsed and warped as though alive. The mother black dragon had finally ceased her frantic clawing at the ground. Her massive form crouched in the fissure, her eyes no longer wild but calculating as they flicked between the shimmering barrier and me.

"You must end this," she growled, her voice deep and resonant, vibrating through my chest like a living force.

I swallowed hard, my throat dry. My anti-magic. The dragon knew.

The dragon's gaze narrowed. "Get down there. Find the artifact. Shut it down." She stretched out one massive forelimb, her other claws digging into the jagged rock as her tail lashed impatiently. "I will take you as far as I can."

The idea of climbing into the dragon's claw frightened me, yet I also felt an odd calm. Perhaps it was exhaustion, or perhaps it was knowing there was no one else able to do it. Or it was simply a far superior option compared to being back in its mouth. Still, the sheer scale of her claw, those talons longer than I was tall—it made the danger inescapably real. Hughelas came alongside me, taking my hand. Someone had to deal with the artifact. That someone was me.

I stepped carefully onto the dragon's outstretched claw, gripping one of her talons for balance, and Hughelas did the same. The scales beneath my feet were warm, the texture rough and ridged like volcanic rock. Kaelith leaped right up with us.

"If you're going in," Kaelith said to Hughelas, "I'm coming too."

The dragon lifted us with surprising gentleness, given the ferocity of her previous scraping, lowering us into the crevice.

"Pyrravyn is dead," Hughelas said. "There's no one to report my movements to. No reason to shadow me." His declaration seemed pointless, as it was too late for her to change her mind.

Kaelith let loose one quick grunt of laughter. "Shows how little you've learned," she commented. "I stopped reporting back to Pyrravyn days ago. Besides, as the last remaining Scion, it's my job to keep you alive, even if you do have a knack for finding catastrophically stupid ways to die."

I agreed with her there, but I also had to take some of the blame for our circumstances. I felt a pang of guilt for how I'd treated Kaelith. She'd done nothing but keep Hughelas—and me—alive. But she'd been close to him while I'd kept my distance, and she was more like Hughelas than I—taller... Saltier?

"Go quickly," the dragon said, her voice softer now, almost... concerned. "That's a Resonant Seal. It was built to trap entities more powerful even than dragons. The Seal attracts, draws in, then consumes. Using *my* life-force, it will sap everything more rapidly. Soon, you—troll in elf's clothing—will be the only thing *alive* in here."

The ground she lowered us to was uneven, the edges jagged. We weren't at the bottom—far from it—but she'd gotten us to a point where the fissure hit the side of the cavern. We could climb down that side into the cave proper—the rest was up to us. I gripped the nearest rock and began climbing down, Hughelas and Kaelith doing the same. The black dragon's massive eye lingered on me for a moment before she withdrew, her shadow retreating from the crevice. She dangled her neck over the edge, and her eyes slowly faded and closed.

As my mother was fond of saying, *Mother of rotting Trees!*

The climb was rough. My palms scraped against the sharp stone, every foothold precarious, as if the earth itself might crumble beneath my weight. Several times, the ground shuddered, once pelting me with small rocks from above. But we all held on. Noise from the far edge grew louder as we descended, suggesting a battle took place below. A shouted command from a familiar voice drew both our heads.

"Dad!" Hughelas shouted, the word slipping out raw, unguarded—a boy's voice breaking through the man's composure. But whatever was going on kept them busy. We barely heard them—in the thick of whatever fight was going on, Beldroth wouldn't be able to hear us.

Keeping close to the fissure's edge, where the slope wasn't as sheer, I carefully descended, each handhold testing my strength. My muscles, still weary from the climb on the cliffs of Shattercove, protested with every move. At last, my boots met the uneven floor of the cavern, the solid ground beneath me a welcome relief despite its rough surface.

"Which way?" I asked Hughelas as he finished his descent, my voice tight with urgency.

He squinted, glancing around the cavern, but the space was massive, the echoes disorienting. The artifact wasn't in plain view, hidden somewhere deeper.

"It could be anywhere," he muttered. "We need to—"

A shrill cry of *song* from the direction of the fighting halted him mid-sentence. Then Beldroth's voice once again shouted orders I couldn't quite make out.

"Father!" Hughelas whisper-shouted, spinning toward the sound. The desperation in his voice was unmistakable.

"Hughelas, go," I told him. "He needs you."

His eyes locked on mine, torn. He took my hand and squeezed. "I can't leave you again," he said, his voice trembling.

"You don't have to do this for me," I said, trying to push him away. "This is my responsibility. Your father—"

"I'm not leaving you," he interrupted, the conflict in his face hardening into resolve.

I didn't argue further. There wasn't time, and truthfully, I didn't want to do it alone.

"Kaelith," Hughelas begged. "That's my father. He needs help."

"As my Scion commands," Kaelith said with a smile. "But if you die without me, I'm going to kill you." Kaelith turned and jogged as well as one could over the rough rock toward the sound of fighting.

A soft trill broke the tension, and both of us froze.

"Wait, is that…?" Hughelas turned toward the sound.

I followed his gaze and spotted the black hatchling we had seen earlier. It perched on a nearby ledge, its luminous eyes darting between us and a passage. Its tail flicked nervously, but it made no move to retreat.

"It knows," I breathed, the realization striking like a whisper of fate. "Maybe it's drawn to the artifact."

Hughelas glanced at me, then back at the hatchling, his face conflicted. "You're sure?"

"No," I admitted, "but it's the best lead we've got."

The hatchling let out another soft trill before scampering ahead, vanishing down the passageway. Without another word, we followed.

Once we made a couple of turns, Hughelas cast a magelight, then cursed as it faded and disappeared. He tried again and failed to light another. But we stumbled forward, feeling our way along the left-hand wall.

I quickly decided we were on the right track, as the air grew heavier with each step, and after several twists, soft light became visible ahead. Something… the air… the magic.. pressed against my skin like a physical weight.

At last, we emerged into a small chamber.

The hatchling stood at the edge, its gaze fixed on a pedestal glowing with runes.

"That's it," I whispered, though my throat was so tight the words barely escaped. My heart thundered in my chest, each beat louder than the last.

The pedestal stood in the center of the chamber, its glow pulsing faintly like a heartbeat. The runes carved into its surface shifted and flickered, their patterns mesmerizing and impossible to track. Just standing near it made the hairs on my arms stand on end, like static electricity before a lightning strike.

246

I wasn't waiting for a perfect answer. There wasn't one. There never had been. I had been pushed, pulled, and cornered by fate and bloodline until this moment stood before me—one more step along a path I never chose.

But the choice to take it? That was mine.

My blood. My life-force. The weight still pressed down—heavy, unrelenting—but this time, I didn't just bear it. I chose it.

"Elliah," Hughelas said softly behind me. His voice brought me back, grounding me.

"Take this," I said, giving him the hammer. I needed my anti-magic.

I forced my legs to move, one step at a time, until I was standing before the pedestal. Up close, the runes glowed brighter, their hum as deep and reverberating as the mother dragon's growl. The hatchling took a cautious step closer as if sensing the tension, but she stayed just out of reach.

I pulled out my dagger, the blade catching the faint light of the runes. For a moment, I simply stared at it, my hand trembling. My pulse raced, fear clawing at the edges of my resolve.

"Will it hurt you?" Hughelas asked, his voice breaking the silence.

"Yes," I admitted, my voice barely audible. "But if I don't do this, it won't matter."

He nodded, his expression unreadable.

I tightened my grip on the dagger and pressed the blade to my palm. For a heartbeat, I hesitated, the edge biting into my skin but not yet drawing blood. Then I pushed harder.

The sting of the cut was sharp and immediate, but I barely registered it through the pounding in my head. Blood welled up, dark and sluggish, pooling in my palm. I turned my hand and pressed it firmly against the glowing runes.

For a moment, nothing happened.

Then the artifact drew my anti-mana, maybe my life-force, right out of me, just as it had with the artifact of a living sculpture. It pulled more and more of something indefinable from me, until I was naked, raw, and dry as old bones.

The hum of the magic faltered, leaving the air heavy and expectant, as though the world itself had drawn a breath and held it. Then, without warning, the pedestal erupted in blinding light, a searing brilliance that carved through the chamber like a blade. I stumbled back, the oppressive weight of the magic lifting all at once, leaving the air trembling in its wake.

Three days had passed since the storm lifted and the harbor lay in ruins. Three days since we'd stood beneath the storm-black sky, clutching the stolen egg, wondering if we'd survive the dragon's wrath. Three days since Pyrravyn died.

And somehow, the world already moved forward without him.

The council chamber felt cavernous and hollow without Pyrravyn presiding. The air was thick with unease, the weight of so many unresolved questions hanging over us like storm clouds. I stood at the edge of the room, my hands clasped behind my back, trying to ignore the subtle glances cast my way.

I was the only living Scion. Oddly, a relic in a room that contained the newly freed Miryndel and Jade, each a Daughter of the Nine Winds in their own right.

Pyrravyn had never told me they were alive. Never mentioned they'd entered the Abyss. He'd spoken of the Nine Winds like they were legacy—symbol, not presence. And yet, he'd known it was at least possible they lived. Of course he had. He kept them hidden, even from Bella. Because their return meant a power shift. Because their voices, freed, might have drowned out his own.

The two of them sat next to each other: Miryndel sad but resolute, Jade old but more celebratory. I'd never seen an old elf before—no one had—and my eyes drifted to her repeatedly. Wrinkles. Saggy skin. Remarkable. The Resonant Seal's collapse had freed them, but years— decades—of imprisonment still showed in the tension of their shoulders and the hollow edges of their faces. Bella was too young to lead, and while either of the Daughters might reclaim the mantle, neither seemed eager to wear it again.

And then there was Kaelith, who guarded the door closest to me, her piercing eyes moving between Miryndel and Jade. Though she said nothing, the tension in her posture spoke volumes. For all her recent loyalty to me, I could see the pull of her heritage—the allure of the Daughters.

The Daughters who appeared content to let me shoulder the day's burdens. Notably absent? Drevin.

Drevin and his Tidewardens had disappeared. Vanished. Janelle had railed to Elliah about it, affronted by the books they'd taken with them. Drevin was too clever to run without purpose. He hadn't fled because of guilt—he'd fled to prepare for something else. That couldn't be good for Deara. Anyone on the Dreadwake had witnessed Pyrravyn's use of magic—they would all have connected the dots to Drevin and his acolytes' sudden departures without ships. But only I *knew*.

The council had convened today for the first time since the disastrous chain of events. The losses were staggering—the Tempest Crown gone, more than half the harbor destroyed. And with Pyrravyn dead, the Peacekeepers and the merchants were already circling the wreckage, looking to claim what remained.

When Maelith finally wandered in, I took my seat as well.

"Eryndra saved her fleet," Yselda opened, her voice sharp and indignant, cutting through the murmurs. "She pulled the Peacekeepers out of the harbor, leaving us defenseless when the blues poured in!"

"She acted before the dragons breached the Shield," I countered, my voice steady but firm. I turned to Gormar, whose prophecy had shown a Peacekeeper vessel sailing amidst a fleet in flames. He'd been sure it was a sign of victory over a foe. In fact, the prophecy had shown Eryndra wisely removing her ships from the harbor. Gormar kept his eyes down, his shoulders slumped. "If she hadn't, we would have very few ships left. What fleet we have remains intact because of her foresight. To my understanding, you still have the Salty Squirt and a few others?"

The merchant scowled, but a few heads nodded in agreement. "Yes," Yselda admitted with a frown. "Captain Striker convinced a few merchants to follow the Peacekeepers out." When the black dragon had flown us over the harbor, it had looked emptied. In the moment, I'd wondered if it was an illusion of seeing it from above, but Eryndra had, in fact, left orders to move her ships outside the storm wall.

The blue dragons had decimated the harbor when the magic of the Tempest Crown failed. Some fishing vessels and a couple of trading vessels had been out to sea, avoiding the carnage, but the dragons, in their mindless rush to get to the Resonant Seal, destroyed the docks and the ships still moored to them. It would be months before the harbor would fully functional again.

I turned to Eryndra, hoping that she would speak for herself.

"Pyrravyn was planning to steal the egg of a dragon," she said. "I told you it was idiocy. Retribution was a distinct possibility. It was not on the prophecy that I acted. Just prudence."

Ironically, that wasn't what happened at all. When the storm shield came down, the blues had charged in, drawn by the Resonant Seal. They were unable to reach it from the harbor, but they didn't know that. We were lucky more hadn't gone in through the passage on the east side of Deara that led to Saltreach Lake—they would have overrun the elves in the trap.

The discussion continued, spiraling into complaints and blame. My thoughts quickly turned elsewhere. Pyrravyn's death weighed heavily on my mind—not out of grief, but because of what I now understood.

The journal Elliah had given me revealed Pyrravyn's secret—Drevin's secret—though I hadn't understood it until I'd seen it in action. Pyrravyn had escaped the ship and avoided death by teleporting—a feat I hadn't imagined possible. With that context, I'd gone back through the journal more carefully.

Dragon teeth.

He'd used three of them, each anchoring a part of the magic that represented a coordinate. The journal outlined the theory and the part Elliah hadn't copied had undoubtedly chronicled some of their early experiments. It was all Drevin's work—a fantastic mind that didn't consider the implications of what he'd done. Or maybe he had.

How deep had Drevin's ruse run? Was collecting the baby dragon a fake mission just to get more material for his experiments? Had he purposefully crafted spells he knew would backfire in order to remove Maelith's Tidewardens from the Tempest Crown, creating a heavier burden that supposedly required the dragon? I didn't know. But the fact that he fled spoke to his culpability.

I clenched my fists.

The knowledge of Teleportation would change everything. If public, it would render Deara's fleet obsolete, shift the balance of power among the factions, and open avenues of exploration and conquest. But it would put a lot of power into unready hands.

I didn't want to share the knowledge. Not yet. And Drevin had not done so either. Except with Pyrravyn. And possibly his Tidewardens, given their absence. And, if Drevin shared what he knew with the wrong people... he could do massive amounts of harm. Deara, still reeling, wasn't ready for another crisis.

But I *did* have something else to propose. I stood, clearing my throat, halting their finger-pointing. "I have one final matter to address." The room quieted, and I scanned the faces—tired, expectant, wary. "The Alluvium are gathering in Alenor, preparing to march with the High Elves to Bellon, and from there, to the Witless Tarn to confront the trolls. But their march will be slow. Our remaining vessels can't harbor here for some time—we should put them to good use. I propose we send what remains of our fleet to Alenor to help transport their forces."

A sharp intake of breath from Kaelith behind me made me smile—she wasn't unflappable.

Murmurs rose again, some surprised, others skeptical.

"It's too big a risk," Yselda said, narrowing her eyes. "We're stretched thin as it is. You would have us gamble what's left of our ships on the *High Elf* war?" Yselda's tone was sharp. "What if they fail? What if the trolls win?"

"Then, at best, we will have no one to trade with," I countered. "The trolls won't stop at Bellon."

250

I wondered how the traders chose who sat on the council—had Captain Striker earned a seat? If Kaelith could read my inner monologue, she would have laughed and told me I was thinking like a Scion.

"I fear the enemy already knows the elves prepare for war," I said. What the trolls knew, I wasn't sure. Whatever enemy had broken into Elliah's mind when she'd communed with the Mother of Trees had done so before Elliah knew our plan. Maybe the trolls prepared for our attack, and maybe they did not. "The more time it takes to get troops in place, the more time the troll Warlord has to enact his nefarious plans. True, you will be safe, far away on your island home." I turned to Yselda. "But who will you trade with when the mainland is overrun?" Then I turned to Eryndra. "Is there a more noble peace than an action to save the world?"

Eryndra nodded, a rare flicker of approval crossing her face. "It's the right move," she said.

After a few more exchanges, the council, weary from loss, reluctantly agreed. Yet, as the decision settled over the room, I sensed a shift—a faint but undeniable energy sparked by a renewed sense of purpose.

It wasn't just the plan—it was them. The Daughters. In the streets, in the port, whispers traveled quickly: the Daughters of the Nine Winds had emerged from the Abyss. Survivors. Symbols. Some called it a sign of Deara's rebirth. I wasn't sure what I believed—but I felt it, too. The air had changed. Their expressions carried something beyond weariness. The Daughters of the Nine Winds exchanged approving glances, their subtle smiles like embers catching flame.

Jade Galefinger, the legendary pirate who had once ruled the seas with daring exploits, leaned forward with a grin that held the power to steer a storm. "Eryndra," she asked with eager boldness, "which ship will I captain?" Her enthusiasm rippled through the room, stirring an echo of the bold, reckless spirit that had once defined Deara.

Her daughter, Miryndel, the visionary who had turned the pirate's cove into a bustling city, took a more measured approach. Turning to the council, her gaze sharp and calculating, she asked, "Who are Deara's most promising architects?" She didn't wait for an answer; her words carried the weight of inevitability. She would rebuild the harbor—a task I had silently hoped someone would take on.

And just like that, the weight on my shoulders lifted. They had purpose again, and the rebuilding would begin without me.

I was free..

Almost unnoticed in their planning, I stood and walked over to Gormar, who sat dejectedly. It could have gone much worse for him—Yselda could have attempted to push more of the blame for the loss of her ships, as well as Pyrravyn's death, on his prophecies. But, admittedly, it could also have gone better. They might have asked for a new prophecy. Might have leaned on his visions of the future to make plans. Instead, they'd confirmed that, without Pyrravyn to champion him, they had no use for him.

I put a hand on his shoulder. It was a miracle he'd survived the Crown's collapse. I'd seen him vanish in a cloud of smoke and debris. Part of me had already grieved him. But here he was—bruised, dusty, one arm in a sling, and stubbornly alive. I'd told him he couldn't contribute. I hadn't been wrong about that. But I'd also never tried to help him find a way to assist.

He jerked, surprised, but immediately recovered. "Wynruil warned me," he said. "Fire lies."

He looked hallowed out, and he likely was. He faced the reality that he'd built all his beliefs upon a cracked foundation.

"It does, and it doesn't," I said enigmatically. He frowned. "The essence of what Fire showed you was true. The Peacekeepers avoided destruction. Pyrravyn used the dragon's egg. It just wasn't what you thought the prophecies meant."

"What good are prophecies that can't be understood?" he asked in a quiet wail. "What does it say about all of Elandra's Prophecies? What if everything I've been told, and everything I've told others, is *wrong*?"

"Then we must spend time and care if we wish to use them as guides," I answered. "Knowing that fire burns doesn't keep us from using it to cook our meals."

Gormar nodded his head, pursing his lips at my shallow, but pithy, wisdom. "I'll go back and read them again. With a more discerning eye. You truly believe you saw Elandra's corpse in the swamps of Fael Themar?"

I nodded.

"Maybe," he said with a sigh that breathed out decades of beliefs, "if I re-read her prophecies, knowing she is truly dead, I will see something different."

I patted him on the shoulder again and wondered whether it was time to make my escape. Miryndel had a map or blueprint unrolled before her. Janelle stood beside her with more scrolls and papers that she laid out on the council table. Jade and Eryndra stood on the elegant council chairs, attempting to hang a woven map from two braziers in the corners, blocking an exit with its bulk.

The council room had become crowded with architects, shipwrights, lieutenants, even cartographers. Bella sat atop the big table to get a better look at the biggest map and her legendary great-grandmother who hung it. Deara had lost its appetite for secrets.

Mostly. I still kept *one*—the truth about Teleportation. Not because I thought the council corrupt, but because no one wielded that kind of power lightly. Even good people often made terrible choices when handed something too big, too fast. Even me.

I found Kaelith still guarding the door behind where I'd been sitting and approached her. "What will you do?" I asked her quietly.

Her gaze flicked to me, then to Bella, who sat staring wide-eyed at the map and the surrounding discussions. "I don't know," she admitted, her voice low. "Part of me thinks I should stay here, help rebuild. Another part wants to follow the Peacekeepers, where I can do something that matters."

I nodded, not pressing further. "Thank you again," I said. "For saving my father."

She nodded like it was nothing. I didn't press her, though the story my father told was extraordinary—his injury, retreats defending small chambers, then the desperate return to the cavern. Jade Galefinger, standing atop a white dragon, singing songs and flinging *mushrooms* at the blues like they were spells. How Kaelith had arrived, balancing the odds and keeping my father alive.

Then, after Elliah took down the artifact, lightning crackling through the chamber—not from the sky, but from two storm elementals who appeared as if summoned, herding the remaining blues back into the sea. Elliah said they approached her when the dragons were gone—quiet, wordless. That it felt like a thank you before they vanished without a trace.

I would not forget Kaelith's role in keeping my father alive.

"What will you do?" Her piercing eyes bore into me, asking a deeper question than where my immediate interests might lie.

I turned to see Elliah, her expression unreadable but her eyes sharp.

"She's waiting for us," Elliah said simply.

The mother black dragon. Lairras.

Kaelith nodded, giving me a half-smile and flicking one of her braids behind her shoulder. Then she returned her attention to the discussions at the table.

Elliah and I left the chamber together, walking in silence. Once away from the chamber, I took her hand. My loyalties were bound to one who couldn't stay in Deara. "Can we check in on our parents first?" I asked.

"You're the Scion," Elliah said, hitting me with a hip so I would know she was teasing. I grabbed the other side of the offending hip and pulled her close. She spun on me and stretched up onto her toes, bringing her lips to mine.

Once I was able to breathe again, I went chasing after the woman who'd left me breathless in the hall with thoughts of stopping by the luxurious room she had agreed to share with me. Being the last Scion had its perks.

We found our parents in a courtyard with a burbling fountain for a centerpiece. Illiara tended long-neglected plants—wildflowers and resilient herbs—in one of six corners, her efforts evident. My father sat with a chisel and a piece of stone, carving. I had no idea what he attempted to create.

"Mom," Elliah said, as Illiara climbed to her feet. "I've been meaning to ask you…"

Illiara brushed her hands together, smiling at her daughter and nodding for her to go ahead.

"Talena Talonforged. Who wrote it?" A book from Elliah's childhood that she carried around with her, though she hadn't pulled it out in ages, but I'd noticed her stare at it when she'd emptied her pack in the room we shared.

Illiara smiled, even blushed. "I wrote it." Elliah's mouth dropped open, then shut. She sat down hard on the edge of the fountain.

"You wrote it," Elliah repeated, as if saying it might make it less strange.

Illiara smiled, brushing her hand down Elliah's arm. "When I found out I was pregnant with you, I wrote down stories. Axilya encouraged me to do it."

Elliah looked at me like I might further elaborate on the matter, but when I didn't help, she turned back to her mother.

Illiara smiled softly. "You carried that book everywhere. I thought you knew."

Elliah shook her head. "I thought… I thought it was just a story."

"It was," Illiara said. "And it wasn't. Those are all places I went as a child. Or things I'd heard."

"You drew all the pictures? Wrote the words?"

"Of course," her mother said simply.

Then it hit me. Janelle had brought a copy to Bella when we'd arrived on the island. "How did the library on Deara have it?"

Illiara's face scrunched. "There was a copy *here*? That, I cannot explain."

Elliah squinted, thinking. "I'll ask Janelle when I see her," she said.

My father still focused on what he was doing—though we weren't far behind him, he hadn't turned.

"Creating a statue?" I asked, raising my voice so he could hear me. Illiara had Healed his leg in time, once the Resonant Seal came down, but his hearing had not recovered. Illiara had explained what they'd attempted to break out of the trap, and that it hadn't gone well. Likely, he would never hear perfectly again.

Beldroth shrugged, his tongue sticking out of his lips as he concentrated on the rock before him. He took one delicate tap on his chisel with a tiny hammer and sat back. "Marinna seemed to take a great deal of pleasure out of it," he said in explanation.

In fact, many Warders carved. My father was not one of them, as evidenced by the blob of rock before him.

"He's terrible at resting," Illiara said. "I thought this would keep him out of trouble."

Beldroth squinted at her. "Keep me out of rubble?"

Illiara sighed, pinching the bridge of her nose. "Trouble," she said more loudly, walking closer so he could hear. She dropped her shoulders, saying in a normal voice. "I suppose both are true."

My father tilted his head, a mischievous grin spreading across his face. "I'm perfectly fine with rubble. Trouble's more fun though." He reached out and grabbed Illiara, pulling her into his lap.

"Well, okay then," Elliah said, pulling on my hand to get us out of there as quickly as possible.

"Don't do anything we wouldn't do!" Illiara shouted as we stepped back into the hallways of the building.

"I don't think that precludes *anything*," Elliah said. Her fingers tightened in mine, and I laughed, not because it was funny, but because I could.

Outside, the air was still heavy with the aftereffects of the collapse of the magic from not one, but two ancient artifacts. Lairras awaited us in a distant clearing between the city and the former site of the Tempest Crown, her massive form coiled like a shadow made flesh. We made the long hike to see her, passing many Salts who had found reasons to work outdoors. Though fear still etched their faces, curiosity kept them close, their eyes lingering on the distant dragons. Lairras seemed unconcerned with the onlookers, her focus entirely on her hatchlings. The smallest of them, with surprising authority, nudged its larger siblings into some semblance of order, its chirps sharp and insistent. Nearby, Flurry remained watchful, her white scales a stark contrast to the black dragons around her.

As we neared, Lairras's eyes, dark and piercing, settled on Elliah.

"You did well," she rumbled, her voice resonant and ancient. "But there is more to do."

I exchanged a glance with Elliah before stepping forward. "What do you mean? What more?" It wasn't that I thought we were done—there was a war brewing with the trolls, dragons were stirring, ancient magics awakening. But the dragon had remained enigmatic, focusing on her children, but doing it in the open on Deara instead of hiding away on Shattercove. Deara's citizens didn't find themselves doused in the storms of Shattercove, but the dragon hadn't explained herself—nor had anyone the courage to ask why she'd suddenly become a degree less antisocial.

"To see the Mother," the dragon replied. Elliah stiffened. "To find Kryhryzar and Jenat," she added, looking at Flurry. "Dragons collect their dead."

The dragon continued, her voice softer now, almost mournful. "The blue dragons… they are not like me nor Arsyli. Their queen is long gone, and with her, their history and purpose. They cling to geodes because they hold the echoes of her memory. It is a futile effort to preserve what has already faded."

"Dragons have queens," Elliah said, like she'd figured out where a piece of a puzzle belonged. "Something they are born to be?"

"Indeed," the mighty dragon said, looking at her tiniest hatchling, who had the other, larger dragons bringing her fish.

"Arsyli is the queen of the whites," Lairras said. "But she knows only what she's lived, which is very little. She can know more with the bones of her mother and grandmother, but not everything. Not with the cage still in place."

"Wait," I said, ignoring that last, confusing piece of information. "'Dragons collect their dead,'" I quoted. "You want Flurry to have access to her parents' bones. You collect your dead because—"

"Because they hold our past," Lairras said, her tone ancient and weighted. "When we die, our children consume our bones, and our memories become theirs. They become us. I *am* my mother, *and* her mother, *and* hers. I remember the day the Mother created us." She paused, her dark eyes swirling with stars. "At least, that was true until the Breaking. I was the youngest queen when the Mother returned and Broke our world. Only Shaythyl and I remember the time before the Breaking, and Shaythyl far exceeds her allotted time. Blue dragons cling to the geodes because their queen put pieces of herself in them—a failed attempt to transfer her past even with the world Broken. But when Shaythyl lets go, then the reds, like the greens, blues, and whites, will be Lost. I will be the only one left carrying our legacy. And once I'm gone, dragons will become nothing more than instinct and hunger. No purpose. No memory. No reason not to burn the world to ash. And that," she said, her eyes boring into Elliah's, "is why I must insist that you speak with the Mother again."

"Again?" I said, trying to pull the attention away from Elliah. How did she know Elliah had spoken to the Mother before?

Flurry spoke up. "I told mighty Lairras of the previous visit, which I learned from your parents. How the Mother hides, comatose, fading. How *something* found its way to you through a connection with her."

"I do not intend to send you to her unprepared," Lairras said. "Have elves lost all connection with their past? Do you not know that you were once disciples of dragons?"

Disciples of dragons? There was that statue in Aendolin. Wynruil was Old Guard—long-lived enough that perhaps he could verify the truth of Lairras's claim. But I shook my head. "No, I did not know that."

Lairras huffed, lightning dancing around her nose. "I trained the High Elves. A white trained the Warders. Red, Alluvium. Blue, Salts. And a green trained the Wood Elves." Her eyes again bore into Elliah. "I trained the High Elves," she repeated. "I can prepare you for whatever lurked in the Mother's mind. But if there is a way forward, I must know."

Elliah's gaze sharpened. A month ago, she might have resisted. Or lashed out. Or refused altogether just to prove she could. But she'd changed.

"You'll prepare me?" Elliah's tone was level. Calculating. "Like you prepared the High Elves?"

Lairras's dark gaze narrowed. "Exactly."

Elliah's chin lifted slightly. "Good. Then I have only one other condition."

Lairras's nostrils flared. My chest tightened. Elliah was bargaining with a dragon!

Elliah's gaze shifted to me, steady and deliberate, then back to the dragon. "You'll teach Hughelas the secret to Teleportation."

My breath caught. "What?" I stammered.

Elliah didn't look back my way. Her gaze remained fixed on Lairras. "I want you to teach him," she repeated. "Not just the theory. The working magic."

Lairras's tail lashed. "You ask for much."

"As do you," Elliah replied.

A sharp tension coiled in the air between them. Elliah had experienced being inside the mighty dragon's mouth once—risking it again... was I watching courageous liberation, or a return to her prior reckless impulsiveness?

I held my breath. Teleportation wasn't just power—it was the power to shape the future. The ability to cross oceans, to outmaneuver armies, to redraw the map of the world. Drevin had unlocked the secret—Elliah was trying to hand it to me, whether I was ready for it or not.

Then Lairras huffed, the sound low and charged with static. Her gaze lingered on Elliah with something between amusement and respect.

"Very well," Lairras said. "You will have what you ask. And bear the weight of it."

Elliah's gaze didn't waver. "Add it to the pile."

I swallowed hard as Lairras's gaze shifted to me. I stood at the edge of a storm while the dragon weighed me against something unfathomable.

Lairras's galactic eyes lingered a moment longer. Then she inclined her head toward Elliah. "You were shaped by dragons before," she said. "You will be shaped by them again."

Elliah's eyes darkened. "We'll see," she said, her tone even.

Elliah ~ Epilogue

Weeks had passed since the Tempest Crown and Resonant Shield fell. Repairs to the harbor were well underway, thanks to Miryndel's leadership, and already the fisherfolk moored their vessels in safety. Watching the Salts adapt had been fascinating—their ingenuity and determination seemed boundless. Just as remarkable, the first geode-transmitted messages had arrived from Alenor. The Salts were there, spreading news of Deara's innovations and their ability to transport troops quickly. It was a relief to know that the world beyond the Tempest Crown still turned, even though local struggles loomed large.

But my focus wasn't on the harbor, the Salts, or even Deara. It was on Lairras, the dragon whose mind shimmered with ancient wisdom. She perched in the clearing, her black scales glinting in the sunlight, her presence commanding. She had been training me in mind magic for weeks—preparing me.

Hughelas, Beldroth, and my mother stood nearby, their expressions varying from grim determination to quiet apprehension. Lairras had promised to teleport us directly over Alenor, sparing us the weeks of travel it would have taken by ship. From there, we would fly to the silvervein where the Mother of Trees waited.

Marinna had decided to stay with the Peacekeepers, to help them on their ships in an effort to move troops to the intended attack on the trolls, and Trentius chose to stay with her. Their odd conversation had stuck with me.

"It's best I don't travel back to Alenor," Trentius had said. "I'm remembering too much." Then he'd shut his mouth rather uncharacteristically.

"What?" Hughelas had asked, shaking his head in confusion.

"Smoky is helping him remember things," Marinna explained.

"And if I go back," Trentius said slowly, "I'm afraid the change will be evident. And then someone is going to want me dead."

He certainly *sounded* much more coherent: the entire conversation lacked alliterative declarations. But when we'd pressed him on who he feared, his face had scrunched up like it hurt him, and Marinna had chased us off, telling us they would be fine.

Gormar, too, had chosen to remain behind—not out of fear or rejection, but with the quiet conviction that he had more to learn. Whatever clarity he'd gained in the fire had shaken him, and he no longer clung so tightly to prophecy. He said he needed time. It appeared he meant it. I hoped, though, that he would not do it in a bubble. Like Hughelas, I regretted the way we'd left Gormar outside the tight circle of our trust. When he made trust hard, I should have tried harder.

We had splintered—not abruptly, but with the slow ease of people growing into themselves. Once, all of us had planned to leave Deara the first chance we got. Now some were staying—*choosing* to stay. It wasn't the pull of the island, but of purpose. And, for the first time, we weren't running, driven by fate, chance, or circumstance. We were choosing the paths that fit us, even if it meant parting ways.

I would leave others behind, too, of course—those whose ties to Deara ran deeper. Janelle had returned to the library, her influence spreading quietly once more. Grenthis had taken up her offer to help restructure it without Drevin's influence and in a way that would minimize the consequences to apprentices of warring Stormwrights. I hadn't expected him to, after what he'd endured. He still flinched at shadowed corners, but he walked into them anyway. That counted for something. For a lot.

Lairras's deep voice interrupted my reverie, echoing in my mind. *Are you ready, Elliah?*

Was I? I had been fortifying my mind against illusions, against whispers that sought to twist my perception. I had grown stronger, but the memory of my last encounter with the Mother and the monster I'd let in still sent a shiver down my spine. Our lessons had been strange—I couldn't work magic, only resist it. Lairras had proved herself an outstanding teacher in a domain only passingly familiar to her. She knew the spells, and she guessed, suggested, and helped me work through how to resist them.

"Yes?" I answered, the tilt of my voice giving away my hesitation.

Nevertheless, the dragon who had become my teacher cast her spell.

The world shifted as Lairras's magic wrapped around us, a sensation like falling upward into a vast expanse of light. And after a blink that lasted forever, the forests of the Heartland appeared with a *bamf* of sound.

I immediately recognized our surroundings. To my left lay a High Elf fortification established to keep the riffraff away from the Mother of Trees. To the right, the walled-off silvervein which housed the goddess.

My father, Felaern, leaned against the gateway to the silvervein, as though it were a perfectly normal place for him to be. He should have been in Alenor. He closed the book in his hands, calmly taking in Lairras and our group as though a dragon magically popping into the clearing with a company of elves was an everyday occurrence.

I hadn't expected him. But I should have.

"Elliah. Illiara. Beldroth." His voice was smooth, almost cordial, but the undercurrent of self-assured authority made my skin crawl.

My mother stiffened, her hand brushing the hilt of her dagger. "What are you doing here?"

Felaern tilted his head slightly, his lips curving into a faint smile. "The same thing you are, I imagine. Seeking answers."

"You're supposed to be in the capital," I said, though I kept my voice even.

He raised a brow, unfazed by my tone. "And yet, here I am. Surprising, isn't it? But I suspected you'd make another attempt to commune with the Mother of Trees. It seemed prudent to meet you here."

My mother crossed her arms, her glare sharp as a blade. "Prudent? Since when have you ever done anything that wasn't for your own gain, Felaern?"

He turned his gaze to her, his smile fading but his composure intact. "You wound me, Illiara. Do you truly think I've come all this way to meddle? The war is escalating. The Mother's foretellings could mean the difference between survival and annihilation—for all of us."

My mother's hand tightened on her dagger. "You always speak of peace while sharpening a blade."

Felaern's gaze didn't waver. "Peace always comes at a price. This question is: who pays it?"

My mother stepped forward, tension crackling between them. Hughelas tensed beside me, the rise and fall of his breath sharp and controlled. A few months ago, I would have stepped into this tension the same way as my mother—sharply, instinctively. But I saw it differently now. This wasn't a fight to win. This was an opportunity to control the field.

I placed a hand on my mother's arm, gently but firmly stopping her advance. Then I met Felaern's gaze directly.

"You seem prepared," I said. "Which means you've already considered what you want from this meeting."

Felaern's brow lifted slightly, his smile returning. "How astute."

I smiled faintly. "If you're here to listen, you'll have to trust me."

Felaern's gaze sharpened, a glint of calculation beneath the surface. "Trust you?"

I inclined my head. "The Mother won't speak to you. She'll speak to me. If you want to understand what's coming—what needs to happen—you'll need to hear it from me."

My mother's head snapped toward me, her eyes flashing with betrayal. "Elliah, you can't be serious."

"I am." My gaze remained steady on Felaern. "You've come all this way, Father. You want insight? Then you'll have to rely on me."

For the first time, something in his expression cracked—a flicker of surprise, quickly masked. He studied me, the calculating edge to his gaze sharpening. "You would position yourself as the intermediary?"

I tilted my head slightly. "I already am."

"Elliah!" My mother's voice cut across the clearing, sharp and dangerous. "You don't know what you're doing."

"I know exactly what I'm doing," I said calmly.

Felaern's gaze darkened, his mouth thinning to a thoughtful line. "And you would relay the truth of what the Mother says?"

"Of course," I said. "Or... perhaps just enough of it."

A thin line of tension curled at the corner of his mouth—a subtle gesture, but one I recognized. Pride. And maybe, for the first time, respect.

"I see." He inclined his head, the movement slow and deliberate. "Very well."

My mother's mouth opened, but I caught her eye. The betrayal simmering beneath her expression made my chest tighten—but I held her gaze, steady and unyielding. "I'm not handing him power," I said softly. "I'm keeping it."

My mother's jaw tightened. Slowly, she stepped back toward Beldroth, her hand still resting on the dagger at her hip. Her gaze lingered on Felaern, sharp and suspicious. *If he oversteps,* her eyes seemed to say, *I will end this.*

Felaern smiled faintly. "Perhaps I have underestimated you."

"Most people have," I said.

Felaern's smile deepened. "Then this will be... educational."

I turned toward the arched entranceway to the silvervein, walking ahead without looking back. The others fell into step behind me.

Lairras's gaze flicked toward me as we approached the silvervein. Her black scales caught the light, fracturing the sunlight into sharp, glassy patterns on the ground.

Her voice curled through my mind like a blade slipping between soft fabric. *Steady your thoughts, Elliah.*

I am steady, I replied, keeping my mental walls firm. *I've trained for this.*

A pulse of quiet amusement touched my thoughts. *We'll see.*

Her words, the mimic of my own to her, were a gentle barb reminding me of all the times I'd failed while she trained me.

Lairras reminded me, *If you encounter anyone else while you are in there—*

I will hide, I answered.

She'd taught me to *hide* beneath my own mind, shielding my thoughts from intrusion. She claimed I was a natural at it. A declaration, perhaps a compliment, similar to one my father had once given me. She had forced me to withstand her mental pressure until my mind had broken like glass. I'd learned to push back—to reshape the pressure into silence. If the thing I'd encountered while communing with the Mother tried to push into my thoughts, I wouldn't just block the attacks—I'd redirect them.

She'd also showed me the little helpers my father had left in my head. Tiny things, whispering encouragement in my mind, that he'd placed there when he'd helped me regain consciousness after my previous encounter with the Mother of Trees. She'd showed me how to root them out, then watched me do it.

I pressed a hand to my temple, centering myself. *If anyone tries to intrude again, I'll know how to stop them.*

Lairras's dark eyes narrowed. Then her mind brushed against mine in a quiet hum of approval. *Good.*

A pulse of quiet satisfaction lingered between us, deeper than words. It wasn't pride—not exactly—but something close. Recognition.

As I climbed the stairs of the silvervein, my previous visit flashed through my mind. We'd been running from guards with no time to take in the details. I'd missed the exquisite craftsmanship. Each step was a story—magically grown images of animals and plants weaving together into a narrative as I ascended. Yet no one maintained them. Leaves, dirt, and even branches obscured their beauty.

The Wood Elves near Alenor must have grown the stairs on the silvervein long before, but the High Elves had stopped them from entering for decades. Loss pressed down on me as I climbed into the heart of the silvervein.

"How is Axilya?" I asked my father over my shoulder, distracting myself with a stray thought.

"Axilya?" he asked, startled. "Zoras's helpmate? I haven't spoken with her in… a century." My question genuinely surprised him.

He didn't know then. Didn't know that Axilya, like Zoras, had created webs of her own. Janelle had revealed the secret of the book my mother had written showing up in Deara. I'd almost laughed when I'd realized that the woman who had her fingers in every pie on Deara communicated freely with Axilya, someone outside of Deara.

"Surprising," I said lightly. "Considering her reach."

His gaze sharpened, but I didn't elaborate. Janelle wouldn't tell me more—but in a sense, Zoras still pulled strings from beyond the grave. At least it provided something else to ponder than my dread.

When I reached the top, the Mother of Trees slouched against the great trunk, her massive form as still as death. Her bark-like skin seemed grayer, and cobwebs once again clung to her lids. My eyes drifted from her to the branches that had fallen to the magically created floor of the room. Hughelas had told me what to expect—the fallen branches had grown into the floor when the Mother of Trees had awoken during our previous visit. One of them had killed Zoras, and I couldn't stop my mind from trying to guess which. Decaying logs in the swamps of Fael Themar came to mind.

"Mother," I called softly, stepping forward, weaving through the branches. My voice was insignificant in the vastness of her presence, though it still disturbed the quiet. Not that I expected anything different, but she didn't stir.

The others stopped when we passed the last of the branches that lay like barricades. My mother's hand tightened on her dagger, while my father lingered with his arms folded, his expression unreadable but intense. Hughelas's eyes kept darting between Felaern and me, while Beldroth stared at the Mother with a sad frown. As an afterthought, I took several steps back to Beldroth and handed him the hammer.

I couldn't help but think She needed us. Yet I knew saying so wouldn't comfort the Warder, and I wanted to comfort him.

"She created us for a reason," I said instead, walking the tightrope between words that worked for his beliefs and mine.

Then I walked back to the slumbering, probably dying, Mother of Trees. I glanced back at Felaern, recognizing that my father would use whatever knowledge he learned to his own advantage. But I controlled that flow of information, not him. Same with Lairras—I controlled what she would learn. Would I be wise enough to use it well?

I'd spent my life running. Following. Reacting. *But not this time.* I wasn't there by accident. I wasn't there because fate demanded it. The world was not on fire. I was there because I chose to be.

This is the moment where I decide what happens next. No one else.

I closed my eyes hard, gathering my resolve. I sighed out my worries, opening my eyes and placing my hand on the Mother's foot. A spark jumped between us, but it wasn't electricity. The Mother's eyes fluttered open, dim and unfocused. "Child," she murmured, her voice a blend of rustling leaves and distant thunder. "You return... though you should not."

Her words gave me pause, but I pressed on. "Mother, we need your guidance. The elves march on the trolls, and the dragons..."

Her hand twitched, the movement slow and laborious. "No... I will not See."

Confusion rippled through me. "What do you mean?"

"To See is to touch the thread of what could be," she said, each word a labor. "And to touch it is to change it. I have Seen too much... interfered too often. The bindings are fraying. I cannot risk unraveling them further."

"But without your insight—"

Her gaze sharpened, green fire sparking briefly in her cobwebbed eyes. "Without my insight, the choice is yours. The burden, yours. That is as it should be. What I see... cannot be unseen."

Illiara stepped forward, her voice hard-edged. "What use is a Mother who won't protect her children?"

The Mother flinched, her massive hand dragging across the ground. "I have protected. I have guided. But I have bent the river's course too many times, and now the river fights back." She exhaled, a sound like rustling leaves in a dying wind. "You. You were the last good path. I will not touch the thread again. I will not be the hand that unravels it."

She closed her eyes. Done with us too soon, just like the last time.

The burden was mine. Whether to push her or let it go—that was my choice too. I put my hand back on her foot and closed my eyes. I used what I'd learned from Felaern and Lairras to seek the Mother with my mind.

***

The world melted.

No, not melted—shifted. Rearranged. I no longer stood in the silvervein. Instead, I was falling forward and backward at once, my mind stretching across centuries.

And then, in the silence between moments, the first world blinked into being. A world of crystal and light, almost as bright as the stars that bathed it. Then it disappeared into darkness and, just as I wondered whether I'd failed, another world of green and growing plants spun by. More came, faster and faster, until worlds sped by, uncountable.

Abruptly, a rumbling laugh echoed in my mind, freezing me in place. The worlds receded, creating a clearing surrounded by planets, where I stood with *something* that didn't belong there.

"No need to press her further, little sister," came the monstrous voice I remembered all too well. "I told you before that you shouldn't be here."

The air thickened, every breath a struggle. But I'd trained and prepared. There was no air—it was a manipulated illusion. My confidence increased when I rid myself of the fear of suffocation.

"You also told me to come see you," I said. "Where are you? How will I know you when I see you?"

Shadows knit themselves into form.

A troll. A Warlord.

His armor gleamed, the scales of dead dragons woven into it, as if he carried the histories of a thousand burned cities on his back. His eyes—the same ones that had haunted my mind before—burned like embers.

I shuddered as his gaze turned to me. He smiled—a chilling, jagged grin. "We meet again, little sister. I see you're stronger now. Good. You'll need to be."

"What do you want?" I demanded, my voice trembling but firm.

"Want?" He chuckled, the sound a low rumble that vibrated through my chest. "I want what you want. Survival."

I didn't believe him for a moment. "You're somehow destroying the

Mother and unraveling everything the Mother has protected."

"Am I?" His tone was almost mocking, but there was a hint of weariness beneath it. "You couldn't be more wrong. I have no intention of harming the Mother," the troll said, his tone softening. "I need her to live. At least for a while longer."

His trap wasn't ready to be sprung?

"Turn them back," he said, his voice holding the weight of a thousand dying stars. "Turn them back, or what dies will live again. Allow them to reach the Dragon Fangs and all hope will be lost."

"What?" I said, shocked beyond belief. He knew where the elves were going. If he didn't want the elves to march, the trolls must not have been ready to stop them. I tried to hide the spark of joy that thought ignited. "Why should I believe you?" I asked, my voice breaking.

His grin faded, replaced by something close to sorrow. "Because the one you think is your enemy... is not. I am trying to stop the true enemy from breaking free. The Devourer of Souls waits, and if the elves reach us..." He looked at the worlds spinning by around us. "...the bindings will shatter."

I stared at him, my thoughts spinning. His words didn't make any sense. Wasn't *he* the Father of Stones, the Devourer of Souls?

"In fact," he said, "you shouldn't come." But for the first time, his voice faltered.

He exhaled, slow and deliberate, his jagged grin fading. "Not anymore. You shine too brightly—he will see you. I've kept you from his sight so far, but if you come here..."

Something flickered behind his ember-bright eyes. A shadow of regret. A weight, heavier than even he could carry.

"If you come, I will have to kill you."

Regret? That he would have to kill me? It was all trolls wanted, killing elves. But his regret sounded real. The magical statue of the Warlord under the swamps had made jokes. What if what I knew about trolls was wrong?

"You've been warned," he said, his voice fading. "I hope for both our sakes that you listen." And then he was gone, the crushing weight of his presence lifting like a storm passing overhead.

After several seconds, I removed my hand, letting go of the stream of worlds, the Mother's life. The real world snapped back into view. My thrill of having stood firm in the face of the monster faded rapidly. No one was going to like the message I'd brought back. Not Felaern, not Beldroth, and not the gargantuan midnight dragon that waited below. *But this time,* I thought, *I hold the reins.*

Author's Note

Thanks for reading Secrets of Deara! If you enjoyed the journey, please consider leaving a review on Goodreads (https://www.goodreads.com/book/show/231225372-secrets-of-deara), Amazon (https://mybook.to/trb3),
or Bookbub (https://www.bookbub.com/books/secrets-of-deara-an-epic-fantasy-thaumatropic-roots-book-3-by-steven-j-morris). Ratings help new readers take a chance, and even a short review can help someone discover whether this world is the right adventure for them.

The story continues as Elliah, Hughelas, and their allies take the fight back to where the adventure started—the troll invasion. Look for Book 4, *Shepherds of Truth*.

If you didn't know, the *Thaumatropic Roots* series is a prequel to *The Guardian League*, an urban fantasy series that takes place centuries later, here on Earth (assuming you're on Earth). That story begins with *The Guardian of the Palace* (https://mybook.to/lklH).

You can also sign up for my newsletter: (https://pages.sjmorriswrites.com/ebook-landing-page) to get updates, sneak peeks, and short stories featuring characters from both *Thaumatropic Roots* and *The Guardian League*.

Visit me at: http://sjmorriswrites.com.

Thanks for joining the adventure,
Steve

Acknowledgments

I joked in the acknowledgments for *Bones of Cenaedth* that I'd have to rewrite *Secrets of Deara completely*—and I wasn't wrong. What I thought would be a quick continuation turned into a full reimagining of the second half of this series. But it was the right call. This book now stands on much stronger ground than the original draft ever could have.

Huge thanks to Libby James, who did the structural editing for this book and continues to sharpen my thinking about character depth, scene structure, and emotional payoff. I finally managed to absorb some of her advice (thank you, Libby, for your patience), and some will no doubt keep echoing in my head into the next book. If you're looking for a writing coach to push your writing to the next level, consider Libby (http://libby-james.com/).

Thanks also to the incredible group of writers and friends who helped with blurbs, ad ideas, character voice questions, and general encouragement: Janelle & Brandon Forteza, Bobby & Amber Montgomery, Brett & Karen Green, Marla Taviano (who also copyedited this book and continues to rescue my grammar—http://marlataviano.com), and Erin MacPherson (who meets me for coffee and/or beer—as the situation dictates—with writing advice). If you're looking for someone to help you launch your first book and make the journey less terrifying, Erin's a great place to start (https://www.rovacommunications.com).

Special thanks to Matthew J. Holmes for his marketing classes and guidance. His help on Facebook ads, Amazon ads, and platform building has given me more time to write—and more energy to pour into these worlds.

And most of all, thank you, readers. You're the reason indie fantasy continues to thrive. Every rating, review, and recommendation you make helps new readers find these stories and keeps the magic alive. Thank you for sailing the treacherous waters of Deara with me--and occasionally shouting advice at the crew along the way.